HER CHRISTMAS BABY CONFESSION

SHARON KENDRICK

A WEEK WITH THE FORBIDDEN GREEK

CATHY WILLIAMS

MILLS & BOON

First published in Great Britain 2022
by Mills & Boon, an imprint of HarperCollins*Publishers* Ltd,
1 London Bridge Street, London, SE1 9GF

www.harpercollins.co.uk

HarperCollins*Publishers*
1st Floor, Watermarque Building,
Ringsend Road, Dublin 4, Ireland

Her Christmas Baby Confession © 2022 Sharon Kendrick

A Week with the Forbidden Greek © 2022 Cathy Williams

ISBN: 978-0-263-30101-4

10/22

MIX
Paper from
responsible sources
FSC™ C007454

HER CHRISTMAS BABY CONFESSION

SHARON KENDRICK

MILLS & BOON

For the ace pilot Captain Matt Lindley
and his (equally ace!) co-pilot Paul Newrick.

They vividly brought to life the world of planes,
emergency landings, quick thinking and plenty of
adrenaline—and their help was invaluable.

Thank you.

CHAPTER ONE

THE WEDDING WAS over and Bianca was glad.

Even though all the guests had proclaimed it to be *'the most wonderful wedding in the history of the world'*.

It had been a jaw-droppingly photogenic occasion.

A Christmas wedding in a golden palace.

A handsome king marrying an ordinary woman and making her his queen.

What was not to like?

Bianca stared across the elaborate palace entrance hall. She hadn't liked being a bridesmaid for a start, even though the bride was her sister. And she hadn't particularly liked being back in bMonterosso—the wealthy mountain kingdom where she'd spent many of her childhood holidays.

The marriage had taken place two days before Christmas and the great cathedral had been decorated to reflect the holiday. Swathes of holly and ivy had hung from the mighty pillars and, as Bianca had squeezed herself into her crimson bridesmaid's dress, she had tried to absorb the joy of the occasion and reflect some of it back.

But all sorts of unsisterly thoughts had started flooding into her mind as she'd followed the vision of shimmering white up the wide aisle, even though she loved her sister from the bottom of her heart and was happy Rosie had found the man of her dreams. Yet Bianca kept thinking that *she* was the older sister. That *she* was still unmarried and, given her history of love and relationships, that situation showed no signs of changing.

She probably could have dealt with the growing awareness that her life wasn't going exactly to plan, if her travel arrangements hadn't been suddenly altered. Bianca had intended to catch a scheduled flight back to England to spend a low-key Christmas at home. No fuss. No fanfare. She'd been looking forward to a bit of peace and quiet after the busy build-up to the royal wedding. Until her sister had forced her to accept an aeroplane ride from the last man she would ever have chosen to spend time with.

Just thinking about him made her shiver. Made her body tingle and her mouth grow dry.

Xanthos Antoniou.

The powerful Greek American billionaire who had proved to be an irresistible magnet to every woman under the age of ninety during the royal nuptials. Dazzlingly muscular, with sinful good looks, he had been like a dark meteor crash-landing binto the golden splendour of the royal wedding. Nobody had been able to take their eyes off him. Herself included.

She hadn't known why her sister had been so insistent she accept a ride with him—especially when she'd made it quite clear she hadn't wanted to—but insistent she most certainly had been.

'Please, Bianca. As a favour to Corso. You'll get a lift in his private plane—*and* he's a crack pilot.'

Bianca had briefly wondered why her sister's royal husband was so keen to do Xanthos a favour, but at that point Rosie had rushed off to speak to someone else and it seemed the matter was closed. Which was why the man in question was currently heading purposefully in her direction across the marble foyer of the palace.

She tried not to glare as he made his way towards her, but keeping her expression neutral was a challenge. She didn't know what it was about the black-eyed billionaire which made her react so strongly, but she didn't seem able to control it. From the moment they'd first been introduced, she had felt a weird kind of reaction to him. A slow flush of heat to her cheeks. An uncomfortable awareness which made her breasts sting. Yet Xanthos Antoniou typified everything she disliked about the opposite sex. He exuded hard, masculine power and soft, sensual danger. He was alpha man personified. And those things did not turn her on.

She liked quiet men. Bookish men. Safe men.

Men who were the polar opposite of him.

'Bianca?'

His voice sounded like gravel being poured over honey as he said her name, which was presumably why her nipples had started pushing against her bra as if they wanted to escape from their lacy confinement and her heart to race as if she were running for a train. Breathing in, she curved her lips into the kind of polite smile she might have given a new client who had come seeking her legal advice.

'That's right. Bianca Forrester,' she replied briskly. Determined to put proceedings on a formal footing, she raised her eyebrows. 'I wasn't sure if you'd caught my surname when we were introduced yesterday, Mr Antoniou.'

'Oh, I never forget a surname, Ms Forrester,' he responded silkily. 'Just as it seems you haven't forgotten mine.'

But the mocking smile which accompanied his words made Bianca feel even more uncomfortable. She wasn't impressed by the fancy trappings of his wealth and couldn't care less that he had his own private jet. Her sister might have tried to big him up but she didn't want any part of it. She lowered her voice. 'Listen, I know you've been roped into offering me a lift and it's really very kind of you. But it won't be necessary.'

He frowned. 'Why not?'

'Because I already have a ticket and I'm perfectly happy to fly commercial. In fact, I'd prefer to travel that way. It means I can work on the flight, rather than have to make conversation.'

As her words clipped over him Xanthos felt a sudden flash of irritation because wasn't this scenario exactly what he had anticipated? It didn't matter that she was one of the most beautiful women he'd ever seen, with her coal-dark hair and eyes the colour of emeralds, the woman had attitude. The kind of attitude he didn't like. Cold and judgmental and…condescending. As if she'd already made up her mind about him and found him wanting.

And didn't that press all the wrong kinds of buttons?

Didn't it remind him of where he had come from and why he was here?

'But your sister specifically asked me to ensure you got back to England safely,' he said coolly. 'And I could hardly ignore such a request, could I? Who could possibly refuse the new Queen?'

He didn't mention the other reason. The main reason. Which was his connection with the groom. The most powerful connection of all.

Blood.

The blood which bound the two men together, even though neither of them wished for that particular bond. It was the dark secret which smouldered in Xanthos's heart, reminding him of how deeply he had been betrayed. The secret which had taught him that no woman should ever be believed or trusted. For he was King Corso's half-brother and nobody else in the world knew, other than bBianca's sister, Rosie.

And that was the way both men wanted it to stay.

Xanthos didn't know why Corso had wanted him to attend his wedding and had initially refused the coveted invitation. But the King had pushed and pushed, and in the end Xanthos had let him have what he wanted. He suspected his half-brother wanted to keep him sweet and thus guarantee he would make no claim on the throne. But not only was Xanthos illegitimate, he had no desire for Corso's bcrown—or his kingdom. He couldn't think of anything worse than being a public figure. He liked his freedom and being answerable to nobody but himself. And if the last thing he wanted was to ferry the ungrateful Bianca Forrester home, he had given his word to her sister, and he was a man of his word.

But as he stared down into her dark-fringed eyes, an unwanted jolt of awareness reminded him of just how incredibly green they were and for a moment he was mesmerised by them, just as he was mesmerised by the soft pink lines of her lips and the undulating lines of her body. 'Are you ready?' he questioned unevenly.

'I don't think you understood what I just said.' The hands she held up in silent appeal did not minimise the patronising quality of her smile. 'I'm giving byou a let-out.'

'But I don't want a let-out. The airport is swarming with paparazzi, which your sister thought you'd be keen to avoid.' This time he didn't bother to disguise his impatience. 'Most people would accept the offer of a lift in a private jet with good grace or even—dare I say it?—gratitude. So unless you want to make a scene, or to upset your sister on her honeymoon, I suggest you accompany me to the waiting car and we ride out to the airstrip.' His mouth hardened. 'Because the sooner we get going, the sooner this will be over.'

'You're making it sound as appealing as a trip to the dentist.'

He gave the ghost of a smile. 'Your words, Bianca, not mine.'

'Wow.' She flashed him a tight smile. 'This is going to be fun, isn't it?'

'I can barely contain my excitement.'

Past the giant fir tree they walked, with its spangle of silver stars and hundreds of tiny white lights which adorned the fragrant branches. Past boughs of holly and giant bunches of mistletoe. Past silver and golden balloons left over from the nuptials. The festive vibe of Christmas was still very much present, but Bianca was so riled by her companion's attitude that she barely took any notice.

Other guests stood chatting and they turned to watch as Bianca and Xanthos walked by.

'A striking couple,' Bianca overheard someone remark.

'Who *is* he?' someone else asked.

'I don't know, but she's a very lucky girl.'

But Bianca didn't feel in the least bit lucky as they sat in tense silence while the royal car whisked them to the airfield. She felt as if control had been snatched away from her and it was a sensation she didn't enjoy. The wind was a biting howl as she emerged from the limousine, and as a snowflake fluttered down and melted on her lips she saw Xanthos's dark gaze linger on her mouth, before he turned to speak to the driver. And the crazy thing was she *liked* him looking at her lips like that. She liked that sense of reluctance as he had dragged his gaze away and she couldn't understand why. How could you desire a man who made you feel so awkward and self-conscious? Hugging her coat around her, she followed him up the steps of the plane, ducking her head as she entered the cabin.

The interior of the aircraft was sleek and the fresh roses and glossy magazines gave the cabin a sumptuous feel, but it was smaller than she'd imagined and strangely silent. Had she been hoping for the distraction of other people? A co-pilot perhaps, or a gorgeous air stewardess or two, who might flirt with Xanthos and stop Bianca from entertaining her increasingly rogue thoughts about him.

'Aren't there any crew?'

'Nope. I'm flying solo. It's a relatively short flight and I think you'll find everything you could possibly need on board.' Dark eyebrows shot up to disappear into the ebony tangle of his hair. 'Unless you have a chronic need to be waited on? Is that what living in a palace does to you?'

'I don't actually live in the palace and I never did,' she returned. 'I used to spend my school holidays in a grace-and-favour house there because my father was an employee of the late King.'

'Then I'm sure you're perfectly capable of pouring your own champagne, Bianca,' he drawled, with a smile.

Was he aware of the impact of that smile? Did he realise that it made her want to shatter into pieces and then ask him to glue her back together? 'I only drink champagne when I'm celebrating,' she answered repressively. 'And the only thing I shall be celebrating is when we touch down.'

'Has anyone ever told you how ungrateful you are?'

'You have. I make that twice now. Has anyone ever told you how repetitive you can be, Xanthos?'

The ghost of a smile hovered around the edges of his sensual lips. 'No, I think you hold the record for making insulting observations,' he observed drily. 'So why don't you just read the safety card and buckle yourself in, while I prepare for take-off?'

Xanthos had been expecting yet more resistance, because she seemed determined to make this experience as difficult as possible. But to his amazement she was instantly compliant, removing her coat and reaching up to put it in the overhead locker—a movement which had the unfortunate side-effect of emphasising the luscious swell of her breasts. As she sank into her seat he lingered for a moment or two before heading for the flight deck, telling himself he needed to ensure she knew where the oxygen masks and life jackets were kept, but in reality it was more than safety concerns which kept him rooted to the spot. Because wasn't the bald truth that he was finding her intensely captivating?

Yesterday she had appeared as the bride's attendant, wearing a fitted red dress which had emphasised her ridiculously tiny waist and petite frame. Her black hair had been studded with scarlet roses and her lips had been scarlet, too, and she had looked like something out of an old-fashioned fairy tale. He'd noticed men sitting up bolt upright and watching her as she passed, her heavy silk gown brushing the stone cathedral floor, but she'd been too busy fiddling with her sister's heavy train to notice them. Or maybe she was one of those women who pretended to be ignorant of their own allure.

But today there was nothing remotely old-bfashioned or fairy tale about her. The jeans and soft green sweater which clung to her curves were bmodern and practical. The thick waves of her black hair had been pulled back from her face and rippled in a ponytail down her back, and she appeared to be wearing little or no make-up. But with lashes that long and that black he guessed she didn't need to. Her only adornment was a pair of golden hooped earrings. No rings. No bracelets. She looked faintly forbidding and somehow unapproachable, and yet... He narrowed his eyes. Was it her lack of height—for she must be barely five feet four—which made her seem so provocatively feminine? Or was it her spirited attitude which he found so alluring?

Xanthos felt his heart miss an unexpected beat. Despite his professed disdain of women with attitude, it was a hypothetical rather than a real dislike, because it hardly ever happened. He was used to adoration and acquiescence. He'd never had to try very hard with women and sometimes he wondered what it would be like if he did.

But his momentary flicker of interest was quickly replaced with a sense of impatience. He didn't want to think this way about Bianca Forrester. In fact, he didn't want to think about her at all. She was the sister-in-law of his unacknowledged royal brother and, as such, she was nothing but a complication. All he needed to do was get through the next few hours before he was free of her and then on to Switzerland for some fun and games...

Sitting in the cockpit, he methodically went through his checklist before getting the all-clear from air traffic control and making a smooth ascent into the wide blue ribbon of the winter sky. He looked down as the famous red volcanic mountain of Monterosso grew ever smaller and thought it unlikely he would ever return, no matter how much Corso should try to persuade him otherwise. For he had no real desire to deepen the relationship with his brother. He did not want a newly discovered family, because families were nothing but a drain. They brought with them pain, and heartbreak, and disappointment. They had the power to wreck your whole life from the inside out. Who in their right mind would ever want a family?

He settled into what should have an uneventful flight and the journey proceeded with textbook ease—reminding him of the pleasure and satisfaction he always got from flying a plane.

And then, out of nowhere, things started to happen.

At thirty thousand feet, air traffic control informed him they could no longer get his flight read-out. He frowned. It should have just been a blip, but it wasn't. With mounting disbelief Xanthos watched as both transponders failed and then the radar flickered ominously before packing up completely. He felt the rush of adrenaline, but despite the tension in his body and mad race of his heart, he was strangely calm. Because, like every experienced pilot, he had trained for an eventuality such as this and was almost prepared for the sudden whiff of smoke from behind him and the thundering of feet as Bianca came running into the cockpit, her lips a gasping gash in her terrified face.

'S-smoke...' she managed and then again. 'Smoke!'

Quickly, Xanthos glanced over his shoulder and saw ominous grey clouds billowing from the bulkhead as the emergency systems suddenly kicked into overdrive. Alarm bells sounded and red lights were flashing and he went into crisis-management mode. Glancing down at his map, he calculated that the nearest airport was forty minutes away and knew an aircraft had twenty minutes' sustainability in case of fire. His mouth dried.

Twenty minutes.

He met the terror in Bianca's eyes as he punched out the four-digit Mayday signal and scanned the screen in front of him, his heart hammering with relief as he located a nearby disused airfield in the valley of a mountain.

'We need to make an emergency landing. Go back and strap yourself into your seat. When I yell "brace" you do just that and we get off the plane asap. Leave everything behind. Do what I tell you and don't ask questions. Understand?'

To her credit she nodded and disappeared and then all Xanthos could think about was bringing down the craft safely, as he'd been taught. His concentration was total as they made a spiral descent and, just before bumping onto the icy runway, he yelled at Bianca to brace. The plane lurched and slid sideways on landing, careering towards the high white wall of a snowbank before coming to a juddering halt. And then he was charging into the cabin and undoing her seat belt and lifting her from her seat as smoke billowed all around them, making it hard to see.

He helped her outside into the bitter chill and never had it felt so wonderful to connect with the earth, even though the snow was hard and impacted like metal against his feet. For a moment it was difficult to keep his balance and he heard something like a sob escape from her lips. Their eyes met and something unfamiliar stirred deep inside him as he read the naked fear in hers. The need to protect her. To keep her safe. But first he had to get her away from the damned plane in case it exploded. Putting his arm tightly around her waist, he pulled her close, so close that her breath was warm against his cheek.

'Now run!' he yelled, leading her away across the runway, the cold wind leaving them both gasping bfor breath.

CHAPTER TWO

THE SENSATION OF Xanthos half carrying her across the airstrip was the only thing in Bianca's world which felt real right then. Everything else was like the worst disaster movie she'd ever seen. There was no colour in this unknown place, with its heavy grey sky and snowy landscape. No sound of traffic or birdsong—nothing but the wild howl of the wind as it whipped around them, with its icy fingers. The distant plane with its nose embedded in the snowbank added yet another nightmarish element and she wanted to scream and run as far away as possible—back to civilisation and everything she knew.

'L-let's get out of here!' she shouted, aware of his arm fixed firmly around her waist. 'Come on!'

But Xanthos didn't seem to be listening. He was scanning the area, as if committing every forbidding inch to memory. 'At least the smoke coming from the plane has subsided,' he said, almost reflectively. 'Which means it's unlikely to explode. We've been lucky.'

Lucky? Was he insane? Bianca stared at the distant aircraft. 'Please,' she whispered. 'I want to go.'

'Go where?'

'I don't know. Anywhere!' She looked around distractedly. 'There must be a village or town nearby. We need to go and find help!'

'No, we're not going to do that.'

His calmness was freaking her out and Bianca wondered if he'd bumped his head when he'd landed the plane during that scary descent, when the craft had been spinning like the slow cycle of a washing machine, leaving her dizzy with fear. Why was he refusing to see sense? Was she expected to take charge—as usual—and mightn't that be the best thing if Xanthos wasn't thinking straight?

'We must,' she said. 'We must!' In desperation she began to drum her bunched fists against the solid wall of his chest, but he didn't even seem to notice that either. 'I want to get away from here! As far away as possible.'

'You see that building over there?'

His continuing coolness had the effect of removing some of her panic and Bianca let her hands fall from his chest as she mirrored the direction of his glance to see a rudimentary stone building, topped with snow. It was possibly the most unwelcoming place she'd ever set eyes on and, instinctively, she shuddered.

'Of course I can see it.'

'That's where we're going.'

'If you think I'm setting foot in that place—'

'Now listen to me, Bianca,' he interrupted, his coolness now replaced by a grim note of determination. 'We can do this one of two ways. You can choose to walk with me and do what I tell you, which would be preferable. But if you continue to resist, I'll be forced to put you over my shoulder and carry you.'

'Because you want to prove how big and tough and macho you are?' she accused in a trembling voice.

'Because I've done enough survival training to know what I'm talking about and you've never been in a situation like this before.' He lowered his voice. 'Listen, I know you're in shock and I know the landing can't have been easy for you, but you need to take my advice.'

'Why should I? Twenty-four hours ago you were a total stranger to me—yet now I'm expected to depend on you for life and death decisions?'

'I'm afraid so.'

But maybe he registered the fear which was still trembling her voice because he reached out and pulled her towards him again and Bianca felt herself sinking into the hardness of his body. And she wanted this. Needed this. She wanted him to continue to hold her tightly because he felt warm and strong and dependable. As if he were her rock. Her anchor. And he was neither, she reminded herself severely, as she resisted the stupid desire to reach up and rest her cheek against his. He was someone she didn't particularly like and the feeling was obviously mutual.

'Let me go,' she said, without any real conviction.

He did exactly as she asked—and she was annoyed with herself for missing his touch—but when he next spoke, his voice had gentled by a fraction. 'You're going to have to trust me on this, Bianca. Do you think you can do that?'

Bianca chewed her lip, the irony of the situation not escaping her. One of the reasons she'd instinctively disliked Xanthos Antoniou was because she preferred men who were safe and she'd decided he wasn't. Yet right now she couldn't think of anyone safer, or anyone else she'd rather be with.

Wordlessly she nodded and began to follow him towards the small building which, on closer examination, appeared even more inhospitable than it had done from a distance. The stone walls were as grey as the darkening sky and she watched as he began shoving his shoulder against the wooden door in a brutal display of strength, until eventually it gave way with a damp-sounding creak and splintering noise. Cautiously, he entered the building with bBianca right behind him—not wanting to let him out of her sight. Her cheeks were burning with cold as she half stumbled into the welcome dryness and a huge cobweb floated onto her face. Instinctively, she brushed it away, her heart pounding with terror.

It took a moment for her eyes to become accustomed to the light. Not that there was much to see. The room obviously hadn't been used for a long, long time and had a damp, stale air about it. There was an empty desk with a wooden chair on either side and a battered armchair beside an old fireplace, which was lined with dust and ancient embers. The walls were bare, with pale rectangles where maps or photos might once have hung. In one corner, a narrow single bed was shoved up against the wall. In the other corner, a door led into a tiny room containing a toilet and a sink, above which hung a rusty mirror not much larger than a grapefruit. And that was it.

'What is this place?' she breathed.

'Obviously some kind of caretaker's hut which certainly won't be a match for the kind of luxury we experienced in Monterosso,' he observed drily. 'But we'll be protected from the elements, at least.'

Bianca began to shiver, realising that there'd been no time to grab her coat and that her sweater offered little protection against the clawing insistence of the icy temperature. 'Now what?' she whispered.

'You stay here. I'm going back to the plane—'

'No! Please.' The words sprang from her mouth before she could stop them. 'Don't leave me!'

His black eyes gleamed. 'A couple of hours ago you couldn't wait to see the back of me.'

'Don't remind me. Maybe if I'd listened to my instincts, I'd be safely back in London by now!'

'Good to see you're reverting to type, Bianca. We stand a much greater chance of survival if you're back to being your usual combative self—rather than some wilting little flower which needs tending all hours of the day and night.'

'I can assure you that wilting has never been part of my make-up.'

'I'm delighted to hear it. But you're cold. Look at you. You're shivering. You need warmth and so do I. Stay here,' he commanded softly as he pulled open the door. 'I'll be as fast as I can.'

She didn't know what made her say it. Was it the sudden tight clench of apprehension as she saw the forbidding bleakness of the winter landscape outside, or the fear of how she would cope if he didn't come back? Or was it the way he'd noticed that she was shivering and had ordered her to stay put, which seemed to introduce a level of intimacy which hadn't been there before?

'Be…careful.'

His mocking smile was unexpected and, again, she was reminded of its potency.

'How touching you should be so concerned for my welfare.'

'It's actually my own I'm worried about.'

The door slammed behind him and Bianca peered out through the window, watching him make his way across the airfield towards the crashed plane, his powerful body etched darkly against the bleached landscape as he negotiated the icy ground. It had started to snow again and already the light was beginning to fade. Soon it would be dark and at some point they would be expected to sleep. Her gaze swivelled to the narrow bed and ropey-looking mattress and she swallowed down the sudden lump of anxiety which had risen in her throat. How could two people possibly sleep on that?

She paced around the small room—mostly in an attempt to keep herself warm but also to try and make some sense of the thoughts which were spinning like cartwheels inside her head. As Xanthos had instructed, she'd left everything behind—but she dragged her phone from the back-pocket of her jeans, her heart sinking when she saw there was no signal. What a nightmare. She hadn't even asked any sensible questions about what their chances were, or whether anyone would ever find them.

And if they didn't?

She swallowed.

She wouldn't let herself go there.

She heard a pounding on the door—as if someone were kicking it—and she pulled it open to find Xanthos standing there, his hair covered in snow and his arms full of various paraphernalia. A blast of icy air followed him inside and she closed the door behind him as he unloaded most of the stuff onto the desk. He threw her overcoat across the room towards her, along with a dark scarf she recognised as his.

'Put those on,' he instructed tersely.

Although he was back in command mode, she was pleased enough to obey, doing up the buttons on the thick coat with unsteady fingers which felt like sticks of ice and then winding his soft scarf around her neck. Had the emergency fine-tuned her senses? Was that why she breathed in deeply, wanting to inhale the woody, masculine scent which seemed to have permeated the fine wool?

'Have you got gloves?' he demanded.

She nodded.

'Put those on too.'

She did as he asked while he slid on his own jacket and she couldn't seem to tear her eyes away from the powerful set of his shoulders and that broad chest.

'Stop staring and start unpacking,' he said abruptly, sliding his gaze towards her. 'I'm going back to the plane.'

'But why? You've only just got back!'

'Because, contrary to popular opinion, I'm not Superman. I couldn't carry everything in one trip. Just shut the door behind me, Bianca. I won't be long.'

This time she didn't beg him to stay, in fact she was pleased to see the back of him. *Stop staring*, indeed. But she had been, hadn't she? She'd been no better than all those women who'd been fawning over him at the wedding party last night. No wonder he was so arrogant.

She began to sort out the stuff he'd retrieved from the stricken aircraft, putting it into neat piles on the desk. Blankets, travel socks, a big container of water and, bizarrely, broken-off bits of rubber. When he reappeared, he was carrying her suitcase, and what looked like the entire contents of the minibar. 'I don't suppose you brought my hand luggage?' she questioned hopefully as he shut the door on the howling wind.

Xanthos felt a flicker of irritation flare up inside him. 'No, I did not bring your damned hand luggage,' he answered carefully. Was she expecting him to take a risk negotiating the treacherously icy airfield, just so she could get her manicured fingers on her no-doubt highly expensive face creams? Didn't she realise that from now on theirs was a new reality, where the pampered sister of the new Queen might be expected to rough it more than she was used to? Maybe he needed to spell it out for her.

They were going to be in close confinement for... how long? A pulse began to hammer at his temple. Who knew? But it was going to be difficult enough as it was. There was no point in falling out. He needed to forget her ingratitude and their mutual dislike, which had been simmering beneath the surface from the get-go. More importantly, he needed to ignore those wide-lashed eyes, which looked like green stars, and lose the memory of the red bridesmaid's dress which had outlined her tiny frame to perfection.

But wasn't it strange how sometimes your mind did exactly the opposite to what you wanted it to do? An image of creamy breasts constrained by blood-red satin swam into his head and, silently, he cursed. His libido might have chosen the most inconvenient of times to rear its head, but this was only going to work if he stopped thinking about her as a desirable woman. All he needed to focus on was the fact that she was the King's sister-in-law and that, somehow, he needed to keep her safe.

'I've just brought the essentials,' he elaborated. 'Why don't you start unpacking—while I go and investigate the bathroom?'

'Perhaps you'd like me to salute every time you shout out an order?' she demanded.

'Now that,' he said softly, 'would be something to see.'

Her sudden blush surprised him but he turned away from the arresting pinkness of her cheeks, shutting the bathroom door behind him with perhaps more force than was necessary. Inside the dingy washroom he located the stopcock, grateful he'd taught himself the practicalities of life, despite the immense wealth which had surrounded him until his ignominious fall from grace at the age of sixteen. But still it gave him pleasure knowing that he never paid anyone to do a job he wouldn't be able to do as well himself.

He checked everything was working and walked back into the hut, but although everything had been unpacked and was laid out with commendable neatness on the old desk, Bianca's face was set and tense, as if she'd been rehearsing what she was about to say.

'I need you to tell me what's happening,' she said, in a low voice.

'I've just made sure you have running water and a flushing toilet. Which must be some cause for celebration.'

'That's not what I meant.'

'No?' He raised his eyebrows.

Bianca felt the slow build of frustration. This was *exasperating*. And also confusing. She was a lawyer. She dealt with facts every day of her life. She asked incisive questions and had the ability to view a situation objectively. Yet now it felt as if her mind were composed of cotton wool and her normal powers of reasoning were slipping away from her. And you wouldn't need to be a genius to work out why.

It was him.

Without actually doing anything, he was unsettling her. Big time.

He was making her feel things which were disturbingly unfamiliar. Softly clawing, erotic things which were way out of her comfort zone. And she didn't want to feel this way. She didn't want to be aware of suddenly stinging breasts or the low curl of hunger deep inside her. Her focus should be on the gravity of their situation, not the curve of his sensual lips or the loud thundering of her heart.

She cleared her throat. 'My phone doesn't have a signal.'

'That's because there isn't one. I wouldn't expect there to be in a deserted mountainous region like this.'

'Are you trying to increase my anxiety levels, Xanthos?'

'No, I'm giving you the facts.' He fixed her with a speculative look. 'Or maybe you're someone who doesn't like dealing with facts?'

'I'm a lawyer.'

'Ah.'

'Go on,' she goaded. 'Say it.'

'Say what?'

'Make one of the many terrible jokes about lawyers which I've heard a zillion times before.'

'I wouldn't dream of it.' He slanted her the glimmer of a smile. 'Scoring points strikes me as something of a time-wasting exercise when we should probably be thinking about the night ahead.'

The night ahead. Cold and dark and miles from anywhere. Bianca drew in a deep breath as, once again, icy fear crept over her. 'How are you proposing we get out of here?' she croaked.

'We wait for someone to rescue us.' He glanced out of the window, where night had fallen, the thick snow clouds masking the stars with a dark mantle. 'Though I don't reckon it's going to be tonight.'

Bianca found herself wondering what lay out there in the impenetrable darkness and, despite the overcoat she was wearing, she gave a convulsive shiver. 'But how can we expect someone to rescue us if we haven't got a phone signal?'

'I sent out an emergency call just before I brought the plane down. They know we're here. We just have to be patient, Bianca. And survive.' His voice suddenly became harsh. 'That's really the only part which matters. That we make it through the night. Do you understand what I'm saying?'

His narrowed gaze was edged with doubt and Bianca knew she mustn't crumble. She mustn't let him see she was vulnerable, or scared—even if she was. She needed to be strong and independent—just as she'd been throughout her life.

'Yes, you're right,' she said, but suddenly it was very hard to stop her teeth from chattering. 'So what's the best way of ensuring we do? Survive, I mean?'

He reached over to grab a miniature bottle of whisky from the desk. 'Most of all, we need to keep warm.'

'I don't think drinking's a very good idea,' she said repressively. 'Isn't it counterproductive if we try to escape the reality of our situation by blotting it out with alcohol?'

He looked as if he were trying not to smile. 'I have no intention of hitting the spirits. I prefer my drinking companions to be a little less prickly around the edges. I was intending to use the Scotch as fuel—to help me start a fire. But first, I'll need to smash up those old chairs.'

She frowned. 'Isn't that criminal damage?'

'Technically, I suppose it is. Let them sue me.' His black eyes glinted as he headed for the door. 'Who knows? You might be called on to litigate in my favour, Bianca.'

Unsettled by his sarcasm, Bianca turned away as he went outside to demolish the chairs—smashing them against the stone walls of the hut, judging by the deafening noise he was making. But the jarring sound which had broken the silence of the night was the wake-up call she needed to shake her out of her shock. She couldn't allow Xanthos to do all the work, could she? For a start, it was much too cold to sit still, and maybe the gnawing fear which had taken root at the pit of her stomach would dissolve if she started being active and thought about something else.

She needed to consider how they were going to spend

the long night ahead, and somehow that disturbed her almost as much as their isolation and the icy temperature of the room. The narrow bed seemed to be taunting her with all sorts of dangerous possibilities—and throwing into stark relief some of her own insecurities. She didn't *want* to think about the fact that this was the first time she'd ever contemplated spending the night with a man. She bit her lip. And that the circumstances couldn't be more bizarre.

So she set about keeping herself busy, shaking out the soft cashmere blankets Xanthos had brought from the plane and thinking what a contrast they made, laid out over the ancient mattress. Next she examined the selection of food he'd brought back from the plane— which was bizarre to say the least. She was just hunting around in her suitcase to locate her toothpaste and some clean underwear for the morning, when Xanthos returned bearing a commendable pile of firewood and suddenly she was stricken with embarrassment, her fingers closing over the little scrap of black silk, in a vain attempt to conceal her panties from him.

'Oh,' she said, her expression as self-conscious as her words. 'I wasn't expecting you back so soon.'

He kicked the door shut with more force than was necessary. 'You thought the night so pleasant I might want to linger?'

'No, of course not,' she said, stuffing the panties bback inside the suitcase.

Xanthos put the wood down beside the fireplace, trying to forget what he'd just seen, telling himself he didn't give a damn what she wore next to her skin.

And you are a liar, taunted a mocking voice in his

head. *Because of course you wanted to know and now you do.* Black and silky and lacy and surprisingly brief. Briefs for the lawyer. How appropriate.

The bland smile he offered her was supposed to reduce the sudden drying of his mouth, but unfortunately it did no such thing. Nor did it go any way towards alleviating the sudden aching at his groin. 'We need to build a fire,' he said roughly, perplexed by the effect she was having on him and wondering why he was so attracted to her. Because she wasn't like the other women who came into his orbit. She didn't bat her eyelashes, or simper, or smile. She didn't throw her head back and giggle uncontrollably whenever he said something mildly amusing. On the contrary. At times she seemed almost to be judging him—and not in a particularly positive way. Yet her green gaze was a temptation as well as a challenge and, no matter how hard he tried to fight it, he couldn't deny finding the tiny woman powerfully attractive, though he'd barely spoken to her before she'd been foisted on him today. He hadn't even asked her to dance at the reception last night and that had been a deliberate omission, despite her being the most beautiful woman in the room.

Was that because he'd known it made sense to keep his distance from someone unknowingly related to him by marriage? Or because some bone-deep instinct made him suspect that to touch her would be to make him lose his mind and, ultimately, control? And control was an essential component of his make-up. Once, it had been taken away from him and he had vowed it would never happen again. Which was why he always needed to be in charge. To be the decision maker. It was one of the elements of his character which had made him so successful in business. The same element which had left a litter of broken hearts behind him, because most women failed to understand the futility of attempting to control or to change him. They had an inability to accept him as the man he was. Instead they tried to tie him down and stultify him with a domesticity he had no appetite for.

Crumpling up one of the magazines, he laid it in the grate, wondering how he was going to endure the hours which lay ahead, unable to blot out the images which were streaming into his mind with disturbing clarity. Of *course* getting up close and personal with Bianca would make the time pass more quickly, but that wasn't going to happen. He was stuck here with her for the foreseeable and didn't intend saying or doing anything he might later regret.

For tonight, at least, there was no escape from the green-eyed temptress and he was just going to have to get by the best way he could.

He struck the first match.

Because no way was he going to have sex with her.

CHAPTER THREE

HE LIT A fire and it was the sexiest thing Bianca had ever witnessed.

Her throat tightened and so did her breasts. She knew Scouts were supposed to be able to create fire by rubbing two sticks together and she'd always thought it a bit of a myth.

But Xanthos was doing something on exactly those lines. Not with sticks, but with some alcohol-soaked wood from the chair he'd smashed up, along with bits of rubber he'd retrieved from the plane. One minute the temperature had been sub-zero and the next, he'd conjured up roaring flames which were licking at her skin with seductively warm tongues. As the flames engulfed the whisky-soaked pieces of wood the dank interior of their shelter suddenly felt almost luxurious. Warm colours of coral and gold were splashed over the walls and the fire's crackle was almost hypnotic.

'Wow,' she said, her voice full of unwilling admiration as he stood up from his crouching position.

'You like that?' he questioned softly, stepping back to survey the result of his endeavours, and Bianca wished he hadn't because now he was standing beside her and her body had begun to react to the proximity of his. The fire had magnified his shadow and thrown it into stark relief, so that it dominated the room with its darkness. He was so tall and so muscular, radiating a powerful energy she'd never come across before, and she could feel the slow curl of something sweet and insistent deep inside her, something she realised was desire.

She nodded. 'It's amazing,' she said, through lips which had grown annoyingly dry.

She still couldn't really relax around him, but she couldn't deny that his behaviour was a dramatic departure from her expectations of him. She'd had him down as yet another arrogant man with more money than was good for him, who just waved an entitled hand to get people to do his bidding. She'd pictured his life as smooth and effortless—screened from the nitty-gritty of the real world in some chic New York penthouse. Yet here he was in this derelict old building, creating fire out of practically nothing but the dextrous flick of his fingers.

Fire-making was a primitive skill, she acknowledged reluctantly. It spoke to her on an elemental level she couldn't seem to understand. Everything seemed to have slowed down, and her senses had become raw. She could hear the crackle of the fire and smell the woodiness of the smoke. She thought how ironic it was that fire could be their saviour as well as their enemy. For the first time since the plane had crashed, she felt warm—and safe. That was the craziest thing of all. With him she felt safe.

But the plane *had* crashed, she reminded herself. Surely they shouldn't just be lazing around like this as if they were on some unexpected glamping vacation? So do something. Take back some of the control you seem to have relinquished so willingly to Xanthos Antoniou.

Because independence was the only thing she'd ever been able to rely on, after her father's terrible accident. Her mother and sister had been in bits and started to lean on her, until it had become a habit for them all. Yet she recognised that there was a certain comfort to be derived from being the one who always made the decisions. It was Bianca who had concluded at a family conference that it was best to switch off her father's life support after years of being hooked to a ventilator, with her mother tearfully agreeing. After that Bianca had concluded she could survive anything life threw at her, if she had all the facts at her fingertips and kept her emotions in check.

She cleared her throat. 'Shouldn't we be trying to attract attention?'

He shot her a questioning look. 'And how do you suggest we do that?'

'I don't know. Have you…um…' she shrugged her shoulders a little helplessly '…thought about lighting a fire outside?'

'No, I haven't. Because only an idiot would do that. It's dark, it's deserted and we're in the valley of a mountain, in case you hadn't noticed. Even in the unlikely event that someone might see us, I'd probably freeze to death making the effort.' His dark eyes glittered with an emotion she couldn't make out. 'And while I appreciate I'm not your ideal choice of companion, presumably even you aren't hard-hearted enough to wish me dead?'

His remark hit home. Of course it did. Quickly,

Bianca glanced out of the window, determined he shouldn't see her expression and realise that he had the power to hurt her. Did he think she was hard-hearted? A flicker of insecurity ran through her. Was that the person she had become? A cold and controlling robot? She clenched her fingers, trying bto quash her suddenly rampant feelings of self-doubt. No, it was not. She was just careful, that was all. She protected herself against the heartache which other women just seemed to lay themselves open to, because she'd learnt that nothing was as bad as emotional pain. But maybe she had taken self-protection just a step too far and now was the time to be conciliatory. 'Don't be ridiculous.' She drew in a deep breath. 'If you must know, I'm very…grateful for everything you've done.'

Their eyes met. Held. Was she imagining the flicker of something responsive in his? Some glint of fire in their ebony depths which made her heart clench with pleasure. For one crazy moment she thought he was about to reach out and touch her, but all he was doing was looking at her and she found his dark gaze immeasurably comforting. It felt like an innocent form of intimacy, if there was such a thing. Was that why she blurted out the first thing which came into her head?

'Why don't I make us some tea? When I was unpacking the provisions, I noticed you'd brought an ice bucket from the plane, presumably to hold water. We could boil some up on the fire and use some of those peppermint teabags.'

'Resourceful,' he murmured.

'You sound surprised.'

'Maybe I am. Maybe I'm used to women who like to

be waited on.' He slanted her a smile as she carefully positioned the bucket on top of the smouldering logs. 'Why don't I watch that for you?' he suggested. 'You might want to go and wash that smear off your face.'

Smear? Instinctively, she reached her fingertips to her face. What smear? Grabbing her soap bag, Bianca hurried into the bathroom and shut the door, her heart beating very fast as she stared into the tiny mirror and saw the large dark mark on her cheek, which must have resulted from her earlier close encounter with a cobweb. Not a pretty sight. Maybe that was why he had been staring at her so intently. Of course it was. In which case, she really needed to lose the schoolgirl fantasies about him, as of now. She washed her face—but the water was icy cold, the soap failed to lather and, of course, she had no towel. She patted her cheeks dry with her hands and then brushed her teeth, ignoring the taunting voice which demanded to know why she thought that necessary.

Then she freed her hair from its ponytail and began to brush it out, convincing herself it would be warmer to leave it loose. But there were other justifications for allowing the ebony waves to fall over her shoulders in a glossy tumble. She stared back at her grapefruit-sized reflection with a touch of defiant feminine pride. Wasn't the truth that she wanted to look good, because that would make her *feel* good about herself and give her back some of the confidence which seemed to be in short supply? She felt awkward in the company of Xanthos—as if she didn't quite know how to behave around him. Somehow, the powers of reasoning—which had balways been her calling card—had slipped away from her. And she needed to get them back.

With a resolute air, she reknotted the scarf he'd given her and returned to find him sprawled on the floor beside the fire, as the water bubbled up to a boil. Did he have any idea how gorgeous he looked? His long legs were spread out in front of him—the faded denim pulled taut over the definition of powerfully-muscular thighs. Her heart gave a mighty kick and it took a huge effort to drag her gaze away, especially when he leaned over to remove the bucket of boiling water from the fire.

Focus, she told herself severely. Just focus.

Working as efficiently as she could with limited resources, she dunked peppermint teabags in two incongruously delicate bone-china mugs which must also have come from the luxury aircraft. She handed one to Xanthos, which he took with a nod of thanks, before perching with her own on the edge of the armchair, which he had pulled closer to the fire. She cradled the cup between her hands and took a sip, thinking how the simple pleasure of being warm again could make her temporarily bforget the precariousness of their situation. 'Mmm…good, isn't it?'

But he didn't respond as he sipped his own tea—he seemed lost in thought. And as Bianca put her cup down and sneaked a glance at her watch, a sudden sense of isolation hit her, along with a hefty dose of realisation. It was only just gone eight o'clock and although she was amazed how much time had passed, and even if they were rescued at first light—*if*—there were still hours to get through. With him.

He was staring into the fire, the firelight licking at his

hard profile and highlighting his body in red and shadowed detail. She thought that he managed to look both relaxed yet alert to danger—like a jungle cat which had momentarily ceased its relentless prowling. He represented all the things she inherently shied away from and yet Bianca was aware that her feelings towards him were changing. Was that because he had taken command of them both in a life-threatening situation and somehow made her feel secure?

She wasn't used to a man making decisions on her behalf yet, disturbingly, she was finding she rather liked it. His imperturbable manner was almost as attractive as his undeniable good looks, and she was rapidly becoming aware that Xanthos Antoniou was the kind of man who could burrow underneath her defences. Was that what was happening to her? Was that why all she could think about was wanting to *touch* him—to run her fingertips over that hard body in a slow and very thorough exploration? She wanted to break the rule of a lifetime. To find out if he could possibly feel as good as he looked. To discover whether his skin really *was* like silk, or the honed ridges of muscle as rock-like as they seemed.

And she had to call a halt to what was nothing but madness. She had to change the dynamic between them, as of now. To move from infatuation to impartiality.

But how? Her flippancy and stonewalling of earlier hadn't worked, had they? If anything it had only increased the spiralling tension between them. It had created a dialogue which bordered on flirtation. So try something different. Pretend he's a colleague you've met at some out-of-town conference. Pretend he's got a wife and two children waiting for him at home. Do that chatty, superficial thing—knowing that once this is over, you need never see one another again. Leaning back in the battered armchair, she tucked up her legs beneath her, and slanted him a companionable smile. 'Well, I must say, this is the last place I ever imagined spending Christmas.'

He lifted his arms above his head to give a slow stretch and Bianca found herself thinking that none of her work colleagues had ever displayed a physique as achingly muscular as his.

'Ditto,' he growled.

She cleared her throat. 'What are you supposed to be doing for the holidays?'

Dark eyebrows were elevated. 'Do you really want to know?'

Bianca felt an unexpected flutter of nerves. 'Of course,' she affirmed brightly. 'And after all, what else are we going to talk about? The likelihood of anyone ever finding us? The rapidly plummeting temperature outside?'

Or the most pressing question of all, Xanthos thought grimly. Which was, where the hell were they going to sleep? And how was that going to happen when his groin felt so heavy that he could barely move? He sighed. Better to humour her, he supposed—while remaining as detached as possible. Which meant ignoring the shapely legs she'd just crossed, sending a battery of erotic thoughts fizzing to his starved senses. Maybe the boredom of making small talk would help him forget how much he wanted to kiss her. 'I was intending to catch up with some friends in Geneva for a short skiing break. I'm supposed to be meeting them on Christmas Eve.'

'That's tomorrow.'

'I know when it is, Bianca.'

'Do you think they'll miss you?'

He thought about Kiki—the supermodel he'd met briefly in Monaco last summer, who had been chasing down a meeting with him ever since. She would certainly miss him. But disconcertingly, he wasn't the least bit disappointed at passing up on what could have been a delicious booty call, not even when he thought about the model's traffic-stopping long legs and her stunning blonde beauty, which had graced the covers of so many magazines. Was that because, in the here and now, the voluptuous frame of the petite Bianca curled up in the armchair opposite was a far more tantalising prospect?

'I'm pretty sure they will,' he said wryly. 'But since I'm hoping we might be rescued before that happens, I might still make the slopes for Christmas morning.' He forced himself to enquire about her own plans, reminding himself that women liked to talk about themselves, which would curtail the inevitable questions she might ask him. Because he didn't like answering questions. He preferred enigma to openness. More importantly, he didn't want her to know who he really was. He had no desire to open that particular can of worms.

His mouth twisted. The truth of his conception had sickened him—coating his already difficult past with yet another unsavoury layer. He had thought it might be possible to overcome it, wondering if Corso's persuasive words were true and that maybe they could form some kind of relationship. But deep in his heart he knew that was never going to happen. He should never have gone to the wedding. Should never have agreed to see his brother again. He had felt like a fish out of water. He didn't need Corso. He didn't need anyone.

'What about your own plans?' he asked.

'Oh, very quiet. Just me. Well, I had a couple of invitations from friends to spend the day with them, but you know what it's like…' She shrugged. 'I'm not really a big fan of the holiday.'

'You don't like Christmas?'

'Well, that's going a bit far. It's just never really meant very much to me. Not like it does to other people. It's mostly about family, isn't it?'

'But you have your sister. And your mother was at the wedding, wasn't she?'

'Yes, with my aunt. They're both staying on at the palace to be waited on hand and foot, while Rosie and Corso are on honeymoon. They wanted me to join them, but I said no.'

He raised his eyebrows. 'Because the idea didn't appeal to you?'

Bianca stared briefly into the golden-red heart of the fire, wondering if he was actually interested in her answer or whether, like her, he was simply going through the motions of conversation. The latter, she suspected. But surely it was safer to concentrate on the subject of Christmas, rather than on her hardening nipples, which were thankfully hidden by her overcoat. 'Not really,' she admitted. 'I used to spend the holidays in Monterosso when I was growing up and—well, so much has changed. I never particularly enjoyed my Christmases there. They always seemed to be about the royal family and nobody else. And I didn't want…' She hesitated. 'I had no desire to go back there.'

'No. I can understand that. Connecting with the past is often difficult.'

It was an observation she wasn't expecting him to make and although she wanted to know more about what had made him say it, something told Bianca to hold the growing silence, to let *him* be the one to break it.

'What was it like as a child in Monterosso?' he questioned at last. 'Did you spend Christmas with Corso and his family?'

'Gosh, no, nothing like that,' she said slowly. 'Our worlds were miles apart. Inevitably. He was the Crown Prince, and although my father might have been the palace archivist, essentially, he was still a servant. And the late King was a stickler for protocol.'

'Was he?' he questioned, and Bianca realised that his voice had grown very harsh. 'Was he really?'

'Oh, yes. He was very particular about everyone knowing their place. All the cooks and butlers and maids used to be working round the clock for days leading up to the holiday.' She hesitated as her mind took her back. 'But he used to throw a party for all the palace staff at lunchtime on Christmas Eve. It was all very old-fashioned. And afterwards we would all gather round the tree and be given our presents from the King.' She remembered how much she'd hated that sense of being an inferior. The sense of being a recipient of the King's patronage and having to be excessively *grateful* for everything which came her way. Hadn't it been that which had spurred her on to work so hard at school and forge for herself her own career, knowing that financial and emotional independence were more important to her than anything?

'And did you like him?' he questioned suddenly. 'The King?'

'Did I like him?' she repeated slowly. 'I've never really thought about it before. He was just there. Ruling everything and everyone. His power was absolute.' But as Xanthos continued to regard her curiously, she knew she was short-changing him. And since she would never see him again once they were rescued—*if* they were rescued—why not articulate something she could easily tell a stranger, but would never admit to her sister or her mother? 'I didn't really like him, no. He was a cold, cruel man and sometimes I felt sorry for Corso.'

'Why would you feel sorry for the sole heir to such a wealthy kingdom?' he demanded. 'A man who would one day have untold wealth and power at his fingertips.'

She wondered what had caused that sudden bitterness to enter his voice. 'His mother died when he was young and I think… I think that hit him very hard,' she explained falteringly. 'He used to come to our house and have meals with us sometimes, and I used to get the feeling that those times with our family were the only warmth and real company he'd ever known.'

'Lucky Corso,' he said hollowly.

'Maybe.' She hesitated. 'You haven't said how you know the King.'

'No.' There was a pause. 'Let's just say we have business interests in common.'

But he didn't do the polite thing of elaborating on what those interests might be, even though Bianca sat there in silence, giving him the perfect opportunity to tell her. Instead, he scrambled to his feet and once again, his shadow seemed to devour the entire room with its darkness.

'At some point we should eat,' he said, his voice assuming a familiar note of command. 'It'll pass the time as well as keeping our strength up. I'll fix us something.'

He was doing it *again*. Taking charge and assuming control. And even though it might be a very old-fashioned way to behave, Bianca was finding it dangerously seductive. So don't let him get to you. Show him that you're perfectly capable of looking after yourself.

She stood up, feeling immediately dwarfed by his immense height. 'That's okay. I can just as easily do it.' She gave him a polite smile. 'Why don't you let me fix something while you tend the fire?'

'Why don't I?' he echoed as he bent down to pick up a log.

Glad for the distraction, Bianca went over to the desk and rifled through one of the boxes. 'Caviar, chocolate, fine wine,' she listed. 'Perfect for upmarket snacking on luxury jets, but not exactly what you'd call a balanced diet. Still, I suppose it'll have to do.'

She did her best, smearing the costly black caviar onto crackers and arranging them on bone-china plates in as attractive a way as possible. She spread the bizarre feast out in front of the fire and sat down while Xanthos walked over to the desk and pulled out a half-bottle of champagne, his black eyes mocking in the firelight as he held it up. 'Something to help wash it down, or are you still vetoing alcohol?'

Bianca shrugged, not objecting when he tipped the

fizzy wine into her empty teacup and handed it to her. 'Peppermint-flavoured champagne,' she commented wryly, as she took a sip.

'Could be the next big thing,' he murmured, before flicking her a shuttered glance. 'By the way, thanks for dinner. Under the circumstances, it looks delicious.'

His unexpected praise pleased her and for a while they ate and drank in a silence which was almost companionable. As the fire warmed her skin and the luxury food provided a burst of energy, Bianca could almost have forgotten about their predicament. But she couldn't ignore the subject they hadn't yet discussed. The invisible elephant in the room, which was now looming so huge that it seemed to be sucking all the available oxygen from the air.

'So.' She surveyed the hard set of his profile and tried not to wonder what it would be like to kiss him. 'Where are we going to sleep?'

He turned to face her, his expression unreadable. 'I would have thought the answer was obvious. There's a bed over there.'

'I can see that for myself.' She sucked in a deep breath. 'And since it's a bed for one person, that creates a bit of a problem.'

'Does it?'

'Of course it does.'

Xanthos could see which way this was going and kept his tone studiedly casual. 'So you'd like me to sleep on the stone floor, would you, Bianca?'

She shrugged awkwardly. 'Obviously it isn't ideal.'

'Damned right it isn't ideal,' he snapped, thinking what a spoiled little princess she could be—bdespite her protestations that she was nothing but a royal servant's daughter. 'Sooner rather than later that fire is going to die out and we need to conserve our fuel because we don't know when we're going to be rescued.' He thought how confident he sounded about the possibility of someone getting to them in time.

Because what if nobody did?

But surely it was easier to concentrate on practicalities rather than his incipient desire for this woman, which was building by the second. A desire to crush those pink lips beneath his and to kiss her until they were both gasping for breath. To explore her luscious curves, which were currently sending out a siren call to his starving senses. He clenched his fists so hard that the knuckles cracked, because this was madness.

He wanted Bianca Forrester, yes. At this precise moment he couldn't remember ever wanting a woman quite as much. He wanted her with a hunger which felt raw and visceral, and he wondered if their life-threatening incarceration was intensifying a desire which was obviously mutual. His mouth hardened. He had seen the way her gaze had roved hungrily over him earlier, her emerald eyes darkening in the firelight. But he forced himself to think rationally—because wanting a woman and having sex with her were two very different things. And denial was no hardship for a man who liked to test himself.

He raised his arms above his head to fabricate a yawn. 'Every survival manual printed will tell you that the best way to keep warm is for our bodies to be in close contact. It's also the best way to maximise the blankets we have,' he drawled. 'Which is why we're going to share that bed.'

'Are you completely crazy?'

'What's the matter, Bianca? You reckon you're so irresistible I won't be able to keep my hands off you?'

'That's not what I said.'

'No, but it's what you implied.'

Their eyes clashed and Xanthos knew he had to come clean, because what other choice did he have? He couldn't just walk away from her. Couldn't plead business, or a meeting, or the need for an early night— or any of the other strategies he used whenever a woman was starting to burrow beneath his defences. 'Look, I can't deny finding you attractive,' he admitted slowly. 'Why wouldn't I? You're a very beautiful woman and you've got a lot going for you. But you're not my type— and I don't have sex with women just for the sake of it. I grew out of that a long time ago.'

She was shaking her head with what looked like fury, so that her hair rippled like glossy jet in the fire-light. 'You think I'd ever have sex with *you*?' she flared back. 'Why, I'd rather walk barefoot through the snowy mountains of this godforsaken country to try to find my way back to Monterosso before I did that!'

'Perfect. Then we're both of the same accord. You don't want to have sex with me and I don't want to have sex with you. What could be simpler?' He splayed out his palms and held them in front of the flicker of flames. 'Which means we can share that bed over there with impunity.'

CHAPTER FOUR

His body was warm and hard and strong. His arms were clasped tightly around her waist.

It felt like heaven.

It felt like hell.

Bianca sucked in a disbelieving breath as her eyes fluttered open and she took in the full extent of her predicament—if such a situation could ever be described as a predicament.

She was in bed with Xanthos Antoniou. Lying wrapped in his arms, actually, beneath a pile of blankets whose cashmere luxury was at odds with their derelict surroundings. She could feel hard, honed muscle pressing against her. The circle of his arms enclosing her. Keeping her safe. Because—against all the odds—hadn't she just enjoyed the most incredible sleep of her life, despite the fact of being stuck out in the middle of nowhere?

The middle of nowhere. She stiffened. *With a man who was dangerously sexy.*

'Relax,' came a rich voice from beside her. 'It wasn't that bad, was it?'

She turned to see his face mere inches away from

hers, strong jaw shadowed with new growth, black eyes narrowed and watchful. Desperately, she tried not to let her panic show, but the panic was there, all right, and it was rising by the second. And who could blame her? She'd slept with a man for the first time in her life and couldn't remember a single thing about it.

Surreptitiously touching her palms to her thighs, she was relieved to discover she was still wearing her jeans. She wriggled her toes. Bed socks, too. And her thick jumper. And even... Her fingertips moved exploratively over her torso as they began to explore an unfamiliar fabric. It felt like a fleece, which must belong to him because she had never owned such a thing.

'What wasn't that bad?' she demanded, her imagination still playing tricks on her.

'Sharing a bed with me.' His black eyes glittered. 'Don't worry, Bianca, your honour remains intact.'

'That's not what I meant!'

'Sure it was.' He gave a lazy smile. 'So why not look on the bright side? We kept warm and we stayed alive, and that was our main objective.'

She supposed he was right. Fractured memories of the night returned to haunt her, like a shattered mirror being pieced back together. She remembered a bizarre supper of caviar and chocolate. A cup of champagne, which had tasted like toothpaste. The awkwardness of who was going to use the bathroom first. Well, awkward for her, since she'd never shared a bathroom with a man before but she hadn't liked to say so. And then there had been the bed. She remembered him stating how they must conserve fuel and it would lower their chances of survival if they halved the meagre supply of blankets and then froze to death as a result. He had made sharing body heat seem like a necessity rather than a pleasure.

But it *had* been a pleasure, hadn't it? That was the awful truth of it. It still was, even though they were bundled up in warm clothes and their faces and their hands were the only pieces of flesh on show. She knew she ought to get out of bed, but she felt so deliciously warm and secure that she was reluctant to move anywhere. Her position could almost have been described as comfortable, were it not for the distracting thud of a pulse at her groin and the small matter of her breasts. Well, not so small actually. They seemed to have swollen to twice their normal size and were extremely tender as she lay glued against him.

She wondered what he would say if she asked him to kiss her, then silently cursed herself for thinking such a thing. Because hadn't he stated most emphatically last night that she wasn't his type, which was presumably why he hadn't touched her in any way which could be considered inappropriate. She chewed on her lip. He had somehow managed to turn what could have been a very awkward encounter into something which had left her wistful and aching for something she seemed to have been denied.

'I suppose we ought to get up,' she said half-heartedly, hoping he might try to change her mind.

Xanthos nodded, forcing himself to pull away, resisting the temptation to explore the compact little body which had been pressing so provocatively against him all night long, sending out the unmistakable message that she was as aroused as he was. Her green eyes were wide, the pupils dark and dilated, and her bottom lip was trembling, no matter how hard she dug those little white teeth into the rosy cushion to try to curtail it. He thought how easy it would be to kiss her. And then? His mouth hardened, rivalling the persistent ache at his groin. Did he really want to complicate an already complicated situation by having sex with her, despite all his protestations that she wasn't his type?

He nodded. 'Good idea. Why don't you go and…?' Was that really his voice? So slow and so heavy, as if he were speaking underwater. 'Use the bathroom first?'

'Okay.'

He missed her softness the moment she slid from the narrow bed, forcing himself to close his eyes as she made her way towards the bathroom—because visual stimulus was the last thing he needed to add to his already overloaded senses.

When the door had slammed shut behind her, Xanthos remained exactly where he was, willing the exquisite aching of his erection to subside, though for once his body was refusing to obey him. He wondered if Bianca had any idea of the torture she'd put him through during what had felt like the longest night of his life. She had slept deeply. He had not. After an initial tense silence when he had joined her on the narrow mattress, she had fallen asleep surprisingly quickly, her head falling innocently against his shoulder. And that was when his torture had begun.

He had endured her cosying up to him as if he were a giant hot-water bottle and pressing herself against him. Endured? Who was he kidding? It had been the ultimate sensation of frustration and fantasy—and a surprisingly potent mix. The gravity of their situation had temporarily dissolved as he had inhaled the shampoo sweetness of her hair and felt her dewy cheek resting against his. He wondered if his newly awoken desire had anything to do with the fact that she had confounded all his expectations of her, proving herself to be both resourceful and not afraid of taking on her share of the work.

And he had enjoyed holding her. A surprising discovery for someone who had never shared a bed with a woman without having sex with her. Yet the chasteness of their situation had inspired a fierce sense of protectiveness in him. Some primitive instinct had kept him alert and watchful, knowing he needed to keep her safe. He had lain awake for countless minutes, listening to the steady beat of his heart and thinking that here, in this bare, bleak room, life had suddenly acquired a fundamental simplicity. If you discounted the immediate and present danger, it provided a strange kind of comfort to realise that the stresses of the modern world had receded—and one in particular.

The unsettling discovery about his birth had been digging insistently at the back of his mind ever since Corso had turned up in New York last year, and he'd been confronted with the reality that he had a brother, of sorts. Not just any brother, but one who was now a king. It had troubled him on many levels, not least because essentially Xanthos was a loner. A very private man with no desire to endure any of the problems brought about by families.

But in this bleak mountain hideaway he had discovered a curious kind of peace. It was almost as if he had been given a clean slate to start over. With his arm around Bianca's waist, he had watched the snow clouds clear to reveal an indigo sky, pricked with the diamond glitter of stars. As a cold, pale dawn had illuminated the stone floor and the sheen of her ebony hair, he had wondered what the day had in store for them. And instead of dread he had felt nothing but expectation, and acceptance.

He could hear the sound of running water next door as he got out of bed and busied himself with making a new fire, so that by the time Bianca walked back in, the temperature of the room had lost some of its icy edge. Her face was shiny-clean, her hair a glossy bounce. She'd put on a sweater the colour of a sunrise, blue jeans were hugging her hips and Xanthos couldn't help acknowledging bjust how...*amazing* she looked. Fresh, yet hot. It was yet another unwanted punch to his jangled senses and, cursing the sudden erotic trajectory of his thoughts, he rose to his feet.

'I'll use the bathroom,' he said abruptly. 'Just keep the fire going.'

'Of course.'

At least the icy temperature of the water was enough to restore his equilibrium and he washed and dressed as quickly as possible. By the time he returned, Bianca was staring out of the window and she turned round as he entered.

'I want to talk to you.'

'So talk.'

Her green eyes were very clear and unblinking. 'Do you think—?'

He could hear the sudden fear which had entered her voice and she hesitated, looking around at the bare, bleak walls as if she were seeing them for the first time. Her mask of bravado had slipped to reveal the frightened woman beneath and Xanthos felt his heart go out to her. He walked across the room towards her, resisting the desire to pull her into his arms—framing her cheek with the palm of his hand instead.

'If you're about to ask me whether I think anyone's going to find us, the answer is that I don't know,' he said softly. 'But I do know it's pointless worrying about things we can't control.'

'What, so we just sit here and *wait*?'

'Not necessarily. We could go outside and walk.'

'Yeah.' Her gaze was darting around the tiny dimensions of the room as if it were a prison. 'I feel as if I'll go crazy if we have to spend much longer in here.'

'Come on, then.'

They pulled on extra clothing and she reached for a bobble hat and gloves, before they stepped out into the freezing morning and a very different world from the one which had greeted them the day before.

For a moment Xanthos just drank it in. Gone were the oppressive grey clouds and icy flakes which had swirled so relentlessly from the sky. In the sunlight, the snow was glistening, turning the high bank into a glitter of whiteness. Behind them the peak of the huge mountain soared up into a cloudless blue sky. Even the crashed plane seemed to have lost its ability to shock or terrify. Total silence engulfed them.

'It's…beautiful,' breathed Bianca, at last.

Yes. Very. Just like her. Xanthos felt the sudden beat of his heart as he met her emerald gaze beneath the brim of her grey bobble hat. The most beautiful woman he'd ever laid eyes on and, ironically, the last woman he might ever see. He thought about the restraint he'd employed throughout that long night and the effort it had cost him. There had been yet more restraint this morning, when she had brushed her lips over his jaw, and if she hadn't been asleep he might have kissed her back. It had been a masterclass in self-discipline from which he had derived a certain amount of masochistic pleasure, but now he wondered whether he should have instigated something else.

If he were to die here in this valley—would that be his one regret? That he *hadn't* had sex with Bianca Forrester?

'Come on. Let's walk,' he said abruptly. 'We need to keep moving.'

He was careful not to let them stray too far from the hut and when he noticed her start to shiver, insisted they go back inside, where he stoked up the fire and made more tea while she doled out squares of dark chocolate, which they ate mechanically. Yet as the minutes ticked by, he could feel the tension mounting in that small room and it wasn't just the unspoken fear that they might never be rescued. Desire shimmered in the air—so real it was almost tangible.

'Maybe we should try and read to pass the time,' she said, her prim words shattering his erotic thoughts. 'Do you have any novels with you, bXanthos?'

'You go ahead and read,' he growled. 'I'm going to take that desk outside and dismantle it for firewood.'

She raised her eyebrows. 'Is that really necessary?'

'You think I just like breaking up furniture for the

hell of it?' He stared her down. 'That I'm channelling my inner caveman?'

'I have no idea.' She met his gaze with a look of challenge. 'Are you?'

But despite his words, the action of smashing the desk to pieces was infinitely satisfying and not just because it was so alien to the way he lived in New York. The physical exertion sublimated some of his sexual hunger and his brief exhilaration was compounded when he heard a sound in the distance. At first he wondered if he had imagined it. It seemed too faint to be real, yet in the overwhelming silence of that stark white world it was as deafening as a bolt of thunder. He stood stock-still as it increased in volume and that was when he yelled at the top of his voice. 'Bianca!'

Dark hair flying, she came running out—her gaze swiftly taking in the approaching vehicle before looking into his face, as if seeking confirmation. And when he nodded, they both looked upwards—towards the steep road which wound down the side of the mountain, where a sturdy-looking vehicle was making slow but steady progress towards them.

'Xanthos,' she said, her thin whisper hopeful on the frozen air.

'Yes,' he said simply.

She reached out to clutch his arm for support—as if without it she might slip to the snowy ground. Was that why he clamped his fingers over hers, to anchor her— or was it simply because he wanted the opportunity to touch her again? Her hand felt tiny beneath his palm and the touch of her gloved fingers pressing against his jacket made it seem like a double dose of sensuality.

They watched in silence as the vehicle slowly made its way towards them, not wanting to jinx it. As if words might reveal the Jeep to be nothing but an apparition— a wintry mirage which would merge into the bleached landscape and disappear. But the sounds grew louder. The hefty chains on the thick tyres were making easy work of the frozen road. Eventually it bumped its way down onto the airfield and the craziest thing was that all Xanthos wanted was to pull Bianca into his arms and kiss the breath out of her. To ask if they could have a few minutes alone, so that he could take her back inside that hut and do what he should have done last night.

But he gently disengaged her fingers and stepped forward as a man about his age jumped out of the passenger seat. Framed by a fur-trimmed hood, his face creased in a wide smile as he spoke in accented English.

'Bianca Forrester and Xanthos Antoniou, I presume?' He grinned. 'We've been looking for you.'

CHAPTER FIVE

'I AM NOT doing this,' Xanthos stated, with grim emphasis. 'I am not sharing a room with you again, Bianca.'

Silently, Bianca counted to ten because Xanthos was being about as insulting as only he could be, but since she had already decided to rise above it, she adopted her most diplomatic tone. They had managed to survive almost twenty-four hours in a deserted mountain hut without killing each another—surely they could manage a few more? At least here there were other people around, so there would be something else to focus on other than the sexy Greek. 'I can assure you it isn't my idea of fun either, but—'

'But what?' he demanded, the sweeping movement of his arm drawing her attention to the snowy village square outside the window, where a giant conifer was decked with coloured lights. For a moment her imagination drifted away from her. She thought how pretty it looked in the moonlight and how sweet the little children seemed, who were gazing up in wonder at its sparkling branches.

'Why are we having to spend Christmas Eve in some godforsaken hotel in the middle of nowhere?' he continued, in that same harsh voice which completely broke the spell.

All her best conciliatory intentions forgotten, Bianca scowled. 'Will you please keep your voice down?' she hissed. 'I don't know how you can be so ungrateful. Especially as you treated me to a lecture on that very subject before you gave me a lift on your plane.'

'That's different.'

'How is it different? The most important thing is that we're safe, Xanthos. We were rescued, weren't we? By the village doctor, no less! We've been examined and given a clean bill of health and told that we can leave—'

'When?'

Bianca sucked in an unsteady breath. 'Dr Druri explained all that, too. You know he did. The road to the main airport is still partially blocked and it's not safe to attempt to get there tonight—but they've said it'll be okay tomorrow once the snow ploughs have been out. Plus, it's Christmas Eve and apparently that's a big deal in Vargmali. We were lucky to get the last room in the hotel *and* they've invited us to their big festive feast downstairs tonight.'

'I'm not interested in attending a festive feast,' he growled.

'Surely you're not so much of a Scrooge that you want to spoil everyone's fun?' she demanded. 'What else are we going to do—sit and stare at each other all evening and demand that an already overworked kitchen prepares something especially for us? That would be a big slap in the face for their hospitality, wouldn't it? At least up here we've got…' She let her words trail off, terrified that her forced her air of bravado would slip and she would give away the precarious state of her emotions. She wished she could wave a magic wand to transport her back to England—and yet the thought of having to say goodbye to this enigmatic man with whom she'd spent a night in a snowy mountain hut was bothering her far more than it should have done. 'Here we've got more than one place to sleep, so we won't have to share a bed,' she continued gamely. 'That fold-up divan over there looks comfortable enough.'

'You think so?' he questioned repressively. 'It looks more like a bed of nails to me.'

'Well, I don't mind sleeping on it, so that's settled.' She breathed out an unsteady sigh. 'I don't know why you can't just accept the situation we're in, Xanthos. You were the one who came out with all that stuff about accepting the things you can't control, which is exactly what I'm trying to do. What's the matter—is it really so awful, the thought of having to endure another night with me?'

Xanthos didn't reply immediately, mostly because he was still having difficulty getting his head around the fact that he remained trapped. With her. And there didn't seem to be a thing he could do about it. After a bumpy ride up the mountain road, to the accompanying chatter of the village doctor who had examined them both in his small surgery, they had arrived at this gothic monstrosity of a hotel, where he and Bianca had been shown into a large and rather draughty room.

After their snowy hut, the accommodation seemed almost luxurious—but continued proximity to a woman who was strictly off-limits was something he wanted to avoid at all costs. She was unsettling him, big-time, and he still couldn't work out why. The situation wasn't helped by the fact that everyone thought they were a couple and any attempts to dissuade them of this notion seemed to get lost in translation. Was that because when the search party had arrived, Bianca had been clinging to his arm, with him holding onto her as if she were a fragile piece of porcelain which might shatter if he let her go?

At least the hotel had a phone signal—of sorts—and on arrival he'd received a blitz of messages, most of which he'd ignored. His first priority had been to text Bianca's sister to reassure her she was safe, resisting the urge to comment that if she hadn't insisted on him giving her a ride in his plane, her anxious night of worrying could have been avoided.

And wouldn't you have found the experience much harder on your own? taunted a voice inside his head. *Didn't having Bianca Forrester there give you something to fight for?*

He had also received several texts from Kiki—her initial understanding about his emergency landing having morphed into a flurry of inappropriate questions about the nature of his relationship with his female passenger, because it seemed that the press had got hold of the story of their rescue and speculation was running rife. It struck him that the supermodel was behaving like some wounded lover when he barely knew her. But that, he reminded himself grimly, was women for you. You gave them the glimmer of an opening and, inevitably, they attempted to prise it apart.

And wasn't the truth that he *was* slightly obsessed by Bianca? He found himself plagued by a flurry of unwanted memories, which kept hitting him at the most inconvenient times. The shampoo scent of her hair and the sleepy brush of her lips against his jaw. The way her petite body had moulded so naturally into his. How easy it would have been to...

To...

But he mustn't think about that.

Why was he even thinking about her at all?

'Do you think there's any danger of getting a drink round here?' he growled.

'Why don't you go downstairs and investigate while I have a shower?' she suggested sweetly.

Xanthos left the room without another word, blotting out images of her standing in a steamy cubicle and lathering soap over those magnificent breasts. He made his way down the echoing flight of stairs to the hotel entrance, past several glass counters in the foyer which—bizarrely—were displaying root vegetables for sale. There was also a large Christmas tree—big and bushy and hung with rudimentary paper decorations which had obviously been crafted by children. Compared to its glitzy counterpart which sparkled outside the Rockefeller Center in his native New York every year, it was about as humble as you could get— yet there was something about the simple decorations which made him linger for a moment, before shaking his head with impatience and quickly walking away.

He passed a large dining room, in which several women were hanging swathes of festive greenery and chattering happily in their own language. The small bar was empty but eventually he found someone to serve him, then sat nursing a glass of malt whisky, until he heard the sound of people arriving in the main foyer, clearly in celebratory mood.

Finishing off the final mouthful, he made his way unenthusiastically back upstairs, wondering if he could plead a headache and spend the evening working, but these thoughts slid from his mind when he found Bianca dressed, her hair a glimmer of shiny waves set off dramatically by her black dress. Indignation vied with desire and indignation won. Wasn't it enough he had lain there like a rock during the long night when she had snuggled into his arms? Was she *trying* to test his resolve still further? To elevate his heart-rate to dangerous levels and make him ache for her with frustrated longing?

Steadying his suddenly erratic breathing, he tried telling himself that no way could her dress be described as provocative. Not when it was buttoned all the way down the front and hung in modest folds to her knees. So why this kick of lust so potent that it was making him unable to think about anything other than how much he wanted to touch her? Actually, he wanted to do a lot more than touch her. He wanted to be inside her. To shudder out his seed and fill her until he was empty and dry.

His body tensed.

Why the hell was he thinking like some kind of caveman?

'You don't like it?' she croaked.

Dragging himself out of his erotic daze, he stared at her uncomprehendingly. 'Don't like what?'

'My dress.' She shrugged. 'The way I look.'

'Why are you asking me that?'

'Because…' Bianca swallowed down the lump which had risen in her throat. His face had grown so incredibly *tense*. Golden olive skin was stretched taut over the high definition of cheekbones and his mouth had hardened into a forbidding slash. Her lawyerly articulation seemed to have deserted her in her time of need, as she struggled to find the right words. Or were they the wrong words? Wouldn't the wisest thing be to keep her mouth shut and not stray into the dangerous territory of the personal? But she couldn't seem to hold back her curiosity and, after the night they'd shared, surely she should be able to speak frankly to him. 'Because you're staring at me as if you couldn't…as if you've never seen me before. As if you don't know me.'

'Because I don't,' he asserted harshly into the brittle silence which followed. 'Just like you don't know me. And that's the way I would prefer it to stay, Bianca. We were trapped on a mountainside but it's over. We have a few more hours to get through and then we can go our separate ways and need never see one another again. So if you'll excuse me, I'll go and wash up.'

As the bathroom door closed behind him, Bianca told herself he was rude and cold and positively obnoxious and she couldn't wait to be rid of him. Looking around for something to distract herself with, she picked up her phone to text her mother and sister again, this time to wish them a happy Christmas. And, even though she was on her honeymoon, Rosie's dramatic reply came winging straight back:

What do you think of Xanthos???!!!!

Bianca was certain her sister would derive little comfort from her opinion that she found him brave and strong and yet extremely hurtful. And that, bizarrely, she really wanted to have sex with him.

She kept her reply vague.

Very capable in an emergency! Enjoy your honeymoon.
B xx

Putting the phone back down, she stared out of the window at the Christmas tree in the snowy village square below, thronging with people enjoying the festivities. Did children hang up stockings in Vargmali? she wondered, when the bathroom door opened and Xanthos walked into the room.

Perhaps if she had been prepared for his sudden appearance she might have been able to do something about her reaction but, as it was, she could do nothing to prevent the lurch of her heart or sudden shivering of her skin. He had changed into dark trousers and a pale silk shirt left open at the neck, revealing a tantalising triangle of gleaming skin. He looked utterly irresistible, she acknowledged reluctantly, every pore in her body unfurling into sensual life as he raked his fingers back through his still damp hair. Their eyes met. Their gazes held. She could almost *hear* the crackle of sex and danger in the air and suddenly she was glad they were going downstairs to eat—anywhere but staying up here, cocooned in this bedroom and susceptible to the ever-present temptation he represented.

'Ready?' she questioned briskly, with a quick glance at her watch. 'They said they're starting the meal at seven-thirty.'

'I can hardly wait.'

She turned to him. 'You're not going to be in a foul temper and ruin the night for everyone, are you?'

'No, Bianca. I give you my word. I will be diplomacy personified.'

'That will be a first.'

They made their way downstairs and as they entered the dining room and everyone looked up, Bianca suddenly realised that she felt like part of a couple—which had never happened before. Wasn't that a sad indication of how insular her life had become? At her all-girls school she'd worked hard to get the grades she needed and had kept to that same rigorous pattern all through uni. And yes, of course she had dated along the way, but no close bond had ever been formed. Her single-minded goal of independence had always seemed more important than being with a man.

But she could never remember feeling more *alive* than she did as Dr Druri's smiling young wife—who was called Ellen—handed them both some mulled wine and introduced them to the other guests. It was a mixed gathering and everyone was fizzing over with yuletide merriment. There were little children and teenagers. Long-married couples and a pair of newly-weds. A babe-in-arms and a very old man who lovingly kissed the forehead of his wife, as she sat in her wheelchair. Most people spoke a smattering of English but Bianca quickly realised the effectiveness of sign language and it transpired that Xanthos could speak fluent Italian, on which the Vargmalian language was based, so was able to give a succinct account of their plane crash.

She looked around the dining room, taking in the way it had been decorated—inexpensively but beautifully. In fact, she couldn't remember ever seeing anything quite so lovely and she whispered as much to Xanthos. Fragrant fresh greenery was looped around the window frames as well as along the top of the stone fireplace, where an enormous log fire crackled. More greenery was wreathed in startling contrast against a snowy-white tablecloth, where tall red candles lit the room with their golden and flickering glow. It was old-fashioned and simple. It was like Christmas was supposed to be and suddenly Bianca found herself overcome by a great yearning for...

What?

There was absolutely no evidence of luxury or vast amounts of money here. It was a world she didn't really recognise, yet somehow it felt real. More real than anything she could ever remember.

'Come and sit down!' exclaimed Ellen. 'Over here! Our guests of honour.'

Bianca slid into her seat as Xanthos took his place beside her and she turned to him. 'Isn't this wonderful?'

'Absolutely wonderful,' he murmured, and she prayed that nobody else had picked up on his sardonic undertone.

Course after course of delicious food arrived. Fish and pastries, berries and bon-bons—all served on what was obviously the best china and accompanied by glasses of the rich local wine. Fortunately the chatter around the table was so voluble that nobody seemed to notice that she and Xanthos merely picked at their food, or if they did they were too polite to mention it.

When the feast was over and Bianca was wondering whether they should make their excuses and leave, the old man got up from the table and went to a corner of the room. Picking up his accordion, he started to play a tune which brought shouts of delighted recognition and, immediately, several people got up to dance.

'Dance with your wife, Xanthos!' urged Ellen encouragingly.

'She's not—'

'A very good dancer!' interjected Bianca hastily, jumping to her feet and smiling as she held out her hands to him. 'But who cares about that?'

Which left Xanthos with no choice other than to pull her into his arms—something which, contrarily, would have been at the very bottom and very top of his wishlist, at exactly the same time. 'Why the hell did you say that?' he growled, into her hair.

'Say what?'

'Implying we were married.'

'It just seemed easier,' she whispered back, her breath soft and warm against his ear. 'Relax, Xanthos. I'm not planning on frogmarching you up the aisle any time soon.'

He closed his eyes as the jaunty chords of the accordion echoed around the room and other couples swayed nearby and thought how good she felt as she moved against him. Indecently good. When had been the last time he had danced with a woman? He frowned. Had he *ever* danced with a woman? He didn't really *do* dancing, but maybe he'd been missing out for all these years. He could feel her breasts pushing into his chest, sending arrows of desire straight to his groin. 'Mmm…' he said, without thinking.

She drew back, her green eyes questioning. '"Mmm..." what?'

'I guess it's not so bad after all,' he conceded, as he whirled her around and he could hear the sound of her soft laughter beneath the notes of the accordion.

They danced until trays of sour-cherry drinks were handed around and the evening concluded with a group of children who arrived to entertain them with a medley of Vargmalian Christmas carols. A mixed clutch of pre-teens began to sing, including a boy whose voice hadn't broken—and whose delivery of the top notes sounded like an angel soaring through the now silent room. It was an emotionally charged moment and, as Xanthos observed wistfulness on the faces of the old and hope on the faces of the young, for the first time in his life he understood the appeal of Christmas.

But he understood too why he had always turned his back on it.

Then, and maybe now too.

'Let's go upstairs,' he said roughly, once the carols had finished, and he saw her nod, resignation darkening her eyes, as if she never wanted the evening to end.

'Okay,' she said.

As they said goodbye and mounted the stairs towards their room, Bianca knew she mustn't read too much into what had just happened. He had danced with her. And just because it had felt as heavenly as anything she could ever remember doing it didn't *mean* anything. It was Christmas, that was all—and Christmas was notorious for putting a dangerous spin on things. She knew she needed to cultivate a degree of impartiality before they spent their final night together, but as the door closed behind them all she could think about was how powerful and sexy he looked. The moonlight was splashing his dark hair with silver and making her want to run her fingers through those luxuriant metallic strands. She longed for the music of the accordion. She wanted to be back in his arms.

As he walked over to the window to stare out at the starry blaze of the Christmas tree in the village square, Bianca wanted to rail against the fact that he had managed to captivate her, despite all the defences she'd erected. That somehow he had made her want him, and that couldn't be allowed to continue. So why not defuse the situation? *You've still got a whole night to get through. At least let him remember you as someone who knows her manners.*

'I still haven't thanked you properly,' she said quietly.

He turned round. 'For what?'

'Oh, you know. For saving my life. For looking after me so well. For going back to the plane. For building a fire For...' She hesitated. 'Well, for behaving like such a gentleman.'

'Don't push it, Bianca.' His smile was wry, his words coated with something unfamiliar. 'Because I can assure you I'm not feeling in the least bit gentlemanly right now.'

Something in the way he was looking at her made rational thought drain from her mind, like the trickle of sand through open fingers. 'Oh?'

'Do you say "oh" like that because you know it makes your lips soften into the perfect pout?' he probed silkily. 'Meaning that I'm powerless to do anything except think about kissing you?'

'I can't imagine you ever being powerless, Xanthos.'
His mouth hardened. 'You'd be surprised.'

'Maybe I like surprises.'

But if she was expecting him to start confiding in her—to explain what had infused his words with that layer of bitterness—then she had misjudged him. Because clearly it wasn't understanding he sought. She could see from the blaze of his eyes that his needs were far more fundamental than that. Just like hers.

And suddenly she wanted her secret fantasy to take shape. She wanted him to pull her into his arms, only this time, not to dance. She wanted him to kiss her in this moon-washed room on the night before Christmas and take that kiss to its natural conclusion.

'I want you,' he stated softly.

'I didn't think I was your type.'

'I'm pretty sure you're not. But right now, that doesn't seem to matter.'

'Doesn't it?' she questioned, as if she had this kind of discussion every day. But although she'd never had sex before, she was certainly familiar with negotiation.

'Maybe it's that survival thing,' he continued, narrowing his dark eyes as he studied her. 'Needing to celebrate the life force when you've lived through the possibility of imminent death.'

'Is that what it is?' she said slowly, bitterly disappointed by his factual assessment.

Did he detect that his unsentimental words—although commendably honest—were threatening to undermine his ultimate goal? Was that why he walked over and touched his palm against her cheek, as if to frame it, or to revel in its softness? Or was he just clever enough to recognise that the romantic gesture was as seductive as the moonlight? To recognise that once he touched her she would be lost.

And she was.

Totally lost.

CHAPTER SIX

HE'D FANTASISED ABOUT kissing her lips for so long and now they were soft and trembling beneath his. Xanthos tangled his fingers into the soft, rich spill of Bianca's hair and as she brought her curvy hips in line with his, he groaned. Could she feel the imprint of his erection through the thin silk of her dress and did she find it daunting?

It would seem not, for she kissed him back with a hungry passion he hadn't been expecting from the cool and independent lawyer. And now she was circling those delicious hips against his legs and he was uncertain whether she was teasing him or testing him, and he drew back.

'You do know that if you don't slow down, this is all going to be over very quickly,' he warned her unsteadily.

He might have imagined her brief uncertainty, but he definitely didn't imagine her familiar challenge. 'And do you have a problem with that?'

He groaned again and his breath felt as if it were being ripped from the base of his lungs, because her provocative question appeared to give him permission to behave, not badly, no, but without any of the restraint he had been clinging onto since he'd landed that plane. Usually, he was the master of slow seduction and finesse. He always took his time. And in a way, didn't his protracted pleasuring of his lovers intensify his own satisfaction by demonstrating his steely self-control?

But there was very little self-control in his body now. Was it that ridiculously sentimental dance downstairs which had robbed him of sense and of reason? As he scooped Bianca into his arms and carried her towards the bed, he felt as if he were on fire. His kiss had never been so hot or hard or hungry, especially when he felt the imprint of a pair of hold-up stockings against his fingers. He toppled her down onto the bed and lay down beside her and his fingers were actually trembling as they began the interminable prospect of releasing the buttons of her dress. How many were there?

'I feel like ripping the damned thing off,' he growled.

'Rip away,' she invited insouciantly. 'There's plenty more clothes in my suitcase.'

And, God forgive him—but he did. With no regard whatsoever for the silky gown, he clasped the delicate fabric on either side of the buttons and wrenched it open. It came apart with a splitting sound, revealing her magnificent breasts—the globes encased in shadowy black lace, which were rising and falling in time with her rapid breathing.

'*Evge...*' he breathed, lapsing into a language he rarely spoke these days. His mouth twisted. His *mother* tongue. The word filled him with disdain, but his bitter contemplation dissolved the moment he bent his tongue towards the proud nipple which strained through the black lace, just begging to be licked. And when he obliged with the slow flick of his tongue, she squirmed her hips against the mattress with restless hunger and he felt himself grow even harder. His throat dried as he dealt with the skimpy lace panties—her open-thighed invitation consigning them to the same sorry fate as her ripped dress. His finger slid irresistibly over the slick heat at her core and, although he hadn't intended to, he began to stroke her until she was gasping and pleading with him.

'No,' he said, still filled with that delicious sense of the primal which was influencing his behaviour in the most uncharacteristic way. 'Not like that. Not the first time.'

'How many times are we going to do it?'

'That depends.'

'On what?'

'On this.' He kissed her some more, and then more still. She seemed unwilling to let him drag his mouth away from hers and he certainly wasn't objecting. At least, not until he thought he might explode if he didn't get inside her. Unzipping his trousers with difficulty, he hauled his shirt over his head until at last they were both naked and she was running her gaze over him with greedy fervour, almost as if she'd never seen a naked man before. But wasn't he doing exactly the same? Feasting his eyes on the black hold-up stockings which he had left in situ. Her hair was dark against the pillow and her teeth looked very white in the moonlight. As her gaze roved down to study his aching groin he thought he saw her bite her lip and wondered if she was reconsidering her options. Had she changed her mind?

And didn't some bone-deep instinct tell him it would be better for them both if she had, even though it would half kill him to walk away from her now? Because there was still her connection to his brother—the brother he had decided he was never going to see again.

'You want me to stop?' he questioned, through a throat so raw it felt as if someone were throttling him.

'Are you out of your mind?' she breathed, with a shake of her dark head. 'I want this, too, Xanthos. bSo badly.'

Her honesty was flattering and, again, surprising. In his experience, women usually held back their true feelings until they were hopeful they might be reciprocated. But Bianca Forrester had broken the mould. He frowned. Did she imagine this was going to end in a hail of confetti in County Hall, with flowers in her hair and a shiny gold band on her finger?

But maybe he was guilty of patronising her. She was a woman in her mid-twenties and a successful lawyer— not some guileless young innocent unused to the wicked ways of the world. They were stranded in an unknown country after sharing a dramatic experience, and then being shown the kindness of strangers on the most unashamedly emotional night of the year. What could be a more perfect ending to a roller coaster of a day and a lucky escape than a long night of delicious sex?

'You and me both. Very badly,' he echoed. The pragmatic interchange reminded him to get up and delve around in his suitcase, because he always used protection. He thought how wanton she looked, lying waiting for him in the moonlight, her black-stockinged legs bent and drawing him irrevocably towards her. He bent his head and kissed her until she was writhing with long-ing. 'You are exquisite,' he whispered.

'Am I?'

He could hear the uncertainty in her voice and that surprised him, too. 'Utterly.'

'Oh,' she breathed.

His fingertip lightly feathered the silken flesh at her thigh. 'Is that good?'

'You know it is,' she said thickly.

He licked her neck, her shoulders and her upper arms, tasting the salty perfume of her flesh. He licked the pouting tips of her breasts and took one into his mouth as he positioned himself over her, her warm thighs parting eagerly beneath his questing fingers. And when at last he pushed into her slick heat, it was…

He grew still.

Was it because he was so aroused that she felt so un-believably *tight*?

'Bianca?' he ground out, every sinew in his body tensing with fierce control.

'Yes,' she whispered back.

But he heard the slight break underpinning her reply and knew instantly what had caused it.

'Bianca—'

'Please don't stop,' she urged him softly. 'Not now. Please keep doing exactly what you're doing.'

Stop? It would have been easier to command his own heart to cease beating, than to have held back from that next delicious thrust. 'You mean, like this?' he ques-tioned unevenly.

'Y-yes. Ex-exactly like that,' Bianca whispered back as a wave of delicious heat flooded through her. And as he filled her, she couldn't hold back the thought that maybe she had been born to have Xanthos Antoniou inside her like this. Would it be insane to admit that somehow he made her feel complete, for the first time in her life? A sense of exhilaration accompanied her soaring joy as he thrust deeper inside her and, weirdly, she seemed to know exactly how to respond. It felt instinctive to wrap her legs around his back and tilt her hips to accommodate his hard rhythm. And didn't his ragged sighs of appreciation thrill her even more, letting her know how much she was pleasuring him? She had never felt so uninhibited, nor so in touch with a side of herself she'd always kept buried and, willingly, she let go. Of thought. Of control. Of everything. So free did she feel that her orgasm startled her. One minute she was opening her lips to the urgent plunge of his tongue and the next she was gasping as her body contracted ecstatically around him.

She could feel his urgency as he slid his palms beneath her buttocks, making those last few thrusts like a man possessed, before giving a shuddered moan which seemed to split the night. For a while he didn't move. He just stayed on top of her while the pulsing of his body grew quieter. Reaching down, he pushed a strand of hair away from her hot cheek, and though there was only moonlight to see by, it couldn't disguise the question in his narrowed gaze.

But Bianca didn't want to spoil what had just happened with some forensic question-and-answer session about why he was the first. She didn't want him thinking it was anything more special than simple sexual chemistry.

Because it wasn't.

Willing the crashing of her heart to subside, she curved her lips into a smile and attempted to take charge of the conversation. To take back control. 'Wow,' she said softly. 'That was amazing.'

For a moment there was a silence punctured only by the sound of their laboured breathing.

'You know, I am rarely surprised by a woman, Bianca,' he said eventually. 'But it seems you have broken the mould.'

'Isn't Christmas supposed to be about surprises?' she questioned glibly.

But he didn't take the hint and shut up.

'You certainly are a total mind-blowing contradiction to the woman you appear to be,' he mused. 'An apparently sophisticated career woman in her mid-twenties, who sends out the very definite message that she's modern and liberal—who turns out to be a blushing virgin.'

She huffed out a sigh and, despite her best endeavours, started wondering whether some kind of explanation was inevitable. Maybe it was, but she made one last attempt to deflect it. 'I don't remember blushing.'

'You certainly are now,' he offered drily.

She ran her fingertip over the outline of his lips. 'Please don't worry about me, Xanthos. I am as modern and as liberal as they come–'

'And you certainly did come,' he observed.

'I'm just not very experienced, that's all.'

'I think I managed to work that one out for myself.' There was a pause. 'And I'm wondering what the reason is. You're under no obligation to tell me, of course.'

Bianca hesitated. Why *not* tell him the truth—

especially if this relationship was going to go anywhere? 'I've never really had time for men, that's why,' she admitted slowly. 'I've spent most of my life working very hard to make something of myself—'

'Even though you grew up in the grounds of an actual palace?'

'Why do people always jump to the same conclusion? The palace was like living in a very fancy rented house! Honestly. We had no real money of our own. Everything we did was dependent on what the King wanted and I knew I didn't want to live like that. That whatever I wanted to achieve, I was going to have to do without any outside help from anybody else.' Now it was her turn to study him questioningly. 'Could you honestly say the same, Xanthos?'

'You think I was born with a silver spoon in my mouth?'

She shrugged. 'I don't know. To be honest, I don't really know anything about you. Were you?'

Xanthos looked out of the window at the snowy rooftops of Vargmali, recognising that it would be the easiest thing in the world to clam up. To shut down her questions about his formative years with a kiss, because that was what he always did. But on this strange Christmas Eve in this faraway land, the normal rules didn't seem to apply. They had been thrown together in more ways than one and the bizarre sequence of events had an air of impermanence about it, like the tall tree which glittered in the village square, which would be taken down before the new year was very old.

And maybe his uncharacteristic introspection had something to do with seeing his brother again—because hadn't that thrown up the kind of questions he would usually have buried? Wasn't it inevitable he should have started comparing Corso's bupbringing to his—and to have been reminded just how grim his own had been? It would be a mistake to reveal too much of himself to Bianca, of all people—yet his need to talk to someone was stronger than it had ever been. And lawyers were trained to be discreet, weren't they? So maybe he would give her some of the facts. Just not all of them. Especially not the ones which impacted on her own sister.

'My mother got married very young when she discovered she was pregnant,' he said. 'And for the first sixteen years of my life I knew wealth on a scale which most people can barely imagine.'

He waited for her to come back at him with a triumphant retort. To say something like, 'So you *were* rich!' But she didn't.

'And was it a happy childhood?'

'Is there such a thing?' he questioned bitterly.

'Wow.' The single word was soft. 'That's a very cynical thing to say, Xanthos. Cryptic, too.'

'It might be—but that's the way I think. It's one of the reasons I don't intend having any children of my own.'

She nodded at this, as if storing away the knowledge so she could take it out and look at it later. 'So it wasn't happy?'

No need to document the gnawing acknowledgement that there had always been a strange kind of tension around his parents. He'd thought it inevitable, given the huge and often embarrassing age gap. He didn't mention the way his father used to look at him sometimes—as if he had crawled out from beneath a stone. His mother had looked at him that way too sometimes, hadn't she? And somehow that had been much, much worse.

'Oh, I wasn't beaten or starved,' he said flippantly. 'But on my sixteenth birthday, my father decided to give me a highly unconventional present.'

'Not a car, then?'

'No, nor a watch. He decided I needed a DNA test.' He paused. 'So a doctor came to the house to take blood.'

He saw the consternation which creased her face. 'But…why?'

'You're an intelligent woman, Bianca,' he prompted silkily. 'Why do you think?'

'He suspected he wasn't your father?'

'Indeed he did.' His jaw hardened as he gritted his teeth. 'And he was right. Because he wasn't.'

'Oh, my goodness,' she breathed. 'How difficult must that have been? What…what happened?'

Xanthos shifted his position on the bed, his gaze lifting to the silvery moon outside the window as he wondered what was happening to him. Why were all the defences with which he had surrounded himself for as long as he could remember, now threatening to crumble? And even though an insistent voice in his head was urging him to shut down the conversation, he found himself wanting to break the rule of a lifetime and tell her, because he'd never admitted this, not to anyone. 'What happened was that he gave my mother an ultimatum. He said it was either him, or me. She could stay, but only if I went.'

She gave a slightly nervous laugh. 'But she chose you, right?'

Xanthos could feel his throat constrict because this was the hardest part of all, even now. *This* was the reason he had locked it away. *This* was the shameful part. Because a mother who rejected her only child...

Had he really been that unlovable?

But it was good to remember these things, no matter how painful it might be. It helped him put things in perspective. It stopped him from painting reality with unrealistic shades of longing. It reinforced his certain knowledge that there was no such thing as love.

'Wrong,' he corrected caustically. 'She figured that, of the two of us, I stood a better chance of survival on my own than she did—since she was totally dependent on her husband financially and had no money of her own. So I was kicked out of the house and told to fend for myself.'

She turned onto her side, propping herself up on her elbow so that a stream of dark waves tumbled over her bare breasts. 'How did you survive?'

He shrugged. 'I already attended a very prestigious school in New York City who were reluctant to see me go, though it wasn't unusual for boys to have to leave the school due to reduced circumstances. But they arranged for me to take a scholarship exam and I ended up staying there as a boarding-school pupil.'

She twirled the end of a strand of hair round and round her finger. 'But what about school holidays?'

'I had some very wealthy friends and one in particular. His name was Brad Wilson and I used to stay with him and his family.' But Xanthos had been a cold, proud youth, suspicious of kindness—mainly because he had experienced so little of it. Hadn't his willingness to accept what he perceived as charity from the Wilsons been because their East Side reserve had meant they never asked him any painful and personal questions? And hadn't one of the principal reasons they had taken him into their family been because he *hadn't* emoted?

'And was that…okay?'

He thought about it. *Okay* seemed a pretty accurate description of a period of his life at that time—because he had been obsessed with his own independence and wondering when he would be able to gain it. 'I was grateful to them,' he said at last. 'But it reinforced my belief that family life is claustrophobic. Soon after that I went to Stanford to do computer science and dropped out after two years to start my video gaming company.'

'And do you still see Brad?' she said slowly, as if it mattered.

It was a curveball of a question and the punch of pain was unexpected. It reminded him of why he functioned best when he avoided any kind of emotional attachment. 'That would be impossible, I'm afraid,' he said slowly. 'He and his father died in a boating accident soon after he left college. His mother never really recovered from the blow, and she died within the year. Within the space of eighteen months, they were all wiped out. Gone.'

Bianca saw the sudden tension in his face as he lapsed into an uneasy silence. She was deeply moved and taken aback by what he had told her, which just went to show that you never knew what anybody was really like on the inside. Who would have thought the outrageously sexy billionaire should have had such a tragic upbringing? That he should have endured so much pain and sorrow, as well as a mother who had chosen her husband over her only son. Couldn't he be forgiven some of his harsh arrogance in the light of this new knowledge?

'And did you ever ask your mother who your real father was?'

'No.'

Something about the flat delivery of his reply made her ask her next question. 'Do you still see her?'

'I haven't seen her since that day she kicked me out. I have no idea where she lives.'

'And don't you...?' She hesitated, recognising that this might be overstepping the mark. 'Don't you think maybe you should try to find her?'

'Why the hell should I do that?' he demanded.

She shrugged. 'It might help you move on, if you could see her again, understand her perspective more.'

'No.' The single word was clipped out like a bullet and as his features became cold, he looked so different from the man who had taken her into his arms and told her how much he wanted to kiss her. Was it that which made her reach out to frame his cheek with her palm, mirroring what he'd done to her just before they'd had sex? She thought how wonderful his lovemaking had been. How he had managed to help create the most magical Christmas Eve she could remember and made her feel properly alive for the first time in her life. She didn't want the night to end with him looking angry and bitter as he recalled the acrimony of his past. She wanted to hear him moan with pleasure again.

Tentatively she let her thumb rove over the strong

curve of his jaw and he stirred in response, the stoniness leaving his face and making it flesh again. His eyes gleamed with sudden fire—as if he had just remembered there was a naked woman in his bed. And maybe he was as loath to miss this opportunity as she was, for he pulled her into his arms, bringing her to lie on top of him.

'I don't want to talk about it any more,' he gritted out.

'I sort of guessed that for myself,' she whispered back.

'In fact, talking is the last thing on my mind right now.'

And Bianca nodded, because she was right there with him. All she cared about was the hardness nudging so insistently against her thighs and the answering rush of heat as her hungry lips sought his.

CHAPTER SEVEN

'WE WILL SHORTLY be coming in to land in London. The captain hopes you have both enjoyed a pleasant flight.'

The flight attendant's smile was wide, and the glass of wine she had recently served had been cold and delicious, but Bianca's heart was pounding with anxiety as the plane began its descent through the wintry bleakness of the English morning sky. Everything was happening so fast that it felt like being on a non-stop merry-go-round and she thought, not for the first time, that this was turning out to be the most bizarre Christmas morning of her life.

Opposite her sat Xanthos, his long-legged frame reclining in the leather seat of the private jet he'd hired to fly them from Vargmali where, earlier today, they had left the tiny village of Kopshtell. With the Christmas bells peeling in their ears and big fat flakes of snow beginning to fall, many of the friendly villagers they'd met last night had turned up to wave them off. Bianca's heart had leapt as she had hugged Ellen and promised that they might try to come back one day. Had it been presumptuous of her to include Xanthos in her impulsive declaration to the local doctor's wife? Was that why he had been so *distant* towards her during the two-hour flight back to London?

After a long night of rapturous lovemaking when she had thought they were as close as two people could be, she had been given a short, sharp shock this morning. Because once they had dragged themselves from their rumpled bed at a hellishly early hour, there had been no touching, or complicit eye contact—no physical contact at all. For a start, Xanthos had dressed in an immaculate city suit and silk tie and that too seemed to set him apart since her own outfit was decidedly casual. Then he'd spent the entire journey working, giving no hint to the crew—or even to her—that they had been lovers. Looking at their body language, no one would have guessed that he had introduced her to pleasure after pleasure, or confided some pretty disturbing things about his childhood before clamming up completely—confidences she suspected were rare. Was he now regretting having made such frank disclosures to a woman who was little more than a stranger?

Consequently, Bianca now felt exhausted and over-sensitive and wished she were back in that rural hotel. Somehow she had felt safe in that snowy village, high in the Vargmalian mountains—as if the normal cares of the world couldn't touch her there. She wondered what was going to happen between them now. If anything. What did she know? Had it just been a casual hook-up for him? Was she supposed to act as if nothing had happened? But if their passionate night *was* to be a one-off, she would accept it. She wouldn't chase him, or beg him or behave as if she was in any way *dependent* on him. Because she wasn't. She wasn't dependent on anyone.

She was just leaning forward to watch the green fields of England growing ever closer, when Xanthos's gravelled voice broke into her thoughts.

'So, what are you planning on doing when we touch down?'

Bianca turned to look at him, steeling herself against all his dark and golden beauty. That didn't sound very promising, did it? 'I told you.' She tried to inject a note of enthusiasm into her voice as she thought of going home to her silent Wimbledon apartment. 'I'm just going to have a quiet Christmas Day on my own.'

Dark eyebrows disappeared into the ebony tumble of his hair. 'And is that what you really want?'

Of course it isn't what I want, you stupid man! I want you to pull me in your arms and tell me I'm beautiful and then kiss me, the way you did last night.

She experimented with a little cool flirtation. 'Why, is there an alternative?'

'I'm staying at the Granchester. I've booked a suite.'

He said it as if she would have heard of it—which of course she had. 'Just like that?' She blinked. 'One of the best hotels in London and you just happened to be able to get a suite there, on Christmas Day?'

He shrugged, drawing her unwilling attention to the broad width of his shoulders. 'The owner is a friend of mine.'

Of course he was. 'I thought…' She fiddled unnecessarily with her seat belt. 'I thought you were going to Switzerland.'

'I was, but I've altered my plans. I'm staying in London for a couple of days.' He subjected her to a steady gaze. 'And I thought you might like to join me.'

'Right.' She sat very still as those dark eyes washed over her. If she were here in a professional capacity she might have asked him why he had changed his plans, and her tone would have been crisp and direct and confident. But she wasn't here in a professional capacity. She was here as a woman who'd spent the previous night having sex and she wasn't sure how to handle the aftermath. What to say or how to react. If there were games people played after being intimate for the first time, nobody had ever told her the rules. Part of her wanted to fling herself into his arms and cover his face with kisses which although last night would have been welcomed, today she suspected would not. As always when she was uncertain, she sought comfort in procrastination. 'Let me think about it.'

Xanthos nodded, not sure whether to be amused or insulted by her lukewarm response, because his head was still all over the place. His night with Bianca had turned out to be the hottest of his life, even before he had made the astonishing discovery that she'd been a virgin. But even more surprising than that was the fact that he had *told* her stuff. Stuff buried deep which never usually saw the light of day, because he wasn't a man given to introspection.

But she needed to understand this wasn't going anywhere. She still didn't know who he really was, and there were all kinds of reasons why that shouldn't change. If she knew, it would alter everything. For both of them. He just wasn't willing to let her go…not just yet. And didn't he have the perfect excuse for suggesting they prolong their liaison—one which wouldn't fill her with false hope about the future? He gathered up the documents he'd been reading during the flight. 'My office have been in touch while we've been in the air. Apparently journalists are waiting for us to land.'

She looked at him blankly. 'Journalists?'

'You know. They usually write or broadcast features of interest to the general public.'

'Very funny. Why would they do that? Be waiting for us, I mean.'

She pursed her soft lips and he was momentarily distracted by the memory of those lips locked around a very intimate part of his anatomy, which had started to ache with unbearable precision. 'Think about it,' he said huskily. 'Your sister is a newly crowned queen, and I'm not exactly unknown in the world of gaming and finance. Our plane recently crashed in the snowy mountains of a distant country and we were rescued by a village doctor in an ancient truck. We spent the night together in a quirky hotel, and I'm afraid that being rich and single inevitably gives rise to speculation about the women in my life. It is also Christmas Day, which is a light news day.' He fixed her with a mocking look. 'Doesn't that give you a hint about why they might want to talk to us?'

'Well, I'm not talking to anyone!'

'Neither am I. Which is why I've arranged for a car to drive me straight from the airfield into London. Have you thought about it for long enough, Bianca?' His raised his eyebrows. 'You could join me at the Granchester and we could spend Christmas Day and night together, or I can drop you off somewhere else on the way.' He shrugged. 'Up to you.'

Bianca was tempted to turn him down because his

attitude was so…*offhand*. As if she meant nothing to him, and the occasional tenderness she'd glimpsed when they'd been in bed had been nothing but a figment of her imagination. Or maybe tenderness was acceptable within the shadows of the night, but vanished when it met the cold scrutiny of daylight. Couldn't he at least have kissed her and pulled her into his arms and told her that he really, really wanted her to spend some time with him? He was being so…*cool*.

She stared down at her fingernails. She knew you weren't supposed to let other people's moods affect the way you felt, but right now that didn't seem to make any difference. She felt like a balloon which had been lanced by a needle. And although it was tempting to want to extend her time with him—wouldn't that be dicing with danger where her emotions were concerned?

But a solo Christmas dinner had definitely lost its appeal and the thought of returning to her small apartment made her feel flat. She pushed at one of her cuticles. Her seduction last night had felt binevitable—as if she would never stop regretting it if she said no. This one felt more considered and the decision was all hers. She knew what would be the right thing to do. To thank him for the memory and say goodbye, thus eliminating the chances of getting her heart broken. Yet hadn't she spent her whole life trying to do the right thing? She had adopted different roles when her father had become ill and her mother had found it so difficult to cope. She'd been hard-working Bianca. Reliable Bianca. But now she'd discovered passionate Bianca, surely she was allowed to savour that side of her personality before normal, sensible service was resumed.

'I suppose I could spend Christmas Day with you,' she said, after much deliberation. 'At least it'll save me from having to do any cooking. Or washing up.'

He smiled and Bianca felt vindicated in her decision when she saw the rabble of press in the distance as they descended the aircraft steps. The waiting car felt like a haven, though she was half blinded by the flash of cameras as they were driven at speed towards the exit. Leaning back, she expelled a long sigh of relief.

'Thank heavens that's over.'

His gaze was curious. 'Had many dealings with the press before?'

She shook her head. 'Not really. I had to refuse a couple of magazine interviews when the engagement was first announced, and shortly before the wedding I was papped leaving a corner shop near where I live in London after buying a carton of milk.' She pulled a face. 'It was an extremely unflattering photo, leaving them to speculate what on earth I was going to wear at the wedding which wouldn't make me look like a gatecrasher.'

'And did that bother you?'

'It did, because that kind of scrutiny was totally unexpected,' she answered slowly. 'From being a fairly anonymous person, I was slightly alarmed to discover that Rosie's new-found fame seemed contagious.'

There was a pause. 'And did you approve of your sister marrying the King?'

She tilted her head consideringly. He really could be quite surprising. At times he was insultingly offhand, while at others he did seem genuinely interested in her life, and her past. She shrugged. 'I didn't always like Corso, no.'

'Oh? Why not?'

The purring consideration of his question was at odds with the sudden tension which had invaded his body and Bianca wondered what had caused it. Was it simply a competitive aspect of his own bcharacter—that of one exceedingly successful man curious to hear about the defects of another? But he had confided in her last night, and surely she must trust herself to do the same. 'I thought he was arrogant,' she confessed. 'And that he would probably break her heart.'

'Because?'

'Because he's a rich royal who's had countless lovers in the past and Rosie has always been fairly naïve and was probably completely out of her depth.'

'But it all ended happily ever after?'

'Yes, it did. The power of love, I guess,' she added, unable to keep the curl of wistfulness from her voice.

He screwed his brow up as if she had just uttered some kind of profanity. 'You don't honestly believe in all that stuff?'

Bianca hesitated. She knew it wasn't cool to admit it, but something made her want to tell him the truth. Was it to ensure that he knew exactly where he stood with her? To warn him—or maybe to issue a silent plea—not to mess around with her own, innocent heart? 'I do, yes,' she said quietly. 'My mother and father loved one another very much and things were great between them until my bfather had his accident. But they provided a loving home for me and Rosie and I'd like…well, one day I'd like to recreate that sort of family life for myself, if I ever meet the right man.'

'Bianca—'

'Oh, please don't worry,' she said quickly, anticipating his words. 'I'm not including you in that consideration, Xanthos. I want someone, yes, but a nice safe man who doesn't make waves—who also wants a family of his own. And you're the antithesis of that man. The wrong man, if you like. Please don't be offended.'

'Why would I be offended when it's nothing but the truth? To be honest, it's a relief to hear you say it. Marriage has never been on my agenda and love is just a word which gets misused all the time. Whereas to be acknowledged as something of a scoundrel, which is what you seem to be doing, well, that's a much better fit.' He gave a dangerously sexy smile, his voice dipping into a velvety caress. 'Do you have any idea of how much I want you right now, Bianca?'

Her throat constricted. 'Maybe.'

'So what are we going to do about it?'

'You tell me,' she whispered. 'You're the expert.'

'Yes, but…'

She could see him swallow as he unbuttoned her jacket, cupping her breast through the thick wool of her sweater and caressing the covered nipple until it peaked against his palm.

'But, what?' she prompted.

'Right now you're making me feel like a novice,' he admitted huskily.

Was that good or bad? Bianca wondered as his hand continued to work its provocative magic. But by then he had turned his attention to the other breast and her head was tipping back helplessly against the squashy leather of the car seat. She could feel the tiptoeing of his fingers moving slowly up towards her thigh and as she felt irresistible hunger spiralling up, she managed to prise a splinter of logic from the befuddled depths of her mind, because surely she ought to stop him. 'What about…the driver?' she breathed weakly.

'Don't worry. He can't see us.' His lips began to brush along her jaw and she could feel the warmth of his quickened breath against her skin. 'Or hear us.'

'Are you…sure?'

'I'm certain. Total privacy is always a non-negotiable whenever I get a chauffeured car.'

She wished he hadn't said that because it conjured up pictures of other women who had been in exactly this situation. But she did nothing to stop the automatic parting of her thighs, nor the questing forefinger which had alighted with aching precision over the denim seam covering the crotch of her jeans. Her throat dried. 'Xanthos,' she breathed, her bottom writhing with frustration as he began to stroke her through the thick material.

'Xanthos, what?' he questioned, the mocking caress of his words turning her on even more.

She wanted to beg him to unzip her jeans and touch her properly. To place his finger against the bare flesh, or even use his mouth—as he had done so shockingly and so beautifully last night. But she was powerless to speak. Powerless to do anything other than try to contain her moans of pleasure as he took her to that exquisite place again.

She came quickly, almost violently, shuddering against his hand, her body clenching with sweet spasms as his head swooped down to claim her lips in a kiss. Blindly, she groped for the hard ridge in his trousers, but he bucked away as if she had scalded him, capturing her wrist within the curl of his fingers, his lips pressed close against her ear.

'No. Not now and not here,' he warned softly.

The spasms of her own pleasure still receding and aware that she was probably never going to get another sexual education like this, Bianca plucked up the courage to ask him directly. 'You mean, you don't want me to?' she questioned, unable to keep the confusion from her voice, and the silence which followed seemed to go on and on.

'More than you will ever know,' he answered in a strained kind of voice, before leaning back in his seat and straightening his silk tie. 'But I've always found deprivation to be good for the soul. Particularly when—'

'When, what?' she prompted.

But he shook his dark head with an air of finality, as if he'd already said too much. As if he wanted to distance himself from her both mentally and physically. Why else would he slide to the far end of the seat as the car drew up outside the Granchester and the liveried doorman sprang to attention?

CHAPTER EIGHT

THE CHRISTMAS TREE which dominated the atrium of the luxurious Granchester was enormous and Bianca gazed up at its laden branches, blinking her eyes against its bright shimmer. The fragrant fir was decked with expensive lights and baubles and, according to the breathless commentary from the concierge who was showing them around, the tiny pink glass pomegranates were a nod to Zac Constantinides, the hotel's Greek owner.

But all she could feel as she gazed up at its splendour was an aching sense of something which felt like *disappointment*. As if recognising that nothing could be as magical as the beauty of the simple tree they'd left behind in Kopshtell.

Her heart was racing and her skin glowing as a result of Xanthos bringing her to that shattering orgasm in the back of the luxury car just now, but it had been curiously a one-sided experience. He hadn't allowed her to touch him back and his expert ministrations had been delivered with the impartiality of someone who'd been following an instruction manual. It hadn't felt as if he were *involved*.

But then he wasn't involved, was he? Not really.

From the moment they'd left the airfield, he'd shown her a completely different side to his character. He was no longer the man who had whirled her breathlessly around the dance floor last night, but a powerful and sophisticated entrepreneur with untold wealth at his fingertips. From the moment they'd walked into the Granchester people had been practically falling over themselves to talk to him. And he was used to that. She could tell. Suddenly, his exalted status had become very apparent.

She was quiet as they rode the private elevator to their vast suite, with its floor-to-ceiling windows and glittering chandeliers.

'Isn't this an improvement on what we've left behind?' he said, tugging off her coat and placing it on one of the giant leather sofas.

Bianca shrugged because her world had started to feel curiously disjointed. Here she was surrounded by nothing but opulence but all she wanted was to be back in that rustic hotel or even the snowy mountain hut, where their needs had been so basic and yet everything had seemed uncomplicated.

'I suppose so.'

He raised his eyebrows. 'You don't sound very enthusiastic.'

She shrugged. 'I liked it in Vargmali.'

'Then let's see what we can do to make you like it here, shall we?'

He unzipped her jeans and peeled away her sweater—his economy of movement belying the slight unsteadiness of his hands. Very soon she was lying unselfconsciously on a giant sofa in just her bra and panties and he was walking towards her, stripping off his clothes and letting them fall. His body was clearly aroused—but the shuttered expression on his face was unreadable and she wondered if she had imagined that warmer version of him yesterday, or whether the mountain air had briefly gone to his head. She lay back against the heap of silken cushions as his suit trousers hit the silken rug and tried to focus on the moment. She could see the unashamed power of his erection and ac-knowledged, with a touch of incredulity, how amazing it was that her body could accommodate something as big as that. The perfect fit. Like Cinderella's slipper, she thought dreamily as he grew closer.

'Please don't look at me like that,' he instructed un-evenly.

'Like what?'

Xanthos felt his throat tighten even more. Like she wanted to devour him. Or bewitch him. Or to suck him deep inside her body and never let him go. But she had already done that, he reminded himself. She had of-fered him her virginity while he, in turn, had told her things he'd never told another soul. How much more of himself was he going to give this woman, and how much more of himself did he wish to expose? He needed to be in control, he reminded himself grimly—not re-linquish any more of it to her, because of this strange physical alchemy they shared. 'It doesn't matter,' he said abruptly. 'Move over.'

She made room for him on the giant sofa and he dis-tracted his wayward thoughts by removing her bra and her panties as slowly as possible—as if to demonstrate that not all his self-restraint had left him. Yet he couldn't prevent himself from drinking in her nakedness as she lay there, as if he were seeing her properly for the first time. And maybe he was. In the hut, the temperature had been icy, their thick layers of clothing vital in helping keep them alive. Even in the rural hotel, the air had been draughty enough to make them snuggle beneath the old-fashioned eiderdown. But here in the centrally heated luxury of the Granchester, he was able to feast his eyes on her body for the first time.

And she was *incredible*. Tiny and soft, her shape was curvy yet compact. Creamy breasts were crowned with nipples the colour of damask roses, and between her thighs a triangle of dark hair, which shielded the honeyed mound he had licked with such intensity. Caressing one lush breast between his fingers for an exquisitely long moment, he watched her emerald eyes darken and her hips wriggle with unconscious invitation.

'I can hardly believe you were a virgin,' he confessed slowly as he continued to stroke her.

The tip of her tongue roved over the cushion of her bottom lip and he wondered if she had any idea how provocative that was.

'Because…because I wasn't very good at it?' she ventured.

'It?' he mocked.

'Sex,' she elaborated shyly.

Shaking his head, he moved his hand down between her legs and felt her squirm with pleasure as he encountered her sticky heat. 'On the contrary,' he murmured, his finger moving lightly against her responsive flesh. 'You behaved as if you were born to it.'

'I suppose everyone is, when you think about it,' she answered, quite seriously, though the stilted delivery of her words suggested she was having difficulty concentrating when he was rubbing his finger against her like that. 'Otherwise, how would the human race ever have survived?'

His response was a short and surprising laugh. For a woman to amuse him was rare enough, but to do so when he was just about to have sex with her was unheard of. 'Tell me what you like best about it, so far,' he questioned, with a sudden indulgence.

'Everything. I like everything.'

Her eyelids had fluttered to a close and Xanthos was relieved, because that had sounded too much like unconditional praise for his liking. He hoped she wasn't going to start *caring* for him, and not just because she was the sister-in-law of his royal brother.

He stared at her flushed flesh. Yes, their bodies had met and matched with mind-blowing chemistry, but that was only one side of intimacy. Emotionally, she would be out of her depth and liable to mistake physical satisfaction for something else. Because that was what women did. It was how they operated. They attached emotions to actions which were never intended to be anything more than actions.

'In that case, let me show you some more of my repertoire,' he suggested on a silken boast.

'You're making it sound like performance art,' she grumbled.

'All life is performance.'

Bianca might have been tempted to continue the debate if he hadn't started kissing her and before too long he was easing himself into her body again and making her concerns vanish like dust on the wind.

Some time later, she went into one of the bathrooms and stood beneath a torrent of hot water and when she emerged, wrapped in a white robe, she realised that Xanthos must have used another of the bathrooms for he sat in a matching robe at a linen-draped table, which had been set up in front of the tall windows, overlooking the park. He was looking at something on his phone as she walked in, and if she was a little disappointed that he hadn't joined her in the shower she was sensible enough to keep her complaint to herself.

He put the phone down, but she noticed it was screenside up.

'I've ordered us a very late lunch,' he said. 'Come and sit down.'

Obediently, she slid into the chair opposite, but she must have been hungrier than she'd anticipated for she tucked into lobster and a feta and spinach pastry, which was one of the most delicious things she'd ever eaten. It was certainly an unconventional Christmas dinner. There were grapes the colour of rubies, accompanied by slivers of French cheese, followed by stewed plums and thick, clotted cream. They drank iced water and, afterwards, champagne—served in faceted crystal flutes which sparkled like diamonds.

'This time it doesn't taste of toothpaste,' Xanthos bobserved wryly.

Bianca nodded but put the glass down after one sip, for the wine was making her feel vulnerable. Because wasn't the recollection of memories dangerous? Didn't it have the potential to create the idea that they shared some sort of history when they were just two people who had found themselves in an extraordinary situation and allowed sexual attraction to take over?

It made her realise just how quickly things had happened.

Too quickly.

'Is the owner of this hotel really a friend of yours?' she asked, deliberately redirecting her thoughts as she glanced out at London's famous Hyde Park.

'Zac?' Xanthos took a sip of his drink. 'We knew each other way back and our paths have crossed from time to time. In fact, you'll meet him later.' There was a pause. 'If you'd like to.'

She looked at him blankly. 'You mean, he's here? In the hotel?'

'Not right now. He and his wife live in Hampstead, but apparently it's a tradition to bring their children to see the Granchester tree on Christmas afternoon. He said it would be good to catch up as we haven't seen each other in a while, and I saw no reason to say no.'

She put her napkin down and gave a hesitant smile. 'Yes. Yes, I'd like that.'

'Good.' His dark eyes glittered with obsidian fire. 'But first I think you need to wipe that faintly concerned expression off your face and come over here so that I can kiss you.'

'Or you could come over here?'

'I could. But in order to do that I'd have to move.' His tone was dry as he directed a wry glance at his lap. 'And right now, I'm not sure I'd be able to.'

Bianca flushed with instinctive pleasure at the erotic inference and did as he asked, unsurprised when he untied her robe and placed his lips against her peak-ing nipple, and she gave a small moan of pleasure as his hardness sprang against her hungry fingers. The outcome was predictable, yet as Bianca began to rock back and forth on his rocky shaft, it felt as intense as the first time they'd made love. It was blissful when he closed his eyes like that and bit out a whimper of pleasure which sounded almost helpless. It gave her a heady rush of triumph which briefly obliterated all her doubts and uncertainties.

Nonetheless, she felt the skittering of nerves as she extricated herself from his embrace and hunted around for something suitable to wear, wondering what Xanthos's friends would think of her. Had they met many of his lovers in the past? Pulling out a short dress in festive scarlet, she held it up in front of her, hoping the couple were sophisticated enough to be polite, even if they didn't automatically approve of her.

But it seemed her fears were unfounded because handsome Zac and his blonde English wife, Emma, were delightful. As were their two children—Leo, a solemn, dark-eyed little boy of five, along with Eva, his thirteen month-old baby sister, who was the spitting image of her mother. The baby took an instant shine to Bianca and, in particular, her long hair—clamping a tight fist around one of the long black waves and refusing to let go, no matter how much her protesting mother tried to disengage the little fingers.

'Honestly, I don't mind,' said Bianca, with a smile. 'Though it might make it easier if I held her?'

'You could *try*, though she probably won't go to you,' said Emma doubtfully, bursting into a peal of laughter as Eva immediately launched herself into Bianca's arms. 'Oh, it seems she will.'

It was a different kind of assault to the senses from the ones she'd been experiencing of late but as Bianca breathed in Eva's clean, baby scent and a pair of chubby arms were draped around her neck, she was overcome by a wave of longing so powerful it felt almost visceral. A thought crossed her mind so quickly it was barely there, but it left an imprint as deep as if it had been branded there.

Will I ever hold a baby of my own like this?

As she pressed her chin against Eva's head, she met the ebony slice of Xanthos's gaze over the softly tousled curls and a pang of something unknown tugged painfully inside her. Was that a warning she had read in his eyes? With an unexpectedly heavy heart, she handed the baby back to Emma and prepared to accompany the Constantinides family into the main lobby.

Most of the Granchester staff were lined up on either side of the Christmas tree to welcome their boss, and a teddy bear and toy drum were produced for Eva and Leo, to delighted squeals. Afterwards, they went to the hotel's famous Garden Room, where tea was served. The courtyard outside was lit with hundreds of white lights, and tiny silvery stars were laced through the bare branches of the trees. In a far corner of the restaurant was a miniature battery-operated ice rink, on which tiny skaters in festive clothes of green and red whirled round and round. The two men took the children over for a closer look, while Bianca and Emma surveyed the glut of Christmas fare piled on the table with slight dismay, before ordering nothing stronger than ginger tea.

'You have two very beautiful children,' Bianca commented as the two women sat down.

Emma smiled. 'They like you. You're obviously a natural.' Her voice was soft but when Bianca didn't answer the unspoken question, she carried on speaking. 'I gather you've just come through a pretty horrendous experience.'

Bianca nodded, because she could hardly confess that what had happened subsequently had been enough to erase the plane crash from her mind. 'Yes, it was.' She hesitated. 'But Xanthos was absolutely amazing. I don't know whether anyone else would have coped as well as he did.'

'Mmm... I imagine he'd be a good person to have around in an emergency.' Emma's expression grew curious. 'He said he met you in Monterosso, at your sister's wedding.'

'That's right.'

Emma glanced across the room. 'That man is a constant surprise. We had no idea he knew the King. But he certainly looks more relaxed than I've ever seen him.' There was a pause. 'You're obviously very good for him, Bianca.'

Bianca wanted to beg the elegant blonde not to say things like that, because it sparked the kind of hope she wasn't supposed to be entertaining. Hope for a future which could never be hers, with a man who wanted different things.

As Xanthos walked back across the restaurant with Zac and his children, he couldn't seem to tear his gaze away from Bianca, who was sitting next to Emma and chatting easily to her—as if the two women had been friends for years. A sense of apprehension was rapidly building up inside him—yet another brick to add to his growing disquiet that here was a woman with the potential to destabilise him. He had watched the way she'd bbehaved with baby Eva—how her expression had grown tender and dreamy as she had cradled the little girl in her arms. That had been the clucky behaviour of a woman aware of her biological clock ticking—and whether or not that had been unconscious, he needed to heed the implicit warning in what he had seen. He had become so lost in her innocence, so bewitched by the wonder of her sexual awakening, that he had failed to look ahead. And he needed to.

They drank their tea and eventually rose to leave and, amid invitations to visit the Constantinides villa on Santorini any time they wanted a Greek vacation, he and Bianca returned to their suite.

'Oh, they're such a lovely family,' she said, breaking the silence which had fallen during the elevator ride to the top of the hotel.

'Yes,' he agreed steadily. 'They are.'

'Do you see much of them?'

'Not really. Our lives are very different now.'

But he could detect her sudden nervousness as they surveyed each other across the vastness of the luxurious suite, as if unsure of what to do next. Was that why she hurriedly walked over to the window, even though darkness had fallen?

'Oh, look—it's snowing,' she said.

He could hear the rush of relief in her voice, though whether that was because she was a lover of snow, or because it gave her something to talk about other than the thing they most definitely weren't talking about, he didn't know. But Xanthos knew he couldn't keep skating around the subject. Didn't he have enough unspoken stuff on his mind already, without adding even more to the heap?

'Bianca—'

She turned round and instantly he could sense that something had changed between them. Was it the tone of his voice which helped pave the way for that, or the way he let her name hang in the air—like a feather which was stubbornly refusing to float to the ground? Because suddenly he could see a different Bianca—a more brittle and watchful version of the woman who had given him her innocence. She was no longer the lover, eager to embrace her new-found sexuality. Her expression was cool and mildly questioning. He could imagine her adopting that look if she were dealing with a client in her lawyer's practice, perhaps twirling a pen in between her long fingers as she prepared to take notes. And if now he wanted to wipe away all her sudden froideur with the urgent press of his lips—he realised that to do so would be self-indulgent.

'I'm sorry,' he said heavily. 'But I can't give you what you want.'

'You can spare me the prepared speech, Xanthos.' bHer voice was quiet but her dignified smile touched something buried deep in his heart.

'You don't know what I was going to say.'

'No, but I can probably guess. You were going to tell me there's no future in this thing between us—or something along those lines.' She shrugged. 'But that's okay, because to be honest—I agree.'

He frowned. 'You do?'

She gave him a frowning look, as if he were being either dense or disingenuous, and he felt himself resenting her cool logic.

'Of course I do. I'm not stupid. I may not be experienced with men but that doesn't mean I can't read the signs. What did you think I was going to do—pin you down for a date? Or demand that we start synchronising our diaries, even though I live in London and you live in New York?'

'I saw the way you were with Zac and Emma's children,' he growled. 'You want a family of your own one day—that much was obvious. You'd already told me that, but seeing you with Eva and Leo made me realise that carrying on would be crazy, because we want different things.'

'I know that...' she breathed, brushing her fingertips against the scarlet hem of her dress. 'And, just for the record, I wasn't expecting a relationship simply because you were the first man I had sex with. Believe it or not, I really am a modern woman—though, admittedly, a late starter. So why don't we just agree to part on the most amicable of terms and enjoy the memory of what happened?'

And for the first time in as long as he could remember, Xanthos was completely lost for words.

CHAPTER NINE

'So…' Rosie's voice was heavy with implication. 'Did Xanthos actually *say* anything?'

Bianca was trying very hard to hold back her mounting irritation—which was surely more to do with her own stupidity at having allowed herself to get involved with the Greek billionaire in the first place, than the fact that her younger sister was annoyingly trying to interrogate her.

'Of course he did,' she said calmly. 'Unless you think we spent the entire time in the mountain hut and then on subsequent flights in total silence?'

'That's not what I mean!' Rosie protested.

'Then perhaps you'd like to explain what you *do* mean!' Bianca knew she was being unreasonable but she couldn't seem to stop herself. It was as if her defensiveness had become a sturdy shield she could hide behind now that her bravado had started to slip away. 'I know you're a queen now, Rosie—but I'm not one of your loyal subjects who has learned to intuit your words before they've even left your mouth.'

'That's not fair, Bianca!'

'Then just say what you want to say, because I am

time limited. Don't forget that most of us don't have a wealthy monarch to support us and still need to work for a living.'

'And that's not fair either!' Rosie's exasperated sigh echoed down the phone. 'You're hopeless when you're in this kind of mood, so why don't we change the subject? When are you coming out to Monterosso to see us?'

'Not any time soon,' said Bianca, before relenting a little. After all, it wasn't Rosie's fault she was hurting so much. The force of missing Xanthos had been like a sudden storm whose fierceness had taken her by surprise. And no matter how much she tried to reason that she barely knew him or to convince herself that she didn't really like him, it didn't seem to make the slightest bit of difference. Maybe their forced incarceration had provided an extra layer of intimacy. Or maybe the man to whom you so eagerly gave your virginity always occupied a special place in your heart. Yes, that must be it.

But she wasn't going to tell Rosie about bXanthos—about what they'd done or what they'd said—because if she shared her pain, it would only prolong it. She needed to draw a line under the whole affair and the best way to do that was to avoid going to Monterosso for the time being because, annoyingly, the place now reminded her of meeting Xanthos. Her voice softened. 'I'll try to get out in the spring if I can. Promise. But right now, I really do have stuff I need to do.'

But after she had terminated the call, Bianca didn't resume work immediately. She sat at her desk, staring at the calendar she insisted on hanging on her office wall every year, despite such things being considered old-fashioned. The January photo showed a clump of white snowdrops clustered around the trunk of a tree and although usually she adored the first flowers of the year, for once the scene looked as bleak as she felt inside.

She felt the wash of despair, wondering why she had allowed Xanthos to get so close and why she couldn't seem to get him out of her mind, no matter how hard she tried. Was it because the sex had been so incredible? Or because she'd enjoyed the unfamiliar experience of being part of a couple?

She thought about their matter-of-fact conversation late on Christmas afternoon, when she had calmly taken the initiative and told him there was no future for them. The truth was that her pride had wanted her to say it first—to signal the end before he did—because his growing distance from her had been obvious. But if her words had brought him brelief, there had been surprise on his face, too—as if she had broken the mould. Did his lovers usually cling on to the bitter end? Probably. No wonder he was so arrogant.

She stared out at the dome of St Paul's cathedral, which dominated her particular patch of London skyline. It didn't matter *why* he seemed to have taken stubborn root inside her mind—all that mattered was the manner in which she dealt with the aftermath of their heady affair. She needed to move on. To start dating, like other women her age. To find a nice, steady man with whom to settle down and have a family. And perhaps Xanthos had been the catalyst she needed to put that in motion.

So what was she waiting for?

She downloaded the apps recommended by her assistant and quickly learnt the rules of Internet dating, discovering never to agree to dinner on a first date, in case the man was so boring that you couldn't make your escape. But all the men seemed boring, even though in her heart Bianca knew they weren't. There was the hunky heart surgeon who invited her on a winter picnic in Hyde Park. The businessman who had rowed across the Atlantic with his brother and raised a shed-load of money for charity in the process—and the fine art expert who took her to a private view at a groovy gallery where they could see lights twinkling all over Shoreditch.

The trouble was that none of them were Xanthos bAntoniou and he was proving an impossible act to follow. Didn't matter how much she tried to reason that he wasn't the right man for her, deep in her heart Bianca wasn't convinced. It was like having tasted a morsel of rich, sweet chocolate then being told you would have to eat stale bread for the rest of your life.

And then one day in early spring, he rang.

His name flashed up on the screen because, naturally, they'd gone through the civilised motions of exchanging numbers before they'd parted. For a moment Bianca stared at it blankly, wondering if she was seeing things. She knew she should let it go to voicemail but suddenly she was sliding her thumb across the screen and praying that her voice sounded normal.

'Hello?'

'It's Xanthos.'

'I know.'

There was a pause. 'You don't sound overjoyed to hear from me.'

'How should I respond, Xanthos? Would you like me to burst into song?'

His low laugh did dangerous things to her blood pressure. 'How are you, Bianca?'

Oh, you know. Missing you. Obsessing about you. Trying not to view the past through rose-tinted spectacles or think about how it felt to have you deep inside my body.

'I'm fine!' she said brightly, looking at the wall calendar, which today was displaying the frilly yellow daffodils of March.

'What've you been up to?'

She saw no reason to lie, nor to be coy and *of course* she wasn't trying to make him jealous. 'I've been dating.'

There was silence.

'Xanthos? Are you still there?'

'Dating?'

'Yes. You know. Two hopefully single people meet in the hope of finding a mutual attraction.'

'And did you?'

'Not so far, no,' she said cheerfully. 'But I'm on several sites, so, by the law of averages, something should come up soon.'

'You're on a dating site?'

Wasn't it pathetic how that darkly dangerous note in his voice made her skin shimmer with pleasure? 'I am.'

'Are you out of your mind?' he exploded. 'You could end up spending the evening with a psychopath!'

Resisting the desire to make the very obvious retort,

Bianca watched as a sparrow hopped onto the window-sill to peck at a crumb of bread from her lunchtime sandwich. 'Why not? Everybody does it.'

'I don't,' he growled.

No, of course he didn't. He just had to walk into a room and women started throwing themselves at him. Remember *that*. 'Was there a reason for this phone call, Xanthos?' she questioned.

There was another pause before he said the words she realised she was longing for him to say. 'I'm coming over to England next week and wondered if you'd care to have dinner with me.'

And although the logical side of her mind wanted to remind him that they'd both agreed this would be a bad idea and her aching heart was pleading for her not to canvass any more potential pain, she ignored them, using two careless words to seal her fate.

'Sure. When?'

He sent a car to pick her up from her Wimbledon apartment and was sitting waiting for her in a discreetly expensive restaurant situated on one of Mayfair's sumptuous streets. And although it registered in the back of Bianca's mind that the luxurious eatery was only a short hop to the Granchester, she made no comment as she slid into the seat opposite him. And if she'd been hoping—which she had—to have acquired some immunity to his powerful brand of sex appeal, then her hopes had gone unanswered.

He looked nothing short of spectacular in a dark suit and a pale shirt. His thick black hair was ruffled, his firm jaw shadowed, and the only negative she could find was that his eyes appeared tired. But it was none of her business what might have produced a fatigue which had the effect of making him appear a little battle-drawn and very, very sexy.

'Bianca,' he said, rising to his feet as she approached.

'Hello, Xanthos,' she said, but her heart was beating very fast and she knew she needed to protect herself if she didn't want to end up in bed with him.

But if she didn't want that, then why else was she here?

She was barely aware of the food they ordered and deliberately stuck to water in order to maintain a clear head and noticed he did the same. They chatted about his work, her work. The record New York snows and the latest political scandal in England. He made her laugh, and she reciprocated, and on every level it was the most enjoyable date she'd had for many weeks, by a mile. But it wasn't enough. Not with him. Because suddenly Bianca knew she didn't want this. She didn't want to skate over the surface and spend the evening making superficial conversation. She didn't want to second-guess his motives, or to push them away and ignore them. The question was whether she intended to be passive or proactive about her fate.

She put down her knife and fork. *Ask* him. Stop playing games and just ask him. 'So why the sudden invitation to dinner, after radio silence for so long?'

Xanthos wondered what had taken her so long, because he'd been expecting this question a lot sooner. But he still took a heartbeat of a pause before he answered, because this was an admission which didn't come easily. 'I haven't been able to stop thinking about you,' he said simply, waiting for the inevitable response to his surprisingly honest statement and when she failed to deliver it, he raised his eyebrows. 'Have you been thinking about me, Bianca?'

She took several moments to fold her linen napkin into a neat square before looking up at him, her green eyes narrowed. 'Are we being honest?'

He felt a nerve tug at his temple. 'Of course.'

'Then, yes.' She shrugged. 'I would have to say that I have.'

'Internet dates proving a disappointment?' he mocked.

'Don't push it, Xanthos.' She folded her lips together. 'I'm perfectly aware that there's a perfectly logical reason for our mutual obsession.'

'Oh?'

'It's because we've undergone a traumatic and dramatic experience together, which means it's probably had a more profound effect than if we'd met in a cocktail bar.'

'And *that's* another thing I've missed about you,' he said in a low voice. 'Your intelligence and your judgment.'

She raised her eyebrows. 'Those are two things, actually—and I find that a very patronising thing to say.'

'How can it be, when I agree with you? Our near-death experience has left an aftermath which probably just needs to burn itself out. So let's burn it.' He reached across the table and took her hand, turning it over so that the palm was uppermost. 'If I were to ask you very nicely, would you stop dating other men and consider having an exclusive relationship with me?'

He saw her lips open and then shut again as if she were having trouble computing this and she pulled her hand away, as if his touch was only adding to her confusion. 'A transatlantic relationship, you mean?'

He frowned. 'Well, I have no intention of moving from New York and you certainly haven't said anything about leaving London.'

She pulled a face. 'Yes, I can see we really *are* being honest.'

'My boundaries haven't changed, Bianca. Have yours? I haven't suddenly transformed into the *nice* man you claim to want, who can commit to you long-term. If that's what you're expecting from me then I'll walk away right now, but if you're open to an exciting alternative, then...'

He let his words trail off but it took so long for her to answer that he thought she was going to turn him down and the prospect of that was something he didn't care to contemplate—and not just because of the unfamiliar impact it would have on his ego. But then he felt the deliberate brush of her knees against his underneath the table and suddenly her eyes were emerald-bright, her cheeks flushed as their gazes locked.

'Okay,' she said, her voice trembling a little. 'Why not?'

'Shall we go back to the hotel?'

'Or you could come back to mine? I know it's on the other side of the river, but Wimbledon isn't that far.'

He shook his head, thinking that perhaps, with his assistance, she could be persuaded to buy somewhere a little more central. 'I think neutral is better.'

He called for the bill and once they were alone in the

back of his waiting car, she fell into his arms and they kissed like teenagers. He realised how much he had missed her as, instantly, he was aroused to an almost unbearable level of desire. With her sexual heat perfuming the air with its earthy tang, it was as much as he could do to resist the desire to touch her intimately and bring her pleasure with his fingers, as he had done once before. But he made himself resist, and of course that turned him on even more. As the car drew up outside the hotel, his blood was pulsing around his veins like hot lava and walking took a monumental effort as they made their way towards the private elevator.

'Oh,' she said, once they were delivered directly into a suite of monumental proportions and she went from room to room, examining the layout like a prospective buyer. 'This is different to the suite we had last time.'

He nodded as he hung up her coat in the hallway. The other booking had been last-minute while this was reputedly the best hotel room in London. But he hadn't booked it in order to impress her. It was more that he wanted to forget the past and live in the present.

But you could never really push away the past, could you? It still came back to haunt you when you least wanted it to.

'Do you know how many nights I've lain awake thinking about all the things I want to do to you, Bianca?' he groaned, as he pulled her into his arms. 'Was it the same for you?' And when she didn't answer, he placed his lips against her ear. 'Tell me,' he urged.

'Yes,' she blurted out unsteadily. 'Yes, I missed you.'

'Show me how much.'

But all she did was to tip her head back in silent submission so that he could kiss her again and he realised that this was a battle of minds as well as bodies, making the prospect of physical release all the more tantalising. She moaned his name as he stroked her curves through her closely fitting dress—her slurred incitement making his gut clench and his groin grow even harder. Every nerve ending in his body was aroused, as if she had torn off a layer of his skin and left him raw. Again he could scent her arousal perfuming the air—musky and provocative—and he picked her up and carried her into the bedroom, thinking how light and fragile she felt in his arms.

Her eyes were wide as he placed her in the centre of the bed and, without ceremony, he ran his fingertips up her leg until he had encountered the black stocking he knew he'd find there. Unable to sustain his teasing caress, he began pulling off her clothes with an urgency which only ever seemed to happen with her and suddenly she was doing the same. As if neither of them could bear to wait a minute longer. As if they had already waited too long. His throat dried and he felt as if he might explode. Because wasn't that how it felt? As if they had wasted too much time during these weeks apart?

He tried to claw back some of his habitual control, but, despite his best efforts to temper his reaction, he couldn't hold back his shudder of admiration as he reacquainted his gaze with her luscious curves and the rose-dark nipples which were crying out for the hungry plunder of his lips. Nor could he contain the sharp spear of lust which cut right through him, as he nudged the heavy tip of his erection against her moist folds and eased himself deep into her waiting wetness and she cried out even louder than she had done the first time he had entered her.

For most of the night he remained deep inside her, with sleep only arriving as the pale light of dawn filtered through the windows. The sun was high when she awoke and took him in her arms and the rest of the morning was lost in a haze of sensual abandon. The weekend spread out in front of them, awash with the bright sunshine of early spring, and while she was in the shower Xanthos had a toothbrush and fresh lingerie delivered to their suite, along with a pair of jeans he thought might fit her, with an accompanying cotton sweater.

'Clean clothes,' she observed when she emerged from the bathroom, before fixing him with a questioning look. 'Do you kit out all your lovers like this?'

'No. Normally, I would have sent you home in a car first thing and arranged to meet you later for dinner.'

'"Sent"?' she echoed, her tone acerbic. 'Like a package, you mean?'

'I prefer to think of it as creating a little necessary distance, because I'm someone who likes my own space. But since I'm only in town for two days, I find myself unwilling to waste a single second of my time with you.' And although she was still frowning, he brushed his mouth over hers in a kiss intended as much for manipulation as for pleasure and it had the desired effect as she whispered and wriggled and begged for more. Still he held back, enjoying a rare and heady sense of domination, until he could resist no more. And suddenly he was lost on a wave of something he didn't recognise.

Suddenly, *he* was the one who was helpless, and the distribution of sexual power seemed far less one-sided than it had been before.

He tugged open her robe and tumbled them down on one of the wide leather sofas, choking out an urgent gasp of pleasure as he eased into her moist heat. And afterwards, when their breathing had lost a little of its ragged quality, he tilted her chin, his thumb stroking softly at her skin. 'Why don't you wander down to the hotel boutique?' he suggested carelessly. 'Pick up anything else you might need for the next couple of days and put it on my account. Anything you like.'

In his arms, she froze. 'Thanks, but no, thanks. I'm perfectly capable of paying for my own clothes, Xanthos. Why else do you think I've been working so hard all these years?'

He was unused to his generosity being refused, but the novelty value only added to her allure and, once she had sorted out her wardrobe to her satisfaction, he had the hotel arrange a dizzying selection of pursuits to occupy them for the next two days. The weekend culminated with an early dinner on Sunday evening, for he was due to fly out the next morning but despite the dazzling setting and Michelin-starred menu, they skipped dessert and went straight back to bed.

He was so hard. Over and over again he thrust into her—he didn't think it was possible to come that many times. Blitzed with satisfaction, he ran a fingertip over the curve of her hip, a sigh escaping from his lips. 'You really are the most incredible lover, you know.'

'I bet you say that to all the girls,' she mumbled drowsily.

He could easy have denied her accusation because he wasn't known for lavishing praise and most of his lovers complained about his detachment—a reasonable enough observation, but an irritating one all the same. Yet Bianca made him feel different. As if she had somehow peeled away his skin and imprinted herself on the flesh and bones beneath. Her body felt so soft and so pliant as she moulded herself against his that at times he was unsure where she began and he ended. Contentment stole over his skin like a silken snare and later he wondered if that had been the trigger which made him shatter the comfortable and easy silence.

'Did you tell your sister about us?' he asked suddenly.

Slowly, she raised her head, blinking long-lashed eyes at him as if confused. 'Well, up until a couple of days ago, there was no *us*, was there?'

'No. I guess not.'

She tilted her head back and yawned. 'Why do you ask?'

He shook his head. 'No reason.'

Bianca's eyelids felt heavy and the temptation to go to sleep was powerful, but something about Xanthos's tone was making her uneasy—because hadn't she been trained to search for nuance behind the stock phrases which people uttered every day? Up until this moment, her weekend with him had been perfect. Like one of those cheesy romcom films. She'd been on a total high. She'd even turned off her phone so the office couldn't get hold of her and she'd never done that before. But his stilted words made doubts begin to whisper into her mind.

She remembered her sister's question, asking whether Xanthos had *said anything*, and how she'd thought that a very strange question at the time. Half-forgotten fragments began to piece themselves together in her mind. Rosie's insistence that a complete stranger fly her home 'as a favour to Corso'. What had made her say something like that? She hadn't asked at the time because there hadn't been the opportunity and subsequent events made it seem as if it had happened so long ago. But something didn't add up and it was making her tense with bapprehension—and coupled with that was the fear that this was all too good to be true. She pulled away from him.

'How did you say you knew Corso?'

There was a pause. He was still looking up at the ceiling. 'I told you. We have business interests in common.'

'Which struck me at the time as very vague. So that's all?'

This time the pause assumed the dimensions of a gulf and when he halted his study of the huge chandelier above their heads to face her, his black eyes were hooded. 'No. That's not all.'

She sat up, feeling her hair stream down over her bare shoulders, tempted to go to the bathroom to find a robe to cover up the nakedness which was suddenly making her feel vulnerable, but she didn't want to lose this moment in case it didn't come again.

Or that she might not have the courage to ask what she knew she needed to ask?

'What's going on here, Xanthos?' she questioned quietly. 'Why do I get the idea there's a bigger picture and I'm the only one who isn't allowed to know what it is?'

Xanthos's throat felt dust-dry. He wanted a drink of water. He wanted to rewind the clock. He wanted... His mouth twisted, because only fools thought that way. Hadn't he learned by now that wishing never got you anywhere? Meeting the wariness of her shadowed gaze, he knew he owed her the truth.

'You once asked me if my mother ever told me who my father was,' he said slowly. 'And I said no, she hadn't.'

'Only guess what? You've suddenly remembered that she did?' she suggested sarcastically.

'No, Bianca. She never told me. Somebody else did.' He dragged in an unsteady breath. 'Corso, in fact.'

'But why would Corso...?'

He saw the exact moment when she worked it out for herself—faster than he would have anticipated, but then her perception and intelligence had never been in doubt. He saw the dawning of comprehension on a face still flushed with sex. And he saw something else, too— something he didn't want to acknowledge. Hurt, and anger, and disappointment—bitter seeds which would now flourish and destroy what little they'd had.

'Of course,' she breathed. 'Of *course*. It all makes sense now. Why didn't it occur to me sooner? I remember thinking you looked vaguely *familiar* when I first met you. And then there was my sister's ridiculous insistence that I travel with you, though I didn't stop to ask myself why. And you...'

She sprang out of bed and began scrambling around for her underwear and it was making a difficult situation practically unbearable to have to watch her slither into a tiny pair of black panties and matching bra. Like some taunting striptease in reverse.

'I understand it all now,' she breathed. 'You're Corso's brother, aren't you?'

'Half-brother.'

'Don't split hairs!' she hissed, bending down to slide on a stocking.

'You want to know what happened, Bianca? How it happened?'

'Not particularly. This is a story which has missed the deadline. It's too late, Xanthos.'

'Well, I'm going to tell you anyway,' he continued, as if she weren't smoothing sheer black silk over one creamy thigh and making his heart pound painfully in his chest. But more than the physical distraction of her beauty was the realisation that he *wanted* to tell her—and wasn't that dangerous? Because things always went deeper with her than with anyone else, didn't they? Somehow she had the ability to touch into a place which had always been out of bounds to anyone else. 'When my mother was about eighteen, she was brought over to the US from Greece and introduced to Corso's father, the late King, as a potential lover. They began a short affair in New York, for which she was paid—handsomely, bI understand. Believe me, this was never a fairy-tale romance,' he added grimly. 'Apparently she had no idea he was married and certainly not that he was a royal, with the power to ghost her when she became pregnant with his child. Which is exactly what happened.'

'Don't you understand? I don't *care*!' she said, hunting around for the other stocking.

But Xanthos carried on regardless, making sentences out of the bizarre facts which had been torturing him ever since he'd discovered them. Saying out loud the words he'd kept hidden away in a place of shame ever since Corso had blurted out the whole incredible story. 'The money my mother had been paid quickly ran out,' he continued roughly. 'And her family back in Greece would have disowned her if she'd turned up pregnant out of wedlock, without even being able to name the father. So she met another man very rapidly and married him, convincing him that I was *his* child. I only discovered this when Corso came to New York to find me. It still feels pretty new and raw.'

She was shaking her head. 'But you're completely missing the point!' she raged. 'All the time you were having sex with me and supposedly being intimate with me—you were holding this back. Don't you see how it makes me feel?' she exploded, wriggling her soft cream dress over her curvy body. 'As if the rest of you are all part of some exclusive, privileged circle and I'm on the outside and don't count. It seems everybody knew about it except me.'

'Not everybody,' he contradicted. 'Corso knows. Your sister knows. Why would I tell you about something when I still hadn't come to terms with it myself?'

'I don't give a damn whether or not you've decided to embrace your precious royal roots. I can't believe my sister kept your identity secret from me!'

'But she didn't know we were involved, did she?' he pointed out.

'*Were* being the operative word,' she gritted out, before storming from the room.

He lay in that sex-rumpled bed, waiting to hear the slam of the door. But his assumption was wide of the mark because she returned almost immediately, wearing her coat, her face even more furious than before. Her eyes were two green splinters in her pinched face, her lips a tight line.

'I can't believe I've fallen into your arms again, or why I've just accepted whatever crumbs you were prepared to offer me. You couldn't wait to try to turn me into a convenient mistress, could you, Xanthos? Waiting until I was in the shower before buying me expensive lingerie.' Her mouth flattened in disgust. 'It's such a cliché!'

'I wanted to buy you something pretty.'

'I don't need you to do that—I can buy my own lingerie!' she protested fiercely, before sucking in an angry breath as if she'd suddenly thought of something else. 'Is that the real reason why you seduced me, despite your obvious reservations about me? So you could ask me all those questions about Corso, and find out what life was really like in Monterosso? Maybe you needed a few insider facts about the place where some of your ancestors came from, before you decided whether or not to make your association with them public. Was I just a convenient provider of information, Xanthos—who you decided to soften up by being physical?'

'You think I'd do something as underhand as that?' he demanded dangerously. 'That I would have sex with you in order to obtain information?'

'Oh, please. Spare me the righteous indignation. It's a little late to take the moral high ground. The bottom line is that you've misled me.'

But her fury couldn't disguise her hurt nor the clouding of disappointment in her beautiful green eyes and Xanthos felt the hard thud of guilt deep in his gut. 'Not deliberately,' he argued.

'You're splitting hairs. Again. Whichever way you want to look at it, I'd still call it a falsehood—'

'Bianca—'

But Bianca silenced him by lifting her hand, knowing his deception was only half the story. Because hadn't she been guilty of deceiving *herself*? Wouldn't that account for her disproportionate sense of hurt and disappointment, rather than the fact she'd been unaware her lover was a half-blood prince? Xanthos had made it perfectly clear this was never intended to be anything other than a casual fling. *She* had been the one to complicate it by reading too much into it—by wanting and dreaming and hoping. She had projected her wishes and her desires onto him, falsely imagining him to be the man she had been looking for. Was she going to imagine herself in love with every man she had sex with?

'I shouldn't be here,' she said quietly. 'I should never have agreed to have dinner with you. We're not right for each other. We never have been. Nothing has changed, Xanthos. *Nothing has changed.*'

And although the temptation to slam the door was powerful, she maintained her dignity by walking from that luxury suite with her head held high.

CHAPTER TEN

BIANCA SAT STRAIGHT-BACKED in the hard chair and faced the man on the other side of the desk who had caused something of a stir among the staff when he had arrived at her workplace a few minutes ago. Her heart gave another heavy beat of dread and there was nothing she could do about it. She thought about the last time she'd seen him, when she'd walked out of his suite at the Granchester, thinking they would never have to lay eyes on each other again. If only. She cleared her throat but didn't smile, because that would send out conflicting messages. Instead, her body grew tense as she picked her words with care.

'It was good of you to come and see me, Xanthos.'

'I was intrigued.' His black eyes were narrowed in question, his New York drawl a tantalising mixture of silk and gravel. 'How could I resist such a summons? I don't think an ex-lover has ever asked to see me in her *office* before. You aren't about to sue me, are you, Bianca?'

Bianca didn't react to the taunt, or the undeniable flirtation which flickered beneath it like a candle flame. Because she hadn't invited him here to flirt with him.

She had asked him to come to her office because she wanted to be in total control of her benvironment—and herself—in light of what she was about to tell him.

She didn't know what his reaction was going to be, but at least she had her assistant sitting next door in case all hell broke loose. She didn't want the neutral space of a restaurant or a park, where their interaction could be observed by strangers. She wanted to be here in *her* space, surrounded by some of the things she'd worked so hard for, as if they would remind her of who she really was. Not the casual sexual partner of a deceitful billionaire, but an independent woman in her own right. Her legal qualification was hanging on the wall, alongside the wall calendar featuring the pinky-mauve sweet-peas which always bloomed in July. On the desk was a paperweight of a rare Monterossian shell, which her father had given her such a long time ago.

And in front of her sat Xanthos, hard and cool and utterly delicious. It was over three months since she'd seen him but not a day had passed when she hadn't thought about him—usually with a mixture of longing and regret. His black hair was shorter than she remembered but the virile shadowing of his jaw was the same. He wore an immaculate dark suit because he'd been in London on business, which was fortunate—if any aspect of this whole business could be described as *fortunate*. But she was grateful he hadn't been forced to travel thousands of miles just to hear what she was about to tell him.

The situation was bad enough—made worse by the fact that she had lost none of her susceptibility to him. The hot summer day meant she was wearing a new cotton shirt, which was already a little tight across her breasts. But now her nipples had started stinging uncomfortably, as if the only thing which could bring them relief would be to feel his tongue or his fingers working their way over them. And she didn't want to feel that way. She didn't want to be vulnerable to him in any way emotionally *or* physically.

She could see curiosity glinting from his black eyes as if this scenario was something he had expected all along—a change of heart from her bperhaps, with the possibility of sex at the end of it. But there was wariness in his gaze, too—as if something was warning him not to take anything for granted. For one brief moment her heart went out to him, knowing that in a few seconds' time, his worst nightmare was going to come true.

'No, Xanthos,' she said. 'I'm not about to sue you.'

'Okay.' He leaned back in the chair, hands clasped together, two forefingers resting against the point of his chin as he looked at her. 'So why am I here, Bianca? Shoot.'

And because there was no way to soften the blow, the words came out more baldly than she'd intended. 'I'm pregnant.'

She watched as he grew still. There wasn't a flicker of reaction on his stony features and in a way that was worse than anger, or disbelief. As if his impassiveness drove home just how little he cared.

'I'm very sorry,' she continued, the dread inside her growing by the second as she recalled his determination never to have a family of his own. 'I know it's the last thing you wanted. It wasn't what I wanted either, but it's happened and I... I thought you had a right to know.'

He rose from the chair and for a moment Bianca wondered if he was just going to leave her office without another word. He was perfectly within his rights to do that, wasn't he? But he walked over to the window, startling the sparrow which had hopped onto the ledge for its daily donation from her lunchtime sandwich, the crumbs now dried out by the hot summer sun. The bird flew away and for a moment he watched its flapping progress as if he wanted to be gone as well. When he turned back the light was behind him, throwing his face into shadow and making his face impossible to read.

'You must be pleased,' he said. 'As I recall, you expressed a very real desire to have children.'

His words were as emotionless as his expression and Bianca couldn't deny a twist of pain as their coldness washed over her. But what else had she expected? Joy? Excitement? Surely she hadn't anticipated he would behave in the way would-be fathers were supposed to behave.

Get real, Bianca.

'You're not suggesting I *planned* this?'

'I have no idea,' he drawled, dark eyebrows shooting upwards. 'Did you?'

'Please don't insult me!'

He nodded, as if her anger and indignation were in some way reassuring. His gaze rested upon her face. 'What do you intend to do?'

She supposed she should be glad he hadn't asked who the father was, or demanded she take some humiliating DNA test, but his question still hurt. Suddenly her carefully rehearsed speech was forgotten as she failed to keep her voice calm, all the pent-up strain of the past few weeks spilling out and making her voice crack.

'I'm k-keeping my baby, of course!'

'Good.'

The word took the wind right out of her sails and she blinked at him in confusion, before reminding herself that she didn't need his approval. But that didn't prevent the sliver of hope which shot through her, like sunlight breaking through a dark cloud. 'I know you never intended to be a father—'

'No, you're right, I didn't.' His words effectively killed off that brief flash of optimism. 'So what do you want from me, Bianca? Is it a wedding you're after?' He shrugged. 'As you know, I have never wanted to marry but if you're determined to legitimise the birth, I could probably be persuaded to put my signature on a certificate.'

She shook her head, hating the way he made her sound like some kind of amateur trophy hunter. 'I would never marry a man who didn't love me,' she said, in a low voice.

'Then that makes the decision very simple for both of us. Because I don't.'

Did she flinch? Was that why he continued with his discourse, still delivered in that strangely detached way?

'I admire you, Bianca. I like your intelligence and your humour.' He paused, his voice dipping by a fraction. 'And the chemistry between us is off the scale.'

'I certainly don't need any compensatory compliments from you!'

'Our relationship would probably have continued if I wasn't Corso's half-brother,' he continued thoughtfully. 'But it was never going to be for ever, was it? We both know that. Even so, I will support you financially.'

'I earn my own money,' she gritted out. 'I don't need yours.'

'But this isn't just about you and your independence, is it, Bianca?' he challenged softly. 'Not any more. I have no intention of stepping away from my responsibilities. I'm a wealthy man and now it seems I have something into which I can channel that wealth, other than my chosen charities. You can't prevent me from putting aside a sum which will one day benefit this child we have created.'

Bianca flinched. If only his last words hadn't fanned the flames of the longing which still flickered in her traitorous heart, a fact made worse by him choosing that precise moment to step forward, so that he was standing uncomfortably close to her chair. A shaft of sunlight had gilded his face, bleaching out the hard lines and inscrutable set of his lips, and as she thought of the little boy or girl who would one day inherit some of those features, a wave of sadness washed over her. She was filled with a sense of opportunities lost. Of something which might have been but now never would. Even so, she had to make certain. She needed to have exhausted all the avenues before she caved in to the inevitable. Prepared to put aside her own fierce desire for independence, she wanted to know that she had done all the right things by their baby. 'But you don't want to be a part of the child's life?'

'I think not. What child would ever want me as a parent?' he demanded bitterly. 'When I don't know how fatherhood works.'

'You could always learn,' she said hesitantly. 'People do.'

'But in order to do that, I would need to want to. And I don't. I'm sorry, Bianca. You know my story—surely you can understand my aversion to families?' His gaze bored into her—hard and cold as jet. 'I'm just trying to be honest with you. I won't make promises I can't keep because that wouldn't be fair to you, or the baby. You both deserve better than that.'

'But what if…?' Bianca clenched her hands, telling herself she was fighting for her baby but afterwards she wondered if she had been fighting for herself. For the tiny fragment of the dream which still remained. 'What if one day your child tries to seek you out and demands that you acknowledge your paternity? What then?'

Xanthos's eyes narrowed as her words took him to a future he had never intended. He pictured a scenario maybe eighteen years hence, when some unfamiliar and possibly resentful teenager might show up on his doorstep. Where would he be living then, in his chosen unmarried and childless state? Would he be an aging billionaire, still in his luxury penthouse in New York with a series of younger and younger girlfriends—a pattern he'd observed many times in his social circles? He felt a pulse flicker at his temple, for the image held no allure.

But neither did dealing with a newborn—taking ban unknown leap into fatherhood and failing his child.

And he didn't do failure.

And what of his child's mother? Was he planning on failing her, as well? With Bianca it had always gone deeper than with anyone else. Somehow she had the ability to tap into a part of him which he'd always kept hidden from other women. But fundamentally, he remained the same damaged man he'd always been—and who would want someone like that in their life? Better she found happiness with the *nice, safe man* she'd told him she envisaged spending her life with, who could give her the deep and inclusive relationship she craved. Wouldn't the best thing he could do for Bianca Forrester be to walk away from her *and* their baby?

'Then I shall have to deal with whatever comes my way,' he said, feeling the vibration of his phone in the inside pocket of his jacket but for once choosing to ignore it. But his heart was pounding and his throat felt as dry as if he'd been running in a marathon, his unperturbed exterior belying the sudden unfamiliar emotions he could feel surging within him. He felt pain. Regret. And something else…something which remained indefinable.

Walking over to a side console, he poured himself a glass of water, raising his eyebrows at her in query, but she shook her head. He drank thirstily before putting his glass down, staring into a pair of wide green eyes which were filled with wariness.

From the moment he'd walked in here today, he had known there was something different about her. Something which hadn't been there before, which transcended the physical. A mixture of fragility and strength. Something soft and nurturing which lay beneath her cool and professional exterior. Xanthos had thought he'd known exactly what lay behind her unexpected request that he visit her office. He'd imagined that now she'd had time to reconsider her decision to end their affair, she would be regretting it—for whenever had a woman been willing to let him go? He had thought she might lock the door and seduce him. Her lying on the desk, perhaps—her crumpled panties on the floor—with him kissing quiet her shuddered little gasps. And yes, he couldn't deny that he would have been up for some of that because she had proved infuriatingly difficult to shift from his thoughts.

Yet the reality could not be more different, and neither could she. She wasn't dressed for seduction, in her crisp pink shirt and plain skirt, with her black hair piled on top of her head. It was difficult to believe she was carrying his child. He felt a twist of something unknown and intensely uncomfortable. Because children were the glue which bound families together and as far as he was concerned, families were toxic. His father's resentment had threatened to whittle away his self-worth, and his mother had chosen financial security over her only child.

Xanthos had buried the rejection as deeply as he could but now he started remembering how it had felt when his mother had cast him out. That out-of-body sensation of feeling completely alone in the world. Of realising he didn't have anyone to rely on. It had taken him quite a while to realise he could manage on his own—that he didn't actually *need* anyone else. And now, for the first time, he wondered how it had been for his mother. He had been so quick to condemn her. He'd never stopped to think that maybe she'd been hurting, too. And when Corso had burst into his life so suddenly, telling him about his real father—that had brought no relief either. How could it? His real father hadn't wanted him either, had he?

He forced his mind back to the present, seeing the way she was biting her lip. 'So what happens next?' he questioned slowly. 'Are you planning to tell Corso and your sister that I am the father of your child?'

'Why?' She jerked her head back, her brief show of anger unwittingly reminding him of her passion. 'Are you worried Corso's going to come after you with a shotgun, demanding you marry me?'

And despite the undoubted gravity of the situation, Xanthos felt the ghost of a smile haunting the edges of his lips. 'I don't think it works like that any more, Bianca,' he said gravely. 'And if it does, you can tell him quite honestly that an offer of marriage was made, and refused.'

'I would hardly call your disparaging question an "offer of marriage",' she snapped. 'You sounded like a condemned man being asked what he wanted for his last meal. And only someone who'd undergone a total brain bypass would elect to marry a man as cold-hearted as you, Xanthos Antoniou!'

She made him want to laugh. She made him want to kiss her. To unclip her glossy hair and feel those ebony waves trickle through his fingers. Even now he wanted her more than he had ever wanted any woman. But he mustn't allow himself to be distracted by the significance of her pregnancy. Nor her wit, or her beauty, or the pressing need of his own desire. And so he shrugged, as if her words had simply bounced off him like drops of rain, for many such accusations had been made against him in the past. Even if, for once, he suspected they had left their mark.

'Now we deal with practicalities,' he stated flatly. 'I suggest you send me your bank details so we can get those payments progressing.'

'And that's *it*?' she questioned, her voice shaking with disbelief as he headed for the door. 'I send you my bank details?'

He reminded himself that he was doing this for her sake and their child's sake and that one day she would be grateful to him. But even so, it hurt to see the pain and reproach which were written in her eyes. 'What else is there to say? I am all the things you accuse me of and more. So go and find yourself a good man to marry to spend the rest of your life with, Bianca.' He gave a bitter smile. 'Because it will be a better life without me in it.'

CHAPTER ELEVEN

IT HAD BEEN trying to snow. The heavy clouds had been getting greyer and thicker all morning. Bianca stared out of the window to the street below as the first few flakes began to flutter down—fat and white and feathery. But the impending snow brought her no joy, no matter how perfectly timed it was to coincide with the festive period. In her current state, it represented nothing more than a health hazard.

Down there the world was super-charged with the anticipation of Christmas Eve, but up here it was strangely silent. She could see people scurrying towards their homes, laden with bags of gifts and shopping as they walked past shops which glittered with sparkly trees and bright lights. The air was buzzing with annual holiday cheer, but she wasn't really feeling it. How could she, when she was so heavy with child that she could barely waddle from room to room, let alone contemplate dragging decorations up the stairs to decorate her second-floor apartment? It had taken her the best part of ten minutes to put on a pair of boots, prior to braving the wintry elements to buy fresh fruit before everything shut down for the holiday.

She stared down at a woman pushing a buggy and found herself thinking, *In two weeks' time, that will be me.* It was hard to imagine herself with a baby. Hard to think that the precious life she had been nurturing would soon burst into the world. But she was trying to be positive and to count her blessings. She had done all the things pregnant women were supposed to do, while winding her caseload down as she prepared to take maternity leave. She had attended antenatal classes and taken gentle exercise. She had eaten all the best food, read all the recommended books, and her doctor had pronounced himself pleased with her progress.

Her mother and sister she had seen on only a handful of occasions and that had been deliberate. At least being thirty-eight weeks pregnant meant she'd had the perfect excuse to refuse an invitation to spend the holidays at the palace, accepting instead an invite to Christmas lunch tomorrow at the home of a very sweet couple she'd met at her antenatal class. She had wanted to distance herself from any well-meant family interference, determined to forge her own path going forward—as a single mother. It wasn't the life she had imagined, but who could honestly put their hands on their hearts and say that things had turned out exactly as they'd thought they would?

Despite the tentative queries which had come floating her way from Rosie and her mother, she hadn't revealed the identity of her baby's father. Not to anyone. And despite the obvious frustration of her family, that situation wasn't about to change—at least, not any time soon. Being pregnant had extracted a large enough toll on her already volatile emotions, without throwing the weight of other people's opinions into the mix. For years *she* had been the sensible one everyone had relied on and this was the first time she had ever stepped out of line. If people had chosen to benefit from her independent attitude in the past, surely she couldn't be criticised for it now.

She just couldn't face the fallout which would inevitably follow any disclosure about her baby's paternity, or get into some kind of blame game. Xanthos hadn't done something so very dreadful, had he? He had unintentionally made her pregnant—bthe type of 'accident' which had been happening to men and women since the beginning of time. He had grudgingly offered to marry her and, when she had turned him down, had set up a standing order, so that a generous wodge of money now came flooding into her bank account every month. At first Bianca had considered refusing it—sending it back maybe, or donating the money to charity. But second thoughts had made her decide against such a prideful action because what if she couldn't carry on working, for whatever reason? What if—and this was the most worrying question of all—what if she didn't actually *want* to go back to work after her maternity leave?

She heard the sound of the doorbell and inwardly cursed, because she wasn't expecting anyone. Living over a shop in the middle of Wimbledon village meant it was unlikely to be carol singers and her busy working life meant she'd never befriended enough people locally who might just 'call in'—especially on the busiest day of the year. Perhaps if she ignored the summons, they would go away. But then the doorbell rang again—more authoritatively this time, as if someone had just jammed their thumb on the buzzer and left it there.

A click of annoyance left her lips as she peered into the door camera, her knees sagging with shock when she saw who was ringing the bell. A man. A very tall and very recognisable man with the broadest shoulders she'd ever seen.

Xanthos.

Her heart was pounding so hard it hurt. She didn't have to let him in. She could pretend to be out. She didn't trust herself around him, not when she was feeling so strange and disorientated this close to the birth. But something told her he wouldn't give up that easily—and surely she wasn't nervous about seeing him, just because she looked the size of a small whale? She would hear what he had to say then send him on his way, wishing him a happy Christmas, even if the greeting got stuck in her throat along the way.

Laboriously, she made her way down two flights of stairs, leaning heavily on the rail, and was a little out of breath when she reached the ground floor and opened the door. But it wasn't the icy temperature which made her breath freeze and her skin start to prickle with goosebumps, because even though she had known it was him—nothing could have prepared her for the impact of seeing him again in the flesh, standing on her doorstep and looking as if he owned it. She saw a couple of female shoppers turn to look at him, their eyes widening with automatic pleasure, and for some reason this riled her.

Grateful for the support of the doorjamb, she stared

into his face, but his carved features were stern and set—as if anticipating the flurry of objections she might be about to fling at him. But her throat was still dry and suddenly she was finding it very difficult to speak.

'What are you doing here?' she said at last.

'Hello, Bianca. It's good to see you too,' he replied steadily.

'I wasn't expecting you.' She studied him suspiciously. 'I would have preferred some sort of warning you were coming.'

'But wouldn't you have found some excuse to refuse if I had suggested it?'

'Who knows,' she said airily, 'what might have happened?'

His gaze flickered over her, those ebony eyes seeming to burn right into her flesh. 'I've tried ringing you. Several times, in fact, but you never pick up.'

'Usually, I'm busy,' she lied. 'But I always email you back, don't I?'

'Not always, no,' he growled. 'And even when you do, I find it a very unsatisfactory form of communication.'

It was also a very dangerous form of communication, Bianca had decided. It had an immediacy which created a false intimacy, which in turn had the power to fuel her foolish dreams. Once, she had been working at midnight when Xanthos's name had unexpectedly pinged into her email account. Infuriatingly, her heart had started racing but she had replied to his query about her general health with a few polite words.

I'm fine, thanks.

A reply had come winging straight back.

Why are you up so late?

I'm working. What's your excuse?

I'm about to go out to dinner. It's only eight p.m. in Barbados.

A red mist had entered her head and she'd been unable to stop herself from wondering why he was in Barbados and who he was having dinner with, all the while recognising that she had absolutely no right to indulge in something which felt uncomfortably like jealousy. That had been the moment when she'd accepted that casual emailing was not an option for two people with their history and she had been determined not to repeat it.

Was he recalling that conversation, as well? Was that the reason for the sudden frustration which had clouded his eyes, as if he wasn't used to having his overtures ignored, and which for some reason pleased her? It was certainly preferable to focussing on the flush of her cheeks as she remembered the way he could make her feel…as if her heart had grown wings and given her licence to fly.

And hadn't she been trying to forget all that soppy and meaningless stuff? Trying to get back to the person

she'd been before she met him, by not thinking about
Xanthos Antoniou at all.

But it was hard to forget that today was an anniversary, of sorts.

'So what *are* you doing here?' she questioned crisply. 'Doing a bit of last-minute Christmas shopping in southwest London?'

'Not a conversation for the doorstep, I think.' He lifted his dark eyebrows. 'So why don't you invite me inside, so that I can talk to you?'

It was a perfectly reasonable thing to say but Bianca recognised the danger of being swept along with his wishes by the sheer force of his personality. She told herself that allowing him to waltz back into her life—without any kind of warning—would be a dumb thing to do, just because she was feeling lonely and vulnerable. She forced herself to bremember some of the things he'd said during their last awkward meeting. His heartless suggestion that she find herself another husband.

Remember how much that hurt, despite the bravado
you displayed at the time.

Yet he was still the father of her child. She had agreed to allow him to provide for the baby whose life he didn't want to be part of, and wasn't an binevitable part of that equation that it gave him certain rights? Could she really turn him away, even though it was painful to acknowledge that it was exactly a year since she gave her virginity to him?

'Haven't we said everything which needs saying?' she said, feeling some of her resolve slipping away.

We haven't even started, thought Xanthos grimly,

but for once tempered his resolve, because deep down he knew he needed to take this at her speed, not his. Accommodating a woman's wishes ahead of his own was something novel to him and, although it cost him a considerable effort, he forced himself to slow down. 'All I want is a few minutes of your time.'

Their eyes met and he saw curiosity replace caution in her wide green gaze.

'I suppose you'd better come in,' she said grudgingly as she turned her back on him. 'Shut the door behind you.'

He followed her upstairs, noting that she was still as graceful as ever, despite being so much more cumbersome than usual. Once they reached her tiny sitting room he was able to look at her more closely and to drink in her sheer *magnificence* as she regarded him expectantly. Last time he'd seen her she had been dressed smartly for work—and back then the tug of cotton across her breasts had been the only sign she was carrying a little extra pregnancy weight.

But now...

Xanthos felt his gaze drawn irrevocably to her swollen belly.

Now she exemplified everything which was soft and warm and feminine.

The change in her was extraordinary. Like a ship in full sail, her huge bump was emphasised by a dress of pale green wool which fell to her knees, below which she was wearing a pair of black boots. Her hair was loose and even shinier than before, tumbling in dark waves over her slender shoulders.

He had known that this close to giving birth she

would be large, but intellectual acknowledgement of a fact was very different from an emotional one, as he was fast discovering. Random thoughts began to pile into his mind and somehow he wasn't able to control them. He imagined his child's heart beating inside her and he felt…disorientated. And something else, too. Something which was gnawing away at his sophisticated veneer and leaving him raw and aching.

He shook his head. He had grown up surrounded by immense wealth, absorbing the often uptight bbehaviour of the class into which he had been born and recognising that emotional distance was preferable to the messy feelings he had observed in others. But all that composure seemed to have deserted him and as his gaze roved over Bianca's bfecund shape he felt positively *primitive*. As if he would like nothing better than to throw his head back and roar like a lion, before picking her up and carrying her upstairs.

He took a moment to look around, his gaze taking in his surroundings with some bemusement. He didn't know what he had expected, but it hadn't been this. He was sending her a generous allowance. And her sister lived in a palace, didn't she? Had he thought there might be some trickle-down effect and his half-brother might have gifted his sister-in-law an enormous apartment? His mouth hardened. Maybe the offer had been made and that damned independent spirit of hers had made her refuse, just as she'd turned down his offer of marriage.

The room was compact, the furniture unremarkable and, unlike just about everywhere else, there was no sign of any festive decoration. No tree. No holly. No baubles. Nothing. He walked over to the window and looked outside. No garden either, just a street. He tried to imagine her here, with her baby.

His baby.

'Where is the…baby going to sleep?' he questioned huskily, because it was the first time he had referred to his child out loud.

At these words her face softened and it was like the sun coming out—and never had Xanthos experienced such a powerful moment of bitter regret.

'Come and see for yourself.'

She led him into the smaller of two bedrooms and for a moment the breath left his lungs in a painful shudder because he was unprepared for the sight which greeted him, and the sudden answering thunder of his heart. A simple crib, above which hung a mobile of animals. The walls were washed a pale lemon, with a large and vibrant picture of a jungle dominating an entire wall. A room put together with love, not money. It made him think of all the things he'd never had. It made him think of Vargmali. A chair sat in one corner, with a small footstool beside it and even Xanthos, with his complete ignorance of small babies, recognised that this was where she might nurse their child. He swallowed.

'Who decorated this room?' he questioned thickly.

She looked taken aback. 'I did, of course.'

'You didn't think to get someone else to do it?'

'You don't think I'm capable of slapping on a few coats of paint, Xanthos?'

He thought of her halfway up a ladder, swaying precariously, and felt his body tighten. 'But you're pregnant.' And although he knew he shouldn't say it, he couldn't keep the words back. 'Why do you have to always be so stubbornly independent?'

'Because that's how I've always lived my life,' she answered.

She turned away and he followed her back into the sitting room, to stand by the fireplace. 'An empty grate,' he stated reflectively. 'What does that remind you of?'

Mostly to prevent tears from pricking at her eyes, Bianca glared at him. Either he was implying that her little apartment was reminiscent of a derelict mountain hut, or that he was feeling nostalgic—and both these options were as bad as each other. Didn't he realise that in her current volatile hormonal state she could be completely undone by a sentiment like that, even if it was patently fake? How *dared* he make it sound as if their snowy incarceration had been anything other than expedient? Was he playing with her see-sawing emotions in order to get what he wanted?

Which brought her back to her original question. What *did* he want?

A flood of dark possibilities rushed into her mind but one was uppermost. What if, during the months since she'd last seen him, he had met another woman and fallen in love with her, despite all his protestations that love was not for him? He might have changed. People did. And, unlike her, another woman might have softened him. Influenced him. Made him re-examine his beliefs. He and his new partner... She shuddered. His prospective *wife*, perhaps... What if they'd decided they wanted shared custody of his child and she would have no grounds to refuse, because what could she say?

I'm jealous. I don't want any other woman to have you or our baby.

But she couldn't do that. Not to him, who had already experienced so much hurt and rejection. And not to their baby either, who had a right to a relationship with their father. She could not and would not stand in his way, if that was what he wanted. She would do the right thing by their child—or else how could she possibly be a good mother?

Maybe she should have offered him tea, or coffee. If he'd called in anywhere else at this time of year he would probably have received a mince pie, but she didn't have any. In fact, she hadn't bought a single seasonal treat because Christmas had been the last thing on her mind. There had been too many other things to think of. Clothes and creams and unscented bubbles to put in the little baby bath which was wedged up against one of the walls in the bathroom.

She shifted from one foot to the other because her feet were starting to hurt, the boots digging into her swollen ankles. 'So go on, then,' she said encouragingly. 'Tell me what it is you came to tell me. I'm all ears.'

He didn't answer straight away and she wondered why. She had seen him looking all kinds of tense before. She'd witnessed the rush of adrenaline just before he'd made that emergency landing in the snow. She had seen delicious anticipation tightening his body just before a powerful orgasm shuddered through it, and she had seen the way he had grown so still when she'd announced he was going to be a father. But this was different.

'I've been thinking about our situation a lot, and I admit that in the past I may have made some poor decisions,' he said slowly. 'But there is still time to put it right.' His dark gaze grew shuttered. 'I want to marry you, Bianca.'

CHAPTER TWELVE

SHE WASN'T GOING to lie. There had been moments during the last year when Bianca had wondered what it would be like if Xanthos had actually *asked* her to marry him—rather than making it sound like something unsavoury which had been on *her* ambitious agenda. Those had been heady moments. Weak moments. Times of physical exhaustion and emotional stress brought about by a combination of long hours at the office, combined with her pregnancy, when she'd wondered what it might be like to have a big strong man to lean on, instead of having to do it all herself. But it hadn't taken long for common sense and her habitual independence to assert itself and remind her that she was fine on her own, just as she always had been. And right now she needed that common sense like never before.

'Gosh. This *is* unexpected,' she answered, with considerable understatement. 'A proposal of marriage, no less. What's brought about this sudden change of heart?'

'You're pregnant.'

'You don't say!' But as she waved a sardonic hand in front of her bump, a tiny heel suddenly scooted across the drum-tight surface of her belly.

Did he notice the fear and joy and vague discomfort which must have shown on her face as she felt the movement of their child? Was that why he suddenly moved forward to place his hand in the small of her back, gently propelling her into one of the chairs by the side of the fire which she never bothered to light because it seemed too much like hard work? She told herself that if she hadn't been so overwhelmed by everything that was happening, she might have stopped him. But then again, she might not. Because didn't it feel delicious to have Xanthos's fingers touching her like this—the sizzle of physical contact undeniably thrilling after so long apart?

And wasn't it wonderful to have somebody to lean on?

And then, even more disconcertingly, he dropped to his knees and began unzipping her leather boots.

'What are you doing?' Bianca demanded hoarsely.

'I'm making you more comfortable.'

He must have noticed her shifting restlessly and correctly concluded that her boots were hurting. And her stupid pang of disappointment that he hadn't been bending down to produce a diamond ring was quickly superseded by the realisation that having someone remove her footwear in her current inhibited state, felt like the most caring thing which had ever happened to her. As well as spookily erotic. His thumb glided over her insole as he took off the second boot and the temptation to leave her foot resting in his palm and ask him to massage her toes was overwhelming, but somehow she resisted it and wriggled away from him.

'We've already had the marriage conversation,' she

said, forcing herself to face facts instead of indulging in a fantasy which seemed to be getting more real by the second. 'You weren't a big fan of the institution, as I recall. In fact, you suggested I hunt around for someone else to be my husband. And nothing is any different since we had that rather difficult conversation—other than the shape of my body, of course.'

He went to stand by the mantelpiece, a study of power and poise, and although this meant Bianca was able to study him properly, it might have been better if she could have been spared that slow scrutiny. He had removed his snow-flecked overcoat to reveal a cashmere sweater in a cloud-coloured shade of pewter, which complemented his black hair and the olive-dark glow of his skin. His jeans were faded and moulded to his legs—as if they had been specially designed to emphasise his muscular thighs and the narrow jut of his hips.

He looked sexy.

He looked dangerous.

And, oh, how she wanted him. She hadn't thought it would be possible for such a heavily pregnant woman to feel sexual desire, but it seemed that was patently untrue. She thought about the way he'd removed her boots and how indecently good it had felt. About the nights when she lay awake, alone and scared and longing for someone to hold. No, not just *someone*. Him, and only him. Sometimes she dreamt of him kissing her. Touching her. Being deep inside her. And then she would wake up and realise it had all been a dream and a terrible sense of despair would run through her blood, no matter how many times she told herself that such a reaction was ridiculous.

She ran her tongue over the parched surface of her bottom lip, but her thoughts just wouldn't stop racing. Would it be so terrible to allow herself to wonder if a marriage between them could work?

'I think a lot is different,' he said quietly. 'But then, I've had a lot of time to think about it lately. I've spent the last couple of weeks in Monterosso, with Corso.'

She stared at him suspiciously. 'I thought you wanted nothing more to do with Monterosso, *or* your brother.'

'I thought so, too, but I was mistaken.'

'Gosh.' She couldn't resist the tart observation. 'You don't strike me as a man who would admit to that very often.'

He nodded his head in brief acknowledgement. 'You're absolutely right. I don't.'

'So what happened to change your mind?'

Xanthos stared at a photo of her on her sister's wedding day, enclosed in a golden frame, studded with emeralds. He thought how happy and smiling she looked—in contrast to the suspicious mask which Bianca wore today. Had he thought time and distance would have made her more amenable and she would instantly agree to his demands? Of course he had. But he had imagined that his own feelings on the subject would be as rational as they always were and he had been mistaken about that, too. The jolt of possession when he had first laid eyes on her today had been like a violent ambush on his senses and he had been unprepared for his reaction. The emotional fire which had raged through him when she'd opened the door to him was still burning, and he was uncertain how best to douse the flames.

She was looking at him expectantly and he realised that he would get nowhere unless he was honest with her. 'Suddenly, I wanted to know more about my half-brother. The only person in the world who shares my blood.' His gaze became hooded as he gazed at her. 'Apart from the child you carry in your belly.'

He saw the colour leach from her cheeks, as if she was unprepared for the emotional quality of his words.

'And my mother, of course,' he added suddenly.

She blinked. 'You've found your mother?'

'No, but I have someone looking for her. That relationship seemed to be something else in my life which needed to be untangled. To try to understand why she did what she did. And maybe to know how it affected her.' There was a pause. 'You suggested a while back it might be a good idea.'

She absorbed this piece of news in silence before responding. 'And did you tell Corso...did you tell him you're the father of my baby?'

'No, since it was obvious you didn't want them to know, and I respect your wishes. I suspect they've worked it out for themselves, Bianca,' he added wryly. 'But I neither confirmed nor denied the fact.'

'Go on,' she said, a little uncertainly. 'With your story.'

He stared down at the empty grate of the fire, before lifting his gaze once more. 'Spending time in Monterosso gave me a chance to evaluate my life. To examine things I don't usually care to look at. I told you early on that the man I believed to be my father had never liked me. It didn't occur to me at the time why his resentment should grow with every year that passed and why it should eventually turn into the kind of hatred which was hard to live with.' A bitter laugh resonated through him. 'It wasn't until many years later that I realised the physical differences between us must have been remarkable.' He shrugged. 'As a child you never really think about that kind of thing, but hindsight gives you remarkable clarity. He was short and portly and I was not. By the age of twelve I was taller than him. And I was strong.'

'And insanely good-looking, I suppose,' she interjected, almost absently.

He raised his eyebrows but didn't comment, even though it warmed his blood to hear her praise. But his looks had never been in question, had they? She was simply stating a fact. 'I can see now it must have been difficult for him,' he continued. 'People were always pointing out how little we resembled each other. I'm guessing that as his misgivings grew, my mother's paranoia about being found out only increased. Long before he finally demanded a DNA test, he began to take out his suspicions on me, in subtle yet cruel ways.'

'Did he…?' Her lovely green eyes darkened with distress. 'Did he hit you?'

He shook his head, for nobody had ever dared hit him. 'No, but there are many other ways to wound a child. Words are particularly effective. Tell a child often enough he is nothing and will amount to nothing and, sooner or later, he'll start to believe you. It was death by a thousand cuts,' he finished bleakly.

'Oh, Xanthos,' she said and the tenderness in her voice made his heart punch with something he didn't recognise.

'I didn't tell you this because I wanted your sympathy,' he ground out.

'Then *why* are you telling me?'

Unwilling to make any more pronouncements from the opposite side of the room, where he felt curiously exposed beneath that green shining gaze, he pulled over the vacant armchair and sat down so that he was facing her—so close that he could have reached out and touched her. And he badly wanted to touch her, for he had missed the warmth of her body against his. But not yet. Not until they had resolved this. *If* they could resolve this. 'At first I thought that giving you your freedom was the best thing for everyone,' he reflected sombrely. 'You had made no secret about wanting a family of your own. A proper family, in which you could be happy—the kind you'd known yourself, until your father had his accident.'

'But you didn't want that,' she reminded him slowly.

'No, I didn't. Which is why I gave you permission to marry someone else.'

Her short laugh was devoid of humour. 'Believe it or not, I don't actually need your permission to marry, Xanthos.'

'No, of course not.' He winced. 'Put it this way, then. I selflessly believed you might be able to find such happiness with another man.'

'Selflessly?' she prompted. 'Or selfishly?'

He ignored her challenge, just as he attempted to ignore the cushioned pinkness of her lips, as if that would prevent him from thinking about how much he wanted to kiss them. 'But that was before I realised the potential consequences of such an act.'

'You're not making any sense.'

'Hear me out,' he commanded softly, clasping his fingers together, as he sometimes did in the boardroom, when people were hanging on his every word. 'At the time of making that offer I was still reeling with the impact of discovering you were pregnant and I wasn't thinking straight.' He paused. 'But I am now.'

She stiffened—straightening her spine as if unconsciously realising that she needed to pay extra attention to his next words. 'And?'

'And I got to thinking about the man you might one day marry.'

'Let me reassure you that there are no contenders in the offing,' she said, directing a flippant gesture towards her swollen belly. 'Looking like this doesn't exactly elevate me to the status of man magnet!'

'I thought about this unknown man bringing up my child as his own,' he reflected. 'Who might one day look at the strange cuckoo in his nest and start to resent him, just as happened to me.'

'But it's a completely different set of circumstances! My baby isn't going to be a secret to the man I marry!' she protested. 'He'll be going into it with his eyes open.'

'You don't think that biology—and nature—won't make a man naturally wary of a child which isn't his?' he demanded roughly. 'I'm sorry, Bianca—but I can't risk that happening. Once I suggested you might wish to marry me and you refused. But now I really must insist on it.' That hadn't come out exactly as he had intended it to and so he smiled, as if his smile would clinch the deal he was longing to make. 'Think about it and realise how heavily the pros outweigh the cons.'

She was staring at him as if waiting for him to deliver a punchline, but when one failed to arrive, she narrowed her eyes.

'The only thing I need to think about are the words you just used. You *insist* on it?' she verified.

'Perhaps I have expressed myself clumsily—'

'Another classic Antoniou understatement.'

'There are many reasons why a marriage between us would work, for we are compatible in many areas. You know we are. You have never bored me, not once—and that is unheard of. And then there is the insane physicality which exists between us.' His voice dipped. 'Believe me when I tell you that sex with you is the best I've ever had, Bianca.'

'And I imagine you've done some pretty extensive research in the field, so to speak?'

Hearing the bite of sarcasm, he held up his palms in silent supplication. 'I am trying to be honest with you, Bianca. I can be a father to our baby and a husband to you. We can create a family of our own and make it work. You know we can.'

She shook her head with what looked like frustration. 'You just don't get it, do you?' she challenged. 'This has nothing to do with laying down the foundations for a good marriage and family life. That's not what's driving you at all, is it, Xanthos? Examine your motives carefully and you'll discover that your proposal is all about power, and possession. You're a highly successful man who's used to getting his own way and I've done the unthinkable and turned you down. Not only that, but you've suddenly woken up to the fact that I've got something of yours which is pretty rare. *Your child.* And

while your response is predictable, it is also human nature.' She stared at him. 'You only want me and the baby
because you can't have us. And it's a useless yearning—
because the moment you get what you think you can't
have, you won't want it any more.'

Her logic and her intellect drew from him a powerful sense of appreciation, even though Xanthos could
see that both were working against him. Had he thought
this would be a walkover? Yes, and three times yes. His
life might not always have been easy but women had
been, falling into his arms with an eagerness which had
sometimes felt predatory. But not Bianca Forrester. Despite their earlier passion and the very pregnant state
which was a result of that passion, she was behaving
with a maidenly primness which was only adding to
her considerable allure.

'And that's it?'

'That's it,' she agreed firmly. 'And since there is
nothing more to be said and this isn't how I envisaged
spending the night before Christmas, I really would
like you to go.'

CHAPTER THIRTEEN

THE SNOW WAS coming down thick and fast as Xanthos stepped out onto the pavement. Icy flakes flew into his mouth and coated his lashes and cheeks with a thin white mantle. He stared up at Bianca's window but there was no sign of her watching him, no wave of farewell, or even making sure he was safely off the premises and heading towards his car.

His car was parked on the edge of the common, but he turned in the opposite direction and began to walk past the windows of the trendy village shops, decorated for Christmas with their glitter and their lights, his thoughts whirling as fast as the falling snow which was making visibility so poor.

He couldn't believe what had just taken place in his ex-lover's apartment. She had rejected his proposal of marriage as if it meant nothing, her accusation ringing in his ears. That his words had been all about power and possession and nothing else.

What had she expected?

His mouth hardened.

He knew damn well what she had expected—more than he was capable of giving her. She wanted him to delve deep inside himself and to open up his heart completely. A heart he had carefully protected from pain since as long as he could remember. Couldn't she be satisfied with what he'd given her already? His lips tightened. Perhaps he'd had a lucky escape after all.

So why did his shoulders suddenly feel as if they were carrying the weight of the world upon them—as if he had lost something very precious?

He saw a shop door open and something drew his footsteps towards it. Was it the sound of taped carols coming from within, or just his need to shelter from the inclement weather? With snowflakes dissolving on his face, he stepped inside, realising too late that it was a children's clothing store.

Among all the miniature elf outfits and sparkly fairy frocks with wings, he could see tiny cardigans of pale wool and unfamiliar smocked garments, embroidered with carrot-wielding rabbits. Would his baby ever wear clothes as impossibly small as this, he wondered, and would he ever be there to witness it? Pain and regret rose in his throat as the sound of a particularly poignant carol split the air with its heartbreakingly sweet melody, and he was reminded of that night in Vargmali, exactly a year ago, when the children had sung their hearts out to the people of the village. He remembered the wonder and joy on Bianca's face as she had gazed at all the simple festive greenery, professing it more beautiful than all the splendour at her sister's palace. Her eyes had been half closed while those beautiful songs had been sung in a language she hadn't recognised, but which she had loved all the same.

And then they had gone upstairs to that high-ceilinged and chilly room and she had given him the greatest gift of all. He swallowed. Her innocence. She had done so without preface or condition, and back in London she had melted just as eagerly into his arms. He had just taken from her, he realised. He had given nothing back.

Even when she had told him she was pregnant, she had done the honourable thing. She hadn't grabbed at marriage to a wealthy man as many women would have done, but had told him with quiet dignity that he could be as hands-on as he wanted. And he had thrown it all back in her face. He had told her he didn't want to be a father. To go and find a different life and a different father for their baby.

Even now…even *now* he had turned up with a heartless offer of marriage. Perhaps she had been right. Perhaps it *had* all been about power and possession. There had certainly been no mention of love, had there?

'Can I help you, sir?'

He turned to see a young woman looking up at him. She was wearing a wreath of golden tinsel like a crown on top of her blonde hair and a pair of earrings shaped like wreaths, which were intermittently flashing red and green.

'I want something for a baby,' he said abruptly.

'Boy or girl?'

'I don't know. It hasn't been born yet,' he admitted, and he didn't know if it was the brusque quality of his words or the sudden brightness of his eyes which made her expression grow soft, so that suddenly she looked much older than her years.

'Let me help you,' she said gently, and Xanthos nodded.

Minutes later, armed with his carefully wrapped package, he stepped out onto a pavement now coated white, the thick snow still swirling down as he began walking up the street to the shop the young girl had recommended.

Because he wasn't done yet.

When the ring came on the doorbell, Bianca was half expecting it. She knew it was Xanthos. It had to be Xanthos, and deep down she was praying it was. She had told him to go away, yes, but deep down she had wanted him to stay, though she hadn't dared ask herself why. Did he realise that and was that why he'd come back? Had he observed the conflict of interests which was waging a war inside her? Had he noticed that too, along with her aching feet?

This time she buzzed him in, having no appetite for another journey down two flights of stairs—but more than that, she was reluctant to open the door to him, afraid that the bright snowy light would reveal emotions in her eyes which might be better kept hidden.

When he walked into the sitting room the snow was thick on his head—a bright contrast to the ebony of his black hair. But he seemed oblivious to it, or the fact that he was still wearing his overcoat as he walked towards her. Without thinking, she perched on the window seat, not trusting her legs to support her as she met the hard glitter of his gaze.

'I have been arrogant and foolish, Bianca,' he began, without preamble. 'A man unable to see what was right in front of him all along.'

She blinked up at him, not quite sure she'd heard

him properly but forcing herself to stay silent and not to prompt, afraid of influencing his words with her choice of question.

'I keep thinking about that time when we were alone together in the mountain hut,' he continued, his voice heavy and low. 'About the things I confided in you. Things about my past and my upbringing. Not everything, no. Not then. But believe me when I tell you that I have never spoken so frankly to anyone, nor felt so secure in the knowledge that you would never betray my trust. Yet afterwards I chose to push that knowledge aside, because it was easier not to think about the things I'd said, or the reason I might have said them.'

She wanted to tell him not to look at her like that, because it was making her breathless. 'Xanthos—'

But he silenced her plea with a shake of his head. 'For too long I have deluded myself,' he continued slowly. 'I refused to ask myself why everything with you goes deeper than anything I've had with anyone else. I have closed my mind and my heart to the reality of what was happening to me. I thought that if I returned to my carefully controlled world then the pain I was feeling would go away. But how can it ever go away when I miss you so much?'

'What are you saying?' she whispered, unable to bottle up the question any longer, terrified she would misinterpret what she prayed he was trying to say.

'I'm saying the words that I've never said before for fear of laying myself open to unnecessary pain. But I love you, Bianca, and I'll risk that pain. I want to be part of your life and our baby's life. I want us to be a family,' he concluded huskily, shrugging his shoulders with an unfamiliar awkwardness. 'A real family. For ever.'

Bianca wanted to seize on his words as if they were a lifeline but she was scared, too. She had spent the last few months pushing him away, mostly as an attempt to protect herself and maybe it had been the right thing to do at the time. But he was right. Protecting her heart came with a heavy price and she was no longer sure she was willing to pay it.

Yes, his first suggestion of marriage had been clumsy but she hadn't cut him any slack, had she? Nor taken into account his shock at being told he was going to be a father. Essentially her reaction had been about her own pride and her own ego, rather than daring to acknowledge that he might be offering her an olive branch.

And wasn't she discounting all the amazing things he had done since he'd blazed his way into her life with such elemental force? He had crash-landed a plane and kept her safe. He had shown her physical love and ridiculous generosity, and now he had turned up covered in snow and opened up his heart to her, without restraint. Wasn't it time she opened up hers, to him?

'I guess I've always used my independence as a kind of shield,' she admitted slowly. 'I watched my mother and sister go to pieces when they didn't have a man to support them and was determined that was never going to happen to me. I was never going to rely on anyone, especially a man.' She hesitated. 'But maybe sometimes it is okay to lean on someone else.'

'I want to be that man, Bianca. Let me be that man,' he urged softly. 'Lean on me.'

Her heart turned over and she wanted to cradle

his face in her hands, but still she wasn't finished. 'I thought I knew what I wanted from a relationship. That if I defined the parameters, then I would be in control of it. That's why I only ever dated men who made me feel safe but never actually made me *feel* anything.' She gave a short laugh. 'And then I met you, who was everything I'd warned myself against. I thought our near-death experience and the accompanying danger were what made me become your lover in Vargmali. But it wasn't that. I didn't really have a choice. I could no more have resisted you that night, Xanthos, than I could have stopped the beating of my own heart.'

She could feel the unsteadiness of his hands as he reached out to pull her from the window seat into his arms and she locked hers around his neck and buried her face against his shoulder. She thought she could have stayed like that for ever, but he tilted her chin with his finger, his eyes blazing black fire as they captured her within their gaze.

'I want to spend the rest of my life with you,' he said simply. 'That's all.'

'That sounds like quite a lot to me.'

'So you'll marry me?'

'Yes, of course I'll marry you… Xanthos, what on earth are you *doing*?'

'Isn't it obvious?' He reached into the pocket of his overcoat to produce a small box containing a diamond ring of such brilliance that it dazzled as brightly as the snow outside her window, as he dropped to one knee. And although there was a touch of bemusement on his face—as though he couldn't quite believe what he was doing—a trace of sexy arrogance curved the edges of

his lips. 'I saw that crestfallen look on your face earlier
when I didn't propose—'

'I was *not* crestfallen.'

'Honey, you were.'

Bianca started laughing as he slid the ring onto her
finger. 'Okay, maybe a little,' she admitted, leaning forward so that he could kiss her, but he shook his head
with firm resolve.

'No, wait. I'm not finished yet.'

Still getting used to the heavy ring glinting on her
finger, Bianca stared in bemusement as he pulled something else from another pocket—this time bigger than
a ring box, but only slightly. A tiny package in silvery-
white tissue paper, its shiny red bow a decorative nod to
Christmas. Her fingers were fumbling as she opened it
to find a minuscule pair of white baby booties nestling
amid the tissue, and slowly she lifted her head.

'They were the tiniest thing for sale in the shop,' he
explained, his voice growing gruff. 'And I just couldn't
imagine a pair of feet that would ever be small enough
to fit them.'

They were possibly the most beautiful words she
had ever heard, and Bianca made no attempt to blink
away the tears which had sprung to her eyes—but why
would she, when she saw them mirrored in his own?
And then he was kissing her. Kissing her as he'd never
done before. His lips were brushing over hers with unashamed passion but there was tenderness, too. When
she began to move restlessly in his arms, he carried
into the bedroom and lay down beside her and stroked
her for a long time, delighting and exploring this new
shape of hers. Her swollen breasts and belly, and the

soft thighs which quivered beneath the feathering of his touch. He pleasured her with his fingers and she came apart in his arms and called out his name on a note of joy and wonder. With an unexpected burst of energy and an agility which defied her bulky frame, she pleasured him right back, and afterwards he ran her a bath and told her to go and lie in it and relax.

Obediently Bianca sank back into the warm water, gazing with contentment at the massive diamond which was winking at her through the bubbles, and at one point she thought she could hear the muffled sounds of voices and footsteps coming up from the street below.

Warm and glowing, she slid on her robe and walked into the sitting room, her footsteps slowing to a halt when she saw what awaited her there. Had a fairy flown in and waved a magic wand? She blinked in disbelief as she looked around her. Her small sitting room had been transformed. The fireplace was bursting with the warm golden light of a fire, which Xanthos must have lit, and there was fragrant greenery everywhere. It festooned the hearth and curled over the edges of the pictures. On the table was a holly wreath, and at its centre glowed four tall red candles which matched the brightness of the berries. And there stood Xanthos, so darkly beautiful, his expression one of intense satisfaction as he studied her reaction.

She turned to him in bemusement. 'But, *how*?'

'The girl in the baby shop pointed me towards the jeweller's and the florist. After I'd bought a ring for my future bride, I went to the latter and explained that I wanted an instant Christmas.'

'And you certainly got that. Oh, Xanthos, it's so… beautiful. It looks like the dining room in Vargmali.'

'That was my intention,' he affirmed softly.

She went straight into his arms and he pulled her close as they sat and gazed in admiration at the little Christmas he had created. Later still he made her cheese on toast, and she wondered how he managed to make such a simple task look so sexy, unable to prevent herself from marvelling at his ability to concoct such a delicious variation of the dish.

'Oh, come on, honey,' he chided her mockingly. 'I'm as independent as you are.'

Yes, he was. Yet Bianca recognised that their independent natures had become modified through love. Their individual self-reliance had blended into something equally strong, yet mutually compatible.

And because it was their first evening as an bengaged couple they went to bed early, their lazy kissing suddenly interrupted by Bianca's abrupt gasp as she stared up at him with disbelief.

But Xanthos didn't need to see her clutching her belly to know what was happening. He told himself he needed to stay calm—and on the outside he was—but never before had he experienced such a helpless sense of terror as he listened to the instructions she was stumbling out to him. No emergency crash-landing could be more scary than this.

'It's early!' she wailed, when the midwife arrived and made it clear there wouldn't be time to get to the hospital, even if the roads weren't already choked with snow.

'Only two weeks. That's nothing,' said the midwife reassuringly. 'Now, can we ask dad to find some towels?'

Xanthos obeyed every command which came hurtling his way, acutely conscious of the pain and effort it took a woman to give birth. As the minutes passed, he wiped Bianca's brow and caressed the small of her back and told her she was beautiful. And when, on the first stroke of midnight, their baby was delivered, it was to the jubilant chiming of the Christmas bells.

'It's a girl!' said the midwife, cleaning the slippery infant with efficient hands before placing a tiny seeking mouth against Bianca's breast. 'You have a beautiful baby daughter.'

Unable to speak for the emotion which was building up inside him like a dam, Xanthos nodded as he bent to kiss first Bianca, and then their baby.

His baby.

His senses had never felt so raw. He was aware of the primitive tang of blood and sweat and tears. The sound of the Christmas bells, muffled by the falling snow. And here, in this room, his woman and his baby, surrounded by firelight and love.

It felt...

He swallowed.

It felt like home.

EPILOGUE

Three years later...

EVEN FROM THIS HEIGHT, the illuminations of the palace's giant Christmas tree could be seen. Rainbow light flooded in over the child's bed, bathing it in soft, kaleidoscopic colours, but little Noelle was fast asleep.

Bianca stared down at the tousled black curls of her daughter before realising that Xanthos was watching her from the opposite side of the bed and, automatically, her heart turned over with love and longing as she looked at him. It had been an exciting day. He had been out riding with his brother early that morning, while Noelle had played with her young cousin—two-year-old Bartolo Corso, Rosie's child and the heir to the throne of Monterosso. Not that you would have known he was a royal prince to see his older cousin bossing him around, thought Bianca fondly.

'She's so strong and so funny and so stubborn,' she said softly, brushing an ebony curl away from a plump cheek.

'Just like her mother,' murmured Xanthos.

'Or indeed, her father,' she countered softly.

His smile was tender. 'Let's leave her to sleep,' he said. 'She's got a big day ahead of her tomorrow.'

Bianca didn't speak again until they were back in their own lavish suite next door, which commanded a magnificent view of the palace courtyard. She could see snow falling outside the huge windows as she went into her husband's waiting arms, snuggling into the warmth of his chest and feeling the powerful beat of his heart. For all his doubts about his ability to be a good parent, he had turned out to be the best father in the world—endlessly kind and endlessly patient. What child could fail to thrive beneath the tide of love which flowed from him just as she herself had thrived? 'I can hardly believe she's going to be three tomorrow,' she said, and gave a happy sigh. 'That was certainly a Christmas Day to remember.'

'It certainly was.'

'You were brilliant that night, Xanthos.'

'You were even more brilliant, honey. But right now I'm thinking of another anniversary which deserves celebration.' His voice was silky as he captured her face in his palm so he could look at her properly, and even in this muted light she could see the passionate gleam in his eyes. 'An occasion almost exactly four years ago, when we lay together in that bed in Vargmali and you blew my mind with your passion and your innocence.'

Bianca gave a sigh of contentment. So much had happened since that blissful night in Kopshtell. After Noelle's dramatic Christmas Day birth on the floor of Bianca's apartment, Xanthos had bought a large and quirky house overlooking Wimbledon Common, with a wonderful garden at the back. She had thought he might want them to split their time between London and New York, but he hadn't wanted that at all. Because family and home had become just as important to him as they were to her. The nature of his business meant he could just as easily operate out of England, which meant that Bianca had been able to go back to work at her old firm, once Noelle was a year old.

Xanthos had told her he didn't miss his life in New York and that all he wanted and needed was wherever she and his daughter were. So they had married in Wimbledon village, in a beautiful church of grey stone with clear, bright light flooding through the stained-glass windows. It had been a small wedding with just Corso and Rosie as witnesses, her sister holding a squirming Noelle. She and Xanthos had taken their baby to Vargmali for their honeymoon, fulfilling her promise to Ellen—and something told Bianca that they would never stop visiting the place where their love had begun.

The two brothers had made their peace and, as he acknowledged on one of their frequent visits, Xanthos had grown to love the Mediterranean kingdom with a quiet passion which had surprised him. It had been that love which had prompted him to make a charitable donation to the children's hospital in Monterosso's capital, for research into childhood disease. And although before that Corso had offered him the prestigious Dukedom of Esmelagu, bXanthos had refused. Mainly because his beloved wife had no desire to take part in the cloistered world of palaces and crowns. But he felt exactly the same. He didn't need a title. He didn't need any public acknowledgement of his royal connection to the King of Monterosso. Essentially, he had always been a private man and he intended to stay that way.

The only sadness in their lives had been the discovery that Xanthos's mother had died in her native Greece, almost a decade previously. But a professional investigator had tracked down an aunt, and they were planning to visit her in the springtime—on their way to Zac and Emma's villa in Santorini.

Sometimes Bianca couldn't believe how perfect their life was. She had longed for a family of her own but had never been certain it would happen—for it had been nothing but a faceless dream. But now the faces had been coloured in and she could see them quite clearly. Xanthos and Noelle, and very soon a baby brother or sister to join their darling daughter.

'Happy?' questioned Xanthos.

'Are you?'

'More than you will ever know,' he said, his voice reflective.

He led her over to the window where they looked out at the palace courtyard. At the snow-covered grounds, which looked magical in the silvery brightness of the moon. But all the beauty of the external world didn't hold a candle to the beauty of the man who stood before her. She rose on tiptoe to brush her lips over his and felt the wildfire response of the sexual desire which had always flamed between them. His hands reached down to mould the shape of her bottom through her silky dress and to draw her towards him, as if to impress upon her the hard heat of his body, before lifting her up and carrying her over to the bed.

'Have we...have we got time before tonight's formal

dinner?' she questioned breathlessly, as he began to slither her panties down with a speed which thrilled her.

'That depends on how many times I make you come,' he growled, and she gave a little gurgle of hunger as she fumbled for the buttons of his shirt.

And then he was inside her, filling her completely—heart and body and soul—taking her soaring to that place of total satisfaction. It was only afterwards, when they'd showered and dressed and she hoped the flush of her cheeks had quietened down before they presented themselves at the royal banquet, that Xanthos pulled her into his arms again.

'You still haven't answered my question,' he murmured, smoothing her newly brushed hair away from her face.

It was a question which didn't require an answer—bthey both knew that. But she gave it anyway, because she liked to remind herself how lucky she was.

'Hand on heart,' she said, placing his palm over her breast, 'I never thought I could be this happy. And there's something else, Xanthos. Something I was going to tell you tomorrow, but I don't think I can wait that long.' She paused, savouring every second. 'I'm pregnant.'

Xanthos stared deep into her eyes. Once before she had said these words and his reaction had been nothing more than lukewarm, but in the intervening years he had learnt to accept his emotions. More than that—to embrace and to revel in them. From the very beginning he had felt differently towards her than he had towards any other woman. He remembered his fierce need to protect her when their plane had crashed. After that had come his admiration and respect and eventually his love, which had just grown and grown. He thought about their beloved child and the new life which was growing inside her.

Hadn't there been moments when he'd been so full of joy as a result of everything she'd given him that he'd wanted to throw his head back and roar like a lion?

He smiled, then laughed.

Because this, he realised, was his moment.

* * * * *

A WEEK WITH THE FORBIDDEN GREEK

CATHY WILLIAMS

MILLS & BOON

CHAPTER ONE

NICO SPOTTED HER long before she spotted him, but because he wasn't expecting his prim and proper secretary to be *in a bar*, it took him a few seconds for his brain to compute what his eyes were seeing.

Grace? His efficient, predictable and, oh, so self-contained personal assistant? Here? In this smoky, dark, sultry jazz bar in Mayfair? Surely not!

Framed in one of the three old-fashioned arched doorways that opened into a room that was very cleverly arranged around a highly polished bar and a bandstand, Nico straightened and narrowed his eyes.

Next to him, his date for the evening was clutching his arm and gazing up at him.

Nico should have been in New York for three days but the main guy on the other side of the Atlantic had cancelled because his wife had been rushed to hospital and it had seemed pointless to make the trip in his absence.

So here he was. A last-minute arrangement with a woman who had been texting him with intent ever since they had been introduced two months ago at a fundraiser in Mayfair.

Now, Nico utterly forgot the blonde at his side. Every ounce of his attention homed in on his secretary with an intensity that made his breathing slow and set up a steady drumbeat in his temples.

The soulful, sexy tempo of the background jazz faded.

The waiters swerving between tables and round sofas with their large, circular trays of food and drink disappeared.

The soft, feminine, flirty purring of the woman next to him was suddenly an irritating background noise.

Grace Brown, *his* Grace Brown, wore knee-length skirts in riveting shades of grey and beige.

She always, *but always*, kept her hair tied back. Severely.

Her shoes were always sensible. Practical, *sensible* pumps with just the smallest of heels.

And above all else, no make-up.

Sure, she'd attended the occasional conference with him but the uniform had never changed.

Even on her thirtieth birthday a little over a year ago, which he had personally arranged as a surprise do at one of the high-end restaurants not a million miles away from his towering glass office building, she had *still* been in her stalwart knee-length skirt and beige jumper and cardigan.

So who the heck was this woman sitting at the table at the back, reaching for the glass of wine in front of her?

Not even the subdued, atmospheric lighting in the room could disguise the fact that she was *in a dress*. Something with thin straps that showed off slim shoulders, and her hair was loose, a thick fall of chestnut that highlighted her cheekbones and softened the austere look he had become so accustomed to. The table obscured all but her top half and yet Nico's curious, stunned dark gaze still dropped, searching to unearth the slender body encased in the floral, frothy summer dress.

He was so enthralled by the sight of her, so transported by what even he realised was an unreasonable degree of sheer shock at seeing her out of context, that it took him a while to register that there was something a little off with what he was seeing.

She was with some guy.

The man floated into his vision as an afterthought even though he was sitting adjacent to her.

Receding hairline…one hand on a glass of something that looked like whisky and the other reaching towards her even as she skittered back and tucked her hair nervously behind one ear.

People coming and going interrupted his view, but he felt something slither down his spine because he knew her almost better than he knew himself.

The hair might be tantalisingly loose, and she might be in a dress that did all sorts of things to his imagination, but she was still *his* Grace Brown and he could pick up that infinitesimal tremor in the hand holding the wine glass, the nervous licking of her lips as she pulled back.

Discomfort poured off her in waves and Nico was suddenly galvanised into the sort of caveman protective mode that he would never have credited himself as having in a million years.

'I have to go.' He turned to his date and raked his fingers through his dark hair, barely able to focus on the blonde standing next to him, itching to glance back to the unfolding scene at the table at the back.

'What?'

'You have my apologies.' It wasn't her fault, and he was gentleman enough to admit that, just as he was honest enough to also acknowledge that he was doing her a favour.

They weren't going to end up in bed, however luscious the curves. The evening would conclude in disappointment for her and relief for him as they went their separate ways.

'Why do you have to go? We've just got here!'

'I know. I'll get my driver to take you back to your place.'

'But look at me! I'm all dressed for a night out!'

'And you look spectacular.'

'I don't mind waiting for you! I'll… I'll…just sit at the bar until you've done whatever you have to do!'

'It's better for you to return to your apartment.'

'Will you at least meet me there later?'

'If I were to be polite, I would say *perhaps*. If I were to be honest, I would have to say *no*. I'm an honest man.'

'But…'

'I have to go, Clarissa.' This as he was urgently texting his driver, who was on standby, to head right back to the bar so that he could collect her. He tucked his mobile into his pocket. 'Sid will be here in ten. He'll wait for you outside.'

'Thanks for nothing, Nico!'

No point going for another apology. Truth was… Clarissa wasn't going to lose sleep over a broken date, even one she had been angling for for a while. She would flounce off and, within an hour, would be on the phone to one of her model friends probably slagging him off.

Besides, gut instinct about Grace and whoever she was with was already consuming his attention and he barely glanced at Clarissa's departing back before striding off into the dark room and amongst the crowds and straight to that table at the back.

Grace had no idea that her boss was in the crowd, far less that he had spotted her from the across the room.

She was too busy trying to work out how best to extricate herself from her evening.

How on earth could this have gone so wrong?

The profile had looked *so* promising!

Victor Blake: aged thirty-four.
Occupation: lawyer.
Hobbies: theatre, foreign movies and reading.

Six foot three with a full head of hair and a smile that crinkled his eyes, at least in the photo that he had posted of himself standing in front of a sailboat, which had implied a love of the ocean, presumably.

Grace couldn't have been more cautious. Three weeks of emails and several conversations before dinner had been suggested by him at this very venue. Grace had been impressed. She'd never been here but she'd booked it often enough for her boss. Chez Giscard...an uber-expensive jazz club in the heart of Mayfair. She had been thrilled.

First date in for ever with someone she had so much in common with. How awful could it be?

She loved the theatre even though she couldn't actually remember the last time she'd been. She enjoyed foreign films. She read voraciously, largely when she was guiltily aware that she should be going out…and sailing? Well, the very thought of it was enticing. Who would ever object to the wind blowing through their hair and the salty air against their face?

So how was it that she was now sitting here, toying with the stem of her wine glass, her anxiety levels rising in small, incremental degrees as her date poured drink after drink for himself and tried to edge closer and closer?

This was Grace's first foray into the thorny business of trying to find a guy via a checklist of likes and dislikes, dispassionately listed under various Soulmate Perfect headings. It was a world she had never seriously considered exploring until six months ago when she had looked in the mirror and staring back at her had been a woman now in her thirties with next to no experience of the opposite sex. A woman who had spent her life juggling various responsibilities that had landed on her shoulders, almost without her realising their consequences at the time.

A woman who could proudly look back on her youth as a time spent anxiously looking out for her mum and then, later, her brother.

Whatever the opposite of a misspent youth was, she had lived it.

And to top it all off, all those years…*four and a half of them*…spent with a crazy crush on her boss.

She'd been hiding. Life had been happening out there but she had turned her back on it and, instead, taken the easier option of a forbidden attraction that was safe because it would never come to anything.

Except, time was gathering pace. She had found her first grey hair and had realised with shock that if she wasn't careful, she would find herself staring in that very same mirror in ten years' time and the only difference might be that the single grey hair had multiplied and taken over.

So here she was, getting her life back on track.

She felt the clammy hand of her date slap down on her thigh and she squirmed away with palpable distaste.

They'd exhausted polite conversation and for the life of her she couldn't think of anything to say. When he leaned in and asked her where they could go from here, she stared at him with alarm because she knew exactly what direction the conversation was now beginning to head.

He wasn't a threat. Behind the alcohol, he was probably a nice enough guy. She was willing to give him the benefit of the doubt. That said, going anywhere with him wasn't on the menu. She brushed off his hand and was about to launch into a polite *well-hasn't-this-been-fun-but-I've-got-to-head-back-now-to-walk-the-dog* speech while simultaneously leaping to her feet and sprinting for the door, when she heard a voice behind her.

A dark, familiar voice that sent shivers racing up and down her spine.

She froze. Then slowly, very slowly, she turned around

and there he was in all his ridiculously good-looking glory.

Four and a half wasted years and he still had the same effect on her. The man was six feet four inches of sexy, muscle-packed alpha male. Of Greek heritage, he had a burnished bronzed skin tone. His raven-black hair was just slightly too long, curling at the nape of his neck, and he had the classical features of a statue lovingly sculpted to perfection and then turned into living, breathing human form.

Right now, he was dressed in a pair of dark trousers that emphasised the length of his muscular legs and a white shirt cuffed to the elbows.

The crowded room, the mellow jazz and the bustle of people instantly dimmed to white background noise as Grace's eyes widened in alarm.

She was barely aware of Victor until she felt his hand on her arm and heard him say, with the over-enunciated precision of someone who's drunk too much, 'Friend of yours, Grace?'

Before Grace had time to answer that, Nico was dragging a third chair to the table and swinging it round so that he straddled it, arms resting loosely over the low back, his body language somehow oozing aggression.

Yet his expression was mild enough as his dark eyes swept over her companion and then stayed there.

'Oh, yes,' he purred. 'Grace and I are very good friends.'

'Nico...'

Grace was so disconcerted that she couldn't get beyond his name.

What on earth was Nico doing here? Shouldn't he

have been on the other side of the Atlantic? In New York? Hadn't she booked his flight only a week ago, along with the usual five-star accommodation he demanded?

He was staring at Victor with undisguised curiosity and the sort of bone-deep insolence that needed no words to still feel like a threat.

Grace would have been furious but right now she was heady with relief.

Yes, she was absolutely fine when it came to dealing with most things, but she had dreaded the thought of having to deal with a drunk date.

'This is Victor,' she said crisply, while Nico continued to stare at Victor, who had fallen silent in the face of a more powerful and decidedly sober presence.

'Victor...'

'Nico, what are you doing here?'

'Same as you.' Nico shot her a quick look from under lush lashes. 'Having some fun. Except, when I spotted you from across the room, you didn't seem to be having a huge amount of that. Were you? Have I interrupted a fun time? If so, tell me and I'll leave immediately.'

He'd seen the way the man had shuffled his chair closer to hers, the way he'd tried to make inroads with his hands. He'd seen the way she'd politely pushed him back and revulsion had caught the back of his throat, as sour as bile.

The ferocity of his reaction had shocked him.

Since when had he ever been in the business of rescuing damsels in distress?

Nico had been twenty-three when he had last seriously rescued a damsel in distress, if you could call someone squatting next to an old jalopy with a flat tyre a damsel in distress. More a pocket-sized cute little thing who had known where to position that old jalopy of hers and who had stayed there in the certain knowledge that he would come along. That cute little thing had managed to steal his heart, or so he had thought before he'd wised up to the fact that the only thing she'd wanted to steal had been what was in his bank balance. When he'd tried to break up ten months after they'd met, by which time he'd recognised just how keen she'd been on all the material benefits he could bring to the table, she'd given him a piece of her mind and gone so far as to consult a lawyer to see if she could get anything on some spurious 'broken promises' platform.

Since then, Nico had learnt the wisdom of self-control so his utter lack of it when he had seen Grace from across the room confused the hell out of him.

'No answer?' He smiled a crocodile smile at Victor, who was now glaring accusingly at Grace.

Grace could see exactly what was going through his head and she was appalled. He'd insisted on paying for the two glasses of wine she'd had and for the tapas they'd shared. Had he thought that somehow that had entitled him to more than just dinner? Or had alcohol and perhaps nerves skewed his judgement? He'd gone from dull to insistent over the course of two and a half hours and he'd drunk an awful lot.

'Don't even think of outstaying your welcome,' Nico grated in a dangerously low voice. 'In fact, if I were you, I'd do the gentlemanly thing right now. I'd thank the lady for a terrific evening, wish her all the best and then head off into the sunset.'

'Nico...' Grace said again, mortified and suddenly overwhelmed with self-pity. Rescued by her boss. Wasn't that what it came down to? The very boss whose disturbing presence in her life was the reason she'd been here in the first place, trying to galvanise herself into doing what women of her age should be doing. Going out...meeting guys...dating and having fun.

Instead, Nico had spied her from across a crowded room and decided to turn into a knight in shining armour.

How on earth had it come to this?

But, of course, Grace knew, and as she pushed back the tears of self-pity she had a piercing flashback to her life, to the events that had determined the course of it.

She thought back to her mum, now on the other side of the world. Wasn't it, in some ways, because of her that she, Grace, was sitting here right now? Not quite knowing where to look, hating Nico for thinking he had to rescue her from an uncomfortable situation while reluctantly admiring him for the way he'd gone about doing it?

Cecily Brown, her mum, still young at forty-nine, was in Australia and on marriage number three. Cecily wasn't her real name. Her real name was Ann but, as she had once explained to a very young Grace, *Ann* was such a dreary name. How could an *Ann* be anything but dull? And Cecily had been very far from dull. Cecily had been a whirlwind of adventure, a gorgeous, gregarious red-haired beauty who had kicked out her first husband within three years of being married, only to see just sufficient of him over the remaining four years to get pregnant with another child before eventually divorcing him.

Somewhere along the line, she had married again, a marriage that had lasted a handful of months.

We all make mistakes. That had been her mother's casual dismissal of husband number two. Fortunately, the divorce had left her richer than she had been post-divorce number one, rich enough for her to pack in the nondescript office job she had spent years hating to follow the siren call of the stage.

And Cecily had followed that siren call with boundless enthusiasm. Young, vivacious and with not a scrap of common sense, she had enjoyed life in the manner of a single woman with zero responsibilities.

Parenting, for Cecily, had involved putting on little plays in the kitchen. There had been pizza for breakfast and cake for dinner and, of course, there had been days upon days with only the kindness of friends to keep her and her brother, five years her junior, fed.

Cecily had alternately proclaimed herself better off without men while going to pieces if she happened to be between boyfriends. There had been times when she had climbed into bed and stayed there for days on end with the curtains drawn while Grace had kept the home fires burning and then out she would come, in a blaze of boundless optimism, to pick up where she had left off.

Grace had witnessed all her mother's emotional highs and lows and every single one had determined the direction she wished her own life to take, and it wouldn't follow her mother's.

She had become independent from a young age and cautious beyond her years.

She had learnt that, while Cecily had been a fun mother, *fun* didn't go the distance when it came to parenting.

Parenting involved taking responsibility and Cecily had adroitly managed to delegate all responsibility to other people, largely Grace, who had never complained at the burden on her young shoulders.

So now?

She never took chances. Nico, with his revolving-door love life, was the very essence of a guy who only wanted to have fun, and the crush she'd had on him was inconvenient because he was the last person on earth she should be attracted to, never mind the small detail that he was her boss and paid her salary.

Her glamorous mother had needed validation from good-looking, eligible guys. She, Grace, did not and never would.

So, crush or no crush, she'd kept her distance except now, with Victor dispatched and Nico still sitting at the table, with the chair swivelled into its correct position, she had never felt more exposed.

His head was tilted to the side and his dark eyes were resting thoughtfully on her, ablaze with questions that were none of his business.

'What are you doing here?' Grace asked stiffly. 'Shouldn't you be in New York?'

'The guy bailed. His wife was rushed into hospital. Decided I'd spare myself a night in and come here instead.'

'On your own?'

She was gratified to see him flush and for a few seconds, he looked discomforted, which was rare for Nico Doukas.

'Actually, I came with someone.'

'Where is she?' Grace made a deal of looking around her, giving herself a chance to get her thoughts together, to distract herself from the horrendous awkwardness of the situation.

She'd put so much effort into making sure that there were clear boundaries between them.

Four and a half years of effort! Keeping her head firmly screwed on whenever he was around!

It had been vital because Nico knew how to make a woman feel special. He did it without even realising it. Perched on the side of her desk, he could be chatting about spreadsheets and stationery supplies and he *still* always managed to make her feel as though every word that left her mouth by way of response were a fascinating revelation.

God only knew what he must be like in the company of women he was actively trying to impress.

The fact that she secretly lusted after the man had made it all the more important that she erect her barriers and remain well behind them.

It was galling to think that in a heartbeat and through some cruel twist of fate all that effort could be reduced to rubble.

'I didn't think there was much point in her hanging around while I came…over here…'

'There was no need to ruin your evening by rushing over here to rescue me.' Grace straightened in the chair but even as she did so, even as she tried to revert to her usual crisp, businesslike manner, she was conscious of the frivolity of her dress, all froth and flowers and straps.

It was hot outside, a rare, picture-perfect August evening, and she had dressed to impress.

At five ten and slender, she lacked boobs and curves but made a good enough clothes horse and she had gone all out to play up her assets, such as they were.

'You…looked…' Nico shook his head and the flush darkened, delineating his sharp cheekbones and making him look suddenly younger than his thirty-five years '…as though the man was making you uncomfortable. Even from a distance I could tell he'd had too much to drink…'

'And you figured that I might not have been able to handle the situation?' Grace enquired tartly, yet when she thought of him getting rid of his date so that he could come to her rescue, something hot inside her flared into unwelcome life.

She felt the pinch of her nipples grazing against her bra and wetness between her legs made her want to squirm.

He'd seen her and flown over…come to save her from the fool she'd ended up with who'd started to make her feel uncomfortable… It wasn't a compliment, was it? But whatever it was, it made her achingly conscious of him in ways that felt, oh, so dangerous right now…

When she next spoke, her voice was sharper than she'd intended. 'Nico, I can take care of myself.'

'Yes, I realise that but…'

'But what?' She clicked her tongue, eager to re-establish herself as the efficient employee who was never flustered and could deal with anything. 'I'm very capable of dealing with…with anything. You should know that! How many times have you given me an impossible task only to find that I deal with it in record time? You've said that yourself so many times! I don't need anyone to feel sorry for me and I definitely didn't need you to cancel your plans for the evening because you felt you had to save me from my date.'

'Did I mention anything about feeling sorry for you?'

Nico raked restless fingers through his dark hair. In truth he had rushed over here without thought. He had seen her, had felt something shift inside him, something weird and oddly powerful, like a rush of air racing past him, blowing through him and leaving before he had time to bottle it and find out what it was.

She'd worked for him for over four years. He had seen more of her than most men saw of their wives and yet the sight of her here, in this sultry, atmospheric jazz club, shorn of her usual starchy trappings, had kick-started something inside him he hadn't been able to put a finger on.

And when he'd realised that the guy she was with was being a pest…when he'd seen the way she'd shoved his hand aside, polite and firm but with just a hint of anxiety, he hadn't stopped to think twice.

He'd dismissed his date without a backward glance and flown over like just the sort of damned rescuer she certainly hadn't asked for and didn't want.

As she was now taking great pains to inform him.

Nico refused to question why, exactly, he had felt so compelled to fly to her side.

Nor was he going to delve deep into his shock at seeing her looking the way she looked now, still cool and remote but with a sizzle of sexual allure that he hadn't previously realised was there.

Or had he?

He brushed aside that tantalising thought while refusing to apologise for being the perfect gentleman in
coming to her aid. Even if she hadn't asked for it.

'And yes,' he grated, 'you are up to pretty much anything I can throw at you in the work environment, but
we're not in a work environment now, and my apologies if I was out of order in thinking that that man you
were with might have been making you feel a bit uncomfortable. Was he? By the way? Because you didn't
seem too gutted when I got rid of him.'

Grace sighed.

He'd done his good deed for the day. So what if she
wished the ground could open and swallow her up because the last thing she needed was for her sexy boss
to see her as someone he felt sorry for?

Sure, not when it came to work, but here? In a club?
For him, a different matter.

Here, away from the familiar stamping ground where
he knew her for what she was, his reliable, efficient secretary, she was out of her depth. He had spotted that
from across the room and had stormed over because
he'd assumed she was in a situation she couldn't handle.

She was thirty-one years old and he knew her well
enough to know that, underneath the official trappings,
she wasn't a woman who was used to the ways of the
world. She wasn't a woman like the ones he dated.

It made her teeth snap together with frustration but
what could she do?

The more she protested and fought against his act
of chivalry, the more bewildered he would become at
her overreaction.

He wasn't going to politely step aside and leave her be. He was a guy who had no objections to being a bull in a china shop if the occasion demanded, and since when were bulls in china shops interested in polite behaviour?

Nico was curious and she couldn't blame him. She'd made such a big deal of being private that of course he was going to be curious in a situation like this.

'Victor was…becoming a bit of a nuisance,' she admitted. 'It's the first time we've gone out on a date and I had no idea he would end up drinking so much that he…'

Grace fiddled with the stem of her wine glass and her eyes skittered away from his piercing stare.

'Some people can't hold their drink,' Nico rasped. 'One too many and the inner creep takes over. Did he do anything more than just make you feel uncomfortable? Did he try and…touch you?'

'No!' But she laughed. 'Why? Would you offer to go and pummel him on my behalf?'

'Damn right.'

'You're kidding, Nico.' Their eyes tangled and there was a brief, breathless silence. Her pulses leapt and, for a few seconds, every thought was driven from her head because there was a burning intensity in his dark eyes that made her feel giddy and sharply alert at the same time.

'I don't joke about certain things.'

'Well, he didn't. He was just a bore and then a pest. That's all.' He was still looking at her in a way that made her blood sizzle and she rushed into chatter, which was so unlike her. She confessed that he was an Internet date and then launched into a nonsensical monologue about dating apps, growing redder and more flustered by the second. Eventually she lapsed into embarrassed silence, mortified and despairing at how utterly she had let herself down.

'The Internet can be a dangerous place, especially for a beautiful woman.'

Grace's eyes widened. She wondered whether, in her feverish panic at the way the conversation was going, she had imagined what she'd heard. Maybe she'd been hallucinating, having some kind of out-of-body experience.

But then he reached out and covered her hand with his. His eyes didn't leave her face. Just that hand, warm on hers, idly stroking...

And her body went up in flames. They licked past all the defences she had erected over the years, sweeping them under a blast of heat as scorching as a furnace. Her heart was a drumbeat that made her feel sick and faint. She was trembling and her breathing had slowed as her body responded to his casual touch.

It was as if she had been fast asleep and now, eyes wide open, life was rushing at her in dazzling, Technicolour fury.

It was terrifying and she snatched her hand away and rubbed it, lost for words.

'I... I think I'll be heading home now,' she breathed jerkily, and Nico sprawled back in his chair.

'Let me get my driver to take you.'

'No! No... I... I can make my own way back.' His voice was its usual lazy drawl while she had to clear her throat to avoid sounding like someone with a speech im-

pediment. 'Monday,' she gabbled, standing and snatch-
ing at her bag, at once eager to leave but conscious of
the floaty summer dress and her body on fire under it.

'Monday?'

'I'll have those reports for you first thing! I've also…
also done some checking up on the security systems at
Deals, making sure there are no viruses in the system
before I start loading sensitive information.'

'Grace,' Nico said softly, 'I'm sorry your evening
didn't work out the way you wanted it to. Head home,
sleep it off and don't even dare think about anything
work related until you're in on Monday. Nothing is so
important that you need to log onto your work computer on a weekend.'

He slapped his thighs and stood as well, towering
over her, emanating waves of heat that furled around
her like a miasma and scrambled her thoughts.

'Have a good weekend…whatever's left of it…' He
saluted her with a half-smile on his face. 'And word to
the wise…be careful on those dating sites. You never
know what or who you're going to find there.'

'Thanks for the advice, Nico,' Grace countered
sweetly. 'I'll bear that in mind the next time I venture
out into the big, bad world.'

And before he could say anything else on the subject,
she spun round on her heel and walked away.

CHAPTER TWO

FOR THE FIRST time in years, Grace approached the glass and steel building where she worked with trepidation.

She had left the bar two evenings before on the verge of a nervous breakdown. Only on the bus back to her apartment had she got her thoughts in order enough to reflect on just how much Nico had managed to kick ajar the door that had always been closed between them, and all because of a chance encounter, and, wow, had he kicked that door in grand style.

She'd felt like a swooning Victorian maiden when he'd put that hand on hers, softly stroking...his eyes fastened to her face, dragging responses out of her she'd been so careful to hide.

Would her charming, charismatic and way too sexy boss suddenly decide that if a couple of barriers had been broken down, then why not have a go at knocking down the whole edifice? When she had first started working for him, she could remember the way he would look at her, with those dark, slumberous eyes coolly speculating, wondering what lay beneath the controlled, calm façade. He did that sort of thing without even realising it. She was sure of it. It was all part and parcel of his magnetic personality. He was the son of a Greek shipping tycoon and he would have grown up with the sort of bone-deep confidence that came so naturally to people born into wealth, a casual assumption that wherever their interest happened to alight, the recipient of said interest would be flattered to death.

Grace was honest enough to admit to herself that she would find it difficult if he suddenly decided to infiltrate her private life. She didn't want the lines between them to be trampled. She couldn't let her barriers down with him. She was far too aware of her boss as *a man* and one whose casual approach to relationships she found personally distasteful.

Yes, he was the smartest guy she had ever met. Yes, he treated his staff fairly and was generous to a fault when it came to paying them. And yes, she had seen enough of his business practices to know that he played it straight down the line without taking any of the sort of financial shortcuts she knew some business tycoons were guilty of doing.

But he played the field and he did it without any trace of a conscience. Grace had grown up alert to the dangers of people who played the field, who moved on from one relationship to another without stopping to work out what the collateral damage might be. Between marriages, her mother had seldom been on her own, without a guy. Caught on a treadmill of always needing to be needed, always looking for distraction, she had been a part-time parent, even after Tommy had had his accident and had needed her to be a full-time mother. At least for a while. She was vivacious and beautiful and vain and fun, but she had never realised that there was more to life than that when it came to the people around her. Grace had realised because, after Tommy's accident had put him in a coma and then, when he had surfaced, confined him to a wheelchair, she had been the one to do the coping and it had been agonising.

Grace never uttered a word when Nico asked her to order expensive flowers to mark the end of a relationship and she showed no emotion when, a handful of days later, she was on the phone reserving seats at the theatre for his next conquest.

But that love 'em and leave 'em attitude? That ability to take like a kid in a sweet shop and then move on when the sweets got boring? No, those were traits she had no time for. Even her mother had at least moved in and out of men in search of Mr Right. Nico moved in and out of women because he was committed to having a good time.

Yet still her disobedient eyes surreptitiously followed him as he moved with lazy grace in his office, walking and thinking aloud while she did her best to keep up with the lightning speed of his thoughts...and her disobedient mind? It bypassed common sense to have fun with all sorts of taboo thoughts and images that made her quiver when she lay in bed at night, waiting for sleep to get a grip.

In an attempt to bolster her defences, she had chosen a particularly uninspiring outfit to wear. A tweedy grey knee-length skirt, a white blouse neatly tucked into the waistband of the skirt, tights and flat black pumps. She had dragged her hair behind her ears to clip severely into place and, with her laptop bag in one hand and her handbag in the other, she looked and felt as carefree as a teacher employed to keep order in a class of rebellious teenagers.

Of course, he was there before her even though it wasn't yet eight-thirty. She stopped only to dump the handbag, remove her laptop from its bag and was already flipping it open as she strode into his office, briefly knocking to announce her arrival.

She didn't look at him.

She *couldn't*.

And yet, she *still* managed to note that he was in a pair of pale grey trousers and a striped shirt that was cuffed to the elbows and with the top couple of buttons undone, revealing just enough of a hard sliver of brown chest to send her imagination whirring in heated response. She was used to this sort of nonsensical reaction…indeed, it was one of the very reasons she had decided to try her hand at Internet dating, because she finally accepted just how much she needed to remind herself that the world was full of other guys and not just this one unsuitable one. That said, she was hypersensitive to every nuanced heated response racing through her now because of what had happened. For a moment in time, she hadn't been his secretary. She had been a woman without the suit and the computer, for once not transcribing emails or arranging his appointments or discussing whatever deals he had in the melting pot. She had been a woman in a slinky flowered dress on a date.

'I've collated all those emails,' she said, automatically sitting in her usual spot on the chair in front of his desk and peering at her computer, 'on the supplies issue with the freight ship from South America. I can send them off to the lawyer at your say-so? Also…'

brow furrowed, she continued without break '... Christopher Thomas wants you to call him urgently about the takeover of his company. He says he wants to add some further clauses about maintaining staff levels for a certain length of time. Shall I set up a conference call? I've checked your diary and you have a slot between two and three-thirty this afternoon but only if we can shift your overseas call to Australia by half an hour.'

She finally risked looking at him and their eyes met.

'And breathe...' Nico murmured.

Grace pursed her lips. 'I have a huge amount to get through today. I thought I'd get the ball rolling because I... I have to leave early this afternoon, I'm afraid...'

'How early?' Nico frowned.

'Three-thirty. I have a dental appointment. I'm sorry. I should have texted you to let you know this morning, but a free slot's only just come up on my way in...'

She didn't have an appointment. Nerves had got the better of her and it was infuriating because it was the first time it had happened. Her quiet, predictable world had shifted on its axis and now she felt as though she had to get it back to where it had been as fast as possible, and being here all day, dealing with Nico and that alarming inquisitive glitter in his dark eyes, wasn't going to help matters.

'It's crucial that we take care of our teeth,' Nico murmured by way of response.

He stood up, unconsciously flexing his muscles before strolling to the floor-to-ceiling glass pane to briefly peer out before turning to look at her.

Grace reluctantly looked at him. She refused to rise to the bait. She intended to do her utmost to move on from what had happened in the jazz club but she could tell from the gleam in his dark eyes that her boss might not be that interested in playing ball.

'So shall we get down to work, Nico?' she asked coolly. 'I know you'd probably like nothing more than to talk about…what happened…but I would really rather not discuss it. It was unfortunate that you showed up when I was there with…with Victor, but these things happen. Best we put all that nonsense behind us.' There. She'd faced down the elephant in the room because it was pointless trying to tiptoe around it and pretend it didn't exist.

Her gaze held his, as calm and cool as always, but it wasn't hard for Nico to spot the simmering defiance there. She had come, he'd realised just as soon as she had walked through that door, with all her defences back in place. Outside the sun was already warning of another hot, unbearably sticky day and yet here she was in her best protective gear.

Previously, Nico would have been amused, but things had changed and he was frustrated at just how determined she was to pretend it was all back to business and let's forget about that blip. He was even more frustrated at just how keen he was to fight against that, as though now that he had happened to find his foot wedged in the door, he wanted to kick open the door and discover what lay beyond it.

Why? What had changed so much? He had retreated successfully for years from trying to prod and poke a response from her, intrigued against his will by a woman who was so immune to him. He had backed away and settled into a routine of working with someone who'd shaped up to be the best PA he'd ever had. He'd told himself that curiosity was not worth the hassle of having to source someone comparable because he had ignored her *Hands Off* signs.

But now...

Who could blame a guy for having a curious streak? Curiosity had got him where he was today. Sure, he had inherited the family empire and, with that, all the kudos and wealth that came with it. He could have stuck to what he knew and carried on the shipping tradition. Lord knew, his own father had had his work cut out when he had been forced to steer it into safe waters after his brother's reckless handling of the asset base. So it should have been in his nature not to take risks, but he had because there were other worlds out there to be explored and shipping was just one of them.

If he hadn't been curious enough to have a look and then to have a go, he would have remained in Athens to take over the reins of the family business. He would have followed in his father's footsteps. He would have had his youthful drama, learnt his lessons and then married a good Greek girl, just as his father had, and stayed put to toe the family line.

He had wanted more than that and he had explored and mastered so many fields in technology and communication that staying close to home had never been an option. He had made sure that the family business was in robust health, but he had moved on. His own private companies were worth their own individual fortunes.

So curious? It was in his DNA and his efficient and dependable secretary roused all kinds of curiosity inside

him. He was hanging onto common sense by a thread
but when he thought of her in that dress and the way it
cupped her high, small breasts…his libido took off at
supersonic speed.

Nico could enjoy the novelty of it, could be tempted
by thoughts of going beyond what common sense was
dictating and yet know, in his gut, that those temp-
tations were indulgences he would be very wise not
to explore. He'd had his brush with adventure. He'd
been a fool once, had taken his eye off the ball, and it
wasn't going to happen again. Fun was temporary. He
would eventually marry and that would be to a suitable
woman, one whose status equalled his and who came
from a tradition of work first.

Inappropriate thoughts about his secretary made
him uneasy because it was outside known territory.
He enjoyed the company of women, treated them like
queens and was utterly monogamous, but he always let
them know what they could and couldn't expect from
him. Boundary lines were always in place. *That* was
known territory. Sudden idle thoughts about his secretary were not.

He sauntered thoughtfully back to his desk and,
when he sat back down, he pushed the chair back at an
angle and leaned back, hands folded behind his head,
and looked at her for a few seconds.

'Let's forget about work for ten minutes, Grace,' he
said quietly. 'I know you want to pretend that Saturday
night never happened, but it did.'

'I don't want to *pretend* anything, Nico.'

'When I got to that club and spotted you, I was
shocked.'

'I don't know why, Nico. Believe it or not, I do actually have a life that happens when I leave this office.'

'I'm not disputing that, but it's been hard to envisage because you've spent the past four and a half years making sure you never breathed a word to me about what you do when you leave here.'

'Because it's none of your business!'

'You're my business, because you work for me and because I'd like to think that we're a bit more than a couple of strangers who happen to be together because of work.'

Nico watched her fidget. He noted the hectic colour in her cheeks. He'd shocked himself when he'd flown to her rescue two days before and he was astonished that he was now pursuing this in the face of common sense telling him that detachment was what he did best.

'I was worried on your behalf, Grace.'

'And like I said, there was no need to be!'

'Because you can look after yourself?'

'That's right.'

Nico looked at her coolly defiant face—so remote and so oddly alluring. Was he only noticing this for the first time or was it something he had unconsciously noted all along but had chosen to ignore until he had seen her in a different light?

'Look—' Grace leapt to her feet, her cheeks flushed '—let's get something straight, Nico. I made it clear when I joined your company, when I started working for you, that I wasn't interested in putting my private life in the public arena. Nothing's changed on that front.'

'We have very different definitions of private life in the public arena,' Nico returned with a thread of amusement. 'And sit back down, for God's sake. You're not being cross-examined in the witness box with the threat of jail if you don't supply the correct answers. We're having a conversation.' He looked at her with brooding intensity. Every bit of her screamed discomfort. He'd never seen her so agitated in his life before but, then again, he concluded that he'd only ever seen the parts of her she had been willing to put on show. Under that smooth, composed exterior, there obviously lurked a complex, fiery woman.

Grace sat back down.

She was rattled. How to play this? What to do? How far could she insist on being secretive without him wondering why? How long before he began to wonder whether she singled him out because she wasn't relaxed around him? And once he started asking himself questions like that, how long before he found his unexpected answers? That he got under her skin? That she was attracted to him?

'I'm not hiding anything,' she said reluctantly. She raised her eyes to his and forced herself to relax. Also to accept that digging her heels in was only going to make him more and more curious about her. She couldn't kid herself that bumping into him in the most unlikely of venues wasn't going to make him curious, and the more she tried to stuff the genie back in the bottle, the more curious he was going to become. Human nature.

But caution was so deeply ingrained that she didn't know where to begin when it came to sharing, least of all with Nico, and the silence stretched between them.

'Grace…' Nico eventually broke the silence, raking

his fingers through his dark hair in a gesture that was both elegant and sexy and one that she was accustomed to seeing because he did it often. 'Okay.' He sighed. 'I get it that you and I are on a different page when it comes to being upfront. I get it that you're tight-lipped on every single aspect of your private life, for reasons that are frankly mystifying, but you work for me, have worked for me for a very long time, and I like to think that we're…we're *friends*. Wouldn't you agree?'

'Yes!' Grace thought of all those forbidden thoughts over the years. None could be described as in the *friendly* category. 'Of course we are. Of course I consider you my friend as well as my boss. Good heavens, we see enough of one another!'

'I'm glad you agree! Which is why I felt compelled to join you on Saturday. Naturally I would never have intruded had I not got the distinct impression that the man was bugging you. And it's because I care about your welfare that I felt the need to offer you advice rather than sit back and watch you wander into situations that you may find you can't handle.'

Grace gritted her teeth in something resembling a smile. So they were here again, were they?

'You need to be careful. You put yourself out there and…' he shook his head '…you have no idea what could be lurking around the corner. That date of yours? Sure, he'd had too much to drink and maybe he's a paragon of virtue when he's sober, but under the influence of drink you can never be certain what direction a guy might take if he's rejected. There can be a thin line between thinking you're in control of a situation as a woman and realising that you're not.'

'Yes, you said something of the sort when you…came to my rescue two evenings ago,' Grace said sweetly, while she counted to ten and then to twenty, making sure to keep her temper in check.

Nico frowned.

'So we agree…' he murmured.

'Not really, because I don't tell *you* how to run *your* life.'

Lush, silky lashes shielded Nico's expression for a couple of seconds but there was a lazy smile on his face when he drawled, softly, 'Would you like to?'

'That's not my place,' Grace countered quickly. His dark eyes on her made her skin prickle and she licked her lips. She could feel the pulse in her neck beating fast.

She longed for the safety of her desk and her computer and emails that needed urgent attention. And yet, just as when he had surprised her at that jazz club, there was a simmering, dangerous excitement inside her. For someone who had always led a cautious life, never taking chances, it was heady and disturbing and frightening.

So why did she like it?

'We're friends,' Nico encouraged smoothly.

'Yes, but there's also a lot of work to get through…'

'This is more important,' Nico said firmly. 'Seeing you in such a state of panic on Saturday evening—'

'I was not in a state of panic!' Grace interrupted impatiently.

'Perhaps that's a slight exaggeration.'

'I was uncomfortable. Not the end of the world.'

'As I was saying, Grace, seeing you in such discomfort made me realise that you're more than just someone I pay to come in between the hours of nine to five to work for me...' He shifted but kept his eyes pinned to her face. 'You're someone I care about and it's because I care about you that I want these barriers between us to drop. I want you to feel free to express yourself around me, to tell me what's on your mind...' He gestured to their surroundings, which were the last word in plush. 'If I don't know what you think, then how do I know whether you're enjoying your job or not?'

Grace looked at her boss and the sincere expression on his face with frustration.

Had she been the only one to feel that sizzle of something when his hand had covered hers? She had been secretly thrilled that he had rushed to her side in the club even though she might noisily make her stand for independence. It irked her that she couldn't shake all those feelings of attraction, that she couldn't get onto the same page as Nico and see the sudden shift between them as a friendship that would simply mark a different chapter in their relationship.

She was desperate for everything to remain *work only* within the glass walls of his expensive offices.

Anything beyond that scared her because she wasn't sure how she could handle it. Fancying him made her vulnerable and she didn't want to be vulnerable.

She'd been vulnerable as a kid and she wasn't going to revisit that place again.

'I love my job.'

'But what about the guy who gave it to you? Hmm?' He grinned with wicked amusement. 'Less love there?'

'You're playing games.'

'Maybe a little,' Nico admitted, 'but it's true that we've taken a step forward and it's important we keep it where it is because I'm genuinely interested in knowing what you think about me, aside from what you think about the job or the offices or the pay cheque at the end of the month. A happy employee is a loyal employee and if you have any problems with me, then I want you to take this opportunity to air them…'

Grace relaxed and fumbled her way to ground she could understand. Nico, for all his charm, thought with his head. Was he protecting his asset? He valued her professionalism and over the years she had had her salary increased hugely along with her responsibilities.

After four and a half years of seeing only one side of her, was he suddenly keen to make sure there was nothing she was hiding from him that might jeopardise their very successful working arrangement?

Had seeing her with Victor made him realise how little he knew her and therefore how easily she could pull the rug from under his feet by letting him down on the work front because she wasn't happy about telling him what she thought? What she really thought? He suspected that she didn't approve of his colourful love life, as he'd said himself, in passing.

But where he had maybe given it no thought, had he now woken up to the fact that the woman he now realised he didn't know half as well as he'd thought might just be banking her disapproval? Quietly biding her time until the scales overbalanced and she took off for another job?

Nothing mattered more to Nico than work. It was the one thing on which he was deadly focused.

As if to confirm what she was thinking, he said, in low voice, 'Be honest with me, Grace. I value you and if you're storing things up…well, that's a recipe for disaster. You're the best PA I've ever had. I don't want you to suddenly quit on me because…you have issues with me…' He shot her one of those devastating smiles that could make her melt from the inside out. One of those smiles that, in the past, had made her tingle with warmth on the inside even though, on the outside, she had always been able to remain perfectly composed. Unfortunately, because she was fighting for composure, that smile made her feel horribly exposed and vulnerable.

And the twinkle in his dark eyes riled her because she could sense just the tiniest bit of mischief there, however sincere he might be. He'd crossed no boundaries for so long that he was having fun stomping all over them now.

So he wanted her to be honest? Well, why not?

Maybe, in fact, it would dilute this crazy spell he seemed to have over her. Who was to say that all these cloak and dagger, childish yearnings didn't contribute to her ill-advised crush? Didn't clandestine relationships flourish in the thrill of secrecy only to fizzle out the minute they were subjected to the glare of tedious, out-in-the-open reality?

It might be her nature to guard her personal life, purely from habit, but if she opened up a bit, then whatever curiosity Nico might be nurturing about her because he had happened to see her out of context would be killed dead in its tracks.

She would become what he was accustomed to. He

had the sort of lively mind that enjoyed pushing the boundaries. If she had suddenly become one of those boundaries he might be interested in pushing, then getting their working relationship onto a slightly more normalised footing might not be such a bad thing.

If he wanted to invite her to ask questions, then why shouldn't she?

She harked back to what he had said and picked up the thread.

'I don't tell you how to run your life, Nico, but now you're asking, I really disapprove of the way you treat women.'

'The way *I treat women*? You mean with frankness, generosity and consideration? *That* way?'

'You break hearts. I know that. I've dealt with those weeping broken hearts down the end of the telephone.'

'I'm always honest. You couldn't find a more honest guy than me. Women always know the score from the very beginning. Nothing long term. Nothing permanent. But while it lasts, they become my sole preoccupation and I am lavish when it comes to spending on them.'

'They know the score?' Grace's eyebrows shot up. 'There aren't many women who start going out with a guy knowing that it isn't going anywhere…no woman is a mind-reader.'

'Then that's not my fault because I'm very truthful with all of them. I lay my cards on the table and tell it like it is.'

'Do you? Literally?'

'I don't like misunderstandings so I spell it all out in no uncertain terms from the get-go. No cosy meals in… no holding hands in front of the telly in the evening…no meeting the parents…no chats about future plans and no idly gazing into jewellery stores and musing about the joys of family life… In fact, not even sleepovers. I like my space to myself.'

Bombarded by the sort of unequivocal information she had always suspected but never had confirmed, Grace could only look at Nico with her mouth half open and he burst out laughing and held her astonished gaze for a few seconds longer than necessary.

'Okay, maybe it's not quite as bold as that, but I always tell them that I'm not interested in anything long term and they get the message on the rest pretty soon afterwards.'

'But why?'

'But why what?' Nico frowned.

'I mean…' She turned bright red as she realised that the question-and-answer session was in danger of overstepping its brief.

'You mean,' Nico said coolly, 'why I'm not interested in chasing after happy-ever-after scenarios?'

'Most people do want to find love…a companion… a soulmate, if you will…'

'Is that *your* aim? Was that what you were looking for when you decided to go with that Internet guy?'

Grace tilted her chin at a defensive angle. She didn't want to be reminded of that mistake but, then again, wasn't it better to be hopeful of finding love than to accept that it was never going to happen?

She might approach life from a different direction than her mother had, but, in the end, weren't their aims similar?

Of course, there was no way she would ever be prepared to kiss a thousand frogs on her way to finding her prince, as her mother had been prepared to do, but hadn't her mother at least had that goal in sight? And she had found that prince.

If you never had that goal to aim for, then surely life would be a little empty?

If Nico was curious about her, Grace was honest enough to admit that it was mutual.

But this curiosity? It had to be leashed. She knew that. Yet, she wondered what had informed his choices and she was so desperate to ask that she had to clamp shut her jaw.

'I wasn't looking for anything,' she said. 'Just some fun.'

Nico's dark gaze rested speculatively on her fine-featured face. Did he believe her? No. Not really. She was a serious woman who wanted more than just a bit of fun.

Was Internet date number one the beginning of that search?

Nico lowered his eyes. Images rushed into his head of her with a man, finding true love. He'd been goading her. Just a little bit. Just to see the tinge of pink in her cheeks, spurred on by who knew what?

But now, when he thought of his serious secretary in the arms of whatever soulmate she was looking for, he felt something tight and uncomfortable in his belly.

A woman in love was an unreliable employee, he grittily told himself, banking down a little voice that wanted to whisper different things in his ear. *That* was why he was suddenly disconcerted at the turn of the conversation.

'So,' he drawled, 'shall we wrap up this soul-searching for the moment and do what we do best?'

It took Grace a few disoriented seconds before her work hat was back in place as she registered his brisk change of tone and she nodded.

'Back to work.' She smiled and stood up and brushed some non-existent dust from her skirt and flashed him a smile.

'You have a dentist appointment, after all,' he murmured.

'So I do.' She'd completely forgotten. For the past forty minutes, she'd completely forgotten far too much.

CHAPTER THREE

NICO TERMINATED THE forty-five-minute phone call with his father in Greece and sprang from where he'd been relaxing in his sprawling sitting room to prowl to the kitchen for a drink. He needed it. Something very strong to deal with what had been thrown at him out of the blue.

'It is your uncle, Nico,' his father had said heavily, after the briefest of pleasantries. 'You do not know it, but he has been ill for some time. I have had news of his death. Arrangements will have to be made, son. I, myself, would go but you know your mother is still recovering from her operation last month. I am in no position to leave her and the process should only take a few days. I am relying on you to step in on my behalf.'

Now, Nico poured himself a glass of whisky and mused that this was not what he had had in mind when he had decided to head back to his place for one of his rare evenings in on his own. It was Friday, it was only just a little after six and he had planned on kicking back in front of a complex computer program that had been submitted from the small, innovative logistics company he had recently bought. Peace. And a chance for his head to be somewhere else because, for the past three weeks, far too much of it had been taken up with his secretary and her sudden irresistible appeal.

Curiosity was proving annoyingly immune to all the usual stun-gun weapons in his armoury. Things had settled back to where they had once been, before that blip. She was once again the dutiful, highly professional secretary who dealt with whatever was thrown at her without complaint and with praiseworthy efficiency.

If he had imagined that their first truly honest conversation might have opened a door that would stay ajar, then he had found himself to be completely mistaken.

She might have been slightly more forthcoming when he'd asked her how her weekend had been…or what she thought of this or that piece of gossip in the news…or, daringly, whether there had been any more Internet hopefuls on the scene…but the polite *hands off* mask was firmly back in place. As were the suits and the neatly tied-back hair and the lowered eyes as she sat in front of him, her fingers flying over her laptop, doing what she did so well. Working.

Nothing wrong with that, Nico repeatedly told himself. He needed a calm, stress-free working environment and she had always provided that and was continuing to do so now.

He hadn't been exaggerating when he'd told her that she was the best PA he'd ever had. Previous to her, he had endured the nightmare of three too young and too easily panicked secretaries, one harridan with only a passing acquaintance with the software he needed her to know and one efficient older woman who had dramatically had to leave after six months because her daughter in Scotland had had triplets and had wanted her to be on hand to help.

Grace had shown up for the interview and within minutes Nico had known that he was going to hire her.

So he was frustrated and impatient with himself for his sudden lack of self-control now whenever he was around her.

And on the back of that phone call? Well, it was no good trying to while away a couple of pleasant hours playing with all the mathematical intricacies of the computer program, trying to improve some of the complex coding, which would have guaranteed total preoccupation with something else.

His uncle.

A blast from the past.

Nico nursed the whisky and thought about the implications of heading off to a tiny island in the Bahamas for what might be longer than the optimistic couple of days his father had opined, in order to wrap up his uncle's affairs.

Sander Doukas, the disgraced black sheep of the family, was a shadowy figure who had never featured in Nico's life, except anecdotally.

He had brought disgrace on the family name. Photos of him in compromising situations had been so numerous that you could wallpaper a house with the cuttings. He had been in rehab three times. He practically had a loyalty card there.

That was the gossip Nico had gleaned from a variety of sources.

What Nico *did* know for certain was that Sander Doukas had come so close to running the family company into the ground that the ensuing battle for power between his father and his uncle had destroyed whatever family bond they had once shared.

They had shared the inheritance of the company when their parents had suddenly and unexpectedly been killed in a car accident. Sander had been, by then, a lightweight member of the board, rarely seen and largely overlooked. He had been thirty and far too busy having fun to don a suit and go to work.

Five years younger, Stefano Doukas, Nico's father, had already been learning the ropes and proving himself to be as serious as Sander had been frivolous.

Had a substantial inheritance not landed on Sander's shoulders at a young age, Nico assumed all would have continued relatively smoothly because the old man, his grandfather and the head of the company, would have kept his older son on a short lead. However, that wasn't to be.

Through the years, Nico had come to realise just how destructive it was to have no control over your emotional life. He had been young but not so young that he hadn't understood those hushed conversations between his parents and the comings and goings of lawyers as power had eventually been wrested away from Sander, with many concessions to sweeten the blow.

In all events, the upshot had been banishment in all but name.

The banishment had been suitably luxurious. Sander had been sent to open and run a hotel on an exquisite island of the Bahamas in the Caribbean.

'Does he keep in touch?' he could remember asking his father many years previously.

To which his father had shaken his head and said, with-

out emotion, 'Too much pride. So be it. We all get the life
that we deserve in the end. Left to his own devices, your
uncle would have destroyed the company, and the company, my son, was not founded to support a spoiled man's
indulgences. Many people's lives depend on it. Have fun,
but it is important to know when the fun has to stop.'

Nico had had no curiosity about an uncle he had
never known. It was unthinkable that he would refuse
his father's request, but it was still annoying, he thought
as he drained the last of the whisky in his glass, because
he had a lot on his plate at the moment and wrapping
up affairs had an ominous ring about it.

On a small island in the middle of nowhere, who
knew how long the procedure would take?

He would have to carry on working.

He assumed all mod cons would be in place, although
he had no idea what sort of hotel his uncle had set up.
He had been shuffled out of harm's way, with sufficient
money to last more than a lifetime but doled out by a
trusted, designated member of the company, and then
left to his own devices.

Arrangements would have to be made now and urgently.

Nico realised that he had no idea where Grace lived
because he'd never had cause to go to her house.

He wouldn't spring a surprise visit on her now, at any
rate, even if he did know where she lived.

On the other hand, he couldn't sit around waiting
until Monday. Like it or not, she was about to have her
weekend disrupted…

Grace had not been expecting a call from her boss.

Were things back to normal between them? Not for

her. For her, the memory of his hand moving softly over hers was still too vivid. She closed her eyes and could relive the sensation. So when he had disappeared early this afternoon, she had been surprised but not displeased.

It was a Friday and she'd decided that she would relax over the weekend, visit her brother as she always did on a Sunday, and then on Monday she would kick-start the dating site and take her chances again. Did lightning strike twice?

So his name popping up on her phone jolted her. It was a little after seven and, even though she was very happy to be doing nothing, Grace possessed sufficient self-awareness to feel a twinge of embarrassment that she wasn't out having fun.

How had *having fun* ended up on a par with *surviving an ordeal*? When had *having fun* entailed gritting her teeth and girding her loins and taking lots of deep breaths before going for it?

'Nico?'

'Glad I caught you, Grace.'

His disembodied voice sent a little shiver through her.

'Is anything wrong?' This could only be about work and now she frantically tried to think if she'd left something unfinished. For a few pleasurable seconds, she was seduced into fantasising that he was calling her to ask her out. She half closed her eyes and got a grip. She'd wasted too many years on fantasies like this and she'd reached the end of the line with that.

'I did stay on after you left, Nico, and got through

as much as I could. If there's something I should have done, then tell me and I can fit it in over the weekend.'

'Fit work in over the weekend?'

'Yes, of course.'

'You're not paid to fit work in over the weekend.'

'I know, but—'

'Besides, haven't you got plans?'

'Well, yes. I'm busy on Sunday…' Grace thought of Tommy, of how much he needed her, how much he had *always* needed her. Sundays were their day. She was always there for him, egging him on, encouraging him, always keen to try and see what more she could do to make his life a little easier.

Whatever foolish confidences she had shared with Nico, that was one she never would, that was a very private side to her that would not be in the public domain.

'Internet date?'

'Nico, why have you called? Is it about work?'

'Yes and no. I need to have a word with you. I wouldn't have interrupted your Friday evening, Grace, but this can't wait. I need to see you. We can do this one of three ways. I can either come to your house, you can come to mine or we can meet at the office. It should be busy there at the moment. There's a social event happening several floors down, some art exhibition McGregor's giving to try and impress the great and the good in culture, and my people will also be burning the midnight oil working on that computer program I want them to perfect by Monday.'

'You're making me nervous, Nico. Can't you tell me what this is about?'

Come to her house? Grace could think of nothing she

wanted less. Nico had never been to her house. There had never been any reason for him to come and even if something urgent had cropped up, she would have done her best to make sure he didn't put one foot over her threshold. Perhaps, even, one foot in the street where she lived or even the town, for that matter, because she knew that he would have been shocked.

Shocked that she didn't live in a smart apartment in a smart part of town, because she was certainly paid enough to afford somewhere really nice. He would have wondered where her very fat pay cheque went. He would never know that so much of it had gone on supporting her brother. She had managed to buy Tommy a ground-floor flat with adaptations made to cater for his lack of mobility. He had tried to tell her not to but she had insisted. He needed looking after. He always had, even from a young child. He had never had her strength of character, and after his accident Grace had been all too willing to carry on caretaking duties.

After all, who else was going to look after him? And with her mother on the other side of the world, Tommy was the only family she had left here.

So not only had she sacrificed her own dream of owning a property to help him out and buy him somewhere to live, but then there had been the bills for the private therapist, which hadn't come cheap.

Fortunately, those had decreased from twice a week to once a week, but there was no way they could be halted for good. How else would her brother ever be in the right frame of mind to deal with the setbacks he had suffered? To fully pick himself up and look to a future very different from the one he had planned?

'I would rather not on the phone, no.' Then the briefest of pauses. 'Am I interrupting something?'

'I was just about to start preparing my dinner,' she said on a sigh.

'In which case, I have an idea. Why don't you meet me at the office in an hour and I'll make sure to get some food in? I know how inconvenient this is and you have my apologies but, like I've said, I wouldn't have called if it wasn't necessary.'

'I suppose…if it's urgent…'

'Great. See you there in an hour. French, Indian or Italian?'

'Sorry?'

'Choice of food. French, Indian or Italian?'

'I honestly am not fussy.'

'One of your many endearing traits and probably why we work so well together. Leave it to me. I'll make sure neither of us goes hungry.'

At which point he cut the call and, for a few seconds, Grace stared at the phone in her hand before leaping to her feet to hurriedly tidy the kitchen and then get changed into something…

Into what?

Her usual outfit? Knee-length skirt and tidy blouse and *I-mean-business* flat black pumps?

On a Friday evening?

Reluctantly Grace chose jeans and a slim-fitting tee shirt and an old tan bomber jacket she had inherited from her mother, just in case it was cold by the time she left.

For once, she had no idea what she was letting herself in for. Nico, for all his colourful love life and ever-changing parade of beauties, was utterly predictable when it came to his working life.

Nothing ever came in the way of it. The women he dated were confined to life outside his cutting-edge offices and on the rare occasions when one of them had ventured where angels feared to tread, she had learnt that such errors of judgement were not to be repeated.

So what was this about? How could it be *yes and no* when it came to work? He wasn't a *yes and no* man.

It felt strange to be hurrying to the office, dressed down, without her stern work clothes in place, as secure and as reassuring as a chastity belt, keeping her imagination in check and reminding her of the differences between them.

Over the past few weeks, the lines between them had taken a knocking and while she knew that Nico was oblivious to those subtle changes, it wasn't so for her.

She noticed every time the conversation between them veered even slightly off-piste. He had asked her, in passing, whether she had been out with anyone else and how could she refuse to answer when that door had been opened?

If she had thought that being more open might have ushered in a more normal state of affairs for her, then she had been mistaken, because closing some of the distance had only made her all the more conscious of her attraction to him and of the pointlessness of it.

What he saw as normal office banter, she saw as a threat to her composure. When he perched on the edge of the desk and asked her casually about her weekend, all she could feel was the racing of her pulse as she tried to ward off the suffocating effect his proximity had on her.

So right now, jeans and a tee shirt and a bomber jacket felt all wrong as she pushed open the glass doors to the building, flashing her official card to the security guard, who knew her anyway and just smiled and waved her through.

Nico was waiting when, exactly an hour after he had called her, she pushed open the door to the office.

He had never seen her here, in these surroundings, in anything other than a suit of some kind so he did a double take at the jeans and tee shirt and the old leather jacket slung over her shoulder.

In fact, for a few seconds, he was lost for words. First a flowered dress with strappy sleeves and now faded jeans and a bomber jacket…?

How much more wrong could he have been about her? More to the point, how much more egotistic could he have been in vaguely thinking that when she wasn't within the confines of these office walls, she somehow remained prim, prissy and mysteriously clad in skirts and blouses?

'Good timing.' He stood up and flexed his muscles, easing away some of the tension that had been building ever since the call from his father. 'The food has just arrived. We can eat and…talk.'

He strolled towards the floor-to-ceiling window and remained there for a few seconds, watching as she ditched the bomber jacket, admiring the ballet-like gracefulness of her movements, so much more notice-able in what she was wearing. The faded jeans fitted her like a second skin, emphasising the length and slimness of her legs, and the tee shirt clung invitingly to breasts that were just about a handful.

He had to tear his eyes away, tell himself to focus.

He nodded towards the sitting area that adjoined the office, where the food was still in neat black and gold containers, bearing the crest of one of the go-to restaurants he used when he wanted food brought in for him.

She preceded him through to the little table and hovered, waiting for him to take the lead and no nearer to figuring out what exactly was going on.

'Italian,' Nico said, settling into the chair facing hers, separated by the squat, rectangular glass-and-chrome table between them.

He flipped open the lids of the containers and nodded to her to help herself.

'There was no need for anything fancy, Nico, or anything at all.'

'Least I could do for dragging you out of your house.'

'You still have to tell me what this is all about.'

For once, Nico's natural assertiveness abandoned him and Grace saw a shadow of hesitation. Her curiosity was piqued. Hesitant was the very last thing her boss ever was. A charging rhino displayed more hesitancy than Nico Doukas.

For a few seconds he didn't answer, just took his time dishing out food and then strolling to the concealed fridge where he kept several bottles of wine for clients. He lifted one and she shook her head.

'I'll never be able to concentrate if I have a glass of wine,' she said politely.

'In which case, you'll have to excuse me if I don't follow suit,' he returned wryly as he poured himself a glass and handed her some water. 'I got a call from my father today.' There was a dark flush etched across his sharp cheekbones and Grace stilled and looked at him with a slight frown.

'Is everything all right? Is it your mother?' she asked quietly, already braced for bad news. He had gone to Greece previously to visit them and she knew that his mother had recently had a bout of ill health. Nico rarely touched on the subject of his parents, but she had seen from the look in his eyes when he had told her of the reason for his week away from the desk that he cared deeply about them. When he had returned, it had been business as normal. Her enquiries about how things were with them both had been met with a polite but unembroidered response and she had got the message that that was an area that he wished to keep to himself.

He put so much out there in the public domain and yet so much was carefully concealed.

'My mother is doing well. Improving by the day but still in need of rest after her operation. No, this is about my uncle.'

'You have *an uncle*?'

'It's not that unusual,' Nico said wryly, 'although the use of the present tense doesn't apply in this instance. My uncle died two days ago and, with my mother still recovering, it's fallen upon me to wrap up his affairs.'

'Nico, I don't understand. I'm, of course, very sorry for your loss, but I'm not sure why I had to rush over here on a Friday evening so that you could tell me this.'

Grace was genuinely confused, yet there was a thread of pleasure underlying her bewilderment.

Had she been the first person he'd chosen to call to share this heartbreaking news with?

She remembered how he had rushed to save her from herself and from Victor when he'd correctly clocked that she'd been in an uncomfortable situation. It had been an intuitive reaction. He had even dispatched his own date so that he could mount the stallion and charge to her rescue!

Did he actually care about her on some level that he wasn't conscious of?

It was completely taboo to be thinking like this, but Grace couldn't stop a shiver of forbidden pleasure from racing through her, like a dangerously addictive drug.

Belatedly she remembered Cecily and the eternal search for Mr Right. There had been so many times when optimism had trumped reality. Too many to count. Grace had always had to pick up the pieces when the bubble had burst and her mother had finally accepted that the guy who'd paid her tons of compliments and taken her out for two meals wasn't going to be putting a ring on her finger. It had taken her even longer to realise that she was better off without that particular Mr Right. It had always been a long, slow process and watching hope die had taught Grace a thousand and one life lessons.

Never, in all the time she had harboured her secret crush, had she felt herself in jeopardy.

How could you be in any danger of *anything* when you were having secret fantasies about some guy who never spared you a second glance?

Except when asking whether you'd checked the company accounts for his most recent takeover. Or sorted those supply chains that were screwed up because of a boat being docked too long somewhere too far away because of bad weather.

So she'd woken up and realised that the secret fantasies had had their day and the time had come to try and find the real thing, a real, living, breathing guy with whom she could have a complete relationship. She'd accepted that Nico had been a useful, innocent distraction at a time when her life had been in turmoil.

But everything had been turned on its head and nothing was what it had been before. He had crashed through all the red tape and *Keep Out* signs and now...

Her awareness was so close to the surface. She could sense the shift between them even though she'd done her best to return to where they had been before. When he came close to her, she could feel a thread of electric charge pushing between them, a low vibration that meant she was on red-hot alert every single second of every single day she was in his company.

This was no longer an innocent distraction.

Now her harmless crush felt dangerous.

Now, for the first time, Grace felt as though she was being called upon to test all those life lessons she thought she had learnt from her mother's adventures.

She reined in her thoughts and returned to the matter at hand. 'And why can't your dad handle the situation? I know your mother's recovering but surely the funeral arrangements can largely be done over the phone? From what I've seen of your mother when she's been over here, I don't think she's going to go to pieces if she's left on her own for a couple of hours. Do you? When they were over before I remember her telling him that there was no need for him to follow her everywhere… and how could he possibly be interested in what was happening in ladies' fashionwear at Selfridges.'

Nico smiled, momentarily diverted as he thought about the dynamics between his parents.

If his uncle had gone off the rails, his father had done completely the opposite.

It had taken the joker in the pack to produce the King of Spades, needed to assume control and get things on track.

Maybe his father would have been the man he had become whatever the circumstances, but maybe Sander had done that. There had been a vacancy for someone strong to take the reins and his father had stepped up to the plate because, frankly, he hadn't had much choice.

He had chosen his wife with his head. He had put his emotions to one side and opted for a woman from the same elevated, wealthy background who knew the ropes. No room for demanding hysterics, just calm support where it was needed. He couldn't remember a single instance of his parents rowing. When his father had worked late, his mother had patiently been there, her role to take the pressure off and not pile it on by demanding he focus on *her*.

From his own experience, Nico could appreciate how important it was to marry a suitable woman.

You could have affairs with women who wanted to be the centre of attention, but those were affairs.

If he had ever thought that his father's life might have been too regimented, his own fling all those years ago, when he had been prepared to give love and emotions a go, had taught him otherwise. Eva had wanted all of him. She had demanded proof of his devotion and insisted that work be delegated to the back burner. She was either everything to him or nothing at all. But at the helm of his own burgeoning business, which had demanded many long nights and gruelling commitments, Nico had come to realise that he was just too imbued with a sense of responsibility to ditch everything because a woman needed him to prove himself.

Now he accepted that he was a workaholic and, as such, when he decided to move from having flings to settling down, it would be with a woman who had no illusions about what she was letting herself in for.

A lifetime of having everything money could buy. In return, he would get a dependable woman who would accept his priorities and live with them.

His parents loved one another. It had been a good relationship and a wise choice because crazy emotions hadn't been in charge, just common sense and goodwill on both sides.

From that had sprung just the sort of marital stability that worked.

'I forgot about that. Of course, in normal circumstances my father could deal with all of this. Unfortunately, things are a little different in this case and I've asked you here urgently because this involves you. I will have to carry on working while I'm dealing with Sander's situation, and I'll need you there in a working capacity. I can't afford to go off radar for a week. Aside from which, there will be certain business matters to handle when we get there. Not extensive but there'll be business to be done and you know how my work suffers when you're not around. I need you by my side or I become a nervous wreck and end up comfort eating.' He shot her a disarming grin.

Of course, this boiled down to work, Grace thought bracingly. What else? Had she really believed that Nico had suddenly called her up because he'd wanted someone to talk to? To share with?

'There? Where's *there*?'

'The Bahamas,' he said, sitting back in the chair, having finished everything on his plate. 'And the reason this couldn't wait is because time is of the essence. I hope your passport is in date because you'll need to book me on the first flight to Nassau tomorrow and you can follow on Monday. I realise this might come as a bolt from the blue but…any questions?'

CHAPTER FOUR

ANY QUESTIONS?

Two and a half days later, Grace wondered how it was that with so many questions, she had managed to ask precious few.

Caught on the back foot, she had gaped at him in astounded silence while he had filled the yawning space with a detailed explanation of why, exactly, he needed her there.

The deals that were coming to fruition, the due diligence needed on several takeovers, and she had to be at ground zero to handle the paperwork because the damned lawyers were prone to chopping and changing...not to mention the running of the family business, with difficulties cropping up because of supply-chain issues. And then there would be some business stuff of his uncle's to sort out. Nothing much, but it would still have to be done. He couldn't do any of that without her, he had concluded in a voice that had left her in no doubt that a negative response would not be countenanced.

She had thought of Tommy and demanded to know just how long the trip would last.

'Why?' Nico had queried, eyebrows raised. 'Have

you got unavoidable plans if it takes five days instead of four?'

'Are you saying we'll be away for four days?'

'I'm saying,' he had responded in an inflexible voice, the voice of the boss who paid the bills, 'that we'll be away for just as long as it takes to conclude this business. My father would have gone himself but he is in no place to leave my mother convalescing on her own. The burden falls to me, and you'll be coming because you work for me and I need to carry on working over there.'

Nico had never mentioned an uncle. Why would he? Grace supposed. It was none of her business. But what was his uncle doing out in the Bahamas? Why wasn't he part of the family business either in Greece or here in London?

Nico hadn't volunteered an explanation but he had softened enough to ask, 'Why are you concerned about the length of time we'll be gone? I can guarantee that it won't be longer than five days. I have no desire to be out of London for any longer. If I'm honest, I could do without this intrusion into my working schedule, but needs must.'

He'd shrugged and when his dark eyes had rested on her face she'd seen him thinking, *Why so concerned about how long this will take?*

'Has another Mr Internet stepped into the picture?' he'd asked silkily and Grace had glared at him, which had given him his answer without him having to ask further. She realised how effective that had been on shutting the conversation down and making sure she didn't ask any more questions.

The following day, she had duly booked the flights

and he had texted to tell her that there was no need for a hotel. Flights sorted, he would deal with the rest of the details. She should just get her things together and he would ensure all the necessary protocol to get her to him on the Monday evening.

So here she was now, after an uneventful and comfortable trip to Nassau.

The seat-belt sign was going on and the captain was interrupting the film she had been watching to tell them how close they were to landing and what the weather was doing and what the local time was.

It had been a long time since Grace had been on a plane. A long time since she had had any real holiday to speak of. Ibiza with three friends five years ago felt like a lifetime away. Since then, her money had been directed at all the costly expenditure associated with looking after her brother, the buying of the house, the tailoring of the space to suit his needs and of course the private therapy sessions. None of it came cheap and while her own life had largely been on hold, the prospect of going anywhere abroad on a holiday had been vanishingly slim.

Ever since Nico had left her in the office, leaving behind him a state of low-level panic at this departure from her prized comfort zone, she had been busy fretting. Fretting about the fact that she would be with him in such different surroundings. Fretting about how that was going to feel. Fretting about the clothes to be packed, about an itinerary she couldn't quite manage to work out. There would be no comforting office environment in which to feel safe. The barriers between them had already taken a bit of a knock and this drastic change to the normal routine made her feel uneasy and apprehensive.

Now, though, as she snapped shut the seat belt and gazed down out of the window, she was infused with a bubble of excitement.

The plane dipped and she was offered a view of lush green set against a backdrop of startling aquamarine. Trees and mountains rising from an ocean of tranquil turquoise and, even from dizzying heights, the water was such a dazzling blue that it took her breath away.

Nico had told her that her only responsibility was to book the flight for them both.

She'd assumed that he had contacts on the island. If his uncle had lived there, for whatever reason, then he would probably know people, people who would be able to arrange accommodation for them far more satisfactorily than she could.

As the plane rolled to a stop, slowly positioning itself in front of the airport terminal, she wondered what this accommodation was going to look like.

Who was going to meet her at the airport? Would Nico be there? The thought of him made her heart beat a little faster.

The heat struck her with force as she stepped out of the plane. This wasn't the polite summer sun she had left behind in London. This was tropical heat, still and fierce and smelling different somehow. She breathed in and that bubble of excitement swelled a little bit more and she had to sternly remind herself that this wasn't a holiday. This was about work.

She was wearing a pair of light cotton trousers and a loose linen shirt. Within seconds of being in the blasting heat, a couple of minutes out in the open between the plane and the airport, she could feel herself perspiring. It was joyful to be inside the cold terminal. Not knowing quite what to expect, she was surprised when she was ushered through a fast lane to exit immigration and security in record time. She'd brought one bag into which she had crammed her usual summer wardrobe of light suits along with a couple of summery dresses and some sandals. Work-ready gear for a tropical island. She was already beginning to suspect that her choices might not have been the most sensible, given the weather.

There was no Nico waiting for her but instead a young, smiling man in a uniform of Bermuda shorts and an open-necked shirt who leapt towards her, flashing identification and a personal letter from Nico explaining that he couldn't make it to the airport, but giving her details of her onward journey.

It was all a blur. Grace was tired yet energised at the same time. Outside the airport, the noises and the sounds and the sights were all so unfamiliar that she could have been on another planet. Everything was in Technicolour, the shimmering tarmac of the road against the brightest of lush green of trees and bushes and weeds and flowers growing in abundance wherever a spot of earth could hold a root. Cars came and went, as did people, coming and leaving, pulling bags and hugging and saying goodbye, a riot of activity against a backdrop of tropical splendour.

She gaped. Where were they going? Where would she be staying?

Not here, not on the main island. She discovered that soon enough because as they walked Curtis told her that he would be taking her to a private airfield, where she would get an island hopper that would take her to one of the smaller islands.

'Mr Nico's there, waiting for you. He tells me you can stay the night in Nassau, fly tomorrow. You want to do that?'

But Grace was eager to finish the trip without interruption and that seemed to have been the message conveyed to Curtis from Nico because there was an acceptance that she would accompany him, which she did.

All her senses were accosted by the shimmering beauty of her surroundings. She could smell the salty sea in the air and she didn't know where to look as she followed Curtis to another part of the airfield, towards a small bank of island hoppers.

'Where are we going?' she asked breathlessly as she followed him to one of the tiny planes, where a pilot was waiting to take off.

'Another of the islands.' He flashed her a broad, proud smile. 'Plenty islands here. Very beautiful. Mr Nico waiting for you on one of them. You going to be very happy when you get there, Miss Grace.'

Grace smiled back and wondered if she should tell him that she was there for work reasons, but chose not to, and follow-up conversation was lost, anyway, in the hustle and bustle of leaving the airport.

It was a brief flight, bumpy as the little plane barely skimmed the top of the clouds, and from her vantage point she could gaze down at an expanse of aquamarine ocean, so clear that she could discern the shapes of rocks and reefs under the surface. The occasional boat dotted the surface, the interruption of islands like pearls strung into a necklace surrounded by water.

That excitement again, reminding her of just how much she had sacrificed over the years.

It had been a gradual build-up. She had had her childhood snatched from her simply because Cecily had been an irresponsible parent. Her mother had cornered the market on having fun, and in the process had deprived her of her own chances to have it. From latch-key kid, she had assumed responsibilities way beyond the pale from far too young an age, and just when she could have really begun to enjoy her life, to live it free from having to be the resident caretaker, her brother had had his accident and, shortly after, her mother had left the country.

And in her gaily departed wake, amidst the flurry of hugs and kisses and dabbed tears, Grace had quietly resigned herself to the door being shut on her dreams of breaking free.

Someone would have to look out for Tommy and her mother wasn't going to suddenly start auditioning for the Mother of the Year award when she'd spent her entire life turning down the role.

So this—however apprehensive she felt about the change to her routine—felt like a holiday and made her heart soar.

Too soon the little plane was dipping down and the pilot was telling her to make sure she was fastened in.

'These runways are small.' He turned to grin at her. 'Sometimes you have to screech to a stop before you hit sea.'

'That's comforting.' Grace laughed but he wasn't

kidding and the shriek of brakes as the aircraft shuddered to a stop made her clutch the arms of her seat and squeeze shut her eyes.

She opened them to see Nico.

He was walking towards the plane and she wondered whether it was her imagination or whether a couple of days in the sun had turned him an even deeper shade of bronze.

He looked impossibly sexy. His black, too long hair had curled a little in the heat and he was wearing a pair of dark sunglasses, which made it impossible for her to see his eyes. He was in the outfit of nearly everyone else she'd seen—slim, tailored pale shorts and a tee shirt— and as he stopped by the plane, he shoved the shades up and squinted into the sun towards her.

Grace pulled back from the window. The pilot was already opening the door and a burst of hot air flooded in as she quickly scrambled to her feet, reaching for her bag and holding it as close to her as a talisman as she carefully dipped out of the plane and gingerly walked down the metal steps.

On the last step, Nico reached out for her hand, a polite gesture that still sent a shock wave of heat through her.

'Here in one piece, I see,' he murmured, sunglasses back in place, which made her feel immediately disadvantaged.

'The arrangements went very smoothly.' Grace looked away and ran her finger under the collar of her shirt, aiming for some much-needed ventilation.

Looking at her, Nico had to stop himself from bursting into laughter. Honestly. What on earth was she wearing?

Surely she would have twigged that a tropical island was no place for starchy work clothes in which she would be reduced to a puddle of sweat the very second she was exposed to the fierce heat? He shoved his hands into the pockets of his shorts and politely made some chit-chat about flying and aeroplane meals as they headed towards the small SUV parked at an angle in the distance.

Nevertheless, he couldn't resist saying, as they approached the car, 'You must be hot.' He slid his eyes across to her and saw the delicate blush. 'I'm very much hoping,' he murmured gravely, 'that this isn't going to be your standard dress code.'

'I'm not at all hot,' Grace lied.

'We're not going to be in the formal setting of an office,' Nico continued, noting the way she blew the hair from her face and continued fiddling with the collar of her prissy shirt, 'so you're allowed to wear more informal clothing.'

'I thought we were going to be working while we were here.'

'We are, but not in the conventional setting of an office. Of course, the hotel has somewhere we can work but...' Nico paused, opened the door of the four-wheel drive, flung her case in the back seat and sauntered round to the driver's side. He turned to her before starting the engine, his hand loose on the steering wheel. 'But the hotel isn't quite what I had imagined.'

He turned on the engine and accelerated out of the airfield. No air conditioning. The windows were open and as the car bumped up speed Grace's hair was blown back by the warm air.

'What do you mean?'

'I mean...' Nico shrugged, eyes on the road as he manoeuvred the car away from the airport and along the steaming tarmac framed with lush green, beyond which was the flat blue sea '... I was expecting something slightly...bigger and more...how shall I put it? More...tourist-oriented than what confronted me.'

'But how could you not know what to expect? Haven't you been here before?'

Nico took his time answering. When he was growing up, mention of his black sheep uncle had always been accompanied by disapproving frowns and muttered oaths. He knew the story of Sander as much as everyone else did. A waste of space whose vices had come close to threatening the survival of the family empire. A man so addicted to self-indulgence and so willing to fight tooth and nail to feed his habits that extreme measures had been taken to limit the damage he could do. To get rid of him.

Raised on a diet of self-discipline and the mantra that doing the right thing involved making sure the company was never jeopardised because it was bigger than just the Doukas family, Nico found everything his uncle had represented personally unacceptable.

Yes, Nico enjoyed a playboy lifestyle. Yes, he enjoyed women and he enjoyed sex, but when it came to the family holdings and his own considerable empire he had always known that his duty lay in sober considerations. There would be no room for anything other than the path his own father had followed. He would wed a suitable wife and emotions would never be allowed to destroy what had been built.

Secretly, Nico had a deeply buried fear that his own

personality was far more like his uncle's than he cared to admit, which made it all the more imperative that he maintain self-control.

He slanted assessing eyes at his companion in the passenger seat because she had asked a valid question.

It was ironic that, while she knew so much about the way he worked and, frankly, the person he was, she knew so little about the actual nuts and bolts of his life. Although, as she had rightly pointed out, he kept to himself exactly what he didn't want the rest of the world to know. When he thought about it, she was different from any of the other women who had entered and departed his life. Actually, she was *very* different, because she actually knew him, with the kind of intangible familiarity that came when you worked alongside someone for a long time. She could practically read his mind when it came to certain things!

But when it came to the details of his personal life? Those were closely guarded. Nico had long ago worked out that to maintain control of your life where it mattered, it was important that you let nothing go. Start opening up and things stood a good chance of unravelling like a ball of wool.

However, here they were and his secretary, until recently a closed book, would inevitably end up knowing something of his life whether he felt inclined to impart the information or not.

Nico told himself that it didn't matter. Grace was his secretary. She wasn't his lover. Lovers clung to confidences, read meaning into them, hoped for more. As his secretary, she would listen, skim over the personal

and focus on the practical, namely the business of sort-
ing out the hotel along with everything else.

*Except things had changed between them...hadn't
they?*

Nico shrugged off that fleeting thought.

They were driving slowly, the winding road fringed
with trees and foliage, swaying palms tilting up to the
blue sky, houses interrupting the green landscape.

He'd only been on the island for a day and a half, but
he already knew how to get around it because it was
small and the main road was the artery from which
smaller roads meandered off into the hills.

He took one of those side roads now.

At the corner, in front of a patchwork of flimsy
houses, a dark-skinned woman was sitting in front of
a stall that was bursting with vibrant colours of fresh
fruit and vegetables.

Ahead, the broad, smooth road turned into a more
winding track, although it was still possible for two cars
to pass one another. Not that the island was bustling
with traffic. The small town was busy, with a hum-
ming central market, but away from that the tributary
of roads, winding through little pockets of houses and
shops and all leading to beaches of some sort, were
largely quiet.

'I've never been to this part of the world before,' Nico
admitted heavily. 'Why would I?'

'But surely if your uncle lived here... I mean, it's
so beautiful...' She slid a sidelong glance at him and
smiled. 'If I had a close relative living in a place like
this, you'd have to lock me up and throw away the key

to stop me from flying over and demanding accommodation at least once a year.'

Nico burst out laughing. 'I can't relax where there's nothing to do,' he admitted. 'Lying on a beach staring at the sea isn't my thing.'

'I can't think of anything better,' Grace mused. She shrugged. 'But I guess to each their own. Why have you never been here? Aside from not liking holidays that aren't action-packed? Didn't you want to visit your uncle? Or did he prefer to go to Greece to see your family? What brought him over here in the first place?'

'Long story.'

'And one you don't want to tell? Nico, it doesn't matter.'

Nico glanced across to her, but she was turned away, her head slightly tilted to appreciate the warm breeze against her face, her eyes half closed as she gazed out at the stupendous passing scenery.

She hadn't pushed for details and suddenly he felt an urge to do more than just volunteer scant information because, really, what business was his background story to her?

For once, slamming the door on a question that breached his boundary lines felt like overkill.

Besides, did she care one way or another if he answered? Then he thought of that simmering spark that had been lit under them weeks before, the spark she'd made sure to douse.

Maybe she did care...maybe more than those cool eyes revealed...

There was a soft smile tugging her lips as she enjoyed the heat and the sprawling, lush beauty.

He swerved off the road, bumped the four-wheel drive to a stop on the grassy verge.

'What are you doing?' Grace's head snapped round and she stared at him in some consternation.

'Two things. First...' He reached past her to open her door and felt the slight brush of her body against his arm. He impatiently dismissed the sharp physical awareness that accompanied this involuntary touch. 'First...this is a good lookout point to see something of the island from above.' He nodded to a bench that was tilted at a precarious angle a little further down the verge. He slung his long, muscular body out of the Jeep but then promptly turned so that he was looking at her, one arm resting casually on the open door as he leant down towards her. 'I found this spot accidentally when I stopped off to take a call. Come have a look. You'll be impressed. I guarantee that.'

Grace obligingly stepped out of the car. Despite the re-freshing breeze, fragrant with the scent of the colourful flowers by the roadside, the heat was still a solid wall that burnt through the trousers and the too thick blouse. She fanned herself and walked to the bench, which was perfectly solid once she gingerly perched on it, despite outward appearances.

'It's so quiet here. It's like life slowed right down,' she murmured, dutifully looking down and drawing breath at the spectacular scenery. She had been acutely conscious of Nico perching next to her on the bench, the heat radiating from his body, the muscular brown thighs so close to her, the way dark hair curled around the dull matt of his watch strap.

Not now. As she stared down, all she could see was the splendid turquoise of ocean, glittering in the distance, bright blue against dark green…the sway of upright palm trees and the little roads intersecting the landscape like veins and arteries, bordered with small houses, some brightly painted, some whitewashed.

'Small island with not that many inhabitants. The tourist trade is booming because there are a lot of people who want this sort of final escape but, even with that, it's still a very peaceful place. Must have to do with the arduous business of actually getting here. Plane and then another plane or a boat across. A lot of people prefer the one-stop destination.'

Grace glanced across at him and shivered at the aquiline perfection of his profile.

Her eyes drifted to his legs, stretched out in front, so brown with a sprinkling of dark hair that made her imagination take flight as she pictured what the rest of his body might look like. She quickly looked away and fanned herself in a desultory attempt to cool down.

'What was the second thing you wanted to say to me?'

She felt his eyes on her as he shifted, turning to face her, his hands clasped behind his head.

The tee shirt rode up and she glimpsed a slither of flat, hard belly.

'You asked me why I've never been here. You're curious and I don't blame you. I've never been here because my uncle was banished here,' Nico said quietly. 'Exiled from doing damage to the family company because of his bad habits.'

Grace inhaled sharply and turned to look at him.

Their eyes collided but she didn't look away. This was absolutely the first time Nico had ever volunteered anything remotely revealing about himself. The ground seemed to shift a little under her feet.

'What do you mean?' She kept her voice neutral even though curiosity was running riot inside her.

'Sander was a weak man,' Nico said flatly. 'No self-control. He enjoyed drink, drugs and women and he allowed his enjoyment to take over his life, to kill all sense of responsibility. He couldn't give a damn whose lives got destroyed because he was too busy squandering his share of the company that had been left to him when my grandfather died.' When Nico looked at her, his dark eyes brooding, unforgiving, it was to find her gazing straight back at him, her interest calm and modulated, encouraging without giving him the impression that she was desperate to hear more.

'Were it not for my father, God knows he would have ended up dragging the company into the dirt. If it was just a question of Sander on a path to his own self destruction, then the solution might have been less dramatic, but the fact is that my uncle's self-destruction would have involved more than just himself.'

'So your father...?'

'Annexed him, having spent years picking up the pieces. Made it worse that Sander was the older by five years. Of course, he had more than enough money to do whatever he wanted, but the flow of money was controlled. The rift caused was papered over in time but, as brothers, the connection had been broken for ever. I'm not sure whether my parents ever came over here at all. Possibly they communicated by email. I don't know.'

'How old were you when all of this happened?'

'Very young.'

'How sad.' Grace meant it. She thought of her own brother and the loyalty that was so deeply rooted inside her that there was no way she could ever *annex* him. It very much sounded as though Nico was fashioned in the same mould as his father, ruthless when it came to protecting the interests of the family company.

For a split second Grace was tempted to confide, and she pulled herself back from the brink before reckless impulse could take over.

Nico might be sharing this with her now, but it was because they were here and the backstory was tied up to a bigger picture.

Would he welcome a sudden sharing of confidences? Would he expect his cool, calm secretary to start pouring her heart out? No. He'd be appalled.

'There's no room for superfluous emotion when other people's lives are involved.' He paused and said, with a hitch in his usually composed voice, 'My father told me that one of the guys who worked for my uncle lost everything because Sander had dissolved that branch of the organisation for no other reason than to fund a gambling debt. The guy committed suicide.'

'My goodness!'

'Lessons learnt when it comes to the weakness of allowing emotion to run your life,' Nico told her darkly. 'My father made sensible choices. Necessary sacrifices.' He shrugged and half smiled as though slightly embarrassed by confidences he was unaccustomed to sharing. 'At any rate, this all happened a long time ago. Sander has been here doing his own thing and this is the first time I've had any real idea of how he's spent the years since he disappeared from Greece.'

Grace didn't say anything. She thought that tangled in that simple statement, woven into what Nico had just told her, one thing emerged very clearly.

Not only did Nico not know his uncle, but neither did he respect him. His uncle had been ruled by excess and that, for Nico, was abhorrent.

Was that why, underneath the easy charm, there was a core of icy steel that made him so inaccessible? Had it been drummed into him from an early age that self-control was the only thing that mattered?

Grace wondered whether it was that very self-control that made it possible for Nico to have his flings without danger of involvement.

Did he ambush his own chances at having a lasting relationship by dating women he knew would always be temporary visitors in his life? While he bided his time for the woman he would eventually marry? A woman who would be happy to take second place to his work and forgive him his inability to form any close bond? Grace mentally wished this poor, hypothetical woman good luck with choosing a life like that.

She might have developed an inconvenient crush on her handsome and charismatic boss, but there was no way she could ever be in danger of harbouring any deeper, darker feelings for him because she was smart enough to realise that a guy like him, in the end, was the antithesis of everything she looked for in a for-ever guy.

She averted her eyes and returned her gaze to the splendid vista in front of her. 'But weren't you curious to find out what happened to him?'

'He was sidelined and that was sufficient. Get too bogged down in detail and chances are you never surface. That said, I assumed Sander was involved in a more comprehensive business than it turns out.' Nico glanced at her and grinned. 'No idea why, to be honest. Possibly because over the years he supposedly straightened himself out and the hotel, from all accounts, was actually making a decent profit. Now I'm here, I've discovered that the hotel is rather more of an…ah… upmarket boarding house and the money lies in the bar adjoining it and a fishing boat business, which has held its own over the years.'

'What is your role in…um…this? Are you going to dispose of the business?'

'What else?' Nico shrugged. 'It's of no use to me and I certainly don't envisage my father wanting anything to do with it. At any rate, that's where we'll be staying so I hope you're not expecting much by way of luxury because if you are, then you're going to be mightily disappointed.'

Grace returned his stare with sudden amusement. 'Now who's misreading who?' She half smiled. 'Do you really see me as a snob? I don't care where we stay. We're here to do a job and, as you've assured me, we won't be here for longer than a handful of days. I think I'm more than capable of staying in an upmarket boarding house for the duration.' She stood up and stretched and then waited a few seconds before Nico followed suit. 'When we get there, what's the plan? I'm very happy to shower, change and begin work immediately.'

'I'm sure you are,' Nico murmured with just the

slightest hint of laughter in his voice. 'You're certainly dressed for it but no. I think we can start work tomorrow. For the rest of the day? You could always try and relax…'

CHAPTER FIVE

IT BECAME VERY clear over the next twenty-four hours just how dismissive Nico was of the uncle he had never known.

Naturally, in the process of winding up the hotel and the various business concerns Sander had built over the years, he had had to consult with various members of staff. Any mention of his uncle from any employee was met with polite, stony silence unless it pertained to business. Fond reminiscing was shut down at source. Grace wondered whether Nico was even capable of seeing that or whether his inherited disdain for Sander Doukas ran so deep that he wasn't aware of his prejudices.

He would begin the process of finding a buyer for the various concerns, he had assured Steve Donnelly, the smiling, affable manager of the hotel who also seemed to fill a number of varied roles, including captain of the small six-boat fishing rental and head of the hotel kitchen. No one would lose their jobs if he could help it but, of course, that wasn't going to be in his remit. He could only do so much.

Grace thought that if things continued going at the speed they were currently going, then everything would be wrapped up in a couple of days because the nuts and bolts of whatever deals were agreed with potential buyers would be handled by lawyers, who were already on standby.

And several of those potential buyers, Nico had briefed her only an hour ago, had already been found.

Now, sitting here on the wooden veranda of the hotel, waiting for Nico, who was going to be her dinner companion on her first real night here, she remembered her excitement when the plane had begun to descend to Nassau, with a little twinge of sadness.

Her only view of the sea had been in passing, as she had strolled out of the hotel at midday to breathe in the sun and the salt and the heady scent of the tropical blooms that surrounded the hotel.

In the distance a marching army of upright coconut trees was starkly silhouetted against the deep purple, indigo and navy blue of a twilit sky.

The 'upmarket boarding house' could not have been lovelier, as far as Grace was concerned. Nico might favour the impersonal opulence of a five-star modern hotel with its cold marble, glass and granite, but, for her, this place was wonderful. It was small, with maybe a dozen rooms at the most, all tiny suites, some of them self-contained and positioned in between coconut trees, others within the main body of the hotel. Each was quirky and different, but all were tropical in flavour, with bamboo and rattan furnishings and paintings by local artists.

There were mosquito nets around the four-poster beds and overhead fans instead of air conditioning and always the sound of the sea, which was accessible on foot, just a ten-minute walk away.

Not that Grace had had the chance to explore yet.

Probably wouldn't because it was obvious that Nico couldn't wait to clear off as fast as possible.

The veranda was broad, big enough for clusters of chairs and sofas and little tables. With the business on the brink of being sold, the only visitors were the ones currently wrapping up their stay, so the hotel was only half full.

Bookings had been halted.

Right now, there were a few people further along the veranda, sipping cocktails and chatting in low voices.

Grace was barely aware of them. She was so captivated by the lazy stirring of the coconut trees and the quiet insistent hush of waves gently breaking, ebbing and flowing, that Nico's voice made her jump and she spun round to see him standing behind her.

He was nursing a drink and in a pair of light-coloured trousers and a black collared polo shirt.

He looked effortlessly and unfairly impressive as he stared down at her, his face unreadable because the light from the hotel was behind him.

'You're still in work clothes.'

She'd certainly come prepared to work because the travelling attire had been replaced, today, by a similar uniform of linen trousers and a blouse neatly tucked into the waistband. Buttons firmly done up to the neck.

And here she was now, in yet another pair of trousers and another blouse.

The colour was less regimental but the flavour was still *let's-stick-to-business*.

He grinned, sipped his whisky and sauntered to pull up a chair, sitting down alongside her.

'I'm beginning to feel a little guilty that I haven't packed any of my suits.'

'Ha ha, that's hilarious. These aren't work clothes, Nico.'

'My mistake. At close range, it's hard to see much difference. It's been a long day.' He was still grinning as he signalled to a passing waiter for the drinks menu. 'Time to relax. What do you want to drink?'

'I'll have a…tropical fruit punch,' Grace said.

'With lashings of rum,' Nico tacked on, eyebrows raised with amusement as she predictably began to huff. 'You can't sit here, with the sun settling on the horizon and a balmy breeze blowing, and order a glass of juice.'

'I…'

'Yes, you're here to work, but you're not working now and you deserve to let go after the long day we've had, so I won't hear of you having some squash instead of something long and cold and relaxing. Live a little, Grace.' His eyebrows shot up with barely contained amusement. He wondered which of his outrageous encouragements would get under her skin more and he had no idea why he was so tempted to flirt with her wrath now but watching her all day…had been strangely intoxicating. Something about the way she moved, the oddly prissy clothes, her habit of absently puffing her hair from her forehead and tucking it behind her ears when she was concentrating…

True to form, she had immersed herself in work and

true to form they had worked quietly and efficiently together, building up the blocks for selling the various companies, liaising with local lawyers virtually and arranging meetings for the following day as everything sped ahead, promising an early conclusion to business here.

In the blink of an eye they'd be back in London. She'd be sitting dutifully in front of his desk, going through emails and noting what had to be done on what deal or other he was working on, and gradually that small window through which he had glimpsed something of the *real* Grace Brown would be closed for ever.

'And back to the work clothes that aren't work clothes. Look around you. Bold colours…shorts…flip-flops… It's not the sort of place that screams conference-table dress code.'

Grace felt the sting of embarrassment and hurt prick her eyelids.

She looked away briefly and started when she felt Nico's hand on hers. This time when their eyes met, the lazy, amused smile had left his lips.

'I'm sorry, Grace. Out of order. What you choose to wear and what you choose to drink? Not my business.'

The waiter was approaching with two long cocktails and Nico immediately ordered a glass of fruit juice, but Grace shook her head. His show of sympathy was even more embarrassing than his casual teasing, because that was what it had been. Teasing. Yet somehow it had struck at the very heart of her, had made her feel like a fuddy-duddy, old before her time, and what was worse was the fact that he had a point. That was what life did to a person. That was what *her* life had done to her.

'The cocktail looks wonderful,' she said and the waiter smiled back, flashing white teeth and rattling off a list of enticing ingredients.

'We can eat out here. Appreciate the scenery.' Nico sat back and stared out to the darkening horizon. Fairy lights lit the coconut trees closest to the hotel and beyond the lit trees, darkness was gobbling up everything. The sounds of night insects and frogs and crickets were a background hum, insistent but soothing at the same time.

'It's so beautiful,' Grace murmured. 'Don't you feel…just a little peaceful sitting out here? Doing nothing?'

'I'm thinking about what we need to do tomorrow. Does that count as *doing nothing*?' But he laughed.

Grace relaxed. It was nice because they were both staring out at the same dark landscape and without his eyes on her she felt less edgy, less self-conscious of the fussy outfit she had chosen to wear. The cocktail looked bright and jolly and harmless, but she could feel the alcohol cutting a path through her reserve, loosening her inhibitions. She sneaked a sideways glance at him and shivered. The light filtering between the shadows and the mellow citronella candles on the tables made him look rakish, like a pirate somehow transported onto solid ground. She gulped and swallowed some more of the cocktail.

'Not really.' She smiled. 'It's strange,' she murmured thoughtfully, 'but when I sit here and look around, when I think of the lanterns in the bar and the wooden counter and all the bright colours everywhere, the picture I have of your uncle doesn't tally with the one you told me about…'

She met his steady gaze when he angled his body so that he was looking at her.

'Am I overstepping the mark?' She raised her eyebrows, finished the cocktail and thought that throwing caution to the wind now and again wasn't half as unnerving as she'd always thought. Frankly, the wind had done quite a bit of caution-devouring over the past week or so. Every time, she had given herself a little lecture on climbing back into her box and re-erecting the barriers between them but just at the moment she honestly didn't feel inclined to do that.

'You're full of surprises of late, Grace Brown, and I have to admit that I'm liking this version,' Nico murmured in a voice that sent little tingles through her because it was as soft as a caress.

'Am I?'

Their eyes tangled.

Nico drew in a sharp breath. Surely his perfect secretary wasn't *flirting* with him?

He dismissed that notion before it had time to take root but as he looked at her now he was struck by just how beautiful she was. Not beautiful in the conventional sense. There was no flamboyance about her, just a quiet intelligence that was far more potent.

How had he not seen that before?

Right now, he could feel her eyes feather over him, and his erection was suddenly as stiff as steel, throbbing and demanding, a physical ache that made him want to push his hand over it to still its insistence.

'You've spent a long time keeping the outspoken side of you under wraps...what's responsible for the sudden volte-face?' He studied her face with leisurely curiosity until he noted the faint pink that crept into her cheeks. 'And why do you say that?'

'Sorry?'

'That this place...doesn't fit the image of the man I painted to you... Explain...'

Grace could feel the rum from the cocktail swimming in her veins. When the waiter approached to offer a refill, she nodded. Two cocktails! Tame by most standards for someone her age!

'You described your uncle as someone...unsavoury, I guess. Out of control and on the wrong side of excess, and yet here...' She looked around her to the wooden banister, smooth from the sun and the salty air, and the hammock to the side and the tasteful clusters of chairs and tables. 'It's so tranquil and atmospheric.' She sighed. 'It's enchanting. In my mind I see a guy who loved the hotel he had started from scratch and everything to do with it, including the bar, which is like a proper fisherman's hang-out. All the art on the walls and the furnishings and the rugs...how could anyone be responsible for all this if he was looking at the world from the bottom of a bottle? And the fishing business—it's been very well run, very tailored to make the most of a commercial market...'

'Which isn't to say that his strenuous efforts to ruin his half of the family business didn't justify his exile to this beautiful island. They did. Sander's race down to the bottom of the gutter wasn't just something that affected *him*. He had no qualms about dragging hundreds of employees in his hurtle towards self-destruction. So maybe he came here and managed all this because he knew that he was in the last-chance saloon. He'd already used up his three strikes. The choice must have been stark. Ruin his life here and there would be nowhere left to turn. People have a way of snapping out of things when their wriggle room has run out.'

Grace shrugged. 'I suppose...'

'There's no supposing about it.'

No, there wasn't, she thought. She would have liked to have asked him if that was why he was black and white when it came to separating work from his personal life. Two halves never destined to meet, with his personal life doomed to play second fiddle to making sure nothing jeopardised the business that provided an umbrella for so many people.

'You've gone quiet on me,' Nico said drily. He drained his second cocktail and relaxed back. 'We've come this far, don't leave me hanging on now...'

He was gazing intently at her face, as if he were mesmerised by her. The waiter came and he ordered a cold bottle of wine along with a selection of whatever tapas the chef recommended, and when the waiter left Nico was leaning into her, having swivelled his chair to face hers.

'Or maybe,' Grace said slowly, 'your uncle, with all his bad habits, got here and discovered that this was what was meant to be. He wasn't trapped and left without a choice.'

'Anyone with a shred of common sense would know to resign themselves to the inevitable and make the best of it.'

'It feels like more than that.' Grace looked around her at the warm surroundings, the old hand-worn sheen of the wooden railings, the little lanterns on the scattered tables, which were attracting small, curious insects, the quirky chimes tinkling in the night breeze. 'It feels like a lot of love went into this hotel and the same with the bar. I haven't seen the fishing fleet yet...'

'*Fleet* is a big word...it's making me think of a large-scale operation instead of a handful of seaworthy boats with passable equipment on board.' He held his hands up in mock surrender. 'Or am I being a little dismissive here?'

'Okay, maybe not *fleet*. But I'll bet your uncle developed a liking for getting out on the ocean, for fishing.'

Nico gave that some thought. 'I wouldn't know. My father sorted out the business with his brother, sent him out here and I have no idea why this destination was chosen in the first place, and that was the end of the story. If Sander and my father communicated over the years, then those communications were not revealed to me.'

'So your only version was of a dissolute uncle who had to be removed from the damage to the company he was doing and, thanks to your dad, that was what happened...'

'Of course, dead wood must be dealt with,' Nico said coolly. 'You may think that I'm being harsh but, like I said, in the bigger scheme of things, it was what had to be done.'

'I know,' Grace said gently.

'And...?' Nico shifted.

'And what?' Grace shrugged, aware that the conversation had become dangerously intimate, possibly because the alcohol in the cocktails had gone to her head. She had encroached onto his guarded territory and now she anxiously wondered whether he might take offence.

'And you've started this conversation, so don't suddenly start being shy.' He leant forward, his dark eyes glinting with teasing intent. 'You're not playing coy with me, are you? I've always admired your direct approach, and even more now you've decided to clamber out of your shell and peep over the ramparts.'

'Of course I'm not being *coy*,' Grace scoffed, pulling back a bit because his proximity was bringing her out in a cold sweat.

'Don't worry,' Nico purred. 'I'm not suddenly going to start weeping and wailing if you tell me what you think.' He looked at her shrewdly, head tilted to one side. 'And I won't incarcerate you into a nearby dungeon for the crime of speaking your mind,' he added for good measure.

Something feathered through her, setting off warning sparks even though the conversation was light and unthreatening.

Her heart began to beat faster and she licked her lips as nervous tension ramped up, melding into something else, a stirring of excitement that made her want to reach out and close the small distance between them.

Nico's eyes were locked to hers, and he shifted restlessly as the waiter approached, setting up one of the low tables closer to them so that he could arrange the selection of tapas for their enjoyment.

'Say what you have to say,' he murmured huskily. 'I don't bite. Not unless asked.'

Grace sucked in a sharp breath and her eyes widened as she found herself on shifting sands. His eyes... there was a smoky burn in them that made her felt hot and addled. She sifted her fingers through her hair and reached for a plate and a cloth serviette and one of the tapas only to realise that her hand was shaking.

Telling him what she thought would bring this situation back in hand. He didn't like having his walls breached. If she breached them now, then at least it would burst the suffocating tension threading through her, making her feel as though she'd suddenly been plugged into a live socket. Why should she allow him to have fun at her expense?

His irritation would surely be preferable to...to... *this*, whatever *this* was.

'You must have been young when all of this took place.' She took a bite of one of the pastries, which was filled with delicious curry. Her tongue darted out, licking some of the sauce from the side of her mouth. 'Maybe things seemed straightforward then, but if you look at the same situation now you might see things differently.' Another bite of the tapas. It was moreish. 'Aren't you having any? They're delicious.' She reached for another, and just like that she felt the touch of his finger by her mouth and it was electrifying. She couldn't pull away. She couldn't say anything. All she could do was stare at him as he gently wiped something from her mouth.

'Some sauce at the side of your mouth...'

Grace blushed a furious red and wiped where he had touched with the back of her hand. He'd sat back and was staring at her with brooding eyes.

'You were saying?' he asked. He raked his fingers through his hair and glanced away for a few seconds before gazing at her once again.

What had she been saying? Everything had flown out of her head and she had to think hard to remember. Defusing the situation...that was what she'd been aiming to do before he'd sent her thoughts into frantic meltdown by touching her.

'I was saying...' she cleared her throat and dived for another, less tricky tapas '...maybe your uncle was a little wild then he came here and found whatever it was he'd been looking for. Maybe he went off the rails because he didn't know what he wanted from life but here...he found it. You can tell. There's love here. It's in the furnishings and the food and it's there in all the people who worked for him. So he didn't carry on being dissolute. He changed. People do.' She thought of her mother. 'Sometimes.'

'Maybe.' Nico smiled. 'Maybe you have a point. It's not something I've ever considered.'

'I'm sorry if I overstepped the mark but you did ask me to be honest with you.' Grace stared at his mouth, blinked and then found she couldn't tear her eyes away as he reached for an intricate pastry, making far less of a mess of eating it than she had.

'So I did.'

'I hope you're not angry.'

'You veer from spectacular frankness to fawning

apology. Grace, we've worked alongside one another for years. You're going to have to find a middle ground that allows you to tell me what's on your mind without being wary of somehow angering me. I'm a big boy. I can deal with whatever you have to throw at me.' He flashed her a killer smile.

He didn't look angry and the killer smile was doing all sorts of things to her body. If she'd planned on diverting him away from whatever he was doing that was heating her up by getting under his skin, then she'd misread the situation. Nico wasn't fazed by her probing. He was fired up by it because, as for her, the buffer zone between them had been removed and he was enjoying himself seeing what had been hiding underneath it. She wasn't getting under his skin. She was amusing him. *He* was the one getting under *her* skin because she was taking all of this seriously.

'So tomorrow...' She reached for something else and noticed that the cocktail had been replaced with a glass of chilled wine, which she ignored in favour of the bottled water that had been brought to their table.

'Tomorrow?'

'I know we've covered a lot of ground today...' Grace could feel her cheeks getting pinker and pinker as he continued to look at her with an expression she couldn't quite read, an expression that could have been one hundred per cent business or one hundred per cent inappropriate flirting.

'And you have my sincere apologies for that,' Nico returned, pushing his plate to one side with his finger so that he could earnestly lean towards her, his elbows resting on his knees, his hands loosely linked. 'I managed to get things in motion before you arrived, and I figured it might be a good idea to strike while the iron was hot. Get things wrapped up as fast as I could.'

'The employees must be saddened by everything that's happened.'

'They'll get to keep their jobs. I've made it abundantly clear that there will be no sackings.'

'So everything will stay the way it was?'

'That…' Nico frowned '…is not something I can guarantee but why would that be important? Provided they get to keep their jobs, then it'll simply be a change of scenery, so to speak. Of course, if extensive renovations need to be done then I can always write in a clause that protects jobs for the duration.'

'Have you considered that they may have been attached to your uncle? I was chatting to a couple of the guys yesterday who work in the bar and they've been there for ever because they really cared about Sander.'

'They'll recover.'

'Why do you sound so surprised that I'm even asking about this?'

'Because it's just going to be a change of ownership, Grace. Everything else is…emotionalism and I don't have time for any of that.'

'You're so cold, Nico?'

Nico flushed darkly. 'I'm not cold,' he growled, but then he lightened up and sipped some wine. 'You'd be surprised at the number of women who think just the opposite.'

Grace refused to back down even though the heat rushed through her like a torrent. 'I'm sure there are hundreds of them who think just that and have always been more than happy to let you know,' she countered wryly. 'Haven't I dealt with some of them over the years? Crying down the end of the phone, receiving extravagant flowers...because you've decided that you've had enough of them and it's time for your heat to warm someone else up?'

'I always tell the women I date that my heat has a timeline before it burns out. I don't do permanence and I'm upfront about that, so why would I take responsibility for breaking hearts when they've been duly warned to keep their hearts intact?'

'That's not what I'm talking about, Nico.'

They stared at one another and Grace met his gaze steadily, and, with a barely contained sigh of impatience, eventually he shrugged.

'I know,' he muttered gruffly. He huffed an exaggerated sigh. 'Okay. You win.'

'Sorry?'

He smiled and raised both hands in a gesture of surrender. His smile was so sincere, so oddly boyish that for a few seconds Grace felt the ground move under her feet and she expelled one long, shaky breath. She was seeing behind the façade that could be so charming and yet so remote at the same time. He lowered his eyes and her heart flip-flopped inside her.

'I'll...talk to them. Listen to what they have to say instead of...'

'Treating them like chess pieces to be manoeuvred into place?'

Nico grinned, burst out laughing and then said, with laughter still in his voice, 'Is that how you think I treat people?'

'When it comes to business, yes.'

'Never got chess. I don't think I ever had the patience to sit it out.'

'That's a shame because you're probably a natural.' She could have added that the way he treated women was hardly any different, but she knew he would have been offended because, in his eyes, he was the soul of generosity. He was capable of lavishing everything on the woman he dated and what he'd just said confirmed what she had always suspected. He was a commitment-phobe who entered relationships with no intention of any of those relationships outstaying their welcome, and that was just fine because he was a decent guy who laid his cards on the table from the very start.

But she felt a small sense of victory that he would chat to Sander's employees, who would all have some kind of story to tell, she suspected. It would be a shame if he left with that one-dimensional picture of his uncle still ingrained in his head. She ruefully thought that she might have had a bit of a life, been a bit more selfish with her choices, if she'd been able to see her mother as a one-dimensional figure instead of someone lovable but flawed, a parent in need of parenting herself and with a daughter all too willing to take on the role.

'But we were talking about tomorrow.' Grace returned to the safe topic of work. 'I can transcribe everything discussed at the meetings today and have them ready for you by tomorrow.'

'Very efficient.'

'I can actually head in now and get started?'

'That's efficiency beyond the call of duty, Grace.'

'Isn't that why I'm here?'

'Today was full on. Yes, you're here to work but I'm not a slave driver and I'm guessing that you haven't been to this part of the world before. Have you?'

'Well, no,' Grace answered awkwardly.

'Thought not. So you were asking about tomorrow? Time off.'

'I beg your pardon?'

'You're going to have a little time off to enjoy the island. It's very beautiful.'

Grace smiled slowly, too thrilled by that suggestion to press her case for doing what she was being paid to do.

'I have a driver at hand and at our disposal.'

Her smile slipped a little. 'That sounds wonderful.'

'I need to be in town so we can head off first thing in the morning and I insist above everything else...' he leaned towards her and said in a low, conspiratorial voice '...that you visit some of the shops. The choice might be limited but you should find more suitable attire there.' He leant back and waved one hand. '*Not*,' he stressed with vigour, 'that I'm telling you what to wear. Like I said, far be it from me to dictate your choice of clothing. That would be downright tyranny. But if you've just come equipped with stuff you'd wear to work in London on a mild summer day, then you're going to be very uncomfortable in this heat while we're here. And before you say anything...it's all on the company. After all, you're only here because of me.'

CHAPTER SIX

NESTLED AMIDST THE swaying coconut trees and cut into an irregular clearing was the hotel swimming pool. It was small, but then so was the hotel, and was thoughtfully designed to blend in with the surroundings. Instead of the usual blue-tiled bottom and scattering of deck chairs, it was shaped to mimic a natural body of water, with a small, gurgling waterfall at one end and shallow steps carved to resemble a smooth, rocky incline down into the green, still water.

It was five in the evening, still light but with the sun beginning to dip, and it was certainly still hot. Humid and muggy and without the slightest whisper of a breeze.

Even the usual orchestra of insects seemed to have gone into hiding.

Nico was listening, the general manager talking to him, his voice low and urgent, but his eyes were absently on the figure in the swimming pool.

When he had airily told his secretary to have a day off, to enjoy the town, the scenery, the extraordinary beauty of the place and to think about buying herself some more appropriate clothing, he had half expected her to ignore everything he'd said. Years of working closely together had taught him that, underneath the controlled exterior, Grace had a mind of her own and, when it came to non-work-related issues, she would do precisely what she wanted to do even if she remained ultra-polite as she dug her heels in.

Being here on the island had confirmed that suspicion, had made him realise just how much fire burned beneath the cool, composed surface.

But she had done as asked. She had taken a few hours off two days ago, had explored the town with his driver at her disposal, had gone to a couple of the beaches on her own and had visited the limited supply of shops where she had bought...yes...more suitable attire.

Colours. Stuff that wasn't in varying shades of bland. Light, colourful clothes far better suited to the searing heat, which not even the overhead fans in the conference room of the hotel in the town they had used for meetings could temper.

The swimsuit, he noted as he continued to gaze in her direction, had sadly and clearly remained the original one she had brought with her. A black one-piece ideally suited for no-nonsense competitive swimming. Nothing frivolous there.

Yet she was still so crazily sexy in the damned thing that Nico was having trouble focusing on what Steve, the general manager, was saying.

He wasn't sure whether it was the fact that they were not in their normal habitat or whether it was because he was seeing sides of her for the first time that tantalised him, or whether it was a mixture of both, but he was finding his concentration slip far too often for his liking.

Eyes drifting to the slight push of her breasts against her light cotton tee shirt…thoughts turning to what lay underneath that light cotton tee shirt…and dreams in which disjointed images of her made for restless sleep.

He tore his eyes away with some difficulty and firmly focused on the matter in hand.

'Look at the sky.' Steve gave a curt nod in the direction of the indigo blue yonder and Nico frowned.

'I agree it seems more humid than it has been for the past few days…'

'You need to know this part of the world, Mr Doukas, sir, to see the signs. Hurricane coming. No announcement yet, but we know how to read the signs. Not just the humidity, Mr Doukas, but you hear this silence? The insects gone into hiding.'

As far as Nico could see, nothing much was that different, but he was willing to bow to greater local knowledge and, after fifteen minutes, he walked towards the swimming pool, towards Grace, who was doing lengths, her slender body cleaving through the water with surprising speed.

He stooped by the side of the pool. There was no decking. Instead, the pool was built into the earth so his loafers sank a little into the damp grass that inclined down. He watched her swim to him, oblivious of his presence as he waited for her, and he noted the widening of her eyes as she abruptly stopped and clung to the side.

'Oh. Hi.'

Grace had sneaked out to the inviting pool, very much aware that she was overreacting because even if Nico was around, even if he was sitting on one of the rattan chairs dotted in the beautiful clearing under the shade of one of the trees, there was no reason for her to be uncomfortable.

The day had been non-stop. They had gone from hotel to offices and at lunch time had interrupted the schedule with a private plane to Nassau so that they could get signatures on paper for the fishing business. She was exhausted.

That said, she had been relieved when Nico had told her that he planned on carrying on with some bits and pieces in the manager's office at the hotel, which he'd had adapted to use as their on-site office.

But he was here now, and she felt exposed as she trod water. 'I thought you were working,' she said a little breathlessly.

'I was until Steve showed up. You need to come to the office. There's a situation.'

'What? What situation? What's going on?'

'I'll wait for you inside. Don't be long and…apologies for spoiling the party and dragging you out of the pool. I realise it's been a hellishly long day for us.'

Grace watched as he vaulted upright, his expression thoughtful, before striding off back towards the hotel. It was so unusual for Nico to reveal any sign of urgency about anything, however stressful things might be, that her heart was pounding with anxiety as she hurried out of the pool towards the office to meet him.

Should she go change? She slipped on the cotton shorts she had worn over the swimsuit and slung her towel over her shoulders.

The hotel had gradually shed more of its guests, people whose time there had come to an end and hadn't been replaced with new intake, so there were relatively few people around. She headed straight for the manager's office to find Nico standing with his back to the door, staring out of the window, and he didn't immediately look around when she entered, not until she coughed, at which point he slowly turned to face her, face grave.

'Sit down, Grace.'

'What's going on? Has the sale fallen through? Is there an emergency back home? Are your parents okay?'

'I've just been speaking to Steve. Look, this is going to be a long conversation. You should probably go change out of your wet swimsuit.'

'I just want to know what's happening. You're stressing me out.'

'Don't tell me that's new on you.' But his wry humour was forced. 'And here I was thinking how well you've always managed stress, because that was one of the clauses in your contract when I hired you. Steve has told me that rumours are swirling of a hurricane on the way. There has been no announcement yet, but he says everyone on the island can predict a landfall hurricane by a change in the atmosphere. It would seem the atmosphere has changed. When he pointed it out, it did occur to me that there's something heavy in the air today. Have you felt it?'

'It's been a bit sticky.'

'If he's right, then there are going to be some change to our plans.'

'What do you mean?'

'The timeline was for our return no later than tomorrow evening. Enough has been put in place for me to delegate the remaining detail to the lawyers and accountants who have been working on things in Nassau. If a hurricane is en route, then we can try to accelerate the last few changes that need to be cemented into the contracts or else we evacuate now, today, and return at a later date. Failing either of those options, we might just have to ride things out, which means possibly being stranded here for longer than anticipated.'

'Stranded?' Grace thought of Tommy worriedly.

'Problems there?' Nico looked at her narrowly, his antenna picking up more than just routine concern, nudging his curiosity and reminding him of the hidden depths he had glimpsed swirling beneath the unrevealing, predictable façade.

'I have commitments…er…back at home.'

'What commitments?'

'The usual.' Grace shrugged. He had told her things about himself, or rather about his background, but sharing wasn't in his nature, and she had no intention of sharing her own troubles with Tommy or anything about her complicated background. This wasn't because she felt he would not be sympathetic, but some gut instinct warned her that that level of confidence would not be welcome. Not in any way, shape or form.

'It's more than possible that there won't be any hurricane. These things develop out at sea and their path can be erratic and tricky to predict but just in case…'

A lot to do.

That, Grace discovered nearly an hour later, was the upshot. The remaining guests at the hotel were briefed and told that they could choose to stay put because there was no certainty of anything happening, or else they could be transferred to whatever hotel in Nassau they wanted at no personal cost. Or flights back to the USA could be arranged immediately, as they were all from various parts of America.

Five couples and none with kids as they were all elderly, enjoying the freedom of children having flown the nest.

There was remarkably little dithering and, by evening, all had packed and left the hotel for a trip back to the USA, largely because their stays were pretty much finishing anyway.

Grace personally felt that it was all much ado about nothing, because there was not so much as a drop of rain or ominous roll of thunder.

Nico removed himself to the office to power through a series of emails and she enjoyed the evening to herself, sitting on the sprawling wooden veranda that circled the hotel like a bracelet, watching fireflies and listening to the rolling of waves on the shore.

This was the most removed she had ever felt in her life from her problems. Even Tommy, whose welfare was constantly on her mind, seemed more distant, and from this distance, with the slim possibility of not being able to return to London at the scheduled time, she wondered whether her unforeseen absence might not do him good.

For the first time she really thought about the implications of having spent a lifetime mothering him. All those years when Cecily had been missing in action and then, seamlessly, picking up the baton when he had had his accident, when Cecily had cheerfully waved goodbye and vanished to the other side of the world with her new husband.

Had she made Tommy over-dependent on her? She spoke to him most evenings in London, went to see him sometimes as often as twice a week. She had been given permission by him to talk to his therapist about sessions and she did. With regularity. As with his various physios. She was ever present, concerned and encouraging. But had that concern and encouragement stopped her brother from taking responsibility for himself? Had it stopped her from taking responsibility for herself? For a future still waiting in the wings to get going? Had she carved a role for herself and cemented herself in, only willing to indulge a crush on her boss that would never come to anything? Had it been easier to do nothing rather than break free of her cage? One Internet date that hadn't worked out and she had once again retreated from doing what needed to be done to really build a life for herself. And maybe, by focusing so much on Tommy, she had also taken away his independence and his need to build a life for *himself*.

Only here in these peaceful surroundings had she really thought about that.

Grace only noticed the sudden stillness when she heard a very distant rumble of thunder.

It was so far away that she didn't give it a second thought, but she woke when it was still dark, in the early hours of the morning, to a banging on her door, and when she pulled it open, rubbing her eyes drowsily, it was to find Nico standing in the doorway. He looked dishevelled.

'The hurricane warning came through a couple of

hours ago. The meteorologists were convinced that it was going to veer away, straight towards the east coast of America, but it unexpectedly swerved, hence the late, frantic warning.' He raked his fingers through his hair and looked at her with piercing dark eyes.

'What time is it?'

'After eight.'

'What?'

'It's pitch-black outside even though it's morning.' He strode past her to pull back the curtains and the shutters before turning to look at her. 'I've been up dragging anything that could move to safer quarters.'

'You should have got me up!'

Nico was in a pair of jeans and a tee shirt, which belatedly drew her attention to her attire, an oversized tee shirt and nothing else. Bare feet. A pair of lacy knickers under the tee shirt. Underneath her always sober practical clothes she had always worn sexy underwear. She wrapped her arms around herself and as she walked towards him the sudden crack of thunder was so sharp and so dramatic that she physically jumped.

Sudden panic bloomed inside her.

Nico dropped the wooden shutters, plunging the room into a twilight darkness before turning on the standing light.

'The winds are going to gather pace,' he said curtly. 'It's important to stay away from the windows. Don't be tempted to look out because the window panes might shatter under the force of the wind. And don't, under any circumstances, venture outside to see what's happening.' He frowned. 'You look terrified.'

Grace gulped and then jumped again at another crack

of thunder and then the sound of rain, racing along the walls and on the roof, as ferocious as the sound of a thundering waterfall. She felt as though the entire structure of the building was going to cave in.

And the temperature seemed to have dropped. Or was that her imagination? She couldn't move a muscle.

'I'm fine,' she breathed, her voice staccato with fear. She could hear the unexpectedly loud sound of the gale gathering strength, could almost feel it battering against the hotel walls, desperate to find a way in so that it could sweep everything away in its destructive path.

They were in this hotel on their own because the few remaining guests had been dispatched to safety and the employees had been sent to their own homes to batten down the hatches.

She stepped towards Nico. She was barely aware of doing so.

She cried out when thunder ripped through the room again and lightning flashed as bright as a sudden blaze of fire.

And just like that, several things happened at once. She moved at the same time as her boss, fear meeting strength, panic rushing into the arms of calm, and he enfolded her.

Everything faded. The howling of the wind…the clatter of rain…the terrifying darkness of day that had suddenly turned to night.

Grace held onto him. Her arms snaked around his whipcord-lean body and she felt the hardness of muscle pressed against her, strong and comforting.

His clothes rasped against her almost but not quite naked body. Her breasts were squashed against his chest but she could still feel the tightness of her nipples blooming at the contact, tingling, making her want to whimper.

'Are you?' Nico husked, tilting her chin so that their eyes met. 'Fine?'

'I will be.' Grace couldn't look away. Her breath was catching in her throat and just getting those words out was an effort. She was no longer the efficient secretary always in control and, even though part of her knew that she should be doing her best to return to that person, right now that felt more like an aspiration than reality. Reality was *this*. 'I… I'm scared…'

Nico felt her vulnerability and it went to him like a shot of adrenaline.

Fire and ice…remote yet direct…strong yet vulnerable. All her complexities lent her a sexiness that might have been latent before, a tantalising suggestion lying just beneath the surface, but here and now they coalesced into something irresistible although he continued to fight it, common sense struggling to win the battle, even as he lowered his dark head, his lips searching for hers.

He kissed her. The second his mouth found hers, anything gentle disappeared under the force of an eroticism that knocked him sideways.

He tasted her hungrily, greedily, his tongue pushing into her mouth and his arms tightening their grip so that he could feel every bit of her pressed against him.

A hurricane was whipping into a frenzy outside and yet all Nico was aware of was the meshing of their tongues and the feel of her peachy bottom as he cupped it in his big hands.

She wanted him.

Was it just fear of the elements that had thrown her into a temporary state of recklessness? Had it blurred the lines between them to the point where she was reacting in a way she would regret? Would the scrabbling slide of her fingers trying to find a way to his bare skin retreat in horror the minute the rain eased off?

Nico knew that any hint of regret, any passing thought that he might have taken advantage of an unusual situation, would be anathema to him and he detached from her with effort but didn't release her, just lightened his hold.

'I want you, Grace,' he said in a driven undertone. 'And it's not just…' he nodded vaguely to encompass the room although his eyes didn't leave her face '…the hurricane outside making me behave out of character. *I want you.* What I *don't* want is for you to fall into my arms because you're scared and then, when you're no longer scared, you somehow throw the blame on my shoulders.' Nico raked his fingers through his hair. 'Tell me to stop,' he grated, his voice barely audible over the shrieking of the weather, 'and I'll stop. Immediately. And never again will this happen or be mentioned. It will have been a…temporary, fleeting blip.'

Grace shivered. Her mouth was still tingling from his and she could still taste him. It felt surreal because this was what she had fantasised about for such a long time. Fantasy had somehow become reality and if in her wildest dreams she had felt her body burn at his touch, it was nothing compared to the reality of what she was feeling now. As though she was alive, lit from within, every sense heightened to a point where she could scarcely credit that this was *her*, Grace Brown, whose life had always been so cautiously lived.

Between her legs was a fierce itch that made her want to rub them together.

Made her want him to touch her down there, to stroke until the itch was gone.

He would back away.

She just had to come to her senses, but she didn't want to come to her senses. She wasn't a fool, and she knew just what her boss was like, where his limitations lay. No commitment. Suited her. Physical attraction, an inappropriate crush, didn't turn her into a complete idiot. She was no more likely to want involvement with Nico than he would want it with her.

Maybe not for the same reasons but all the same. The net result amounted to the same thing.

And in the meantime?

'Right now,' she breathed huskily, 'I want you, Nico. I don't…want you to stop and I'm not going to blame you for anything. I know you for who you are and, trust me, I'm not going to want more than what's happening between us right here and right now. No tomorrow, just today.' She cupped the thick brown column of his neck with her hand, marvelling at how pale she was in comparison.

She had forgotten what it felt like to live in the moment because the business of fretting about tomorrow had always taken precedence. It felt heady.

She tentatively wriggled her fingers under the waistband of his trousers and his low moan went to her head like incense.

He propelled her back, small steps at a time until her knees buckled against the edge of the mattress.

Half laughing, half serious because the howling winds made for an incongruous situation, she asked him whether they should be doing something.

'Other than this?' Nico growled, standing up to strip off his tee shirt in one swift motion.

Headiness was making breathing laborious. He towered at the side of the bed, a monument to sheer physical perfection, from the arrogant beauty of his face to the bronzed muscularity of his body.

She gasped as he hooked his finger at the zip of his trousers. She could discern the bulge of his erection and for a few seconds she closed her eyes to get a grip.

'You can look now,' Nico husked, and she opened one eye then both, propping herself on her elbows and then downright staring because he was completely naked. His fingers lightly circled his penis, and he absently played with himself while his eyes remained on her face, wickedly amused and dark with intent.

'Like what you see?' he murmured, closing the small gap between them so that he was standing right next to her. 'Because now it's my turn and I'm not going to help. I want to see you get undressed. I want to savour every second of the sight.'

His desire was boldly stamped in his dark eyes and it acted as a spur, so that she stripped off in record time, alive to him in a way that made her daydreams feel like girlish nonsense.

He rifled blindly for the wallet in his trousers to extract a condom, but she stopped him, huskily telling him that she was on the pill.

In a mad moment of moving forward with her life and going on the Internet to find her soulmate, she had done what was necessary and gone on the pill because there was no way she would get herself into any kind of situation where she might be dependent on someone else taking responsibility for an outcome that would enormously and directly affect *her*.

She was realistic enough to know that while she would rather sleep with a guy if she was assured of a positive outcome, that was just not how life worked.

She'd never imagined that the guy she ended up in bed with might be her boss.

He was lowering himself onto the mattress next to her. She had wriggled up to the pillows without realising it and as the mattress depressed under his weight she curved to face him, bodies pressing hot against one another. Outside the driving rain continued its furious attack, pelting against the building, driven by the gale-force winds. Yet here, in the room, Grace was only aware of Nico and the demands of her body, coming alive to remind her that she was still young and with sexual needs that yearned to be satisfied.

She ran her hand experimentally along his waist, along his thigh and then inwards, tremulously feeling the bristle of his hair as she touched the heavy sacs and then the erection pulsing between them.

She wanted to pass out.

She was so wet for him. The taste of this forbidden fruit was so dangerously sweet. She slid her fingers along his shaft and he groaned again, covering her hand with his, stopping her, telling her that it was too much.

'Want me to come?' he joked but his voice was shaky. He cupped her breast and then straddled her, paying attention to the delicate mound that had occupied way too much of his imagination of late. Perfectly shaped, a handful and just about, the pink nipple a perfect disc and swollen with arousal.

He lowered himself to take one nipple into his mouth and its nectar sweetness sent his heated libido into the stratosphere. He suckled on it, licking and rolling his tongue over the stiffened bud while his fingers moved over her flat belly until they found the soft hair at the juncture between her thighs. He slid one finger lower, and Grace let her thighs fall open so that he could insert his finger. He moved it inside her until she was panting and then, with just the right amount of pressure, he gently grooved it over her clitoris and Grace loosed a low groan of pleasure.

Assailed on both fronts, mouth and hands driving her into a frenzy of desire, she could feel herself hurtling towards the edge and weakly tried to regain some control because she wanted him inside her. She didn't want to come against his questing finger even though her body was on a trajectory that made it hard to resist.

She curled her fingers into his hair and tugged and he obediently unlatched from her nipple but only to torment her more by trailing his tongue over her stomach, finding her belly button and briefly stopping to explore the indent before moving further downwards.

By the time Nico was finally inside her, he had taken her body to heights she had never dreamed possible.

He had teased and licked and drawn sighs and gasps and utterances from her that had sounded alien to her ears.

Fantasy and reality had merged into a crescendo of pent-up longing that was as overpowering as a tsunami. Wrapped up in her little cocoon, plodding the same path every day, Grace was ripe for just the sort of response Nico so effortlessly provoked.

She came almost as soon as he began thrusting deep into her, losing herself in sensation, all self-control abandoned as her body soared towards an orgasm that wrenched a sob of utter satisfaction and fulfilment from her.

Only when they were lying, spent, did Grace wake up to the weather happening outside.

She glanced towards the window and the sliver of grey light struggling to get past the shutters.

'What are we going to do?' she whispered. 'How long do you think this is going to last?'

Nico had to drag his sluggish brain back to Planet Earth because his body was still lazily luxuriating in a post-coital glow he had never experienced in his life before.

Who knew breaking with routine could feel so good?

He didn't want to talk about the prosaic stuff about what happened next or how long the filthy weather was going to last. For once, practicalities weren't demanding his immediate attention even though, given the situation, they should have been.

Nico thought that what he really wanted to do was stay right where he was, with Grace curled against him, letting the heat subside before stoking it all over again.

He had been satisfied, mind-blowingly so, and yet he wanted more.

She was gazing at him with a frown. Why was she so anxious about how long they might be trapped by the weather? Did a couple of extra days here throw everything out of sync for her? She was dependent-free and would have been in the office in London anyway. And besides...shouldn't she be yearning to be marooned here with him? After the mind-blowing experience they had just shared? A keen sense of self-irony made him smile at his own over-inflated ego.

'No idea,' he murmured truthfully, distracted by her sweet, newly made-love-to scent. 'The actual hurricane might just last a day or so but that doesn't mean we're going to be heading back to London as soon as it's blown over.'

'Why not?'

'Because...' The *shouldn't-you-want-to-prolong this?* crazy notion side-swiped him again, leaving a sour aftertaste because it smacked of a lack of self-control on his part. 'Because there will be a lot of destruction left in the wake of the hurricane. Trees blown over...damage no doubt to property. We will be fine here because this is a well-constructed hotel, but I have no doubt there will be time needed to clear debris and, of course, the airstrip will doubtless be affected.' He paused and said evenly, 'So if you've made plans in the next week or so, then I'd advise you to think again.'

'A week or so?'

'It's not a lifetime in the great scheme of things.' Nico was astounded that he was the one promoting a laid-back approach when his life was so tailored to put work first.

He felt her stiffen and wondered what she was thinking. How was it that she could writhe with such abandon in his arms and yet withdraw into herself the way he felt she was doing now?

And why did he care?

He propped himself on one elbow then slid off the side of the bed to pad towards the window, doing the very thing he had advised against but needing to get his thoughts in order.

He slid apart the wooden shutters and there, in all its glory, was proof of what he had just said. A hurricane wreaking havoc. The trees were bending at right angles, whipped this way and that by the gale-force winds. Plants had been ripped from beds, flowers torn from hedges and the sky was dark with rage.

A few more days…

She might be anxious. God knew, she might have commitments she didn't want to cancel…but as far as he was concerned?

His body was still on fire for her and a few more days cooped up here was certainly not giving him pause for thought.

It should have been, but it wasn't and, for the first time in years, Nico was disturbed by the grey area where things weren't as clear-cut as he'd want them to be.

But who safer for a brief fling with here than his secretary? She knew him well enough to know that, once they left this island, whatever they'd shared would be relegated to the history books. She knew him for the man he was.

No need for warning speeches, no need to be on the lookout for clinginess, no hinting that a future might lie with someone on a distant horizon.

Just…sex.

Nico turned to smile at her. She might be concerned but he was confident that he would be able to change her mind and make her see that a few days here might just be fun.

CHAPTER SEVEN

GRACE KNEW THAT what she was doing was a dangerous indulgence. What they were *both* doing.

Taking time out from reality. Having glorious sex as though they were a couple of frisky teenagers without a care in the world.

Instead of a thirty-one-year-old woman and her out-of-bounds, sexy-as-hell boss.

The hurricane had swept through, leaving behind a trail of destruction and, yes, the small airport had been out of commission for two days, but it was now up and running, yet she and Nico were still here, and the only place *they* were running to was the bedroom, so that they could lose themselves in wild, crazy passion.

Of course, work continued. Of course she still went through his emails and arranged his conference calls and participated in various Zoom meetings concerning deals coming to fruition.

The difference? The prissy outfits were gone, as were the ramparts she had studiously erected to protect herself against the inconvenient attraction she'd kept under wraps for years. There were no busy eyes in an office that had to be avoided. Out here, they had complete freedom to do whatever they wanted to and what they wanted to do was touch one another.

He stroked her inner leg as he chatted on the airwaves to company directors scattered across the globe. He reached to cup her wetness, his hand moving rhythmically against her panties as he finalised the details about the sale of the hotel and the bar and the fishing business. Only yesterday, as he had lounged on the leather sofa in Steve's office, with her next to him and the computer winking in front, he had lazily slipped his finger underneath her dress and inserted it with devastating efficiency into her wetness. She had zoned out from the conversation he had been having with one of his CEOs on the telephone, which had been on speaker. As he had stroked the engorged slit between her thighs, she had done the unthinkable and spasmed against his finger, barely able to contain her urge to scream out her satisfaction, acutely conscious of the business discussion taking place. He had shot her a wicked smile, mouthed *Have you had fun?* and she had felt her body go up in flames, mortified and blisteringly excited at the same time.

When they were in the company of other people, when they were dealing with various employees, they were the soul of discretion but once those doors were closed behind them, they couldn't keep their hands off one another.

Of course, it was going to come to an end. That was a given. There had been no need for him to tell her because she knew him well enough to know where his flings led and what they had here, in this bubble, wasn't even a fling.

It was more a weakness to which they had both suc-cumbed…a fleeting moment in time soon to be papered over by a return to routine.

Grace didn't know when that return was coming, and she had shied away from asking because she was hav-ing fun. For the first time in her life, she was having fun. Was it so wrong to want to prolong this forbidden situation? She would return to London and head straight back to life on the straight and narrow. Meanwhile, Tommy seemed content enough to manage without her, but by the time she went to see him he would be back to his usual self, dissatisfied and querulous and in need of guidance. That being the case, she would be a saint not to want to snatch this stolen pleasure.

Sitting on the wide porch, to which the outside fur-niture had been returned from the spacious shed that was used for storage in bad weather, Grace drew her knees up to her chest and watched the distant figure in the ocean. It was a little after six and after a day of meetings, calls and the usual tidying of the beach area, Nico was striking back from his ocean swim.

He was a powerful swimmer, had laughed at her con-cern the first time he had sauntered down to the wa-ter's edge and plunged straight into the bright blue sea.

He liked swimming at night. She could feel the build of excitement as he sliced through the water, getting closer and closer.

They had become accustomed to having the hotel to themselves. It was small and cosy, and the employees had been only too glad to be relieved of their duties, not that they were overworked because, aside from the two of them, the place was empty.

The solitude lent itself to all sorts of titillating situations and Grace shivered with pleasure just thinking about them.

Four days felt like four weeks because time seemed to stand still out here.

She straightened as Nico emerged from the water, rearing up from the softly breaking waves like a monolith.

He paused to sweep his fingers through his wet hair and then, eyes locked to her, headed in her direction, a dark silhouette in the fast-fading light.

He stopped just in front of her and then leant down, hands firmly planted on the arms of her chair, caging her in.

'You should try some night swimming with me,' he murmured.

'I don't think so.' Grace smiled back at him and then curled her finger into a wayward strand of dark hair. 'I'm too much of a coward, I'm afraid.'

'What's to be afraid of? When you'd be swimming next to me?'

'Oh, right. I forgot. Nothing would dare attack if they sensed that you were in the water...'

'Correct.' Nico leant into her, kissed her long and slow until her eyelids were fluttering and the ache between her legs made her brain shut down the way it always seemed to. 'Besides, you swim like a fish. Whoever taught at school did a good job.'

He grinned. In response, Grace said nothing. She'd never had swimming lessons at school. They had been an adult treat at the local swimming baths. She could have told him but what they had did not include intimate sharing of confidences. He had admitted to his uncle's past because it had formed the backdrop for their trip to the island. Grace had savoured that titbit, but she had not returned the favour and nor would she.

Nico walked alone. Any girlish desire to share secrets about herself would send him into rapid retreat because it would make him think that she might be reading a depth to what they had that wasn't there and never would be.

In essence, she was his loyal secretary who had stepped outside the box for a moment in time.

He knew nothing about her background and nothing about her circumstances and he hadn't asked. He hadn't asked because this was about sex. When it came to knowing *her*, he knew enough. He knew that she was reliable and did a good job and knew how to take the initiative at work when she had to.

The fact that he had caught her on an Internet date had opened a door between them, but this was where that open door had led to. Great sex.

Yet, if this was just lust, then why did he fill her head every waking moment? If she didn't care, why was there a sneaking suspicion that she would be hurt by all of this? If she really thought that by sleeping with him, she might get him out of her system, then why did the thought of losing him fill her with dread? Why did the prospect of returning to normality, picking up where they had left off, pretending that nothing had happened between them, fill her with panic?

Because she was falling for him? How could that be possible when it made no sense?

For Grace, whose life had always made sense, who had mastered the art of turning chaos into order, the recklessness of falling for Nico Doukas brought her out in a cold sweat.

Even more terrifying was the thought that he might somehow wise up to what she was feeling.

What if he saw past the shiny veneer to the murky, muddy confusion underneath?

What he didn't know about women could be written on the back of a postage stamp. How long before she let something slip, let her feelings for him show on her face…? Then what? He would be horrified. As far as Nico was concerned, they were on the same page. Some unexpected fun in the sun, a break from routine. She knew him, as he was fond of reminding her. She knew the man he was and the one he could never be.

She knew the rules of the game.

The slightest whiff that she had strayed from following those rules and everything would be lost. There was no way he would keep her on because she would risk becoming an embarrassing and needy liability. He would no longer be able to look her in the face and the relationship they had built up over the years would be gone for ever.

'Things…seem to be progressing really well…here… I know we've had to stay here longer than originally planned because of the hurricane but I've been surprised at how efficient everyone is when it comes to tidying up behind it.'

'They're used to it. Hurricanes happen every year

here. A lot of the places, as you've seen, are built in ways that withstand the onslaught.'

Grace was temporarily distracted. She looked at him with curious eyes.

'What did it feel like?'

'Come again?'

'Helping clear the beach...all the debris...sorting out rebuilding some of those houses that were battered. Have you ever done anything like that before?'

'That's a very serious question,' Nico murmured, flinging himself on the beach towel spread next to hers and lying on his back, hands folded on his broad chest.

'Oh, sorry. I forgot that we steered clear of serious questions.'

'Have I ever said that?' He angled himself so that he was looking at her.

'Nico, you don't have to.' Grace laughed lightly. 'And it wasn't a serious question. It was just...a question.'

'To answer you,' Nico said pensively, after a few seconds of telling silence, 'yes and no. The physical exertion felt good. I've never been called on to do anything like that before. There was never any need. No need, growing up, to earn some money by working on a building site during the summer holidays. No need to go fruit picking to grab a bit of freedom.' He was staring up at the twilit sky again.

'Oh, the headache of growing up in a rich family.'

'What about you?'

'Normal.' Grace thought of her far from normal background and wondered what he would make of it.

'Is there ever such a thing?'

The conversation was beginning to feel dangerous, like suddenly staring down into an open fire.

'Of course there is!' She laughed. 'It's getting a little chilly out here.'

She rose and he did as well to begin drying himself with the towel he had been lying on.

'It is.' He spun round to face her, his dark gaze hot with lazy, sexy amusement. 'I have a number of options when it comes to warming you up.' He feathered his finger across her cheek and for a few seconds her head emptied of all intent as her body revved up in expectation of more.

He dipped his finger over her lips then into her parted mouth and Grace went weak at the knees. She sucked it, their eyes locked, her body melting. When he curved his hand to cup the side of her neck and drew her towards him, she didn't resist.

She edged closer, weaved her arms around his neck and pulled him down to press her mouth against his, to savour the wetness of his tongue meshing with hers and to enjoy all the attendant reactions that lingering kiss roused in her.

She would get a grip. The control she'd given up was waiting to be regained. She'd seen the danger in front of her and had known what steps had to be taken to limit the damage that would be caused.

She would save herself but first...

Would it be a crime to take what was on offer one last time? Wouldn't that just be playing him at his own game? When it came to women and from everything Grace had ever seen, Nico took what he wanted. Why shouldn't she take what *she* wanted? Would one more day make a broken heart more difficult to mend?

Because she would have a broken heart. She had made the fatal mistake of giving it to the wrong guy and there would be a heavy price to pay for her misguided generosity.

How ironic to think that she had watched her mother's shenanigans, had resolved to make sure never to go down a similar road of losing her heart willy-nilly in a frantic search for validation from a guy, only to find herself, at the age of thirty-one, so naive that she had gone and done the very thing she had spent a lifetime cautioning herself about.

In hindsight, she could have used some of her mother's experience when it came to playing the field because she might have been better at protecting herself from Nico and the consequences of falling for him.

Grace felt as though the weight of her poor choices would topple her over so she closed her mind to it, closed her mind to everything aside from the need to enjoy herself and let tomorrow deal with the rest.

They staggered in a jerky embrace towards the kitchens, which they had been using for themselves since they had been holed up. They barely made it there. Her hands were scrabbling over him, raking along his spine and cupping his pulsing erection through the still damp swimming trunks. They kissed as they backed towards the kitchens, pushing open the door, which swung back behind them.

The privacy in the hotel was liberating, conducive to sex wherever they landed and whenever they wanted.

For the past few days they had greedily done whatever they had wanted because there had been no one to witness their stolen passion.

Grace felt herself butt against the edge of one of the cool granite work surfaces and gasped as he lifted her off her feet, settling her on the worktop.

She was wearing no more than a flimsy cotton dress and he shoved it up, urging her to wriggle so that he could push it underneath her. He parted her legs with his hands and Grace arched back, hands extended so that she was supporting herself. She was breathing fast, loosing tiny whimpering moans from her parted lips, eyes fluttering shut, holding the image of his dark head lowering with intent between her thighs.

He nuzzled her through her panties, breathing her in and teasing her with little darts from his tongue. He didn't bother taking them off. She could easily have shifted so that he could have pulled them down and done away with them altogether but, instead, he played with her until she was losing her mind with wanting more.

When he finally pulled the crotch of the panties to one side and inserted his tongue into her wetness, Grace was a heartbeat away from coming. She held on for as long as she could, but it was impossible to resist the insistent thrusting of his tongue as it found her sensitive clitoris and probed it with devastating effect.

Her orgasm was so powerful that she wobbled on the counter, almost falling backwards. She was relieved when he eased her off in one swift, effortless motion to deposit her on the long sofa, one of three that made the kitchen such a comfortable space. Groaning from the aftermath of coming, Grace was aware of Nico ridding himself of his swimming trunks and she barely had time to absorb his rampant erection, as hard as steel, when he thrust into her. One move, deep and hard and taking her beyond what she had experienced the first time. One move and he shuddered against her before collapsing to the side. It wasn't quite wide enough for the two of them and he was practically falling off, not that she really noticed because she was spent.

The dress was still on and he primly patted it back over her thighs.

'That's what happens,' Nico murmured, 'when a guy goes swimming and spends the whole time thinking about the woman waiting for him when he gets back to dry land. Think that's what sailors felt when they spent months at sea? Think that's why so many children were fathered when they returned from their trips back to hearth and home?'

'Sometimes,' Grace said drowsily, 'the fathering didn't necessarily include the hearth and home…'

'Very astute.' He chuckled and pushed her hair from her face so that he could plant a gentle kiss on her forehead.

It was so tender a gesture that her heart constricted.

For just a moment, she wondered whether this was what love felt like when it was returned. The gentle kiss after the explosive sex, the whispered words, the holding close. The planning for a shared future and the hopes and dreams waiting to materialise.

How could something so far from returned love mimic the real thing? How could life be so cruel? How could she have ended up where she had when she'd thought that all her defences were up and running?

How?

'Nico…' She sighed and twisted away. There was just the one window in the kitchen and the shutters were half closed. Through them she could just about glimpse snatches of darkness outside, could hear the rustle of night-time insects in the still, hot air.

The beaches looked different after the hurricane, with toppled trees yet to be cleared away and debris that had either been washed in from the turbulent seas or swept down from the battered land, but nothing could disguise the true blue of the water as it returned to its placid beauty or the icing-sugar softness of the sand drying out nicely under the steady sunshine.

Grace would never forget any of it. Not the sights or the sounds of this lazy tropical island. It was so different from anything she'd ever experienced. Nico was resting against her, idly stroking her breast through the dress, and she shifted a little. 'I'm thinking that the airstrip is back open for business and the work we began when we came here is finished…'

Nico stilled.

He was still on a high after some of the best sex he'd ever had. He heard what sounded like a serious conversation in the making and for once, post sex, he wasn't interested. Accustomed to leaping out of bed the very second business between the sheets was concluded, he had discovered a liking here for staying put and winding down with a warm and willing body next to him. *This* warm and willing body next to him. The last thing he felt like was a dissection of deals that needed doing back in London.

When he had first slept with Grace, he had accepted, as a given, that whatever brief fling they had would disappear the second they touched down at Heathrow. The thought of sleeping with his secretary, once back to the cut and thrust of his high-octane city life, was frankly unacceptable.

He was a firm believer in several hundred lines of separation between work and his personal life. There was no way he could see anything but trouble on the horizon if he were to ever take another route.

And it was more than that. He knew the kind of woman he needed in his life when it came to commitment and Grace didn't fit the bill, however hot the sex was.

Out here, he was happy to go with the flow, but that wasn't his nature and it would never be the right path for him.

Now, as she threw that timely reminder into the mix, Nico asked himself why he was so reluctant to admit that she was right, that they couldn't stay here much longer.

Was it because he wasn't ready for this to end?

He hadn't anticipated that taboo sex could feel so good. Just lying here next to her made his erection begin to stir back into enthusiastic life.

Women had always been so predictable. Grace, though...in a heartbeat, things had changed between them. It felt as though bit by gradual bit he had peeled away layers of her and the more he peeled away, the more he sensed there was to discover.

Was it any wonder that he wasn't quite ready to relinquish the challenge of digging deeper?

Would it get complicated once they returned to work? Weren't there exceptions to every rule? Besides, if he lost control physically, he never would in any other area. That just wasn't the man he had conditioned himself to be.

He could think out of the box... Wouldn't he wean himself off this by carrying on? Wean them *both* off this...by not killing what they had prematurely?

Nico luxuriated in multiple scenarios in which what they had might carry on until such time as inevitable boredom seeped in.

Having never had to put himself out when it came to holding onto a woman, he surprised himself with the number of creative reasons he could now come up with to justify hanging onto what they had started.

The disgruntlement he had felt when she had broached the topic of their mission here coming to a close disappeared. He quietly congratulated himself on being able to see everything from all possible angles, thereby finding a solution to whatever thorny issue was at hand.

On this occasion, the thorny issue of them not having reached the natural conclusion to this affair.

'Don't talk,' he purred. Before she could protest, he was silencing her with a gentle finger over her lips. 'Let me do the talking.'

He leapt off the sofa, turned around and held out his hand, which Grace took, though she seemed reluctant. He pulled her to her feet and then to him, so that their bodies were pressed against one another, and he cupped her rear with his hands and gently massaged until she could feel the thoughts draining out of her head.

'Nico...'

'You raise a good point. We have to talk. And we will...just as soon as we have a nice, long shower and get dressed and come back down here to prepare something to eat. Don't forget, I've just swum the equivalent of the Channel crossing...'

'At the very least...'

He was already leading her out of the kitchen and she followed him without resistance. Nico, holding her hand, was brimming over with the exultation of having found a way to quieten his frustration at reality beckoning.

He idly glanced around him as they headed through the small boutique hotel up to the suite where they had taken up residence together.

Of course, he had become accustomed to these surroundings. To start with, he had barely noticed them. He had arrived to do a job and doing the job hadn't included appreciation of what his uncle had done. In truth, he had been so prejudiced against Sander that he had come fully prepared to scorn everything his uncle had touched.

Nico didn't know how and when things had changed but, as Grace had mused on a couple of occasions, the hotel and everything that went with it, from the successful fishing business to the loyalty of all his employees, spoke of a guy who had landed on the island as a confused and washed-up man only to find purpose and direction and a reason for living.

Now, Nico thought that it might have been okay to have known this guy his uncle had become.

He would never have had time for the man who had

wasted his youth and recklessly threatened the future of the family business but, yes, he would have had time for the man who had found his way.

Nico was vaguely aware that Grace wasn't her usual self. He felt that she wasn't a woman who lived in the moment. He felt that sleeping with him would have been her biggest break with caution. With London looming she would thinking ahead to them going their separate ways and if she felt the way he did, then she would be at war with herself, wanting more yet uneasily aware of the siren call of common sense. He knew her so well. Well enough to realise that she would never throw herself at him and plead for more, but she wouldn't have to. He would hold out his hand, she would take it and they would return to London and finish what they'd started.

He coaxed her in the wet room with expert hands that soaped her all over…and he murmured just the right words to have her smiling and then laughing as they headed back down to the kitchen, and when she hesitantly looked at him with a question in her eyes and something close to anxiety shadowing her delicate features, he distracted her by talking about Sander and the thoughts that had come to him as they had walked through the hotel earlier.

She was a good listener. She rarely interrupted and she never threw her opinions into the mix or else, if she did, then they were always opinions he was interested in hearing.

She *got* him and that was one of the reasons why he was so confident that when the time came they would remain…friends.

Beyond that…

He frowned, because there could never be anything beyond that. She had told him that her life had been normal. He'd never expected otherwise. For a few moments, he wondered what would happen if he didn't define what they had with timelines, if he gave it a chance, waited to see where it would lead. Almost as fast, he dismissed the notion. She would always deserve better than a man trained to put work ahead of everything else.

'You were saying,' Nico revived the conversation begun earlier, 'that things we came to do here have been done.' He watched as delicate colour crawled into her face although she didn't turn to meet his eyes.

He could read what was going through her head and he savoured the anticipation of dispelling all her unasked questions.

Filled with a sense of intense satisfaction, he stopped the chopping, dumped the knife on the counter and swivelled so that he was looking at her, hip against the counter, legs lightly crossed.

Grace stiffened, but eventually she couldn't kid herself that he wasn't staring at her.

Even though she'd known that this moment was going to come, she still felt unprepared. Things had to end, and she only wished that she had stood her ground and got in there with her speech first, before him.

Now she was going to be at the receiving end of one of his *Dear John* talks, and the only consolation was that she wouldn't be sending a bunch of flowers to herself.

At least she wouldn't be weeping and wailing and making a nuisance of herself, whatever she happened to be feeling inside. And at least she had not once given in to the temptation to over-confide. She'd respected his boundaries and kept her dignity and pride in place.

She wondered whether she could head him off at the pass, but when she finally met his eyes it was to find determination stamped there along with…a suggestion of satisfaction. Or maybe it was *relief* that she had broached a subject that might have been playing on his mind.

She hadn't got the impression that he was fed up with her, but then he was a guy who knew how to keep his cards close to his chest when it suited him.

Grace felt her heart thud inside her. She wanted to look away, but she couldn't. She had become too used to feasting her eyes on him, appreciating his sheer masculine beauty. She guarded her love like a thief with stolen treasure but when it came to lust, there were no holds barred. He enjoyed her looking at him, devouring him greedily with her eyes, and she had always been more than happy to oblige.

'What we have here…' Nico paused but only for a couple of seconds. 'I don't want it to end.' He gestured and smiled at her ruefully and with some bewilderment. 'I know… I know…this isn't how I expected things to play out but something about you, Grace… I see you and I want to touch.' He shrugged his shoulders with yet more incomprehension.

Nico noted that she was staring at him with a dumbfounded expression and he smiled slowly,

'And you want it too,' he murmured with sweeping self-assurance. He reached out and placed his hand at the nape of her neck and absently stroked the sensitive skin while he continued to maintain the sort of eye contact that would have had most women reaching for the smelling salts. 'I touch you and you go up in flames. Like me. I don't understand it but I'm not going to fight it. I know,' he continued with the same, mesmerising softness, 'you might have some concerns that if we continue with what we have, it might impact on our work relationship, but it won't. Trust me. I've never mixed business with pleasure but there's a first for everything and this is going to be my first…'

CHAPTER EIGHT

'*TRUST YOU THAT* it won't make a difference to our working relationship?'

Grace managed to get her vocal cords into working order, but she was still gaping at him with incredulity.

This wasn't what she had expected. She had expected to be gently given her walking papers. So he was now saying that he wanted things to carry on? That he didn't want things to end? Grace knew him so well that she could read everything between the lines, everything that hadn't been actually *said* but was there as big and as bold as a billboard advertisement.

Nico hadn't expected things to have ended up where they had. She doubted he'd ever looked at her twice until that fateful accident of chance when he'd bumped into her on her pointless Internet date. Maybe he'd seen her for the first time, then, as a woman rather than an extremely efficient robot? Maybe his curiosity had been piqued? He was never one to deny the beckoning of sexual curiosity—being marooned on an island that was the essence of heady romance might have prompted him into doing what he would never, ever have done within the confines of an office. As he'd just said, he'd never mixed business with pleasure.

At any rate, here they were and what he was essentially saying to her in that charming, self-deprecating, humbly confused way of his was that he wasn't ready for the sex to end *yet*.

That it would end was a given. It had always been a given. He was simply, now, laying down his terms for when it ended.

Grace knew that she should not be annoyed by that, and she definitely shouldn't be surprised because that was how his love life functioned. He called the shots.

The very thought of him shoving her into the same category as all the other women he had dated made her grit her teeth and clench her fists and want to throw something hard and heavy at his handsome head.

Did he honestly think that she was now so much under his magnetic spell that she would do as requested? Was their relationship now puppet master with the empowering hand and pliable, mindless puppet with no more self-determination?

Unfortunately, she could see just why he might have come to that conclusion, and she winced with bitter regret that she hadn't had the strength to walk away when she'd had the chance, but her own secret longings had been dry tinder to a match suddenly struck. She had gone up in flames because her fantasies had suddenly come true.

She surfaced to hear him in full flow, and she frowned. 'Sorry, I missed that...'

'For me there would be no problem working with you. Yes, yes, yes... I know what you're going to say.

You're going to say that I was never a man who encouraged work and play to happen in the same place. You're going to remind me of those times when I've complained at calls interrupting meetings and unexpected visits screwing up my work schedule, but aren't there always exceptions to every rule? Isn't that a sign of flexibility? Not being tied down to dogma? It's no good lamenting the fact that we started this. In fact, I don't regret a minute of it.' He shot her a devilish smile. 'Would it be so wrong of me to say that I think we're on the same page with this? Making love has never felt so good. Just thinking of you gives me a hard-on and that's a first for me. So we're both adults and if we break new ground by seeing one another and working with one another as well, then who are we hurting?'

'So to recap,' Grace said slowly, 'what you're saying is that we carry on having this…fling when we return to London because we're both adults and why bother to try and find the energy and willpower to call it quits when we can just carry on going with the flow until… well, until the whole thing fizzles out.'

He'd announced his offer with a note of triumph and all guns blazing, assured of victory.

For him, she was just someone else, another body he wasn't quite tired of.

For her, he was the embodiment of everything she knew she shouldn't want or love but wanted and loved anyway.

The man beyond cynicism had met someone not cynical enough.

'How long do you think that'll take?'

'Who can put a number on something like that?'

'Actually, if I had to think of one person who could, then it would probably be you.'

'What do you mean?'

'Come on, Nico,' Grace said gruffly, 'if I had to keep a diary of how long your relationships last, then I'd say none of them go beyond the three-month watershed.'

'I'm sure you're wrong on that score.' But he was frowning and thinking. 'At any rate, this is different. What we have is nothing like what I've had in the past with…the other women I've dated, so it's impossible to go down the comparison road.'

'I'm guessing I should be flattered?'

'*I'm* flattered you looked twice at me,' he responded with sincerity. 'Seeing that you came from a standpoint of disapproval. Do you remember that conversation we had? When you opened up about my dating habits?'

Grace shivered. From that perfectly accurate assessment, it surely would only be a hop and a skip before he started coming to all sorts of conclusions, some of which might be right.

This time she was definitely going to head him away from the pass before that clever brain of his started joining dots.

'I remember.' She shrugged and smiled distantly. 'Maybe that's why we're in this place now. Neither of us saw it coming but it worked, *out here*, because we took what we wanted and had some fun.'

'Run that by me?'

'You enjoyed the novelty and so did I.'

'The novelty…'

'I mean, we worked alongside one another for a long time, and I guess, thrown together like this…'

She glanced around her and left it up to him to interpret where she was going with what she had just said. 'Curiosity got the better of us. It happens. Doesn't mean it has to keep on happening! Realistically, I think we're both too sensible for that, don't you?'

He liked novelty but there was no reason why he had to have the monopoly on that.

She stepped back and slowly wiped her hands on one of the kitchen towels, then she retreated to the safety of a kitchen chair, swivelling it so that she was looking at him.

Her legs felt like jelly. She could tell from the shadow of sudden uncertainty in his eyes that the conversation wasn't going in the predicted direction.

All of this, the arrogant assumption that she would fall in line…the glib acceptance that she would want to hang onto what he was offering because what woman wouldn't? She hated herself for still loving him because it defied everything sensible inside her.

However, Grace still possessed sufficient common sense to know just where this was going to go, and Nico Doukas was about to find out what it felt like to have the rug pulled from under his feet.

She intended to play by *her* rules, even though this was anything but a game.

'You don't mean that…do you? I can *feel* the desire coming off you in waves. It's telling me something else, another story…' He strolled towards her and then made her treacherous heart flutter like crazy when he leant over, propping himself on the arms of her chair and suffocating her with his unbearable proximity.

What would she do if he kissed her now?

Push him forcefully back? Turn away with freezing intent? Cave in and loop her arms around his neck and return that kiss?

'It's not going to happen, Nico.' This because option three felt dangerously tempting. She placed her hands on his chest, felt the heat of his body burning through the tee shirt and clenched her jaw. She didn't push but the intent was there and after a few seconds, during which she saw bewilderment register on his face, he drew back but remained in place in front of her, staring down with a frown.

'Oh, Grace, my darling…'

'I don't think it's tenable for this to continue after we leave here.'

My darling…if only she were…

'Why not?'

Grace shrugged. 'Because it just isn't.'

'Are you telling me that you've abruptly stopped being attracted to me? Maybe you're saying that once we land in London, the attraction will conveniently disappear…because if that's what you're saying, then we could always put it to the test.'

'Nico…this has been fun.'

Her voice was gentle. She was being reasonable. She was letting him down the way she imagined he was accustomed to letting down the women he inevitably got bored with. In her head she was thinking, *I still need this job, but tomorrow the search begins for a replacement, because I'll never really be able to share space with this man without hurting.*

'But we both know this is going nowhere and *you*

might not have a problem carrying on with it until it fizzles out, but *I* have.'

'Why?' he questioned, eyes narrowing.

Grace could see him thinking, working things out, joining dots that she didn't want him to join.

'Because I want more for myself,' she told him quietly and truthfully. 'I'm thirty-one years old and I have no intention of wasting my time with something that's not going anywhere. We get along and the sex has been great fun but that's where it ends. Essentially, I'm not your type and you're not mine.' Every word that passed her lips hurt but none of that hurt showed in her determined expression. 'And I'm not getting involved on a pointless joy ride that'll be over in the blink of an eye and whatever you say about it not affecting our working relationship, it probably would. There's a very good reason you say that you've never been tempted to mix business with pleasure and even if you're the boss and you can do exactly what you want, it's still not a good idea. How would it work? Practically?'

'What do you mean?' He flushed, and Grace's eyebrows shot up in an amused question.

'I mean, Nico, think about it. I get to the office usual time, bring you a cup of coffee, as per usual, and we spend the day...dovetailing around one another until the clock strikes six and then what? We lock the outside door and suddenly throw ourselves at one another and rip off our clothes and make wild love on your office desk?'

'Don't be ridiculous.'

'I'm not being ridiculous, Nico,' she said wryly. 'It

would be embarrassing, and our working relationship would totally end up suffering.'

Not to mention her heart.

She thought of her mother, always searching for the right one, getting hurt along the way.

She had had little sympathy because of the fallout left in the wake of her mother's never-ending parade of possibilities. When her mother had disappeared to the other side of the world, Grace had resigned herself to it being the full stop to a chequered love life that had seen her have no time to spare for the children she had had.

Now, she had a reluctant admiration for the way Cecily had always picked herself up, dusted herself down and carried on. She hadn't been the most responsible parent on the planet, but all those knocks along the way would have hurt and yet she had still played her acting games with Grace and her brother, like the kid she essentially had been, and dazzled her way through her hurt. And Australia? Perhaps that had finally been True Love. Who was Grace to begrudge her that? She had disappeared leaving her adult children behind to look out for themselves and maybe that was just tough love. Maybe that had been all she had had to give.

Loving Nico had opened Grace's horizons and shown her the nuances in life. It was seldom a case of black and white, with the right guy coming along, ticking all the boxes with no broken hearts along the way because measures had been put in place to protect those hearts. She had been so careful, had assured herself that she had learnt all the lessons necessary to make sure she controlled her love life instead of her love life controlling her, and yet, here she was, ambushed by the very thing she had fought to protect herself from.

At least her pride hadn't been flushed down the drain. At least she had only allowed Nico to see sides to her that she wanted him to see.

How many times, in those lazy moments when they had been flushed and content after making love, had she been tempted to tell him about her childhood? About the stress of having Cecily for a mother? The responsibilities that had been shouldered when she'd been just a kid? About Tommy and all the problems now on her plate?

She had held back because a little voice inside had warned her that oversharing would be a mistake.

Whatever her feelings for Nico, he would never have appreciated that level of depth because, in his eyes, what they had had just been a bit of fun. Exciting and thrilling but just some fun.

Now, she was glad that she had held back because she would carry on working for him until she got another job and she would pretend that everything was fine. She would do what her mother had been an expert at doing. She would put a smile on her face and dust herself off and carry on.

She had to smile when she thought how much she had fought against having anything in common with Cecily. Now, she sincerely hoped her acting skills were up to scratch.

'Of course, I'm very flattered.' Grace offered a placating smile. 'But like I've said, you know that I'm a sensible person…'

'I never thought I'd hate the sound of someone being sensible,' Nico growled.

Grace overrode the interruption. 'I'm sensible enough to know that whatever dying embers of attraction might still be there when we get back to London, it would be sheer folly to fan them into life.'

'That's a very overblown way of saying that the sex is great. So why stop when the going's good? Anyone would think that this is about more than what's on the table.'

'What do you mean?'

'I mean this is great sex. It's not a *Gone with the Wind* searing love story.'

'I know *that*.' She laughed dismissively. 'Do you honestly think I'd be crazy enough to read more into this than what's there?' She raised her eyebrows and rolled her eyes and made a convincing show of indifference mixed with amusement. 'Like I said, Nico, let's put this behind us when we get to London. We have a lot to do...deals that have been hanging in the balance...'

Nico looked at her narrowly for a few seconds, then he shrugged and threw her a shadow of a smile.

He raised both hands in a gesture of rueful resignation.

'You can't blame a guy for trying.'

They were back on track. Grace should have been relieved, but she felt a punch of misery at what was being lost.

'Shall we carry on with our evening? Seeing as it'll probably be the last?' She kept smiling and chatting as she busied herself adding the final touches to their meal. She wanted him to keep asking and yet she knew that her answer would be the same however much he asked. She felt his dark eyes on her and her body tingled and burned, but when she finally turned to look at him, she was still smiling and there was nothing there to give her pain away.

Nico was sitting at his desk three days later, frustrated with himself because things couldn't have been more normal between them and yet the normality, which he should have welcomed, felt like a shard of glass that wouldn't leave him alone. He looked at her down-bent head as she did what she always did, made notes on her iPad of things to do, and he pictured her naked beneath him…on top of him…looking at him over her shoulder…her cool eyes turning him on in ways he'd never been turned on in his life before.

When she wasn't in his presence, he thought of her. He couldn't concentrate. Images of her kept surfacing, interrupting him when he was desperate to focus. It got on his nerves.

Was this preoccupation of his to do with the fact that she had been the one to end things?

Surely he couldn't be *that* shallow? *That* self-centred?

They hadn't slept together after she'd told him to get lost. On the surface, they'd reverted to what they had been before, two people with a successful working relationship. The boss and his secretary. Gradually, conversation had returned to work and the passion they'd shared had been papered over.

By the time they'd touched down in London, it had

felt as though the intimacy that had been so real had vanished like dew in the summer sun.

He swivelled his chair to stare through the window and was frowning and gazing out when he heard her clear her throat.

'Am I interrupting?'

Nico swung the chair round, pushed it back and resisted the urge to scowl. Instead, he bared his teeth in something resembling a smile. A ferocious, slightly terrifying smile.

Naturally the frothy summer clothes had gone. She was back to the serious stuff. Today was a pale grey knee-length skirt and a white cotton top and a cardigan, which she had yet to remove even though it was mid-afternoon and the office was warm.

He *still* wanted to touch her. He *still* had an insane urge to rip off the prim and proper layers and get to her nakedness, feel her bare body, her nipples, the dip of her belly button. He *still* wanted to hear her whimper as he got between her legs and teased her with his tongue.

He emphatically *didn't* want to hear her ask him about some legality on some merger of some company.

'Not at all,' he drawled, vaulting upright and moving towards the pale leather sofa where his jacket had been tossed earlier in the day. 'It's Friday. It's been a roller coaster couple of weeks. I suggest we both knock off early.'

He paused and wondered whether she would pick up on the ambiguity, but she tilted her head to one side, tucked her hair behind her ears and smiled politely.

'Have you got exciting plans for this evening? For the weekend?'

'Not at the moment. But I intend to.' He slung on the jacket and thought, with a distinct lack of enthusiasm, that he could have plans if he chose to pick up the phone to any number of women he knew would happily go out with him wherever he chose to take them.

Hell, why shouldn't he?

And why shouldn't she know what his plans were?

Hadn't they returned to their previous working relationship? The one where she knew him like the back of her hand? The one where she knew what all his plans were because she arranged them on his behalf?

'See if you can get me a table for two tomorrow at that little French restaurant I like in Pimlico, would you?' He didn't look at her. He looked at his phone, began scrolling through it.

'French restaurant?'

'You know the one. Candles and vases of flowers on the tables and waiters with French accents pretending they don't understand a word of English.'

Grace knew the one.

Of course, he wouldn't have waited long before he picked up where he'd left off with his fan club. He was a guy who moved on. She knew that but it didn't help. Every pore and fibre in her body hurt with a pain that was indescribable. She smiled with frozen politeness and nodded.

'What time?'

'Hmm…' He glanced at his Rolex. 'Eight sounds about right. We can loosen up with a drink at the pub opposite before.' He dealt her a slashing smile. She returned with a brilliant, thousand-wattage one of her own.

'And you? Hectic weekend fun?'

Grace hesitated.

She would be seeing Tommy the following evening.

She'd phoned him as soon as she'd got back but he had seemed less enthused to hear from her than she'd expected and she'd wondered what was wrong.

In a flash, all the worries she had blithely cast aside during her heady stay on the island had returned in full force. He could be moody. She didn't blame him because he had suffered so many setbacks for someone as young as he was and he just didn't have the stamina to deal with them.

She had asked him to come to her place instead of her going to his as she usually did.

The change of scenery might do him a power of good. He would stay over and she would pamper him and listen to him and get him back on track.

She surfaced to find Nico staring at her intently and she wondered whether he was making assumptions that her weekend would be an uneventful one. Their eyes met and she shifted and flushed and then said, a little defiantly, 'I have plans, as a matter of fact.' *Completely true,* she thought wryly, although *adventurous* would be a definite overstatement.

'Really? Going anywhere exciting?'

'The excitement will be at my place,' she chirped. 'I plan on cooking a really fantastic meal…'

'Special occasion?'

Grace blushed and shrugged mysteriously and looked away all at the same time and when she spoke it was to throw over her shoulder that she would text and email him confirmation of his dinner booking.

He was still standing, hands shoved into his trouser pockets, a slight frown on his face, but then his expression cleared, returned to one of lazy amusement and he nodded and began galvanising himself back into action.

'Walk down with me,' he murmured, pausing as she bustled out to her desk and began busying herself with her computer.

'I...' Grace glanced at him, heart pounding, desperate to get out of his presence so that she could wallow in her misery that he had resumed his old life without so much as a backward nod to what they had shared. For a few breathless seconds, their eyes locked and it felt as though the air between them had been drained of oxygen. She knew, with dismay, that her cheeks were on fire when she at last managed to break eye contact. 'I...have one or two things to do before I leave, Nico.'

'What?'

'Some emails to get through...that report with the financial figures still has to be compiled for Robert in Accounts...'

Nico sauntered towards her and gently but firmly pressed shut her computer with one autocratic finger.

'No, you don't. I'm the boss and I'm giving you permission to stop work for the day.'

'And also to walk down with you? Is that an order as well?' She'd been aiming for light, but she heard a sarcastic, resentful edge to her voice that he picked up on because his expression cooled.

'Is this where we are, Grace? You'll only actually walk ten steps with me out of this office if I tell you that you have to?'

'No, of course not!' Hot colour stained her cheeks

and she licked her lips, mortified because he was right. This wasn't where she wanted to be. Yet how could it ever be possible to feel normal around him when she was in love with him? When they had been lovers?

She gathered her things at speed, conscious of his eyes on her as he waited.

'What will everyone think?' This to try and lighten the sudden tension between them, but her voice was brittle and her smile was watery. Inadvertently, she had alluded to the relationship they had shared and she went even redder. 'I mean...' she stammered, then fell into awkward silence.

'What *will* everyone think?' Nico purred silkily. 'By everyone, I take it you're referring to everyone we're going to pass on the way to the elevator?'

'This isn't funny, Nico.'

'You're my secretary,' he said mildly. 'I think it's safe to say that no one is going to think anything. Are you afraid your reputation might be ruined?' His eyebrows shot up and he stepped back to open the outer door so that she could precede him. He leant to whisper in her ear. 'Only you and I know the truth, don't we, Grace?' He pulled back and briskly walked away and she hurried after him. 'Your reputation is already so interestingly sullied...'

If the merest mention of *anything* to do with what they'd had opened a Pandora's box, then it was obvious that she was going to have to be very careful to skirt round it all and truly pretend none of it had happened. Her ears were burning and her throat was dry at the flurry of images those wickedly whispered words provoked. It reminded her that her hunt for another job would have to be an urgent one because how much more would it take for her to just be able to control her wayward responses?

He was off on his hot date!

Yet, he wasn't averse to alluding to their brief affair. Did he think it was funny to embarrass her?

She was hot all over as they rode the elevator down to the basement and she looked at him with alarm as it shuddered to a stop.

'Where are we?'

'I'll give you a lift home.'

'No!'

'Why not?' The doors slid open and he stood to one side, which compelled her to slip past him although she immediately turned around, her hands on her hips.

'Because…because…'

'Are you scared?'

'Scared?' Her voice was pitched a few decibels higher. 'Scared of what?'

'Scared of this,' Nico muttered, sotto voce.

And just like that, before she could do anything, before she could pull back or turn away or even get her thoughts in order, he was leaning into her. He held her, a gentle enough hold but powerful enough to stay her and his mouth covered hers.

His kiss was hungry, his tongue probing as it moved against hers, caressing and greedy and *wanting* all at the same time.

Time stood still. Wetness pooled between her legs and muscle memory made her lean towards him, devouring him just as he was devouring her.

She wanted this to stop immediately and she wanted it to go on and on and on for ever.

Disobedient hands strayed upwards to wind around his neck and the heat of his hard body against hers filled her with giddy, guilty pleasure. His fingers lightly threaded a blistering path along her collarbone and her breath hitched in her throat and her eyelids fluttered. Oh, how she could remember the way he had made her body feel!

She heard the clacking of footsteps echoing in the cavernous underground car park and yanked back, half stumbling in the process and automatically tugging her clothes into some kind of order.

Sanity was like a bucket of cold water, drowning her with shame and mocking her for her weakness. She jerked back and stared at him with wide, horrified eyes.

'How *dare* you?'

'How dare I *what*?'

Nico raked his fingers through his hair and looked away. He was furious with himself. Furious with himself for not being able to get her out of his system…for wanting to touch when he'd been knocked back…for not being able to resist temptation when it had been put in front of him. Everything about what had just happened exemplified the sort of weakness he had trained himself to despise.

God, even now, as his dark eyes rested on her swollen lips, he had to fight against moving towards her even if only to breathe her in.

Being on that island had perhaps put the misdeeds of his uncle into some kind of perspective but there was no way he had any time for emotions ruling his head, whatever change of perspective he might have had. Never had, never would.

The frustration right now was intense.

'You have my apologies,' Nico muttered in a driven undertone.

Tension was tearing through her body as she stared at him, her mouth still bruised from his, her body still wanting more, still burning for him.

He'd apologised but there had been no need because there was nothing for him to apologise about. She'd kissed him back as hungrily as he'd kissed her. She'd wanted him with every fibre of her being.

The only difference was he'd kissed her, she knew, to prove a point. To prove that she was still turned on by him. She, however, had kissed *him* because she'd had no choice. Her body had not been able to obey what her head had been saying.

He was moving on where she was standing still, and she would carry on standing still just so long as she was in his presence.

Grace took a deep, steadying breath.

'This isn't going to work,' she said quietly.

'You have my word that nothing of the kind will ever happen again,' Nico said heavily. 'God knows what I was thinking.'

'You wanted to prove to me that you could still... have an effect on me.' She supplied the answer before he could fill in the blanks himself. 'I expect...you must find it all very amusing, that someone of my age could be as—'

'Don't say it, Grace,' he interrupted thickly. 'I could never be that person.'

'I might still find you attractive, Nico,' Grace said, gathering all her pride, 'but that doesn't mean that it's any more annoying than that.'

'Annoying…'

'What else? It's an inconvenient attraction. Nothing more.'

'Of course,' he said stiffly.

'But it's there and it's going to be impossible for us to continue working together. I thought…it might not intrude but…'

'My fault.'

'No one's fault, Nico. It is what it is. Tomorrow I'll begin looking for another job.'

The pain that tore into her as she uttered those words made her feel dizzy and sick. That she had actually already begun the exercise made no difference. She had openly stated her intention and now it was written in stone, a declaration of intent from which she could not, now, withdraw.

'No need.'

'What do you mean?'

'The last thing I would want is for you to…feel uncomfortable at the office. We work far too closely together for that to be a bearable situation. Not that that's the point. I…you deserve better than to feel apprehensive whenever I'm around and I get it that you might, even though you have my word that what happened just then…an aberration…' Nico breathed out heavily, unable to meet her eyes and making sure to step back, to put distance between them. 'You can leave without working your notice.'

'I beg your pardon?'

Nico smiled crookedly. 'This isn't how I ever saw our...working relationship playing out, but you've been the best... I wouldn't even call you my secretary because you've been a hell of a lot more than that. My right-hand...woman. And, Grace...' he pressed his thumbs against his eyes and then looked at her steadily '... I... I'll miss you, but you would be more comfortable not having to come in, so don't. As of this moment, I'm relieving you of your duties. You'll be paid for as long as it takes for you to find another job and I guarantee that I will give you the most glowing reference you could hope to get.'

'You mean...'

'I mean you can return to the office, clear your desk and say farewell to this building with no obligations to ever set foot in it again.'

'But what about my replacement?'

'I'll manage, Grace.' He tipped his hand in a mocking salute. 'I'm a big boy now.'

CHAPTER NINE

NICO LOOKED AT the woman sitting across from him at the table in the romantic restaurant that Grace had somehow found the time to book between clearing her desk and leaving copious notes for whoever happened to replace her.

How had she managed that?

Nico had no idea. She must have worked until midnight. At any rate, he had returned to the office early this morning and it was as if the woman who had been by his side for so many years, the oil that lubricated the engine of his working life, had never been.

The desk had been empty. The two plants had gone. The work computer had been sitting squarely in the middle of the empty desk and the stack of neatly typed notes had told its own story of dedication to the last.

Nico surfaced to the sound of silence and his blonde date staring at him with gimlet-eyed disapproval.

'I thought this evening was going to be fun.' She pouted, toying with the stem of her wine glass.

'So did I,' Nico concurred.

She was everything any red-blooded man could want in a date when it came to looks. Long blonde hair, falling like a sheet over narrow tanned shoulders. Big, baby-blue eyes and breasts that refused to be constrained by the strappy top she was wearing. She was an easily recognised catwalk model and every head had swung round the second they had entered the restaurant.

Unfortunately for Nico, as soon as he had seen her emerging from the chauffeur-driven Bentley he had sent to collect her, he had realised that the last thing he'd wanted was a date with Flavia Destyn. Politeness had prevented him from doing what he had wanted to do and making up a something and nothing excuse to back out but now…having spent the past forty-five minutes in stony silence while his mind whirred with images of Grace, he could no longer pretend that he wasn't bored out of his wits.

And it wasn't Flavia's fault.

'I have a lot on my mind at the moment,' he continued truthfully. He sat back as the exquisite fish dish he couldn't remember ordering was placed in front of him, but he continued to look at his date, aware that he had already concluded that the evening wasn't going to be going anywhere that involved the two of them in the same space.

What was she doing?

Who was she seeing?

Had she gone back on the Internet in the space of a handful of days?

Was she meeting some hunk in her house and cooking him dinner?

He stabbed the fish and scowled.

'I know a very good way of taking your mind off whatever's bothering you,' Flavia cooed, reaching out and covering his hand with hers and turning her baby blues on him with smoky, sultry invitation.

'So do I,' Nico murmured, sliding his plate to one side and feeling a sense of purpose for the first time since he'd magnanimously dispatched his secretary from his life.

He watched the blonde preen coquettishly with triumph and felt a little bad because she was in for a rude awakening.

'You're a nice girl, Flavia, and I'm sure that under other circumstances it would have been nice to get to know you...more intimately...'

But my days of getting to know you or anyone else intimately are at an end because the only woman I'm interested in knowing intimately is doing God only knows what right now with someone else.

Sudden panic swept through Nico. He'd never thought himself a fanciful person but suddenly he was bombarded by very graphic and very unwelcome images of Grace in the arms of another man.

She wouldn't be.

She wasn't like that.

He knew her. He knew her as well as he'd known anyone in his life before, as well as he knew himself.

Maybe she was doing right now just what he was doing. Seeing someone because she needed distracting from an attraction that wasn't going anywhere. Inconvenient it might be, but that didn't mean it wasn't urgent and demanding, an attraction that no one else could erase.

And maybe that attraction was more than just annoying. Could it be that she felt the same way he did?

Under that controlled exterior, was she hiding feelings for him? Because wasn't that what *he* had been doing? Hiding feelings he hadn't expected? Pretending that what he felt was something he could control? Something that hadn't got to the very core of him until it was so embedded that life without those feelings was unthinkable?

He had been so sure that he could plan the outcome of his life that he had had no defences in place to prevent the slow intrusion of a woman who had gradually become indispensable.

He had slept with her and not for a moment had he paid heed to the dangers right in front of him. The klaxons and alarm bells had been shrieking and yet he had gaily sallied forth, utterly oblivious.

Why would he have paid them a scrap of attention?

In his well-ordered world, Nico had set himself the goal of marrying for convenience.

Once, he had tried his luck elsewhere. Once, he had opened the door to a gloriously impulsive woman who'd wanted everything. He had looked at his father's arranged marriage and figured he could do things differently. He'd fallen for a woman who had demanded more than he could give. What had started with the heat and urgency of courtship had crashed and burned in a welter of accusation and anger. She'd needed him there by her side twenty-four-seven. She'd wanted one hundred per cent attention and had complained bitterly when work demands had called him away. He'd tried, but his father's mantra about the importance of responsibility had come back to haunt him. If that was love, then love wasn't for him.

After nine months, he had retreated from the fray and accepted that the lessons he had grown up with had been right all along.

Love and emotions were chaos, and he just wasn't built to deal with chaos.

Chaos had been his uncle. Order had been his father. Experience had taught him that it was pointless to look for the middle road.

Nico had locked his heart away and thrown out the key.

He might enjoy life to the full, but he would never be a fool. He would always be in control of his responses and no one would ever cross the lines he had laid down. He might be less constrained than his father, who had married the right woman when he had been very young and had never strayed from the straight and narrow, but he would never be his uncle.

Nico had quietly believed himself immune to surprises when it came to matters of the heart.

Was it any wonder he had glibly glazed over at all the warning signs that had been posted along the way until he was here now with a growing sense of panic inside him that he might have left things too late?

He focused. Flavia's expression was changing from self-satisfied triumph to growing alarm. Very shortly the alarm would tip over into fury and Nico didn't think he had it in him to face the wrath of a rejected date.

'I should go,' he said quietly. He scrunched the linen napkin on the table and signalled to the waiter without taking his eyes off Flavia. 'My apologies for leaving, Flavia. This isn't your fault. I should not have contacted you.'

'You can't just *walk off* and leave me sitting here,' the blonde hissed, glancing around her at the well-manicured, expensive clientele. 'What are people going to think?'

'That I'm a bastard and a blind one at that for walking out on a beautiful woman.' Nico paused and glanced at his watch. Time was suddenly of the essence. His imagination was fired up with all kinds of scenarios and he didn't like any of them. 'You like Destra?' He named an exclusive club of which he was a member and she nodded, although the pout was still in place. 'You can gather up your friends and go there. Ask for Ronnie and tell him you and your friends are to be treated like royalty. Champagne and caviar until midnight.'

'But when will I see you again?'

'I wouldn't bank on any more dates in the future.' Nico began rising to his feet, asking her whether she wanted to accept his champagne compensation offer and then telling her that he would phone Ronnie in advance so that there were no problems at the door.

He vaguely registered that it was a result that his date hadn't thrown her dinner plate at him. Flavia might be a catwalk model and tough as nails when it came to guys, but walking out on her halfway through a meal was not something he would ever have considered doing, however bored he might have been with the conversation.

In this instance, though...?

He could have contacted his driver but this felt like a very personal mission so he detoured only to grab his Ferrari and, on the way, the most expensive bunch of flowers he could find that late in the evening from a florist's close to the Underground.

His body was alive with edgy restlessness, but he was doing something. He was figuring out his life and he was doing something about it. He only hoped it wasn't too late.

Tommy was talking. He seemed to have been talking for most of the dinner she had painstakingly prepared to the point where most of it was still on his plate.

Grace knew that she should be happy, but she felt as though she were being battered from all sides, which meant that most of the food on *her* plate also remained uneaten.

She'd been on a low when her brother had arrived that morning. She'd plastered a bright smile on her face, but her head had been worrying over the misery sitting like a lump in the pit of her stomach.

No more Nico. No more job. No more *anything*. Fair as he was, he had allowed her to walk away without the discomfort of having to work her notice.

She would have her pay kept intact for as long as it took for her to find suitable employment. His references would be glowing. Could she have asked for more? Hadn't she already concluded that working with him was going to be impossible?

And that kiss...

The nail in the coffin. So much had been given away in her response, in the way she had clung to him with the desperation of a drowning swimmer clutching at a lifebelt thrown in the water. He had seen and smelled and *tasted* all the passion that was still there, simmering under the surface, waiting to be ignited at the spark of a flame.

Good heavens, she had been asked to book a dinner date for him with his latest blonde, and, even knowing that he was back to his old tricks, she *still* hadn't been able to resist his touch. He had lazily and idly tried it on, and instead of pushing him away she had capitulated without even the whiff of a fight.

So now she was staring at a bottomless void and on top of that... Tommy.

She'd expected him to be querulous...in need of the usual soothing pep talk... She'd braced herself to bite down on any hint of impatience. Instead, he had been fighting fit and, having had a break from her, had decided that the time was right for him to launch into what, she assumed, had been on his mind for a while.

He wanted her to back off.

She was too intrusive. He felt stifled. He could manage just fine without her calling him all the time to make sure he hadn't done anything silly. He *knew* she meant well...he *knew* how bad things had been after the accident. But that was years ago, and it was time for her to do her own thing and stop fussing over him.

Then he had gentled his tone and informed her that he had met someone, a girl in the same block as him. They'd been seeing one another for nearly four months and he hadn't mentioned it because he knew that if he had she, Grace, would have given him so many well-intentioned warnings that she would have ruined the whole thing.

Now, as she stared at her beautiful and in her head permanently dependent kid brother, she had to struggle not to feel mortally wounded by everything he had just laid at her door.

He'd finally dived into the chicken pie she had cooked but she shoved her plate to one side.

When, she thought miserably, had she morphed from the sister who picked up the pieces to the sister who became a bore? She felt rejected in her love life, with all her silly expectations, and rejected by her own family, who clearly no longer needed her suffocating concern.

Tears pricked the backs of her eyes, but she squeezed the hand that suddenly covered hers.

'You're amazing, sis,' Tommy told her, his blue eyes caring. 'But it's time you let me live my life and you go and live yours. I feel you've always put your life on hold to look after Ma and then me and, okay, I've been pretty pathetic for a while, but I really thought about stuff when you were stuck out there and it's time for me to stand on my own two feet. Hey! You should be married with a kid of your own by now!'

Grace was struggling not to burst into tears of self-pity at that well-meaning but, oh, so way-off-target remark when the doorbell buzzed.

She wasn't expecting anyone, but she was glad for the distraction anyway.

How much more could she take? She was hopelessly in love with the wrong guy. Married with a kid of her own? She might as well try and find some magic red shoes and float her way to another planet because that was how impossible the dream of marriage and kids felt right now.

'Sorry to interrupt, Tommy. Doorbell!'

She fled, leaving Tommy to his chicken pie, and pulled open the door without thinking.

It took Grace a few seconds to register who was standing outside.

She saw the whole first—tall…male…impossibly handsome…

She noted the clothes—expensive…casual…dark trousers and a perfectly tailored designer polo…

She saw the flowers…well, in truth she'd seen better…

Then her brain tallied all those impressions and she flew back, eyes wide.

'What are *you* doing here?' Automatically Grace barred entry to the house by standing in front of the door, blocking him from sweeping past her.

'I've come…look, here. I got these for you.' Nico thrust the flowers at her and in response Grace looked at him coldly and folded her arms.

So…had he realised, after his bountiful gesture that she could leave without working her notice, that having an empty space with no one efficiently handling so much of his workload was going to be a bit harder than anticipated? Had he met his blonde bombshell and retrospectively realised that he would have to make his personal arrangements himself because it would take time to train up her replacement in the finer art of booking expensive, atmospheric restaurants? Not to mention sourcing just the right goodbye token when the time came. Come to think of it, why wasn't he clinking champagne glasses over a candlelit dinner with the bombshell, looking forward to a night of fun between the sheets? Never mind. Not her business. What *was* her business was the fact that he was planted in front of her door and she didn't want him there.

Had he shown up with a bunch of less than average flowers in the hope of wooing her back behind her desk?

Grace shuddered at the very thought.

'Shouldn't you be at an expensive French restaurant with your latest conquest?' she couldn't resist asking and he flushed.

'Will you let me in?'

'No.'

'Because you're busy entertaining *your* latest conquest?' Nico asked, his mouth twisting cynically, although his hot, brooding eyes were saying something she wasn't sure she quite understood.

'Who I'm with is none of your business, Nico.' She looked at the flowers and was filled with sudden rage. 'And if you think you can renege on your promise and get me back into the office to do my time because you've realised you can't cope with the hassle of finding somebody else, then forget it. And the flowers? Not up to scratch, Nico. If you'd told me in advance, I would have ordered a much more expensive bunch for myself to plead your case. Although my answer would have been exactly the same!'

Nico edged closer and Grace, in turn, feeling the heat from him and the stirrings of her own treacherous body, toughened her stance, stood straighter, her back ramrod straight.

'Grace...'

About to tell him that he needed to go, Grace was interrupted before she could open her mouth by Tommy calling her, asking who was at the door, his voice high and cheerful and then the sound of his slow steps heading towards the front door to join her.

She glanced over her shoulder and there he was, pausing to stand in the small hall, his head tilted to one side. So blond, so angelic and so…*so present at exactly the wrong time.*

'Tommy, please, could you go and wait for me in the…er…kitchen? I'll be with you in a sec.'

'Tommy?' Nico shifted closer to peer over her shoulder.

'Who's that?' Tommy flagrantly ignored Grace's request and padded over so that he was standing directly behind her. She could feel his warm breath on the back of her neck although her eyes were riveted by Nico and the dark, disapproving flush spreading across his handsome face.

'Please, Tommy…' She half turned to her brother, who was grinning at her, eyebrows raised. He looked as though he might launch into a conversation she didn't want.

'Tommy? Pleased to meet you.'

Grace was aghast as Nico reached past her, brushing her arm, to encourage her brother towards him, and she half closed her eyes when they shook hands, which proved awkward considering she had remained standing between them.

Her heart was hammering inside her like a sledgehammer. Her secrecy about her private life now made her burn with discomfort. She had kept her private life to herself as a self-defence mechanism! And what a good idea that had been, all things considered! But now it felt sly and overblown. Now, she wished she had confided in him. He would have listened. He would have given her sensible advice. He would have told her what

Tommy had just told her…that she needed to stop playing full-time carer. He would have braced her for something that had come as a complete shock.

She wished she'd shared. She'd given him everything anyway, everything that really mattered. What had been the point in holding back the little details?

Nico, shifting awkwardly to inspect his competition, noted the guilty pinkening of Grace's cheeks.

Tommy?

Since when was she someone who abbreviated other people's names? Everyone else called James, the sales manager, Jimmy, and it had always amused him that she had never used that abbreviation. In fact, thinking about it, hadn't she once told him in that sexy, prim, husky voice of hers that she didn't have time for the annoying tendency people had to shorten anything and everything?

So… *Tommy*?

Nico felt something he had never felt in his life before and it ripped through him like shards of glass, cutting, wounding, making him bleed inside.

Jealousy.

It was an emotion he had never had time for, but it was very real now, and he felt his jaw ache as he clenched it in something he hoped was a passably indifferent smile.

So she had a guy over. So she had cooked him dinner. That didn't mean she'd moved on from *him*, did it?

He found that he was clutching the flowers so tightly that the stems were breaking and he hurriedly thrust the bunch at her, which took her somewhat by surprise.

'I haven't brought these because I'm trying to woo you back to the workplace,' he muttered.

His mind was occupied with the fair-haired guy who was still looking at him with open curiosity.

He looked like a kid. Fresh faced despite a certain seriousness lurking beneath the surface, something shadowed and disillusioned that spoke of life more eventful than would appear superficially. He wasn't a kid. He was a man with a backstory. He was a three-dimensional guy standing in the doorway of a woman he realised he'd always thought of as *his*. Jealousy tightened its grip.

'I suppose you'd better come in and tell me why you're here.' Grace stood aside reluctantly, shooing Tommy back into the kitchen, relieved when he did as she signalled although she made sure to funnel Nico away from the kitchen into the sitting room. She stood back and watched as he swung round to look at her for a few tense seconds.

'You moved fast.'

'I beg your pardon?'

'Who is he?'

'Nico, what are you talking about?' She narrowed her eyes and folded her arms.

He dominated the small sitting room, standing there, towering over her, his aggressive masculinity threatening every part of her and making her feel unprotected.

'The man,' Nico grated. 'New Internet sensation?'

'For heaven's sake!' Grace looked at him narrowly. 'Are you...*jealous*?'

I should have told you... I shouldn't have been so buttoned up.

'Jealous? I've never been jealous in my life before!'

Nico raked his fingers through his hair and stared at her before swinging away to drop into one of the chairs. He immediately leaned forward, hands on his thighs.

'I think I need a drink.'

Grace hesitated.

Of course, the last thing she wanted or *needed* right now was this man in her house, sending her already frazzled nervous system into yet more freefall.

And she certainly didn't need to feel this *guilt* about drawing the lines she had drawn.

He made her feel *alive* but was feeling *alive* a good thing? Hadn't it been so much easier to live life on one level? Not too high, not too low? The excitement flooding through her made her want to cry because it was a rushing tide she couldn't hold back.

'You need to tell me why you're here, Nico,' she finally managed to say.

'Okay. You're right. I'm… I suppose you could say…' he looked at her with smouldering accusation in his deep, ink-black eyes '…that I'm jealous.'

'You're *jealous*?' Grace quietly shut the sitting-room door behind her. If she knew Tommy, he would finish his chicken pie and reach for his mobile and probably, given what she now knew, immediately get in touch with his girlfriend for an hour-long conversation.

She sidled towards one of the chairs and then perched on it. Her tummy was full of butterflies. She had no idea where this was going but there was no way she could walk away from this edge-of-the-seat thrill sensation swirling inside her.

She linked her fingers and leant towards him.

'You asked me what I was doing here and whether I shouldn't be at that restaurant with a woman and the answer is yes. That's where I should be. That's where I was up until an hour ago but I found that it wasn't where I actually wanted to be.' He shook his head as though clearing it and continued, voice low, 'I couldn't get you out of my head, Grace. Where I wanted to be was with *you*. I came here because I had no choice. I thought about you…and another man and it drove me nuts.'

Listening to Nico, hearing the ragged sincerity in his voice and seeing the urgency in his dark gaze, Grace felt her heart swell but with that came a warning voice of caution.

This wasn't love.

This was attraction. This was lust. He didn't want her back in the office. He wanted her back in his bed and he had come here because he had thought she was entertaining some guy.

The fact that he was jealous…well, Grace had to admit that that did something to her, sent little shivers racing up and down her spine. As did the way his eyes were burning into her.

Little did he know that he had nothing to be jealous about. She breathed in deeply.

'You have nothing to be jealous about.'

'I don't?' Long, lush lashes dropped to conceal his expression but there was a glitter in his eyes when he next looked at her.

'Tommy is…my brother.'

Afterwards, Grace would try and recapture in her head the sequence of expressions that flitted across

Nico's face at that revelation but overwhelmingly it was one of utter stupefaction.

His mouth dropped open and for a few seconds he looked as though that sharp mind of his had been completely emptied.

'Sorry?'

'Tommy's my brother.'

'But you haven't got a brother.'

'What do you mean?'

'We… I thought…we shared…you would have told me if you had a brother.'

Nico felt that unexpected revelation like the force of a runaway train barrelling into him at full speed. It knocked him for six.

A brother?

He'd thought he knew her. Thought he knew her as well as she knew him. He'd shared more with her than he ever had with anyone in his life before. When he thought back to their time together on the island, before, even, he could see a trail of confidences left behind him. Barely acknowledged, just slipped into conversation in passing. He'd told her things he'd never told anyone. And yet, it had not been returned. No like for like.

It felt like treachery and it hurt.

Grace's throat constricted. How could she explain that talking about her childhood had felt dangerous? How could she tell him that she'd been so scared of turning him off her that she'd edited herself to be the person she'd thought he wanted? Someone who was in it just for the fun? That she'd held her private life close to herself because, in her head, she could envision him running a mile if she shared things that overstepped the boundaries between them?

How could she explain that she had made a mistake?

In a rush, she began talking.

She was suddenly desperate to wipe that shocked look from his face. She didn't care if he'd come here just to ask her for a few repeat performances in the sack. She wanted that look on his face *to go away* because it made something inside her tighten with a pain she had never felt before.

'Tommy…yes, Tommy's my brother. I've been looking after him, really, for…all his life.' She paused, licked her dry lips and ran her fingers through her hair but she kept looking at him, trying to gauge what he was thinking. 'I never knew my dad,' she said jerkily. 'It was just me and Mum and then Tommy came along. Just the three of us but the responsibility…well, it fell on my shoulders from as far back as I can remember. My mum…our mother…she wasn't really into parenting. She was more into guys and having fun. When it came to taking responsibility for us…she just didn't have it in her. She was lovely and carefree and, as I got older, it felt as though she was…younger than me in a lot of ways.'

'You…have a mother…'

'I do, Nico. I have one of those.' Grace paused but he failed to fill the silence and so she ploughed on with the backstory she had withheld for such a long time. Nerves were skittering through her and she was perspiring.

'Enlighten me.' Nico's voice was barely audible.

'My mum had a couple of husbands. She was so

young when she had us and she was always in search for the right guy, always being knocked back. All I can remember is taking care of her, picking her up when she was down. She didn't like cooking, at least not the sort of stuff that kids should eat. We used to have pancakes for dinner and pizza for breakfast. Whatever came to hand. When I got old enough, I took over the business of making sure there was nutritious food on the table, at least most of the time.'

'And your brother?'

Grace could scarcely hear him and the expression on his face, while not as shocked, was blank, which almost felt worse.

'Tommy… Tommy suffered more from Cecily's lack of parenting skills.' Grace lost herself in the telling because it was cathartic and because she was desperate to tell him *everything*. 'I filled in the best I could but there was always disappointment when sports day arrived and Mum wasn't there. He was very talented on the playing field. Loved his rugby. He was climbing up the ladder, had been scouted and the future was looking bright but then he had an accident. A severe one and all those dreams came to an end.' Grace chewed her lip, remembering those painful days.

'I… I'm very sorry to hear that.'

'It was a very bad time all round. Worst of all was that just around then, as luck would have it, Mum found her guy. All that time, all those mistakes, but she found her guy. A great guy from Australia. A proper outback rancher who swept her off her feet. She married and then, very shortly after, emigrated to Australia.'

'She left you to take charge.'

'It happens.' Grace pressed her hands to her heated cheeks. 'Tommy was in hospital for ages and when he finally came out, he faced a long, hard struggle to get back on his feet, literally. Lots of physio, lots of setbacks and lots of therapy so that he could deal with what had happened.' She looked around her at the small, nondescript sitting room.

'I had to do my best for my brother. I got him somewhere small but specially adapted to suit his needs. And then the therapist. All private and none of that comes cheap, which is why I live here even though I've been paid a lot over the years. I'm babbling, I know, but, Nico...' Her voice trailed away into silence.

Nico listened. Every word was fresh hurt. He knew he shouldn't feel betrayed but he did, because she had a side to her, a *world* to her that she had denied him.

He thought of the flowers he had bought and the final hurdle he had overcome to let his defences down and thinking about that made him sick to the stomach.

He'd opened himself up, admitted his own vulnerability but he had fatally misread the signals. She had never allowed him in because what she felt for him had never been on a par with what he felt for her.

He had made a terrible mistake. Nico felt he was drowning under the weight of misplaced assumptions and a reckless optimism in something that had always been a chimera.

He stood up.

'It was a mistake coming here, Grace.' He moved towards the door and rested his hand on the doorknob and then said, over his shoulder, looking at her for the last time, 'When I leave here, you won't see me again. Don't try and contact me. The past has gone and that door is now closed for good.' He smiled heavily. 'Adieu for the last time.'

CHAPTER TEN

'So what are you going to do about it?'

Grace looked at her brother, the very same brother she had conditioned herself to believe would always be her responsibility. The very same brother, she now realised, who was perfectly capable of looking after himself. She smiled ruefully.

'He doesn't love me. Hey…since when are you the one dishing out the sensible advice?' But the smile had turned into a grin and for a split second she almost forgot her chaotically beating heart, the very heart that had been wrenched from her chest when Nico had walked out of the house.

Tommy looked at her seriously. 'This is a crossroads for us, sis. From now on, we're equals and, as such, I'm telling you that if you love this guy, then tell him, because if you don't you'll spend the rest of your life regretting it.'

'Okay.' Grace felt a slow fire begin to burn inside her. 'Maybe you're right. No. You *are* right. So, Tommy…' she walked as she talked, throwing words over her shoulder '…if you don't mind, I'm going to love you and leave you and…' She dashed to where

he was sitting and hugged him tightly before standing
back. 'Next time I see you, I want to see this girlfriend
of yours. Understood?'

'Wouldn't have it any other way, sis.'

Of course, Grace knew where her boss lived. Like so
many bits and pieces of information, it was just something else she had picked up along the way.

She didn't know whether he was going to return to
his house or when.

She had no idea if, having walked out of her life, he
might decide to return to the date he had abandoned.

She would wait.

She had enough on her mind to wait a thousand years
and still have more thoughts to process.

The sprint to the Underground was breathing space
she needed. She wanted to analyse everything he had
said to her and every shifting expression on his face,
but a sense of urgency jumbled all her thoughts.

He'd been so shocked to find out about Tommy and
she could understand why. He had always been a man
to value his privacy, but he had ended up sharing a
great deal with her and so to discover that there had
been major things she had chosen to keep to herself
would have hurt.

She had babbled out all the confidences he had been
denied but she could remember the shutters that had
slammed over his dark eyes, locking her out.

Grace knew that she had had the option to walk
away. He had come bearing flowers and an invitation
back to his bed, which was not what she wanted. If he
had been hurt by the fact that she had guarded her pri-

vate life from him, then *she* had had her fair share of suffering, knowing that she had fallen for someone who was incapable of returning her love.

The line could have been drawn underneath it all. Nico would never have returned. His adieu would truly have been final.

But Tommy had been right and she would have reached the same conclusion sooner rather than later. To live with regret was to live a half-life and she would have had a lot of regrets.

It was still and dark by the time she made it to Nico's palatial house in Kensington.

She had been there several times in the past. Twice to drop off urgently needed documents and another time for a Christmas gathering he had hosted for a handful of employees. It had been a grand occasion, with waiters everywhere and a classical quartet playing in the background. She could remember the way she had felt then…painfully aware of Nico in his black polo and black trousers and the woman who had followed him here, there and everywhere, looking at him with adoring puppy-dog eyes.

Why on earth she hadn't got the picture loud and clear then and duly taken herself off to a dating site, Grace had no idea.

So long being careful and responsible had boxed her in. Her energies had gone into her job, and living a life outside that—outside Tommy and all the practicalities that went along with the care he had needed—had been sidelined. All those missed opportunities to meet a guy, have fun, see what the future might hold in store for her…not to mention to give Tommy the freedom from her stifling caretaking. He hadn't put it in so many words but she had understood without having to be told. Instead, she had remained in a holding bay, waiting for life to happen and daydreaming about Mr Impossible.

She had barely recognised her own crush on her boss for what it could dangerously mushroom into.

Now she was here, and she was going to deal with the fallout for all her poor choices whatever the outcome.

Of course, there was nothing convenient anywhere near his house, like a coffee shop. There were just other mansions with forbidding iron gates and precision-trimmed hedges tall enough to protect the occupants of the big houses from riff-raff's prying eyes.

In the absence of a key to his house, she did, fortunately, have the code to his side gate and she let herself in hoping no one saw her, because they would immediately call the police.

This was definitely not the sort of place where random strangers were tolerated, least of all ones letting themselves in via side gates.

Of course, there was no one in. The darkness was a giveaway. Just the outside light illuminating the front door. She rang the bell anyway and, with the predictable lack of response, she went to the bench at the side and sat down. She was braced for the long haul. It was not yet nine in the evening. Thank goodness it wasn't too cold. A bit chilly but nothing her thick cardigan couldn't handle.

It was after eleven by the time Nico got back to his house. He'd left Grace and headed straight to the pub. It wasn't a gastropub with delusions of grandeur. It was one of the few proper pubs not a million miles from his house, because he wanted to walk back. A proper pub where a guy could go and drown his sorrows in a few honest-to-goodness bottles of strong beer.

He had to.

His mind was going crazy. He couldn't assimilate what had been thrown at him and even though he knew he was being an ass, because he, more than anyone else, should know that people were entitled to their privacy, he still felt bitterly hurt. Wounded to the very core. Wounded in places he hadn't even known existed.

The temperature had dropped. He felt the coolness penetrating his lightweight jacket as he clumsily pressed the buttons to the side gate. The walk had sobered him up, but he could still feel the effects of the beer he had drunk. Not enough to block out all his thoughts but enough for a definite improvement.

The sound to his left as he began heading up the Victorian paved path to his front door almost failed to penetrate.

The shape huddled on his bench registered a hell of a lot more and if the night air hadn't quite sobered him up, then the sight of someone on his property did the trick in record time.

And Nico's milk of human kindness was at an all-time low. He strode over at pace and reached for the collar of whoever was curled on his bench and then cursed with shock when the shape unfurled and he saw who it was.

She had gaped in surprise when he had shown up on her doorstep. Now it was his turn. He watched, stunned for a few seconds, as she rubbed her eyes and began sitting up.

'Jesus,' he muttered, swearing again. 'What are you doing on my bench, Grace? How long have you been here?'

'I'm cold,' she whispered by way of response.

Nico barely stopped to think. He swept her up in one fluid movement and carried her through the door and into the warmth of his sitting room, then he gently placed her on one of his wildly expensive leather sofas and stood back, arms folded, staring.

Grace looked up at him. Their eyes collided and she swallowed, at a disadvantage now that she was here, lying on his sofa while he towered over her with an expression that could freeze water.

She struggled to sit up, but her joints ached from how she had fallen asleep on the bench.

'Want to tell me why you're here?'

'I'm sorry.'

'You've come here to tell me that you're sorry? When I walked out your front door, Grace, I told you that I had no intention of ever seeing you again and I meant it.' His voice was cold and unforgiving. 'So what if I knew or didn't know about your brother, about the life you'd had? Not the end of the world. Trust me.'

'I know it's not the end of your world, Nico.'

'You're shivering.' He swore again, told her to stay put and returned seconds later with a glass. 'Drink this.'

Grace took the glass, drank the whisky and felt it burn through her nerves, giving her some much-needed strength.

'I wasn't keeping secrets from you,' she said quietly, nursing the glass.

'I told you—'

'Yes, that it doesn't matter. You came to my house to try and get me back into bed with you. I know that, Nico.' She watched his face darken into a scowl. 'You met Tommy and you were jealous but then you found out that he was my brother and you were hurt and I'm sorry about that.'

'You overestimate your position in my life, Grace.'

That felt like a body blow but she met his cool gaze without flinching. 'I've had a crush on you for years, Nico.' There, it was out in the open. It should have felt like a weight lifted from her shoulders because didn't they say that confession was good for the soul? Sadly, Grace just wanted the ground to open and swallow her up.

'I never thought it would ever come to anything because I always knew the sort of women you were attracted to. Racy blondes who enjoyed all the things money could buy. I wasn't a racy blonde so you were never going to be attracted to me. Ergo, having a crush on you was safe because nothing would ever come of it and I liked that because... I've spent all of my adult life being a coward.'

She looked at him as he shifted closer to sit on the sofa next to her.

This wasn't the equivalent of a welcome mat but at least it wasn't the sound of a door slamming in her face.

'I was brave when it came to looking after Mum and Tommy. I bore the brunt of all the hard work. Tommy was always the vulnerable one and I was always the strong one and, really, they both looked to me to do the caretaking. But I never had a chance to develop in all those areas where girls develop.'

'You weren't allowed *any* freedom to do what you wanted to do?'

The gentleness of his voice made tears prick the backs of her eyes for this was what she'd missed when he had withdrawn from her. She had thought she'd walked away from him, so it was ironic how much it had hurt when he had shown up unannounced only to retreat behind an impenetrable wall when he'd met Tommy and found out who he was.

'I had all the freedom in the world,' Grace said quietly. 'I just didn't know how to use it. My mother never chained me to the stove and forced me to cook and Tommy never asked me to help him with his homework or make him a packed lunch to take to school. I did it all because it just seemed to happen that way and then, somehow, I hit my teenage years and I found that I never learnt how to flirt or talk to boys or get invited to parties.' She smiled. 'Or even have confidence when it came to stuff like that. I had one boyfriend, which was a fumbling, clumsy affair, and it was so much easier to give up on the whole scary thing.'

'Go on,' Nico urged.

'Then, like I told you earlier, Mum married and moved to Australia not that long after Tommy's accident and my life seemed even more closed in. I started working for you and…yes, I developed a crazy crush on you.'

'I like that. I approve of crazy crushes.'

'I would have told you about Tommy and Mum…

but there were lines between us, Nico. You were my boss. Even when we slept together, you were still my boss, and I was very conscious of that.' She paused and gazed at him with a thoughtful expression. 'No,' she admitted with painful honesty, 'it was more than that. Somewhere along the line, I realised that my crazy crush wasn't quite as harmless as I'd thought it would be. That's when I made up my mind to go on the Internet, find the life I'd been missing.'

'The nuisance lawyer... Victor? I remember his name.'

'That was my first foray.' She held his gaze sheepishly. 'I didn't expect to be caught out.'

'I'm glad I did. It showed me a side of you I think I always knew was there, waiting to get out. Tell me about this crush of yours and how it developed.'

'It got serious, Nico. I realised just how serious when I was on that wretched date, trying hard to make an effort and hating the fact that I was there, and, even worse, hating the fact that I wished it were you sitting opposite me. An impossible dream. A stupid impossible dream that had grown completely out of hand.' She sighed and yawned. The whisky had made her feel sleepy, but she was no longer cold and she could finally feel the weight being lifted from her shoulders.

'And then we went to that island.'

'Yes, we did.'

'We made love and it was everything making love is all about.'

'For me, it was falling in love, Nico. And that's why, even in those most intimate moments, when I wanted to rest my head on your shoulder and spill my soul, I didn't because I figured it would drive you away and I didn't want that to happen. I was a coward. I'd fallen in love with you and I wanted to do everything within my power to hang onto you for as long as I could. I was proud. I was greedy.'

'You fell in love with me…'

'That's what I came here to say. I couldn't bear the thought of you walking away and never knowing what was in my heart.'

'Oh, Grace…'

'I know what you're going to say. You're going to tell me that you can't return the feeling and I understand. I've always understood that what I felt for you would never come to anything.'

'In your search for a job,' Nico said gravely, 'I hope you haven't thought about going into fortune telling.'

'What do you mean?'

'I came to your house earlier because I wanted to tell you much the same thing.' He smiled wryly. 'Different backstory but there you go—we've ended up on the same page and maybe it was always going to be that way.'

Suddenly wide awake, Grace straightened and looked at Nico with urgency, although underneath the urgency there was still a thread of caution, guarding against believing something that sounded too good to be true.

'I don't understand,' she breathed.

'You do, Grace. I'm in love with you. I never thought it could happen to me. I've always told myself that I would never allow my emotions to wreak havoc with a cool head. My uncle—well, never mind that in the end I didn't know him, only knew of the reputation that lay in tatters after his exile—shaped my way of thinking. He represented everything that could go wrong when you lacked discipline. I looked at my own father and saw the opposite. An ordered life with ordered choices. He was the cool, calm and collected half of the coin where Sander was the other, and then I made my own youthful mistake.

'I fell for a girl who turned out to be just the sort of demanding woman I had spent a lifetime being warned against. In no uncertain terms I was warned that the woman who ended up at my side for the long haul would have to be someone who understood that I wasn't like anyone else. My father had his own empire and was responsible enough to put his employees first and I had my own and would have to do the same. There would be no time to pander to a woman who wanted all of me. I was too young to see that travelling down one road did not preclude the other. To be in charge didn't automatically mean making sure you never gave your emotions away. Falling in love didn't necessarily entail throwing yourself under the bus and giving in to a life of chaos. I look back on my parents and I can see now that while it may have been an arranged marriage of sorts, it was also a true love match.'

'You had such a varied, colourful love life, Nico...'

'Because I was happy to divide myself into two halves. The first would be the man who played the field and had fun and the second would be the man who gave that up and married a woman who didn't make demands, who left me to put work at the forefront of my life. Hot and cold, black and white, nothing in between. But, my darling, even while I was busy making those choices you were there, and little did I ever suspect that every minute of every day spent with you undermined all my grand plans for my future. Making love to you...it was different from anything I'd ever done before, fulfilling in ways I never dreamed imaginable and, of course, now I know why. I wasn't having sex, I was touching...tasting...*being* with a woman I had fallen hopelessly in love with.'

'So does that mean you forgive me for not telling you about Tommy?'

'On one condition...'

'What's that?'

'No more secrets between us. We talk about everything and anything all the time. Doubts, fears, hopes and dreams...we share everything.'

'I think I can agree to that...'

'And one other thing.'

'That's two conditions!' But she laughed, her eyes gently teasing him, filled with the love she had been so careful never to reveal.

'You marry me. As soon as possible. I want to start our lives together without waiting because I can't live without you.'

'I can definitely...' Grace flung herself at him, the man she'd loved for so long '...agree to that.'

EPILOGUE

GRACE LOOKED AT herself in the full-length mirror of the bedroom and smiled.

She twisted to one side, then to the other. Outside, winter was gathering in cold and darkness even though it was only a little after six in the evening.

Nico was due back any minute, and just thinking about that lock in the front door, and the decisive tread of his footsteps as he entered the lovely old cottage in Richmond they had chosen together a little over a year ago, made her heart thump.

The old, familiar feeling, a love that was so deep and so true that just thinking about him and knowing that she was the only person in the world to really see what lay inside him, made her shiver with pleasure.

Sometimes, she stopped and was amazed all over again at how much had happened in such a short space of time.

He hadn't been joking when he'd told her that he wanted their lives together to start right away.

'But a wedding takes ages to sort out,' Grace had told him a little dubiously, but, as neither of them had wanted anything at all extravagant, it had been remarkably straightforward to arrange.

They had gone back to the island for it and had been welcomed warmly by the new owners of Sander's hotel and by the staff who remembered them from when they had last been there.

Old memories and new ones being shaped. Grace had looked around her to the turquoise sea gently lapping on sand as powdery as icing sugar, with the sun a setting orange ball sinking behind the indigo horizon. The assembled guests had been as struck as she had been by the beauty of the place as she and Nico had exchanged wedding vows.

Her floaty cream dress had reminded her of how she had felt that first time on the island, when she had dumped the starchy work clothes and slipped into the light, soft summer dresses she had bought, and she had blushed when her husband-to-be had looked at her with such love and tenderness that it had brought a lump to her throat. Had he read what she'd been thinking?

His parents had been there and that had been moving as they had touched base with the people Sander had grown to love.

They'd both kept in touch with him, as it turned out, and, much as they had pleaded for him to return to the fold, he had flatly refused, preferring the peace of the island.

Her mother had come as well, along with her stepfather, and Tommy with his fiancée.

It had been a small affair. Relatives, friends…they had stayed at one of the five-star hotels in Nassau and she and Nico had remained back at Sander's hotel, as they privately called it.

'It's not where I started to love you,' Nico had whispered, on that first night after they had married on the beach, when everyone had been shuttled back to the main island, 'because that was something that started a long time before. But this place will always be special because it will always be where I touched you for the first time.'

When Grace thought back to the huskiness in his voice when he'd said that and the love in his eyes, she got a tingle of absolute contentment and a happiness that was as deep as an ocean inside her.

She heard the sound of the front door opening and she sprinted down the stairs just as Nico was shrugging off his coat.

'When are you going to stop doing this to me?' he murmured, moving towards her as she moved towards him.

'What's that?'

'Making me wish that my working day was shorter?' He grinned and pushed her hair back and then held her at arm's length and inspected her. 'I'm sensing something different about you this evening. New dress?'

Grace nodded. Now that she was working from home, editing a financial magazine, she had time to dash to the shops and, yes, the dress was new.

'I thought men weren't supposed to notice those things.' She grinned and spun round, pulling him towards the kitchen, where the table had been elaborately set, at which point he stopped in his tracks and turned her to look at him.

'First…' he grinned back at her and dropped kiss on the side of her mouth, and then, as though giving it a bit more thought, he kissed her thoroughly until she was all hot and bothered '… I'm unique, as I keep reminding you, and second, you need to tell me what's going on, because if you don't I'm going to start thinking that I might have forgotten something important.'

'I have a surprise for you.' Grace led him to the table where a slender box was wrapped with a ribbon round it and she watched as he held it aloft for a few puzzled seconds before peeling back the wrapping.

Then he smiled and the smile got wider and, when he looked at her, his dark eyes were ablaze.

'My day just got a whole lot better,' he growled, pulling her towards him and holding her close, so close that she could feel the beating of his heart under the crisp white shirt.

He held up the positive pregnancy stick and then looked at her and laughed with delight.

'A family. My darling, I can't wait. You've made me the happiest man on earth and I will treasure you till my dying breath.'

As I will you, Grace thought with overflowing love. *As I will you…*

* * * * *

COMING SOON!

We really hope you enjoyed reading this book.
If you're looking for more romance, be sure to
head to the shops when new books are
available on

Thursday 10th November

To see which titles are coming soon, please visit

millsandboon.co.uk/nextmonth

MILLS & BOON

MILLS & BOON®

Coming next month

WEDDING NIGHT WITH THE WRONG BILLIONAIRE
Dani Collins

"It's just us here." The words slipped out of her, impetuous. Desperate.

A distant part of her urged her to show some sense. She knew Micah would never forgive her for so much as getting in Remy's car, but they had had something in Paris. It had been interrupted and the not knowing what could have been had left her with an ache of yearning that had stalled her in some way. If she couldn't have Remy then it didn't matter who she married. They were all the same because they weren't him.

"No one would know."

"This would only be today. An hour. We couldn't tell anyone. Ever. If Hunter found out—"

"If Micah found out," she echoed with a catch in her voice. "I don't care about any of that, Remy. I really don't."

"After this, it goes back to the way it was, like we didn't even know one another. Is that really what you want?" His face twisted with conflict.

"No," she confessed with a chasm opening in her chest. "But I'll take it."

He closed his eyes, swearing as he fell back against the door with a defeated thump.

"Come here, then."

Continue reading
WEDDING NIGHT WITH THE WRONG BILLIONAIRE
Dani Collins

Available next month
www.millsandboon.co.uk

MILLS & BOON

THE HEART OF ROMANCE

A ROMANCE FOR EVERY READER

MODERN

Prepare to be swept off your feet by sophisticated, sexy and seductive heroes, in some of the world's most glamourous and romantic locations, where power and passion collide.

ISTORICAL

Escape with historical heroes from time gone by. Whether your passion is for wicked Regency Rakes, muscled Vikings or rugged Highlanders, awaken the romance of the past.

MEDICAL

Set your pulse racing with dedicated, delectable doctors in the high-pressure world of medicine, where emotions run high and passion, comfort and love are the best medicine.

True Love

Celebrate true love with tender stories of heartfelt romance, from the rush of falling in love to the joy a new baby can bring, and a focus on the emotional heart of a relationship.

Desire

Indulge in secrets and scandal, intense drama and plenty of sizzling hot action with powerful and passionate heroes who have it all: wealth, status, good looks…everything but the right woman.

EROES

Experience all the excitement of a gripping thriller, with an intense romance at its heart. Resourceful, true-to-life women and strong, fearless men face danger and desire - a killer combination!

To see which titles are coming soon, please visit

millsandboon.co.uk/nextmonth

LET'S TALK
Romance

For exclusive extracts, competitions
and special offers, find us online:

f facebook.com/millsandboon

🐦 @MillsandBoon

📷 @MillsandBoonUK

Get in touch on 01413 063232

For all the latest titles coming soon, visit
millsandboon.co.uk/nextmonth